Alison Stuart was born [...] legal secretary and worked in London, where she dreamed of being a writer and indulging her passion for historical drama. She lived in London in the early years of her marriage and became fascinated by the social history of its people. Her first novel, under a different name, was published in 1987. As a dedicated author she is meticulous in her research and enjoys revisiting the settings for her scenes. She now writes full time, and lives with her husband in Sussex. She has two children and is now a grandmother.

Alison Stuart's previous novels, LOYALTY DEFILED, FATEFUL SHADOWS and INNOCENCE BETRAYED, are also available from Headline:

'A very good read. Exciting . . . and full of emotion'
Harry Bowling

'A good read' *Woman Journalist*

'A riveting book that retains the excitement to the end'
Huddersfield Daily Examiner

'A well-written book . . . very exciting, very descriptive and one you can't wait to finish' *Worcester Evening News*

Sin No More

Alison Stuart

HEADLINE

First published in 1996 by
HEADLINE BOOK PUBLISHING LTD

First published in paperback in 1997 by
HEADLINE BOOK PUBLISHING

10 9 8 7 6 5 4 3 2 1

ISBN 0 7472 5368 4

Typeset by Avon Dataset Ltd, Bidford-on-Avon, Warks

Printed and bound in Great Britain by
Cox & Wyman Ltd, Reading, Berks

HEADLINE BOOK PUBLISHING
A division of Hodder Headline PLC
338 Euston Road
London NW1 3BH

To Maureen, Evelyn and Joan
three very warm-hearted and special sisters-in-law.

A special dedication
to the most important people of all – my readers.
Without you I am an entertainer in an empty theatre.

To Margaret May – you saw the spark and
encouraged the flame. Thank you.

PART ONE

It is a public scandal that constitutes offence and to sin in secret is not to sin at all.

La Tartuffe: Molière

Chapter One

'When it's starve or sell your body, it's not a sin, Faith. It's a necessity. And we ain't eaten for three days,' Ruby Simons declared.

It was almost midnight on a freezing February night. Faith Tempest stared at the bright lights of Piccadilly Circus and the women blatantly parading around the statue of Eros, before answering her friend. 'I'm not doing anything of the kind.' She finally allowed her anger to surface. 'Is that why you insisted that we come here? You've had some wild schemes in the past, Ruby, which I've sometimes gone along with. But not this!'

As though in protest her empty stomach rumbled painfully. There was grim determination in the set of Faith's oval face and her aquamarine eyes were bright with an uncompromising light. Pulling her coat collar up to her ears, she tucked an escaping tress of long auburn hair back into her cloche hat. The thought of spending another night on the streets alarmed her. Yet even with hunger snapping at her insides she would not succumb to Ruby's plan.

Ruby groaned. 'That stubborn pride of yours will be the death of us.'

'When all you have left is your self-respect . . .'

Ruby swore roundly and moved off. 'I give up on you, Faith. You can't bloody eat self-respect.'

Faith did not respond. She knew Ruby's temper would cool and she would acknowledge that Faith was right. They had already endured so much hardship that nothing could break their friendship. It would be tested as it had tonight – especially now that it looked

3

as if it would snow to add to their misery – but it would never be severed.

Ruby, the orphanage foundling, had few scruples and fewer morals and preferred to take the easy option. Faith could never forget the middle-class values and principles instilled in her by her mother until she was seven.

'Without references we can't get a job.' Ruby scowled into the night, her lovely heart-shaped face shadowed with the same weariness etched into Faith's expression. At five foot, she was six inches shorter than Faith. What she lacked in inches she made up for in vivacity and impetuousness. Now there was a flinty hardness in her grey eyes; a ruthlessness which saw life as a battle to be conquered which Faith could never possess. Ruby grimaced and her tone was sour as she gritted out, 'Since we came to London two days ago we've done our best to find a job. My feet are killing me from traipsing round scores of hotels and restaurants.'

'Tomorrow will be different.' Faith attempted to sound optimistic, but, weak from hunger, it was not easy. As she rubbed her arms to generate some warmth in her slender body, she tried to resurrect the dream that had brought them here. She had been convinced that London would give them a better chance in life.

Ruby took off a shoe and massaged her foot. 'In the meantime where are we gonna sleep tonight? Do you fancy sleeping out in the park again with winos and tramps? Our bags were nicked when that gang of ragamuffins set on us that first night. They took our money and everything. We ain't even got a clean pair of drawers between us.' Her calculating stare scanned the throng of people illuminated in the bright coloured lights around London's famous statue.

'We've just been unlucky.'

'If I ever get my hands on those sods who nicked our stuff, I'll do for them,' Ruby snapped.

'For heaven's sake, Ruby.' Faith lost patience with her moaning. 'Try and look on the bright side. London is a big city. There must be work for us here. Remember our dreams. Our plans.'

At seeing the resolute expression on her friend's face, Ruby shook her head and laughed derisively. 'We were lucky they were boys who robbed us and not grown men. Otherwise you'd not be so worried now about losing your precious virginity. They'd have had us both and nothing we could do about it. And for bloody free.' She sauntered along the bottom steps of the fountain as a group of men crossed the road, her hips swaying with provocative invitation and her stare bold. 'Any of you gentlemen looking for company?'

'Stop it, Ruby!' Faith grabbed her arm and pulled her back. 'It's my fault we're in this mess,' she said darkly. 'I shouldn't have reacted so violently when Randy Rogers cornered me in the hotel bedroom. We'd still have our jobs as chambermaids in Tilbury.'

Ruby gave a throaty chuckle. 'Just because he was manager of that run-down hotel, he thought all the women staff were his for the taking. No one else had the guts to slap his face and deny him. He didn't sack you though. He fancied you too much for that. So don't go blaming yourself for the mess we're in. It were me what did for us, calling him names when I learned he'd tried to force you. When he sacked me, you, loyal as always, told him where he could put his job.'

She put an arm round Faith's shoulders. 'We still got each other. That's what's important. We've been through rougher times than this at the children's home.'

'Yes,' Faith said firmly, 'and it made us fighters. 'We don't have to sell ourselves. Something will turn up, Ruby.'

'Like getting abducted and sold on the white slave market.' Ruby rolled her eyes heavenwards. 'With your innocent looks, you'd get the sheik who's the image of Rudolph Valentino, and I'd get his ugly brother Fatty Arbuckle.'

Despite her low spirits Faith laughed, inadvertently drawing the glances of several men in evening dress. Their plight was desperate. And the image of being sold in a slave market was not so far off their predicament, Faith thought despairingly.

Faith could not stay cross with Ruby for long. Her friend never took anything seriously and that was infectious. Studying her now, she felt a rush of affection. Ruby was eyeing a balding Lothario in an expensive astrakhan overcoat. His young mistress giggled incessantly and pressed her mink-draped figure against him. Faith saw the man's interest linger on Ruby. Momentary regret clouded his eyes before he stepped into a taxi. Ruby's beauty affected all men. Her pale blonde hair was cut in an Eton crop, only the fringe visible under her bright red cloche hat. Red hat no drawers always came to Faith's mind when she saw Ruby wearing it. Knowing how wild her friend was inclined to be, it was probably true in her case.

They were so different yet their friendship was unshakeable. Ruby was twenty and had already had several lovers, unlike herself. At eighteen Faith was never short of boyfriends, but she was sensitive of her family pride. She might be an orphan, but her parents had been respectable and hard working. The middle-class upbringing of her early years still made her baulk at shaming her family, or cheapening herself by giving herself to a man out of marriage. Not that she hadn't been tempted. Too often for comfort her body stirred strangely when she was kissed passionately, or a man's caresses became bolder. But always she had held back from the final commitment.

Self-respect was important to Faith. Wasn't it worth being hungry and cold for? A loud painful rumble of objection from her stomach made her hunch over. If only her nostrils weren't constantly tantalised by the aroma of cooking food. The smell of hot pies and soups bombarded them from the street stalls and restaurants. It was impossible to blot the thought of food from her mind. Not that this was the first time she had been hungry.

Childhood memories flooded back. Her parents owned a draper's shop in a small parade some distance from Tilbury docks. Her father served in the shop and her mother was also dressmaker to the wealthier residents of the town. Faith's childhood had been happy and surrounded by love. Her pretty dresses were lovingly smocked and embroidered by her mother. Every day her father took her to Miss Morrell's private girls' school in a large house in Grays. She travelled in the side-car of his motorcycle and she felt

6

as grand as Cinderella arriving at the ball in her fairy coach.

Faith had been aware from an early age that she was more privileged than many of the ragged children she saw in the streets. She was warned by her mother to stay away from any children who came from the rough area nearer to the docks. Yet if her father saw these youngsters he'd flip them a couple of half-pennies for sweets.

'Poor blighters,' he muttered. 'No kid asks to be born into poverty. Always remember that, my girl. I don't want you getting ideas you're better than them. You're just more fortunate. I ain't ashamed that I was a docker's son from Poplar. Neither should you be. Me dad worked hard and he played hard until he got killed by some cargo breaking free from a crane.'

It was one of the last conversations she had with her father and she remembered it vividly. His handsome kindly face was sad. They'd taken his favourite Sunday walk along the river bank, past the World's End public house and the redbrick Tilbury Fort.

'I were fourteen when dad died,' her father went on. 'Ma died a year earlier of consumption. I didn't have no relatives. I'd already left school so I did odd jobs for a few years but I wanted to better meself. Without a proper education that ain't easy. So I joined the navy. It was a grand life, took me all over the world. It was the best thing that ever happened to me. Until I met your mother that is . . .'

He ruffled her hair and grinned. He must have loved her mother very much to give up the sea and take on the draper's shop when his father-in-law died. Faith has sensed her father's restlessness in being tied to a shop. He worked there out of duty and love for his family.

Secure in her parents' love and the comfort of a middle-class home, Faith couldn't imagine her life changing. But nothing stays as it is. She hadn't heard of the Kaiser then, nor known the dreadful losses incurred by war.

Henry Tempest had re-enlisted in the navy when war was declared and had been killed when his ship was sunk in 1915.

During the first two years of the war her mother had struggled to run the draper's shop. One night a burglar broke in. Hearing the noise, her mother went to investigate. Faith had slept soundly through it. She came downstairs in the morning to find the living-quarters and shop ransacked. Her mother had been beaten to death. It was then that she realised how pampered and protected had been her early years.

There was no other family. Her mother's elder brother and sister had died in a flu epidemic when they were children. Faith had been placed in a children's home. There was no money after the sale of the business, just enough to meet the debts. Her mother had been too soft-hearted. She listened to any hard-luck story and had allowed her customers to run up large bills on credit. Used to fine living, Gloria Tempest continued to spend extravagantly until all their savings were gone.

At seven years old life in the children's home was a shock for Faith who was still traumatised by her mother's brutal death. She wore hand-me-down clothes and was always hungry. She had stoically adapted and learned to defend herself against the older children's bullying. But the other children resented that her speech and manners were not rough like theirs. They would have made her an outcast if Ruby had not befriended her.

Faith never forgot her upbringing by Gloria, who had valued respectability above all else. Yet Ruby brought out the wilder side of her nature which was her father's legacy to her. Remembering her father's restlessness, she now understood it. Frequently, she could have thrown up her job in the hotel and chanced everything for a more exciting life in London. But the years of poverty and life in the orphanage had made her cautious. Security was also important during her first years at work. Only she had not expected security to be so boring and weigh like a yoke about her neck. Getting sacked had been a reprieve from prison.

When Ruby suggested they start a new life in London, she had been exultant at the prospect. Even now, hungry and almost frozen, Faith adored the capital. There was an underlying pulsing within the bustling streets which energised her. She could not believe that London would betray her and cast her into destitution. Hadn't her father always said, 'You make your own destiny'? She clung to that thought now.

With a frown, Faith watched Ruby step in front of a young gentleman. Despite the cold Ruby had opened her coat to display her figure in the straight waistless scarlet dress. It was short enough to display her shapely calves and trim ankles. Her shoulders were thrown back and her heavy breasts thrust forward in a brazen pose. The cold air made her nipples stand out prominently.

Faith turned away. Ruby was incorrigible. She still couldn't believe that her friend was serious about selling herself for the price of a meal and a room for the night. Then Ruby was capable of anything. She was a true survivor. But tonight she had gone too far. Several malevolent glares were directed at her from the other street walkers, who had neither Ruby's looks nor sultry style. In response Ruby flaunted her figure even more provocatively.

To Faith's relief her invitation was declined. She had tolerated enough. She wasn't about to be bulldozed by Ruby's action into a situation which repelled her.

'Let's get out of here, Ruby.'

'Give over,' Ruby replied. She was eyeing a couple of young sailors in uniform. They were reeling drunk with a bottle of whisky in one hand and a meat pie in the other. 'Those two look like they've just docked and been paid.' She nudged her in the ribs. 'Look a bit more lively, girl. We ain't gonna get any men interested if you glare at them all. Likely they'll fork out for a meal and room. They'll pass out before they can do anything.'

Ruby cursed under her breath as the two sailors were accosted by two brunettes just yards before they reached her. 'What have those old bags got that we ain't, except being riddled with the clap?'

Faith had endured enough. Piccadilly was still bustling with night revellers. The sounds of pianos in pubs and strains of jazz bands in the Soho clubs could be heard in the distance. People were laughing as they left the theatres, picture palaces or dance halls. Beggars whined from doorways, hands outstretched for money. Within an hour or two the crowds would thin and it would

9

become a more sinister place: the haunt of the destitute, the drunks who could become violent or abusive; a place of menacing shadows which could conceal thieves, rapists or murderers.

'Couldn't we try busking again?' Faith suggested. 'You've a great voice. It earned a couple of bob last night.'

'We don't look like buskers,' Ruby moaned. 'We're dressed too smart. People thought we were larking around.'

Ruby was right, Faith admitted. They had tried everything. But as she watched the whores, with their grating voices and cheap gaudy clothes, she knew she would rather endure hunger and another freezing night, than surrender to that life. They'd been standing on the statue's steps for twenty minutes and she was aware that a short man was watching them. She'd earlier seen him bully a young girl into going off with an elderly lecher. His face, illuminated by the flashing electric lights, was cruel and threatening.

'Anything is better than this,' she stated. 'I feel dirty and I haven't done anything wrong. I'm not staying here, Ruby.' She walked to the kerb and was forced to halt as the merging traffic jostled for position in the road.

Ruby joined her, her manner truculent. 'We could wait outside one of the dance halls. They should be turning out now. If we pretended to be waiting for a cab, we won't look so obvious, or desperate.' At Faith's indignant expression, she added, 'We ain't never failed to pull a couple of blokes at a dance. You can handle it if yours tries anything on.'

'No, Ruby!' Faith was about to start weaving through the traffic when a shrill voice accosted them.

''Ere your two. What's your bloody game 'anging round 'ere?' A woman with black hair cut in a bob to her aggressive jawline, bright red lips and thin pencilled brows was glaring at Ruby. She nodded to two other women who joined her and they bore down on Ruby.

Faith quaked not from fear, but from humiliation. She hated scenes and these women meant trouble. Aware that several passers-by were staring at them with a mixture of curiosity and disgust, her skin burned with shame.

'What's it to do with you?' Ruby challenged.

'Yer can piss off, that's what. This is our patch,' the black-haired woman snarled. 'We don't want no flash tarts stealing our trade.'

'Who you calling a tart?' Ruby retaliated.

'Don't start anything, Ruby.' Faith tugged at her sleeve. 'Ignore them and leave.'

'Yeah, sod off!' the other two women chorused. 'If yer know what's good for yer.'

Ruby was bristling with rage. 'I ain't scared of you. No one tells me what to do. But happen I've got better things to do with my life than spend my time staring at ceilings. Or giving someone a cheap thrill in a dark alley.'

'Snooty bitch!' the first woman screamed. 'We'll teach yer, yer stuck up little . . .'

The three women turned on Ruby, one drawing a thin-bladed dagger. 'She won't be so lippy with 'er mouth slit.'

'Leg it, Ruby,' Faith urged. The mortification of being forced into a street fight was the last straw.

'Not so fast!' The short pimp barred their escape. His face was narrow, and his mousy, oiled hair was slicked back, hanging like slugs over his collar. Menace emanated from the cold eyes and brutal face.

Faith had never met a pimp before, but she'd heard of them. This man had the charm of a maggot who would feed off the rotten and sordid business of prostitution. 'No one works here without my say so,' he lisped from several broken and blackened teeth. 'Two fancy tarts like yerselves could do right well.'

Faith's temper exploded. She was hungry, frozen, dog-tired and now this obnoxious, ugly squirt was offering to become their pimp. She was too outraged to be frightened. Her stare flayed him. In a refined accent she intoned, 'Get out of my way, you offensive little man, before I call the police. How dare you suggest such a thing! Chief Inspector Wickham of the vice squad is my uncle. He will hear about this. So call your old dragons off, unless you want them arrested for soliciting.'

Her verbal attack momentarily took him back, his slow wits churning over her words. Before he could recover, she demanded, 'Out of my way. I've never been so insulted.'

With that she strode off. Her heart was hammering so wildly that it threatened to burst through her chest. To her relief Ruby was beside her. Once across the road they broke into a run and jumped on to an omnibus as it pulled away from the kerb. They flopped down breathing heavily and giggling at their narrow escape. The conductor was upstairs and they'd gone several stops before he approached them.

Ruby winked at Faith as she delved her hand into her pocket. 'Two to Paddington, please.'

'You're on the wrong bus, luv. We're going to Holborn. Get off at the next stop, cross the road and the bus you want should be along shortly.'

'Much obliged, sir.' Ruby smiled at him. 'It's our first time in London. This is the third time we've got lost today.'

They jumped off the omnibus reluctantly. At least they had escaped paying any fare. To sit and rest had been too brief a respite and the confrontation at Piccadilly had scared Faith more than she cared to admit. It was darker here away from the bright lights. On the walls of every building was a water line where only a few weeks ago the River Thames had burst its banks and flooded the city. Fourteen people had died. The thought of this mighty city underwater from the force of the elements made Faith feel vulnerable. If it snowed tonight how would she and Ruby fare? It made her more determined than ever to triumph over their misfortune.

'I've had it with your ideas, Ruby. I hope that's taught you a lesson. We were lucky to get away that time.'

Ruby waved her hand dismissively. 'It taught me, we're going to have to watch our step, that's all.'

'We came to London to better ourselves,' Faith admonished. 'Do you want to end up like those whores? Once you start thinking that's the only way to survive you end up in the gutter.'

'Of course I won't.' Frustration brought a tremor to Ruby's voice.

12

Less harshly Faith added, 'Ruby, you're a beautiful woman with a warm heart when it suits you. Don't sell yourself short. Know your own worth and live up to it.'

'You do come out with some sayings.' Ruby sighed. 'When I think how I had such dreams about London . . . It ain't like I thought it would be. What we gonna do, Faith?'

Head down as she walked, her hands dredged deep in her pockets seeking warmth, Faith saw something shining under a piece of torn newspaper. She stooped and her heart pattered with excitement as her numb fingers closed over a silver florin. 'Our luck is changing. I've just found two bob. This will buy us a hot drink and a sandwich.' She linked her arm through her friend's. 'We are going to survive.'

The tea was purchased from a roadside stall. The warmth seeping into their flesh lifted their spirits.

'You're right, Faith. Something will turn up. But I hope it's gonna be quick. I don't fancy another night on the streets. Give us another bite out of that cheese sandwich. In Tilbury we could have got a meal each for what that cost. Bloody London prices. It ain't cheap to live here.'

'That's because we've stayed in the West End,' Faith replied. 'The porter at the last hotel I tried for work said that the south bank of the Thames is cheaper. So is the East End. With all these theatres and nightclubs, it's bound to be pricey here.'

The tea and sandwich barely made an impression on their starving bodies. Within an hour the hunger cramps began again. Ruby hugged her arms about her figure as they trudged the streets. Her shoes pinched and she'd got blisters. At times like this she could throttle Faith for her stubbornness. Why did her friend have such strong morals? Ruby had no such inconvenient scruples. Although she would not have enjoyed bartering her body to just anyone for food and a comfortable bed, she would have done it out of necessity. She prided herself on being a realist.

If you've got something special, use it for all it's worth. That was her motto. And she had that something special. Or so her men friends told her. And she was prepared to use it. She'd never sent

13

a lover away disappointed. Nor had they left her empty-handed. They had all shown their gratitude. She would have been outraged if anyone had suggested that the gifts they gave her were in payment for her favours. They were gifts of appreciation. Any woman would be a fool to keep seeing a man if they didn't appreciate her company, wouldn't she? Also you got nothing for nothing in this world.

Her stare was brittle. It was a lesson she had grown up with. Unwanted by her own mother, she had been dumped on the orphanage steps. She had no illusions about her parentage. A drunken sailor or docker for a father, and a whore for a mother was most likely. What did it matter anyway? Parents – sod them! She didn't need them. She didn't need anyone . . . not in that way, to look out for her. She could look after herself.

Seeing her friend's shivering figure, she experienced a rush of affection. She did need someone. She needed Faith. Faith was special. She was her mentor and her salvation. Their friendship had kept her on the straight and narrow. Well almost. If Faith knew the half of what she had got up to with blokes, she'd have a fit.

Ruby inwardly grinned. Sex had been a wonderful discovery ever since she'd had her first lover at fourteen. Her body had developed early and even though she was petite she easily passed for sixteen. After that she couldn't get enough of it. A vigorous lover could transport her from the drudgery of her life to a world of pleasure and sensation. And weren't that what life was all about? Making the most of it: using whatever means it took to wrench excitement and fun from this existence. She reckoned that life owed her fun and pleasure. She'd had enough poverty and wretchedness at the orphanage.

Bitterness rose in her throat as she recalled the incident in Piccadilly. So far London had not been kind to them. Nevertheless, it had revealed a treasure trove which could be hers for the taking. The West End had shown the affluence of the people going about their business. The fashionable clothes in the shop windows were magnificent and the London roads were crammed with more motor cars than she had seen in her life. The city had class and money. Ever an optimistic, she chose to ignore the poverty and beggars. In London you could make something of your life.

Faith had been right when she said that you had to know your own worth. Any mirror showed her that she was beautiful and had a figure men fantasised over. London was a city of opportunity and Ruby meant to grasp any opportunity which came her way. She'd done with slaving for a living in hotels and making do with a pittance of a wage. She wanted to be rich, adored and successful. She wanted fortune and fame. She yearned to be the orphanage kid who hit the big time. That was her goal. Whatever it took, she would not waver from it.

She saw two men cruising past in an expensive motor car and intended to flash them her most seductive smile. It was halted by Faith, who plucked at her arm and drew her down a brightly lit, more populated street.

Even as her exasperation with her friend mounted, Ruby knew that their friendship was the most important thing in her life. She would not jeopardise it. Faith was the only true friend she'd had in the children's home. They had been through a lot together. Faith had stuck by her when she'd got herself arrested for disturbing the peace by attacking some old biddy for calling her a slut. Faith had been there for her when she'd been heartbroken over a man ditching her. Faith cared for her when she'd been ill, or was too drunk to get home. In bouts of selfishness, when Ruby had forced her friend into impossible situations, Faith had been stoic and remained loyal to her. Faith never judged her.

In the last two years Ruby had tried to curb the recklessness which could drive her to acts of foolishness and into further trouble. Faith was not only her friend, she was her guardian angel and her conscience.

But sometimes your conscience could be a trial, especially when surrendering to temptation was the easier option.

By two o'clock in the morning, Ruby was too miserable to pay heed to her conscience. Temptation was an insidious whisper in her head. With a despondent curse, she leaned against a lamppost. They were somewhere near Covent Garden and across the road a band was playing in a nightclub.

'I can't go any further, Faith. I'm dead on me feet. It's brass monkeys' weather. If we sleep out in this, by morning we'll both be dead from pneumonia.'

Faith stamped her cold feet to bring some life back in them. 'We'll go to one of the main line stations. I should have thought of it before. We look respectable enough to stay in the ladies' waiting room all night. If anyone asks we'll say we're waiting for the morning train.'

Ruby was light-headed with hunger and determined to sleep in a proper bed. She'd had enough of wooden benches to last her a lifetime. When two men emerged from the nightclub opposite, she was struck by their rich attire. She nudged Faith in the ribs. 'Our luck's just changed. Those two are good looking and loaded. Don't you dare do or say anything to put them off.'

Faith had heard that tone often and knew Ruby meant what she said. A night in the park with the two of them had been terrifying but alone . . . She shuddered. It was too awful to consider. She didn't fancy walking to a railway station by herself at this time of night. She would though if she had to.

'Do what you like, Ruby. I'm going to a station.'

'I ain't freezing me tits off sleeping rough again, not even for you,' Ruby warned, undeterred by her threat. 'And, eyes off the blond one with the film-star looks, he's mine.'

Faith stared at the road ahead. It was filled with dark menacing shadows. How would a woman alone fare? At least these two men looked like gentlemen. Perhaps they could get a hot meal out of them. With luck they would accept that they had missed the last train and would not expect more than the pleasure of their company.

Somehow she doubted it would be that easy, or without unpleasant consequences.

Chapter Two

Apprehensively Faith followed Ruby's gaze and saw that the men appeared to be in their twenties. Both wore evening dress, but only the blond man wore a top hat and carried a cane. The other was bareheaded and dark. They certainly looked as if they had a bob or two. The blond man was good looking with smooth boyish features and a narrow moustache. He weaved slightly, clearly intoxicated. His companion was three inches taller at over six foot, thinner of face and clean-shaven. The line of his high cheekbones and fine-boned jaw was striking, giving him a commanding presence. If they had met in a dance hall, Faith would have been attracted to him. Embarrassed by the situation in which she found herself, she kept her eyes downcast as the two men crossed the road.

'Hey, gents, any idea which way Charing Cross station is? We've got lost and missed our last train,' Ruby called out, her voice sultry with enticement.

Cheeks scorching with humiliation, Faith edged back into the shadows. Sometimes she could throttle Ruby. Now she wished the pavement would open up and swallow her. She pulled the collar of her black coat higher around her ears and jammed her hands into her pockets. The brim of her dark green cloche hat was deep enough to hide her face. She couldn't stop shivering and her stomach was again aching with hunger.

Attracting no response, Ruby pursued. 'It ain't much fun spending the night in the ladies' waiting room. I suppose we'd be better off finding a decent restaurant for a meal. How about making it a foursome and afterwards we can have some fun?'

Faith glared at her. Couldn't Ruby be more subtle? Not that she would know the meaning of the word. When Ruby saw a chance, she seized upon it, never stopping to weigh up a situation first. It wouldn't have been so bad if she had allowed the men to address them. No decent woman spoke to strangers on the street.

Panic stifled her breath, making her voice husky as she intervened, 'Stop messing about, Ruby. These gentlemen want to get home.'

'Wouldn't mind a bit of fun myself,' the blond man said, putting his arms around Ruby and drawing her close.

Ruby giggled. 'I like a man who knows how to enjoy himself. With a decent meal inside me I could show you how appreciative I can really be.'

'They're just whores, Tony. I'm not interested.'

The dark-haired man said this with such scorn that indignation shot through Faith, making her forget her embarrassment.

'We certainly are not,' she blazed. Her head came up and her eyes flashed as her temper soared. 'Come on, Ruby. I'm tired of you fooling about.'

As she turned to walk away she dragged on her reserves of strength to straighten her weary shoulders. Although it pained her to abandon her friend, loyalty did have its limits.

She reached the arc of light from a street lamp when her arm was grabbed by Ruby. She was swung round so hard that her hat came loose and fell to the ground. Her thick auburn hair which had been pushed up inside the high crown tumbled down around her shoulders to her elbows. In the lamplight it shone with the vibrancy of a copper sunset brightening the darkness.

'For Gawd's sake, Faith,' Ruby cried, 'why must you be so stubborn?'

Any answer was halted by the loud rumbling of Faith's stomach which completed her humiliation. Through chattering teeth, she forced out, 'It's a matter of self-respect. If I haven't got that I might just as well freeze to death in the park, because I couldn't live with myself.'

'A tart with a conscience, how frightfully novel,' the blond man sniggered.

'She's not a tart, Tony,' his companion corrected. Picking up Faith's hat he held it out to her. 'I apologise for my comments and those of my friend. I was mistaken.' His kindness was the last straw. Although she bit her bottom lip to stop it trembling, Faith could not stem the tears which spilled over her lashes on to her cheek.

A long square-tipped finger lifted her chin and she found herself compelled to look into piercing blue eyes ringed by thick dark lashes. 'You look done in. Hungry too, I expect. How did a lovely woman like you end up on the streets?' His voice was deep with the lyrical brogue of Ireland in its tone.

There was arrogance in the way he was appraising her but for once it did not spark her anger. She drew back so that his hand fell away from her chin. 'We came to London looking for work. Our money and bags were stolen,' Faith said with clipped defiance. 'But it isn't your concern. We'll manage.'

Ruby was flirting outrageously with Tony who was trying to kiss her and get his hand up her skirt. 'Meal first, fun later, that's the deal.'

'Are you coming to the station, Ruby?' Faith's voice was uncharacteristically sharp.

'Please stay,' the Irishman insisted. 'I'm Dan Brogan. Will you do me the honour of dining with us?'

When she hesitated he added, softly, 'No strings attached, I promise. It will get you out of the cold for an hour. Have you nowhere to stay?'

She shook her head, but the defiance remained in her eyes. 'I cannot accept. Ruby has given you the wrong idea about us.'

'I wasn't inviting her.' Dan held her stare, the corner of his mouth lifting. 'I'm asking you. It's obvious that you're a different type of woman than your friend. What are you doing with someone like that?'

'We go back a long way,' Faith defended. 'Ruby is not bad, just a bit wild at times. The last few days have not been easy . . .' her voice tapered off.

'You're loyal as well.' Surprise warmed his husky voice. 'You intrigue me. I would enjoy getting to know you better.'

Still suspicious, Faith hesitated. 'Why?'

To her consternation he laughed. 'Why not?'

'Do you usually pick up women off the streets, for altruistic reasons?' she queried, knowing that she was being difficult which was ludicrous in the circumstances. Dan Brogan was handsome, too handsome to have to pick up whores for female company. There was kindness in his voice, but no matter how tempting his offer, she was wary of his motives.

He surprised her by grinning. She was uncomfortably aware of the magnetism of his attraction. Yet it wasn't attraction which was making her heart pound painfully. It was trepidation. She was ashamed to have met him in these circumstances. Twining her thick auburn hair into a coil, she was about to pull her hat over it, when Dan stopped her.

'Would you leave it down? Your hair is magnificent.'

'Most people call me carrot-top,' Faith admitted, suspecting that he was mocking her.

'Then it shows their ignorance. Please, indulge me. I'm an artist. It's rare to see a true Titian redhead. You see, my motives in asking you to dine are not entirely unselfish.' Now Faith was intrigued. It was her greatest regret she could not afford art lessons. At school she had been top of her class in all lessons including art. Egged on by Ruby she'd often skipped lessons. When Ruby left the orphanage two years before her to work and live in a hotel, they kept in touch and when Faith was fourteen Ruby persuaded her to work instead of taking up the college scholarship the orphanage were trying to get for her. At that time her friendship had seemed more important.

Within six months Faith regretted her rashness. She didn't want to stay a servant all her life. Too late she realised that education would have enabled her to get a better job. She had contacted Miss Morrell, her old schoolmistress. The elderly woman remembered her. She had retired from teaching and was lonely. In exchange for Faith's company she had agreed to allow her to make use of her library and borrow two books each week. Miss Morrell was an art lover with dozens of books on artists and their paintings. Faith had been captivated and had quickly read every book on art Miss Morrell possessed. Sadly, Miss Morrell had died last February, but Faith was grateful for the chance the old schoolmistress had given her to extend her education. Now that they had moved to London Faith had planned to visit all the exhibition halls, museums and libraries to expand her knowledge. That Dan was an artist made him even more exciting.

'Do you paint portraits?'

'Sometimes, if a model inspires me.'

There was an impatient tut from Ruby and she interrupted, 'Are you two going to talk all night, or are we going for a meal?' She shot Faith a meaningful glare and added, 'You ain't going to back out of that are you, Faith?'

Dan lifted a dark brow in question and silently offered her his arm. The first flakes of snow settled on his thick dark hair, a lock of which had fallen rakishly over his wide brow. Her stomach rumbled again. Then the street lamp dipped drunkenly towards her and her head began to swirl. For an awful moment Faith thought she would faint. Taking a sharp breath she combated the light-headedness. To refuse a meal would be foolish. With food inside her she would recover her strength and could always leg it if matters got out of hand.

They walked down another side street and entered a small but classy restaurant. Subdued lighting came from glass wall lamps and candles were on every table. They were shown to a table set between a mahogany and patterned-glass partition. The blue padded bench seats also created an intimate setting. On the table was a bowl of white chrysanthemums. Expecting to sit next to Ruby, Faith was discountenanced when she deliberately sat opposite her. Tony slid in beside Ruby, put his arm around her shoulders and whispered in her ear. That his comments were suggestive was evident by Ruby's laugh.

Ruby looked across at Faith and with a wink silently mouthed, 'We've landed on our feet here.' Then her attention was all for

21

Anthony Chalmers. Just gazing into his eyes and seeing his interest in her, made her forget the rigours of the last three days. That he was rich was apparent by his cultured voice and expensive suit. This was a man who could afford to spend his money on a woman. Ruby was determined that she'd do whatever it took to keep him interested in her. And no one knew better than Ruby how to ensure that he kept coming back for more. Her smile was pure enticement as she laid her hand on his. 'Do you live in London?'

'I wish I did,' he evaded. 'When I'm in London I stay at my club.'

Ruby's spirits dipped. She'd hoped that he'd have his own place to take her to. A seductive smile parted her lips. 'Pity that. They don't allow women in these gentlemen clubs do they?'

He frowned. 'You don't have a place then?'

She shook her head. 'Didn't I tell you that we were looking for the station. Actually we came to London to find work. We had our stuff stolen. All we've got is the clothes we stand up in.'

'I say, that's rotten luck,' Tony said, his gaze calculating. 'Can't have you without a bed for the night to lay that gorgeous body in. Plenty of hotels round here. And you've said that you're a woman who knows how to show her appreciation.'

'A hotel sounds divine as long as it's not a cheap one. Even a girl down on her luck has her pride,' she stipulated. 'And there's another problem. I can't leave me mate. Do you reckon Dan will see her all right?'

His expression clouded and Ruby wondered if she'd pushed too hard. Finally, he said, 'Dan seems taken with your friend, but it's for them to make their own arrangements. He's got his own flat, but . . .'

'That's all right then,' Ruby said, eager to keep Tony interested in herself. 'I always dreamed of living in London,' she added, 'not the rough areas, somewhere a bit more respectable. Perhaps you could advise me.'

As she chatted about inconsequentials, she allowed her knee to rub against his thigh. 'That nightclub you came out of, the music was divine.'

'You like jazz, do you?' His expression cleared.

'It makes your blood sizzle,' she laughed provocatively.

Tony's eyes darkened with desire. When his hand slid under her dress, her fingers clamped on his and steel entered her voice. 'I won't be treated like a whore. If you want a night to remember, then you treat me right.'

Tony often picked up women on visits to London. Most were sluts. He'd never met anyone like Ruby. She was wild, fun and incredibly sexy. The women of his acquaintance and especially his fiancée, wanted a wedding ring on their finger before they even allowed a glimpse of a stocking top. He was getting married in the summer. He wanted a fling before he was forced to spend more time in the country managing both his father's and fiancée's adjoining estates.

Faith saw Tony's hand move beneath the table to Ruby's thigh and her cheeks flushed with colour. She looked away but as she was sitting against the wall she had to stare across Dan's profile to gaze at the other diners. All were dressed smartly. After having her belongings stolen Faith possessed only the navy drop-waisted dress she was wearing. It was her Sunday best. The day they were robbed she was wearing it in the hope of gaining an interview which would lead to employment. The material was good quality wool. A narrow navy velvet band edged the collar and the low waist seam. It had taken her three months to save for. At least she did not feel out of place.

'What are you having, Tony?' Dan asked as the waiter appeared with the menus.

'This delicious bird here,' he quipped nuzzling Ruby's ear. 'You order, Dan.'

Dan ordered two bottles of wine and soup to start with, followed by fillet of sole and then chicken cooked in wine. Faith felt her mouth watering in anticipation of such a feast as Dan turned to her with a smile.

'Now I've ensured that you will not starve, will you at least tell me your name?'

He was teasing her and despite her nervousness, she found it easy to respond. 'Faith Tempest. And thank you for the meal. It's very generous of you.'

His eyes crinkled with amusement. 'I'm sure it will be my pleasure.'

Immediately she tensed, again suspicious of his intentions. At her response his smile broadened. 'I meant the pleasure of talking to you. I find you something of a mystery. You speak well. There's an innocence about you which does not belong on the streets of London.'

Faith blushed. 'I'm so ashamed. I never realised that without references we would be unable to find work, or that the landlords want rent in advance to secure a room.'

His vivid blue gaze bored into her. 'How is it that you have no references?'

Faith told him and finished by saying, 'I despise men who think that women are for their amusement.'

'A man who takes advantage of his employees should be horse-whipped. Since your money was stolen, you haven't yet got a place to stay then?'

This time she could not hold his piercing stare and looked down at her hands as she shook her head.

The soup arrived and Dan added gently, 'I remember what it was like to be hungry when I was a struggling art student. Tuck into that.'

As they ate Dan drew her story from her. She was flattered that he seemed genuinely interested, but was also aware that Tony kept refilling Ruby's wine glass. When he did so again Faith pushed the bottle away, saying sharply, 'Ruby, you've had enough to drink.'

Tony scowled at her, 'Who are you? Her friend or her mother?'

'That's enough, Tony,' Dan warned. Turning back to Faith, he added, 'Ignore him. I'm sure your friend can take care of herself.'

Faith hoped that was so. She didn't want to leave yet. She was enjoying Dan's company too much. Why did Tony have to spoil it?

'Ruby isn't usually this bad,' she apologised. 'We've only had

24

a cheese sandwich between us in three days. Mr Chalmers seems determined to get her drunk.'

'You have had a tough time, haven't you?'

His concerned smile increased her liking for him. He seemed genuinely interested and she relaxed, feeling that she could trust him.

Dan moved the wine away from the other couple. Tony protested. 'She's had enough, Tony,' Dan insisted. 'If you give her any more to drink, she'll be ill.' Reverting his attention back to Faith, he added ruefully, 'I'm no more responsible for Tony's conduct than you are your friend's.'

His assessing stare caused her heart to pound ridiculously fast. Was it the wine that was affecting her, or Dan? Her emotions and thoughts were chaotic. She had been rescued from a nightmare and was in danger of succumbing to this man's charm. To realign her concentration, she voiced her curiosity, wanting to know more about his painting.

'Do you paint full time? Do you specialise in portraits or do you prefer landscapes or still life? It must be an exciting life.'

'So many questions,' he parried. He leaned back on the bench and studied her for several moments before continuing, 'I paint full time when I'm in London. I spend a lot of time travelling to places which I hope will inspire me.'

'You are fortunate to have the means to pursue something which is so special to you.'

Shadows flickered across his eyes and he ate in silence. There was a tension in his shoulders. Concerned that she had offended him, Faith said, 'I don't mean to pry, but an artist's life does seem exciting. I'm fascinated by the great painters and their work. Would it be too nosy of me to ask what you prefer to paint? I'd love to have lessons myself one day.'

He relaxed and laughed. 'The enthusiasm of youth. I had forgotten how starry-eyed I was about art when I was your age. I paint anything which inspires me. Often my work is described as spiritual. It does not appeal to everybody and is vastly different from the Art Nouveau so popular today.'

25

'By spiritual, you mean religious?'

'No. Father O'Hannigan, the village priest where I lived in Ireland, would call them more the Devil's work. He decried them once as heretical. And me at the time a good Catholic boy who attended Mass every Sunday.'

'Do you spend much time in Ireland?'

He shook his head. 'Since my widowed mother died five years ago I've not set foot in Ireland. I fell out with my two elder brothers years ago when they thought painting was effeminate. And my five sisters are scattered across the globe. Two in America, one in Canada, one in South Africa and another in Australia.'

'Don't you miss them?'

At his frown, she went on quickly, 'I was orphaned when I was seven and have no relatives. I suppose I idealise about family life.'

His eyes darkened with compassion. 'That must have been hard for you. But there is little that is ideal about life in a large family, or any family for that.'

His cynicism was so at odds with the kindness he had shown her that it startled her. There was suppressed anger in the lines carved each side of his mouth. What had so disillusioned him?

She was too tired to pursue the mystery, but there remained an uneasy feeling that Dan Brogan was perhaps not the gentleman that he appeared.

Seeing her puzzlement, his mood changed and a smile which she found impossible to resist altered his countenance. When he looked at her with such interest, she could not think straight.

With her hunger finally dissipated and her body rosy from the glow of three glasses of wine, she was beguiled by Dan's smile. He leaned his chin on his knuckles and continued to probe her with questions, until she laughed and held up her hands. 'Enough of me. Tell me more about your painting? Are you famous?'

'Hardly that,' he replied modestly. 'I've sold several paintings and had an exhibition or two, but I'm far from famous. You need something startling to capture the imagination of the critics.

Something magical and different from anything else someone has done.'

'You sound so passionate about your work.' Faith leaned closer, totally absorbed in his words. 'I'm sure you have that magical quality.'

His eyes sparkled with a cobalt fire. 'Perhaps I've not found the right subject.' He lifted a tress of her hair which shone with the richness of a burnished chestnut in the candlelight. 'You have the innocent yet worldly look of the Pre-Raphaelite paintings which were so popular last century. Yet also there is a mysticism and the look of the modern woman of today. Saint, sinner, Madonna or seductress. Your face has the essence of all womankind: the ability to be all things to all men.'

'I've heard some chat-up lines in my time,' Faith said with a laugh, 'but that is the most original and outrageous.'

A flicker of impatience hardened his face. 'I wasn't joking and it wasn't a chat-up line.'

Before Faith could reply, Tony cut in, 'Now we've eaten, where are we going on to? An hotel?'

Faith gasped. 'We most certainly are not!'

Tony glared at her. 'You saying we bought you a meal and you don't intend to keep your side of the bargain?'

'I made no bargain with you.' Her expression was cold as she glared at Ruby who was now giggling helplessly.

Dan put his hand over hers which she snatched away. 'Did you intend to get us drunk so that we would not refuse you?'

His face tightened with anger. 'I don't break my word. If your friend is drunk she has only herself to blame.'

Faith realised that she had been unjust, but Dan was wrong to accuse Ruby so harshly. Tony had been encouraging her to drink. Her manner was cool as she stood up. 'Thank you for the meal, Mr Brogan. Goodnight.'

'And where do you intend to go?' Dan put his hand on her arm. Trapped against the wall, Faith was reluctant to create a scene unless the men became difficult. She had thought she could trust Dan who had appeared so kind and considerate. But what did she know of him other than that he was an artist. Didn't artists lead decadent Bohemian lifestyles?

Turning to Ruby she was appalled to see that she had fallen asleep on Tony's shoulder.

'Wake up, sweetheart,' Tony voiced his annoyance. 'You promised me some fun. Damn woman!' He stood up and Ruby's unconscious figure slid along the bench seat. 'Come on, Dan. We aren't going to get anything out of these two.'

'You can't shirk your responsibilities that easily, Tony,' Dan replied. 'You got her drunk. We can't leave her.'

'I'm not forking out for an hotel room.'

Faith glared at him and tried to rouse Ruby. 'If you wanted more from her, you shouldn't have given her so much to drink. Just leave us. I can look after her.'

'She's out cold,' Dan said. 'Don't be stubborn. I've a studio along the river at Pimlico. You and your friend can stay there tonight.'

Her trust in him was shattered. He was no better than Tony Chalmers. 'I think not.'

A hardness entered his eyes at her change in manner. 'You'll be quite safe. I had intended to sleep on the sofa.'

The repressed anger in his voice made Faith regret her outburst. Had she wronged him? But dare she trust him? Her thoughts spun in confusion. The wine she had drunk had dulled her senses. She no longer trusted her instincts. She regarded Ruby with exasperation for drinking so much.

'Be reasonable, Faith,' Dan went on persuasively. 'Where else have you to go? Don't you trust me?'

How many women in the past had fallen for that self-righteous statement of innocence from a man? But did she have a choice? And she did want to trust him. More than anything, she didn't want Dan to shatter her illusions.

Sensing her wavering, he persisted, 'I'm out of London for the next few days. You and Ruby can stay in the studio until I return. It will give you a chance to get yourself a job and a room somewhere.'

'You'd do that for us! Why?' Faith was touched at his generosity but could not shake her doubts. After all they had endured in the last three days, this offer seemed too good to be true. 'What do you want in return?'

'I'd like to paint you. Would that be too much to ask?'

Faith was dumbstruck. Paint her! She couldn't have heard him right. 'I'm not posing nude, if that's what you were planning.'

'I won't ask you to do anything you don't want to. Will you accept my offer?'

To Faith's dismay tears prickled behind her eyes. 'You're a nice man, Dan Brogan.'

He shook his head, but in the flickering candlelight his handsome face was sardonic and impassioned. 'There is nothing nice about my motives. I've waited years seeking a model with that look you possess. And I don't intend to lose you.'

Desperate for a room as they were, Faith couldn't help wondering if she was about to enter the lion's den.

Chapter Three

Dan's flat was one of three in an impressive porticoed Georgian house at one corner of a tree-lined square. The entrance hall was carpeted in warm tones of red and amber and they took a bronze and gilt, open-cage lift to the top floor. As it clanked to a halt Dan pulled open the doors, saying, 'The flat is more a studio than living quarters although I spend most of the year here. Best of all, it is quiet. The middle-aged couple who own the first floor only use it on occasional weekends and the elderly lady on the second floor spends every winter in Madeira.'

The flat occupied the entire top floor. It was larger than Faith expected and smelt of paint and turpentine. In the glow from two gas mantles she surveyed the large sitting room which held a couch, two leather horsehair chairs and a table. Three thick-piled rugs were scattered on the polished floorboards. Dominating the room was the easel and several paintings covered by a dust sheet were stacked on the floor. A vast window filled another wall. Through the open curtain, Faith saw that this opened on to a balcony which overlooked the Thames. Imposing warehouses lined the far river bank. Behind them pinheads of lights from houses and side streets led away into the distance.

Off this room an open door revealed a small kitchen. Two more open doors showed a black and white tiled bathroom and a spacious bedroom. Even with gas light instead of the newer electricity the studio was luxurious. Dan had described it as though it was scarcely fit for habitation. He must indeed be wealthy if such grandeur left him unimpressed. The knowledge took the edge off her pleasure. Wealth was a barrier between them. She liked Dan and had hoped that he wanted to see more of her, but now she was not so sure.

The fresh air had revived Ruby but she was still unable to walk unaided. Tony Chalmers carried a bottle of champagne in one hand and supported her with the other around her waist. As soon as the door closed behind the couple they began kissing. Faith moved to the balcony window. It had been snowing when they left the restaurant and now it fell in a lacy screen, blurring the far river bank. A foghorn sounding from a passing ship made her start and then laugh.

'I'm afraid the river can be noisy on a night like this,' Dan apologised and crossed to the fireplace to light the gas fire fitted in the grate. He shrugged off his overcoat and slung it across the back of the couch.

Faith shrugged. 'I'm so tired, I doubt I'll notice. I want to start early in the morning looking for work.'

'What kind of work are you looking for?'

'Anything really. Waitress. Chambermaid. Cleaner.'

'Heaven forbid! That's no work for you.'

Faith glared at him. 'It's an honest living.'

'But you've a quick mind. You could do better . . .'

'Don't I just wish.' Everything he was saying was what had been nagging her since she started work, but she resented a stranger putting her shortcomings into words. Her aquamarine eyes flamed with indignation. 'Just what do you suggest? I hated being a skivvy and treated like I'm an imbecile incapable of making a decision. But it was work. It fed, housed and clothed me. I can't even get that in London. The only offer I've had in three days is from you to pose for a portrait. Grateful as I am, it's hardly going to set me up in a professional career.'

His full lips compressed. Had she angered him? She had not meant to. Her heart sank as he snatched at his bow tie, pulled it loose then unbuttoned the neck of his shirt and his jacket. Dressed less formally, he appeared more approachable and Faith was again struck by his dark handsome looks.

'I'm sorry.' She rubbed her brow, a headache pumping behind her eyes. 'You've been kind. I should be thanking you, not making you take the brunt of my frustration.'

'I will pay you for your time as a model,' he declared less harshly.

She smiled to lessen the tension which had sprung up between them. Aware that the giggling and movements from Ruby and Tony had stopped, she glanced across the room. The bedroom door was closed and there was no sign of the couple.

Embarrassment flooded her cheeks with colour and she hung her head, her hair curtaining her face. She was unable to look Dan in the eye.

'Do you want me to turf them out? I can tell Tony to leave now, if you wish,' he suggested.

'What Ruby does with her life is her affair,' she answered stiffly. 'I'm not her judge, but sometimes she can be inconsiderate.'

Defensively, she wrapped her coat closer about her figure. Dan had walked into the kitchen and she heard the rattle of a kettle being placed on a stove. He called out to her, 'I'll give them half an hour. Then I'll chuck Tony out so that you can get some sleep. You look exhausted.'

She leaned against the kitchen doorway. 'You're very kind.'

He shrugged. 'I know what it's like to be broke. When I was an art student I never seemed to have enough money for paint and food.'

'You have done very well for yourself in the meantime.'

His expression shuttered and he turned away to pour the coffee. 'Some would say that.'

His abrupt manner made her hesitate from probing deeper. It wasn't her business. He had done so much to help them, she did not want to offend him. Even so, she felt a quiver of unease. Beneath the apparent wealth and charm, she sensed an underlying sadness. Or was it just his artistic temperament?

A dark winged brow lifted as he regarded the way she continued to clutch her coat tight to her figure. The gas fire had heated the room and she was beginning to feel uncomfortably warm, but her coat was a protective barrier.

Faith was uncertain whether she could trust Dan, especially after the way Ruby had disappeared with his friend. But as she was different from Ruby, she should not judge Dan by Tony's behaviour.

'This isn't Bluebeard's lair,' Dan chided.

After his kindness, it would be wrong to insult him. Impatient with her doubts, she removed her coat and laid it on the chair arm. It wasn't as though she didn't know how to look after herself.

Glancing at him, she decided that she could trust him. She had never yet misjudged a person, even Ruby. She knew and accepted her friend for exactly what she was. A fun-loving, frivolous woman, who underneath her hard shell was desperate to be loved – as only a foundling can want the security of such love. Not that Ruby would ever admit to such a weakness. She saw herself as her own woman, who needed no one and nothing but her own wits to survive.

Taking the coffee cup Faith sat down. After a few sips, she relaxed back in the chair. The relief at taking her weight off her aching feet made her sigh. Kicking off her shoes, she stretched her legs and wriggled her toes in the thick black and red rug. Briefly, she closed her eyes and luxuriated in the warmth and comfort of the room. For the first time since leaving Tilbury she had a full stomach and her natural optimism returned. London was a place to succeed and better themselves. Opportunities for anyone willing to work hard flourished here. The excitement she had felt on the steam train to Fenchurch Street station returned. Now she was warm and replete the future again looked rosy.

When she opened her eyes, she discovered that Dan had picked up a sketchpad and the charcoal stick was flying over the page. She sat up more demurely.

'No. Don't move,' he said abruptly, his manner abstracted as he concentrated on his drawing.

She relaxed and settled comfortably in the chair. The temptation to close her eyes as the warmth of the room cocooned her was too strong to resist.

Ruby was first aware of her head feeling like someone was nailing it to the bed, then the crushing weight on top of her body registered. Pushing ineffectually at it, her hand contacted with naked flesh. With a groan, she struggled to full consciousness and the figure on top of her moved, rolling over to pull her on top of him with a throaty chuckle.

'That's the way I like my ladies, always ready for more.'

There was only a glimmer of dawn brightening the sky and Ruby could just make out a blond-haired man beneath her. An arm thrown back over his head revealed a gold watchstrap and heavy gold signet ring. The dull ache in her lower body told her that their sex must have been boisterous. Hazily, she recalled how they had met. When his hands moved over her hips and his mouth circled her breasts, her passion took control. She moved against him murmuring, 'I hope you've got more of the necessary. I'm not about to risk getting up the spout.'

She might be hot blooded but she never allowed sex unless the man took precautions.

'Always prepared, sweetheart,' Tony answered, his competent hands sliding between her legs, blotting conscious thought from her mind.

She reared up, her breathing coming in hard gasps as she impaled herself on him and began to ride him with deliberate and provocative slowness. Twice she brought him almost to the point of ecstasy then withdrew before repositioning herself to prolong and intensify his release.

'Now, sweetheart. Now!' he groaned, his fingers digging into her buttocks to stop her withdrawing a third time. Her gyrating hips gave him the release he craved, his voice hoarse as he cried out in pleasure. Mercilessly she sought her own fulfilment, riding him with hard thrusts as he moaned beneath her, until she finally collapsed over him, her body contracting in a throbbing explosion of heat.

'Great Scott, you are something else,' Tony murmured against her hair.

'You were dynamite yourself. You know how to make a woman feel so good.' She laughed confidently. In the brightening day, his handsome face was flushed and her body was bathed in contentment. Most of last night was a blur to her, but before they left this bed she was going to ensure that Tony Chalmers was completely under her spell.

'That was some night,' she breathed. Her head was beginning to clear and she vaguely recalled Tony telling her that he knew several nightclub owners and would put in a word for her to get a job. Who knows, with contacts like that, she might finally realise her dream and become a professional singer. Tony could help her achieve that dream.

Faith stirred and rubbed at the painful crick in her neck. She stretched and was surprised to discovered how warm she was. Opening her eyes she saw the gas fire still burning. The extravagance of it made her sit up with a start. To her astonishment she was lying on the couch with her coat placed over her. Hadn't she last been sitting on an armchair? Then her glance fell upon Dan who had pushed both the armchairs together, improvising a makeshift bed. His long form was curled up and he was sleeping soundly though she suspected with great discomfort.

He must have moved her and chosen the more uncomfortable place to sleep for himself. Standing up, she rolled her shoulders to ease the stiffness from them. They had been fortunate in meeting Dan and Tony last night. Just how fortunate, she realised as she crossed to the window and rubbed the window pane. The warmth of her fingers melted the frost crystals which had formed. The balcony and rooftops across the river were covered in several inches of thick snow. The sight made her gasp.

A movement from Dan swung her round. He was staring sleepily at her. 'Is anything wrong?'

'It snowed heavily in the night. I reckon Ruby and I would have frozen to death if you hadn't taken pity on us. That's a debt I can never repay.'

He pushed a hand through his dark hair and swung his legs to the floor. His tousled appearance emphasised his earthy magnetism. Her attraction to him was heightened by her feelings of gratitude.

'I want no more talk of being indebted to me. By modelling for me you will be doing me a service.'

His encompassing stare held a tenderness which made her heart caper. If she wasn't careful she could find herself falling for this man and that would be a mistake. His wealth put him far above her. She steeled herself to counter the fascination Dan was weaving around her. Holding his gaze, she insisted, 'I believe in paying my way.'

There was a devilish curl to his lips as he stood up and drew her to him. Before she could protest he kissed her. A gasp of surprise parted her lips and an answering response was drawn from her before she could check it. The kiss set her body tingling. The probing flick of his tongue against hers was a sensual caress which caused her limbs to lose their strength. She clung to him, her eyes closed, savouring the pleasure his lips so effortlessly evoked. Her blood turned to a lava flow, spilling through her veins. As his hands moved slowly down the length of her spine, her flesh seared and ripples of pleasure sizzled through every sinew. A sensual moan soughed in her throat. The wanton entreaty within it scythed through to conscious thought and following it came the shock that her conduct was as shameless as Ruby's. With a sob she pushed back from him.

'No, Dan. I don't pay my debts that way. I will model to repay your kindness.'

He bowed his head, concealing his reaction from her, but she could feel the tension in his arms. Within his embrace, her resistance was melting. When he made no move to release her, she willed her frantic heart to slow. He was now regarding her with such tenderness her resolution wavered. How could a look cast her willpower to the winds? She fought against the enchantment of his gaze and drew a shaky breath, willing ice to form and freeze the fire still simmering in her veins. When that failed, she dredged her resources to summon the strength to remind him sharply, 'You said you'd make me do nothing I did not wish. Was that a lie to get me back to your flat?'

'Who are you fooling?' he coerced. 'Don't be afraid because of what you felt just now. Surrender to your senses.'

She despised the way her body continued to crave his touch. He thought she was cheap and easy. Indignation turned to anger which she kept fuelled. His kiss, brief as it was, had affected her too deeply. It had stirred emotions which she could not risk erupting. Anger was her protection and she used it ruthlessly. With a harder shove, she freed herself and backed away. She stumbled over her shoes and stooped to pick them up and retrieve her coat. 'Tell Ruby I shall wait for her outside by the river.'

'Don't run off because of one kiss. You're acting like a frigid virgin . . .' He stopped. The anger which had darkened his face was replaced by amazement. 'By God, you are a virgin! What the hell are you doing with a friend like Ruby. She's anyone's for . . .'

'Don't say that. You don't know her,' Faith defended. 'And don't make me sound like a freak because I don't believe in sleeping around.'

Dan rubbed a hand across his brow. 'Believe me, I don't regard you as a freak.'

The respect and admiration in his eyes were as disconcerting as his ridicule. This man tossed her emotions into turmoil.

He spread his hands in a mute gesture asking forgiveness. There was coercion in the velvety remonstrance. 'It's insane to go out in this weather.'

'It is best if I leave.' Stubbornness heightened her resolve. It was too dangerous to remain in his company.

'I find you remarkable and captivating,' Dan assured, then with a tantalising smile, added, 'and desirable . . . but I'd never force you. I apologise if I offended you.'

Suspecting that he was now either mocking or patronising her, she remained on her guard. He didn't move. The corner of his mouth tilted in a roguish smile. 'Artists are selfish creatures. I wouldn't do anything to jeopardise you posing for me. You inspire me. I've a dozen ideas of how to paint you. Does that help you to trust me?'

Faith relaxed. Had she overreacted? She felt foolish and realised that in her inexperience she had insulted him. 'Last night proved that I could trust you,' she amended, but did not add that it was herself she did not trust. She could still feel the imprint of his mouth on hers, the all-consuming heat of passion slow to cool under his steady gaze. She did not believe in love at first sight. The way her body had reacted was a warning that she could easily become infatuated with this handsome artist.

As she hesitated she became aware that there were several pages of the sketchpad scattered around the chair where he had been sleeping. Every drawing was of herself.

Curiosity may have killed the cat, it now drew Faith into its dangerous web. Picking one up, her throat tightened with emotion. It was her, but it was not her . . . She could not be this beautiful creature lying half-drowned in a woodland stream. The woman's long hair was tangled in a briar which had stopped her from drowning. It was tragic, mystical and beautiful.

'I don't look like that. Well, it's me . . . but . . .'

'It's how I saw you last night. A beautiful woman caught in a web of fate who was not yet free from all dangers.'

She could not hold back a laugh. 'Her life saved by a briar. Is that how you see yourself?'

His stare was enigmatic. 'Briar could be right.'

His words again made Faith uneasy. She had meant to be flippant. His reply was serious. It must be tiredness which was making her react so oddly to his moods. Her concentration returned to the sketches. She might not understand this man, but as she studied the drawings it was obvious that he was a talented artist. Most were of her sleeping in the chair but one other had the same perturbing element as the first. Here she was leaning against the trunk of an ancient oak tree. She was gazing up at the stars, one hand raised as though she would draw down the moon from the heavens. Her expression was enrapt. It disturbed her to see that one of her bare feet had the coils of a snake entwined around it.

'This sketch with the snake. What is its meaning?'

Dan glanced at it and frowned. 'It's the image which came into my mind. My imagination sometimes reveals elements of a person which are unknown to themselves or others.' He shrugged. 'It's the Irish Celt in me. When I'm absorbed in my work I sense things about the models. Another time I see colours around them which reveal their personality and mood.' He checked abruptly. 'I've never told anyone that before. It could be the ruin of my reputation as an artist. I'd be labelled some kind of crank.'

'Or visionary,' Faith answered, intrigued. 'Do you see colours around me?'

He looked annoyed that she had asked. 'Well, do you? I am interested.'

He regarded her for a long moment before answering, then said with reluctance, 'Green.'

'The colour of envy and jealousy.' The hurt was sharp in her voice.

'No. Green is the colour of unconstrained love. You were well named, Faith. It is also the colour of nature. Hence the settings of the drawings.'

Fascinated, Faith persisted. 'And Ruby. Did you see colours around her?'

'I wasn't sufficiently interested,' he evaded. 'I have an impression of red interlaced with black.'

'Dramatic colours. Ruby will love that. But the red would be linked with her name,' Faith responded.

Dan was inexplicably afraid for Faith. He could not shake the colours of red and black which had imposed themselves on the image of Ruby. They were volatile colours. Red for flamboyance and also a warning of danger. Black the colour of the sinister and dark side of a personality. Colours he had once glimpsed around a convicted murderer when he had been called for jury service. How on earth had such a tender-hearted woman as Faith become embroiled with a creature like Ruby – a cold-hearted, self-centred and calculating bitch . . . of the type he knew to his cost?

His anger resurfaced at thoughts of Imelda. He was still paying the price for becoming entangled with her machinations. It was too late when he had seen the colours of red and black around Imelda. He'd been a besotted fool too blinded by passion to see the warning of danger. He'd been ensnared by her beauty and the illusion of an idealistic love.

Abruptly Dan took the drawing from Faith, refusing to dwell upon regrets and recrimination. Faith was looking at him with concern and to make light of the matter he said, jokingly, 'Ruby, the scarlet woman. In her case it is apt.'

There was no point in saying more. Faith would not listen. Her affection for her friend was without condition and she would resent him maligning someone she cared for.

'And you see so much when you start to draw a person?' To his relief Faith turned the subject to safer ground.

He expanded. 'To capture a person and make them come alive on canvas you have to be able to see beyond flesh and bone. You need a perception of their hopes, aspirations and personality. Faith, you have the courage and determination to achieve something special in your life. Therefore I drew you reaching for the moon. Whatever you want to achieve, you can. The moon is also the symbol of the Celtic Goddess who my ancestors believed created all life, including creativity itself within ourselves.'

'What then is the significance of the snake?'

Dan regarded her sombrely. 'Everyone's life has some snake in the grass waiting to pounce, to wrap its coils around them and hold them back . . . to stop them rising above their level. Don't let anyone do that to you, Faith. Don't let old loyalties bind you too tightly.'

'The snake represents Ruby, does it?' she said with a flash of ill humour. 'You don't like her, do you?'

'She's not good for you. She will always be governed by her passions, or the need to take the easy option. I know her type. She will use your friendship to her own ends, if you allow it.'

Conscience pricked him. The cynic born in him in recent years rose to mock him. How easy it would be for him to use this beautiful, desirable woman for his own ends. He had been potently aware of the intensity of passion he had aroused in her.

41

Faith regarded Dan with growing hostility. What right had he to make such assumptions, or try to turn her against her friend? Her eyes glinted with anger. 'From your words I assume Ruby reminds you of some woman who played you false. I think I know Ruby better than you. I don't like my friends judged by the actions of others.'

At her retaliation his jaw clenched and he swung away from her to march across the room. He thumped loudly on the bedroom door. 'Tony, I'm leaving for Sussex in an hour and need to get changed. Move yourself, will you.' Without looking at Faith he disappeared into the bathroom and she heard him running water into a basin to wash.

His reaction disturbed Faith. Clearly some woman had hurt him profoundly in the past? Who? An old flame?

She collected up the sketches so that they would not get trodden on and placed the one with the snake at the bottom of the pile. She felt guilty that she had angered Dan. Although she would never allow anyone to malign her friends, he had done so much for Ruby and herself. Even though it was the answer to their problems, she didn't feel right accepting his offer to use this flat whilst he was out of London.

Her thoughts still on Dan, she wandered over to the window to stare out. A footstep behind her made her swivel round. Ruby was yawning and combing her short blonde hair with her fingers to free its tangles.

'That Tony is something. He's going to see about getting me a job in a nightclub. I'm meeting him again tonight. How did you get on with Dan?'

'Fine. Our flat-finding problems are not so immediate. Dan has said we can stay here for a couple of days while he's out of London.'

Ruby studied her with a sleepy smile. 'You spend the night with a gorgeous fella like him and it's just fine. And he offers you his flat. You've got it made, girl. I reckon he fancies you.'

'Give it a rest, Ruby. You're a great one to talk. Since you and Tony hogged the bedroom, I ended up on the couch. Dan, who just happens to own this flat, slept in the chair. How could you act like that, Ruby? Sometimes you're so damned selfish . . .'

'Ah c'mon, Faith. I'd had a skinful and Tony is a persuasive bugger when it suits him. Still, we landed on our feet with this place to ourselves and no rent to pay.'

Faith could hear Dan's voice raised in anger from the bedroom. The words were indistinct but '*selfish*', '*inconsiderate*' and '*only considering yourself*' were clearly audible. Since Tony could have returned to his club in London to sleep, she had a low opinion of him for stealing Dan's bed for the night. In some ways Tony and Ruby had a lot in common and deserved each other. Why was it that Ruby always attracted the wrong type of men? Men who used her. Faith was certain that some of Ruby's past boyfriends had been far from respectable law-abiding citizens.

'We're not staying here for more than two nights,' she declared. 'This is Dan's flat. We'll be gone before he returns. I'm going job hunting this morning.'

Tony ambled into the room and went straight to a cupboard and took out a bottle of whisky and helped himself to a generous measure. He raised his glass and grinned at Ruby. 'Hair of the dog and all that.'

Dan appeared having changed into a black suit. Ignoring Tony, he gave Ruby the briefest of acknowledgements and took Faith's hand to draw her away from her friend. His voice was an urgent whisper, 'If it was just you, I'd be prepared to sleep on the couch when I return, but not for the benefit of your friend. In the meantime use whatever you need.' He pressed a white five-pound note into her hand. 'This will get you some food to tide you over and should be enough to pay a couple of weeks' rent in advance on a flat.'

'I can't take your money, Dan.'

'Nonsense. But promise me that you won't go without leaving me your address. I meant what I said about painting you. And I shall pay you for your time.'

Tony was by the door passionately kissing Ruby goodbye. They had obviously hit it off and Ruby would be seeing more of

43

him. Faith's lips tingled with the memory of Dan's kiss. He had not pursued her when she had pulled away from him. He had treated her with respect and a kindness she wasn't sure she deserved. She felt guilty that Ruby had deliberately set out to get these two men to buy them a meal.

'I shall never forget your kindness last night, Dan. I will happily pose for you. It will repay your generosity in allowing us to use your flat.' Her mouth dried as she conquered her sadness that he was leaving so soon after they met. When he returned he might have forgotten all about the street waif he had rescued from cold and starvation.

He nodded, apparently satisfied. For a moment she thought he meant to kiss her again and her heart catapulted with expectancy. Instead there was a momentary clouding of his expression, then he stepped back, lifted his overcoat from the back of a chair and walked to the door.

Disappointment smote her that he had no intention of kissing her goodbye. He paused halfway across the floor and looked back. His smile was disconcerting. Had he seen her disappointment? For a second she was tempted to follow Ruby's example and hurl herself into his arms. Pride made her chin tilt higher and her shoulders squared.

'Have a safe journey, Dan. I won't be here when you get back, but I shall leave my address.'

He winked at her as though he had seen through her demure veneer to the wanton clamouring of her heart. 'You've a noble, stubborn streak, Faith Tempest. Remember what I said about reaching for the stars.'

Chapter Four

When Dan and Tony had left, Ruby sauntered towards the bedroom yawning. 'I'm going back to bed.'

'No, you're not!' Faith rounded on her. 'We are going out to find work.'

'But Tony said he'd get me a job.'

'Gents like Tony are only interested in themselves. Don't put too much trust in his word. You've been let down before.'

Faith hid the five-pound note in her dress pocket. She didn't intend to use it unless they were desperate. 'There must be work about.'

Ruby pouted. 'Those two are rolling in it. And Dan fancies you or he wouldn't have allowed us to stay here. It's freezing out there. We'll look for work tomorrow.'

'This flat is a blessing, but it isn't permanent,' Faith snapped. 'Have you forgotten that we haven't any money? Or did Tony leave you some to buy food?'

The scowl which marred the beauty of Ruby's face told Faith that he had not.

'You're an old slave driver,' Ruby groaned. 'Truth is I don't fancy being a skivvy no more. It would be more exciting to work in a nightclub.'

'Then get yourself smartened up and do something about it. Stop relying on other people. You've a good voice, Ruby. Why not have a try as a singer?'

Naturally optimistic, Faith visualised Ruby as she had seen her singing in pubs. The customers kept demanding more songs and on top of the piano she always had a line of drinks they bought for her. 'I've seen the way you look at men when you're singing. They find you irresistible.'

'You're right. Nothing ventured, nothing gained.' Ruby placed one hand on her hip and sashayed across the room. She began singing a love song and on reaching the bedroom door turned and blew a kiss to Faith. 'Since I can't help being irresistible, I might as well use it to my advantage.'

'Take care you don't misuse it.'

'So what are you going to do?'

Faith shrugged. Dan's parting words had taken root and were feeding upon an ambition which had always been with her. She wanted to make something of her life. 'I don't know. I came to London to better myself. No more waiting on others for me either. I'll get a paper and see what's in that. I'll walk the streets again looking for opportunities if I have to. I feel our luck has changed.'

'Have you got money for a paper?' Ruby brightened. 'Did Dan leave you a couple of quid?'

For the first time she could remember, Faith lied to Ruby. If she knew she had five pounds, she wouldn't go looking for work. 'He offered. I only accepted enough to buy some food and a paper.'

'You're a fool not taking his money.' Ruby shook her head in despair. 'I don't know what I'm going to do with you. I suppose I'd better get meself dressed then.'

'And we are leaving here together,' Faith warned. 'I've got the only key. Don't think you can sneak back into bed when my back is turned.'

Ruby pulled a face. 'Slave driver.'

While Ruby dressed Faith was beset with worries for their future. She was optimistic that a worthwhile job was out there waiting for her. But Ruby's attitude troubled her. Ruby couldn't go on using people without repercussions rebounding on herself.

Eager to seek employment, Faith paced to the window and gazed out at the river. Tugs and barges were chugging down the waterway which was as busy a thoroughfare as any road. In the distance she could see the clock tower of Big Ben and the distinctive skyline of the Houses of Parliament. The sight of them made her shiver with anticipation and excitement. London was a place of power and importance. A place where opportunities must be grasped and anything could happen.

A watery sun was pushing itself through the clouds casting its golden light upon the glistening snow. She smiled, remembering the story of Dick Whittington who had come to London believing the streets were paved with gold. This morning they were.

'Look, Ruby, the sun has come out and the snow is melting. Isn't that a good sign? Let's each make a wish to achieve something special.'

Unimpressed, Ruby sighed. Her head thundering with a hangover made her sarcastic. 'I'll be top of the bill at the London Palladium and have the world worshipping at my feet. How about you?'

Faith gazed longingly at the paintings stacked against the wall. 'I'd love to be an artist but I could never afford the lessons.'

'Don't most artists die broke?' Ruby grimaced 'Blow that! Only a mug would spend their life starving in a garret and then someone else gets rich by discovering their talent when they're six feet under.' She closed her eyes against the persistent headache. 'My bloody head. I feel rough. I can't go out yet.'

Seeing Ruby's pallor Faith's compassion overrode her impatience. 'Okay, stay here for the morning. No one will employ you while you look like death. But I want your promise that you'll search for work this afternoon.'

Ruby curled her legs up on to the chair and murmured, 'I promise.' She was asleep by the time Faith closed the door behind her.

Four hours later Faith wondered whether she would ever get a job. The snow might have melted but the hazy sun had little warmth in the February morning. She was again half-frozen and determination alone was now forcing her to continue walking and searching. The newspapers had proved unsuccessful. The only work for women was in offices for which she had not been trained. In her wish to better herself she had stayed away from Soho and walked along Oxford and Regent Street inquiring in the large departmental stores for employment. In desperation she would have taken a temporary job as a shop assistant until something more challenging came along. Even that lowly position was denied her. They all wanted someone with experience and the only work they offered was cleaning. She declined. Thanks to Dan's generosity, she wasn't that desperate – yet.

She turned into Bond Street. These elegant shops with expensive clothes and furnishings in the windows belonged to another world where money was no object. She looked into a shop window, her attention held by a large painting of a water pageant in Venice. It was a detailed scene with masked revellers flirting and carousing. It was a masterpiece, but Faith did not recognise the artist. Intrigued she peered into the shop. On its walls were a score of exceptional paintings. She could not walk past without seeing them properly.

A man was seated at an ornate desk with carved gilded legs. He looked haughty, reminding her of a photograph of Noël Coward on the billboard outside one of the theatres. He wore a dark suit with a blood-red cravat inside the open neck of his white shirt and was talking on the telephone. His thick hair was the colour of buttermilk and waved back from his wide brow.

At the tinkling of the door bell, he looked up and grey eyes beneath straight white brows flickered over her disparagingly. Faith inwardly cringed. His assessing glance seemed to calculate the value of her smart but inexpensive clothing as little above that of a ragamuffin. For a moment she expected him to ask her to leave. The telephone call must be important. His voice dropped and he was protesting into the receiver and ignored Faith. Still she hesitated. That look had put Faith amongst the working class and unable to appreciate or afford the art around her. She hated snobbery and intellectual snobbery was the worst of all. Had her parents lived she would have gone on to grammar school and been allowed to take art lessons. Why should she feel inferior to him? She might not be able to afford to purchase any of the paintings, but she could appreciate them.

A seascape was beckoning to her from the far corner. Holding her head high and defiant, she walked slowly past a row of paintings, pausing whenever one was of special interest. Two smaller pictures, obviously a pair, depicting sunrise and moonlight over a craggy moor, had a magical quality about them. Their mystical beauty brought a shiver to her spine. The sunrise was a golden sunburst of colour against dark granite rocks. The crescent moon was reflected in a stream. Its silver light embraced the rocks and heather with its light. When she studied the signature her eyes crinkled with pleasure. Dan Brogan had painted them! He must be famous despite his modesty, otherwise a gallery such as this would not display his work.

It was an added joy that she had been captivated by those paintings without knowing that he was the artist. Reluctantly, she dragged her gaze away and within moments was enthralled by the seascape. In her opinion it was superior to the painting in the window. It was of two fishermen in a rowing boat trying to rescue a companion who was on the point of drowning in a stormy sea. The anguish on the faces of the men was poignant. You could feel the icy water and the horror the men were experiencing. She couldn't take her gaze off it.

How long she stood there she did not know; she was lost in the wonder of the painting. Gradually she became aware that a man with a neatly trimmed brown beard and wearing a bowler hat and cashmere overcoat had come to stand beside her.

The salesman ended his conversation and hurried over to attend a prospective customer. 'Mr Devereux, such a pleasure to see you again. I've had some exceptional paintings in recent months. But I knew you'd be just devastated if I didn't ring to tell you about our latest acquisition.'

'The Venetian scene in the window. It has charm,' the customer replied.

'It exudes the essence of Venice itself.' The salesman rolled his

49

eyes heavenwards. 'It is divine. Simply divine. It's eighteenth century and the artist was little known until Christie's sold one of his works for five hundred guineas in November. I knew it was just right for you.'

When Mr Devereux did not respond, the shop assistant waved a hand expansively towards the seascape. 'Or perhaps this is more to your liking.'

'I will consider them both, Lincoln. But in quiet contemplation.' There was impatience in his voice. The fawning man, Faith realised, must be Mr Lincoln of Underwood & Lincoln Gallery, the name in gold-leaf lettering on the door. Owner or not, he had irritated her by his posturing and pressuring.

'Of course,' Mr Lincoln said with a false laugh. 'Take all the time that you need, Mr Devereux. Both the seascape and Venetian scenes are superb investments.'

'Investments!' Faith muttered. 'It's criminal to possess such paintings for other than the pleasure they give.'

The effeminate owner looked down his aquiline nose at her and swept a hand through his buttermilk hair. 'Madam is an idealist. My customers want good investments for their money.' His sarcasm was like a slap across her cheek.

The unnecessary rudeness of it made her retaliate. 'They do not deserve to own fine works of art, if all they can see is the guineas that they are worth. Art is meant to be enjoyed, to enrich the soul, not one's pocket.'

'How terribly whimsical.' Mr Lincoln laughed, a high affected sound which grated on Faith's nerves. '*Hoi polloi* cannot be expected to understand such matters.'

Mr Devereux put up a hand to silence him. From his air of command, Faith assumed he must be someone wealthy and important. He turned to her. 'You speak so passionately about art, miss. What then is your opinion of this painting?'

Suspecting that he was mocking her, Faith was about to walk out. Then she saw his expression. He was serious. His brown eyes were regarding her solemnly and with interest. He really did want her opinion and she was flattered. She guessed he was several

50

years younger than Mr Lincoln, somewhere in his mid-forties.

'It is beautiful and tragic,' she said, passionately. 'It is a picture which will stay in my mind for years.'

'Don't you find its subject depressing?' Mr Devereux replied.

'No. Far from it,' she enthused. 'Those men are risking their lives to save their companion. It is alive with the courage of men fighting against the elements. It should be an inspiration to us all. I've never seen a storm painted so dramatically.'

'What would you say it is worth?'

'I'm not an expert. Probably more than I shall earn in a lifetime. To me it is priceless because of its beauty. I hope whoever purchases it will hang it in a special place. Somewhere where its owners can sit and gaze at it and feel its presence like an old friend in the room.'

Mr Devereux turned to Mr Lincoln. 'Have the painting delivered to my country house. It will hang in the family parlour where I can enjoy it of an evening.'

'You will not be disappointed, Mr Devereux.' Lincoln minced to his desk and began writing in an order book. 'A wise choice, Mr Devereux.'

'This young woman sold it to me by her enthusiasm.' He smiled at Faith. 'I still need a painting for my grand salon, which is filled with house guests every weekend. Would you recommend the one in the window?'

She was about to say that she was no expert. Mr Lincoln's glare razored into her, the pinched lines about his mouth showing his fear that he could lose a second sale. Unable to contain himself, he burst out, 'It is the perfect choice.'

Faith was indignant enough at his earlier derision to contradict him. 'But only if Mr Devereux feels moved by it.'

Behind his customer's back, Mr Lincoln scowled at her. Mr Devereux was regarding her seriously. That meant a great deal to her. 'It is an atmospheric and noble work. There is no doubt of that. It would look impressive in a large room if you are looking to fill a wall.'

'Fill a wall!' Mr Lincoln wailed in agony. 'This woman knows

51

nothing of art. I have never heard such sacrilege. Mr Devereux, I implore you . . .'

'As I was saying before I was interrupted,' Faith continued, 'if I owned a large house with an impressive staircase I would hang it as a focal point in a hall; such as a curve in the stairs or a division of a staircase. That would be the perfect setting and would capture the attention of your guests in the most impressive manner.'

She studied Mr Devereux intently and asked softly, 'Do you like art? Or are you buying these works merely to impress your guests, or as an investment?'

There was a muffled squeak of outrage from Mr Lincoln. 'Madam, I must ask you to leave. This charade has gone quite far enough. I will not have a customer insulted.'

'I am not insulted, Lincoln,' Mr Devereux replied, his eyes glinting with amusement. 'As a businessman I look on my paintings as an investment to hand down to my children. I also receive a great deal of pleasure from them.'

She smiled warmly. 'I'm glad. If you want something for your grand salon, where people are gathered to talk and for recreation, a more discerning visitor would delight in this pair of paintings.'

She walked to the two moorland scenes painted by Dan. Her action had nothing to do with her indebtedness to the artist, but stemmed from a genuine wish to give Mr Devereux her honest advice. 'Can't you feel the power of the open spaces and the glory of the earth's beauty, sir.'

She broke off, the impact of the paintings reducing her to awed silence. Their beauty brought a tear to her eye and as she wiped it away, she laughed softly. 'How foolish of me. I get emotional just looking at them.'

'Brogan is a modern artist,' Mr Lincoln explained. 'As you know, it is our policy to promote new artists. I was persuaded by my partner, who knows Brogan, to exhibit his work. His style is a bit fanciful for my taste. I prefer the simplicity of art nouveau which is all the rage. We have several such paintings in the gallery upstairs, if you are interested.'

'Fanciful or not, I like Brogan's style.' Mr Devereux regarded Faith with renewed respect. 'You see these paintings with an artist's inner eye, Miss . . .'

'Tempest. Faith Tempest. But I'm no artist.'

'A pity. You have a rare gift of insight. Thank you for your time, Miss Tempest. I have enjoyed listening to you.'

Mr Lincoln was standing stiffly, his figure visibly bristling with indignation. 'Shall I take the Venetian painting from the window for you to view, Mr Devereux?'

'Don't bother with that now,' Devereux waved him away. 'It will hang over the staircase as this charming lady suggested. Send it with the seascape and also these two here.'

Faith was shocked at how much Mr Devereux would be spending on all four paintings. She felt she had to intervene. 'Sir, you must only buy them if you like them, I was not trying to influence you.'

She saw Mr Lincoln's cheeks bleach of colour. Mr Devereux laughed, saying, 'They are all good investments, Miss Tempest. However you have given me a deeper insight into them and I shall enjoy them even more. A woman as knowledgeable as yourself should own her own gallery. You would make a fortune.'

'I'd settle for a job at this moment,' Faith declared.

Mr Devereux regarded the gallery owner, who looked ready to frogmarch Faith from the shop, before she said anything else. 'Snap up this young woman as a sales assistant, Lincoln. She's a natural. Her talent will make your fortune if not hers.' Tipping his bowler to Faith, Mr Devereux walked out of the shop.

Faith hurried after him, unwilling to face the storm brewing in the owner's eyes.

'Miss Tempest, a moment please,' Mr Lincoln rapped out. She froze, suspecting his ridicule. It had all been a joke. Devereux had been mocking her, pretending to be interested in her opinions, when he was probably laughing at her naivety.

Yet Mr Lincoln looked far from annoyed. Instead he was beaming at her. 'Are you looking for work?'

'Yes, but Mr Devereux was just amusing himself at my

53

expense. He walked out without paying for the paintings.'

'My dear child. He's a millionaire. He doesn't pay over the counter like buying penny wares from Woolworths. He has an account with us. He is a very discerning customer. To have purchased one painting would have delighted me, but four . . . you even managed to sell him Brogan's paintings, who has yet to make his mark in the art world. The job is yours if you want it.'

Faith was stunned. 'Really!' She curbed her enthusiasm. The gallery must have made a great deal of money from the sale of those paintings and she had been the one to sell them. Even through her excitement she responded to the stab of loyalty which promoted her to defend Dan's work. 'Brogan is a talented artist. So how much are you willing to pay me?'

He pursed his lips. 'Three guineas a week.'

She stared levelly at him. It was an insult considering how much profit the gallery had just made. To work here she would need to dress smartly and that would cost money. Mr Lincoln was using her naivety to get her cheap. One thing Faith had learned today from Mr Devereux was that nothing of quality comes cheap.

'Double that offer and give me a bonus on any paintings over a hundred pounds which I sell for you.'

'The girl would steal my living,' Mr Lincoln groaned. 'You have no experience.'

'I didn't need experience for Mr Devereux. I learn fast and I will study art in my spare time.'

'Five guineas a week and no bonus.'

Faith drew a deep breath. 'There are other galleries in Bond Street. Mr Devereux has shown me that this is something I could do well. I am sure a reference from him will be well received elsewhere. After all, if I don't sell the paintings I don't earn the bonus.'

'She'll be offering me her grandmother to work for free next – ' Oliver regarded her fixedly – 'and me a poor man.'

She could feel his antagonism. After all, he had only offered her the job because Mr Devereux was such an important customer. Had she gone too far? Faith's heart banged against her ribcage. She really wanted this job. It was a heaven-sent opportunity to work with the paintings she loved. Though she wasn't so sure that she could stomach the snobbish Mr Lincoln as her employer. She would have to swallow her irritation. It was the work which was important and the chance to gain the necessary experience.

Remembering the buzz of excitement she had felt at Mr Devereux's interest, her eagerness for the job tempted Faith to back down, but a stubborn streak kept her silent.

Appraising the cut of his Savile Row suit and white silk shirt, she said, 'May I be as poor as you one day, if I'm lucky, Mr Lincoln. But while we are discussing money I shall need an advance to purchase some suitable clothes. I had all my belongings stolen a few nights ago.'

'Oh, you poor luv.' Oliver Lincoln's haughty manner dissolved with his false accent. 'London can be a vicious city. A friend of mine was robbed and beaten by thugs just last week. Just up from the sticks, were you?'

His look of concern melted her antagonism towards him. Perhaps he wasn't such a snob after all. She nodded. 'But that doesn't mean I don't know my worth.'

He tapped his cheek with his forefinger before adding, 'You drive a hard bargain. But then you have to be ruthless in this game. There's customers who will do their best to knock the price of a painting down so that we'd get no profit from it.' His expression was approving. 'Five guineas and a bonus of two guineas on every hundred pounds your sales exceed a monthly target. But how do I know I can trust you with an advance? I may never see you again.'

'I need a job and I can think of nothing more wonderful than working in an art gallery. I'd be a fool to steal a couple of pounds from you when I could earn a great deal more by working here.'

'If you drive as hard a bargain with the customers as you have with me, Miss Tempest, then I can ask no better from you.' He opened the ornate gilt till. 'Here's ten guineas. I don't want my customers' sensibilities offended by my staff wearing cheap clothes. You can repay me a guinea a week from your wages. Can you start tomorrow?'

She nodded. Five pounds five shillings a week was a fortune for her; she had only earned a fraction of that as a chambermaid.

Faith shopped for her new outfits in Peter Jones. To her delight they had several suitable dresses at sale prices. She chose a kingfisher dress and another in camel which complemented her fiery hair. To ring the changes she selected some plain and patterned long chiffon scarves to drape around her neck. She also purchased a coral pink wool day dress marked down to nineteen shillings and eleven pence which Ruby would find irresistible. The money stretched to a new pair of shoes, some face powder and lipstick and several items of underwear for herself and Ruby to replace those stolen. If they were careful there was enough left to keep the gas meter and themselves fed until she was paid next Friday.

Unfortunately she would have to use Dan's money after all. How else could she pay the deposit on a rented flat? At least she could repay him by posing for him. Although it didn't seem right to be paid for sitting still and doing nothing, especially as it would mean spending time with Dan. She hugged herself, wishing that Dan was back at the flat so she could tell him of her job. Irrationally it was important to her that he approved.

Ruby was sitting in the bar of the Ritz. Having passed the famous hotel, she could not resist going inside. Hadn't she sworn to better herself in London? And you couldn't find anywhere swankier than the Ritz to cheer yourself up. Her day was unsuccessful, but a gin and tonic would lift her spirits.

She downed it in one gulp and ordered another. After Faith left the flat she had slept until midday, then made herself some tea and lazed in front of the gas fire until the meter had run out. With no shilling coins to replenish it the the room soon chilled.

'Might as well drag myself round a few clubs, I suppose,' she muttered without enthusiasm. The sunshine had vanished and without Faith to encourage her, she was more inclined to lounge round all day. Tony would be good for a meal and a bit of a lark tonight. There was time enough to get a job.

She soon became bored with her own company and without any gas she couldn't even boil a kettle to make a cup of tea. There was a ten-shilling note in her coat pocket which she had lifted from Tony's wallet when he'd gone into the bathroom this morning. It would buy her something to eat and a hot drink. She smiled. 'What the hell, I'll even get a bus to Leicester Square,' she said aloud as she left the flat.

With the ten shillings in her pocket she was feeling carefree. 'Live for today,' she added with a grin, 'somehow tomorrow always takes care of itself.'

For half an hour she had been made to wait inside a nightclub for the manager to appear. With the lights turned up and devoid of customers it was seedier than she expected. When the manager's door opened a large man in his shirtsleeves and braces appeared. A buxom blonde woman wriggled past him and giggled. She was in a short black satin maid's uniform.

Ruby smothered her anger. Her coat was unbuttoned and she stood with one hand on her hip, revealing her hour-glass figure. The lecher had kept her waiting while he fucked one of the waitresses. The manager's pale bulbous eyes peeled the clothing from Ruby as he studied her.

'What you offering then, babe? The barman said you reckoned you were a singer. Singers I got, but I could be persuaded to give you a try.'

The man was repulsive. 'Are you gonna listen to me sing?' she challenged.

'That depends on how persuasive you are.'

She knew the type. He wouldn't even listen to her without demanding sex. Now she understood what Faith meant about self-respect. That fat toad was only after a cheap thrill. She shuddered. She didn't want to work for a creep like him. Thank God she wasn't that desperate for dough now they had a place to sleep even for just a night or two. She might be promiscuous but she'd never given herself to a man who did not attract her. There were too many handsome men to bother with the ugly ones. While she had her looks, she would never be short of choice.

'Oh, I can be very persuasive,' Ruby said, leaning forward to rest her hands on a table. 'Only you'll never know just how persuasive, because I save all that for the punters. And I make sure they'll be panting for more.' With a toss of her head she swung on her heel and sashayed across the floor, as proud and assured as a royal concubine. 'Just you wait. I'm gonna be a star and you'll be the mug who turned me away.'

'Stupid tart,' he shouted after her.

Ruby halted at the door. 'Not stupid enough to work here.'

She hopped on the first bus which came along, no longer in the mood to look for work. If the managers were all creeps like that she wasn't so keen on working in a nightclub. When the bus pulled up outside the Ritz, out of devilment she decided to go inside. Gazing at the opulence of the room and the richly dressed men and women seated in the bar, she felt a stab of envy. This is what I want, she vowed. The best of everything. Twice today she'd voiced a wish to be a star. Wouldn't that be something. Her name on everyone's lips . . .

Finishing her drink, she left the bar. She had just enough money for the bus fare back to Brogan's flat. Tony would be calling for her in a couple of hours and she wanted to bathe and prepare herself for him. He had been an energetic lover. More importantly he could afford to keep her until the right job came along. Not that she would tell Faith that. Dear, innocent Faith was an idealist who would work her fingers to the bone rather than accept charity from anyone.

Having seen the splendour of the Ritz and the beautiful women draped on rich business men's arms, Ruby had other ideas. Half the women had been mistresses, not the men's wives. She didn't intend to dirty her hands again with menial work. With Tony as an escort she would move in exclusive circles and who knew where that might lead.

As soon as Ruby walked in to the flat the smell of a pie cooking made her mouth water. From the broad smile on Faith's face as she poked her head around the kitchen door, she had obviously found work. She let Faith chatter excitedly while they ate the meal, sitting on the two armchairs pulled up before the gas fire. Then putting her plate aside she praised, 'You landed on your feet and no mistake. But I failed again. The nightclubs wouldn't even give me a chance to sing for them. Looks like I'll have to try something else.'

'Something worthy of you will turn up,' Faith encouraged.

'That's all right for you to say. You've got a job and new clothes.' Ruby was petulant.

Faith reached across the table to take her hand. 'Don't be downhearted. You'll find something soon. And you didn't think I bought all those clothes for myself without thinking of you?'

She took the coral dress out of its bag. Ruby felt ashamed at Faith's generosity. She hadn't given her friend any thought when she'd squandered the ten bob she'd nicked from Tony. Why couldn't she be more like Faith? She'd wished it so many times, but she never changed. She hugged Faith, her voice tight. 'You shouldn't have spent your money on me. The dress is gorgeous. Thank you. I'll pay you back as soon as I get a job.'

Ruby paraded around the room holding the coral dress to her body. Pity it was on the practical side; she could have done with something sexy to excite Tony. She'd press the scarlet satin which would have to do again for tonight.

Faith was talking enthusiastically, 'At least with me working we are no longer destitute. While I'm at the gallery tomorrow you can look at flats for us.'

'Plenty of time for that,' Ruby said.

There was a brittleness in Faith's eyes as she replied. 'There isn't. Dan returns the day after tomorrow.'

'So what are we gonna use for cash?' Faith pinned her with a triumphant stare. 'Brogan did give you ample money. How much?'

'It's an advance payment for me modelling for him. And it will only be spent on rent.'

Ruby sniffed with displeasure. When Faith had that stubborn

look nothing budged it. She strolled into the bathroom, an unheard-of luxury in most rented flats. They'd never be able to afford a place like this, not even with her working. There'd be a bathroom and toilet down the hall which was probably shared with a dozen other occupants. The thought depressed her. She wanted to live like the toffs and only have the best.

She stared at her reflection in the bathroom mirror. The beautiful face heartened her. 'While you've got your looks, kiddo, there'll always be men like Tony Chalmers to spend their money on you. And London is the place to meet them.'

Chapter Five

Dan viewed the square Georgian manor house with antipathy as he swung his car into the drive. Here he had lost not only his innocence, but his ideals about life. At twenty-nine cynicism had begun to erode even his painting. It was years since he had been uplifted by the spiritual essence which had driven him to paint the two moorland scenes. They had been his best work and he had been loath to sell them. Eventually necessity had driven him. Charles Underwood had given a good price for them and Dan needed to be financially independent. Outwardly he might have all the trappings of wealth, but he despised them. It had distorted his life – shackled him.

The estate's only redemption was its setting close to a river inlet on the Sussex coast near Chichester. With a backdrop of the gently swelling South Downs and spectacular views of the sea and marshland, the landscape provided solitude: a respite from duties he felt obliged to honour. Today the sky was tarnished with weighted snow clouds but none had fallen this side of the Downs. The grey mist which secreted the reed beds and distant spire of Bosham church was as comfortless as his mood. Once the mist had inspired him, making his landscapes timeless. They had sold well in local galleries. In recent years he had changed and so had his paintings. The darkness in his heart crept into them, masking inspiration. These paintings he destroyed as they revealed too much of his inner torment.

He stared at the house. From an age renowned for its elegance the building was an abomination. Everything about it offended his artistic eye. It was as architecturally stimulating as an overdressed hat box. The six columns on the porticoed entrance aped the grandeur of more stately residences and looked absurd. The variegated coloured brickwork in red, ochre and black bands gave the tessellated effect of a badly rendered mosaic. The four-storey monstrosity had been built on the profits of the slave trade by Joshua Passmore, an unscrupulous eighteenth-century sea captain. Dishonourable conduct was a family trait which Dan had not discovered until it was too late. By then he was already enmeshed in a mockery of a marriage and a prisoner of his Catholic religion to remain bound to a woman he despised.

On entering the house a thin, harassed-looking maid took his hat and coat.

'Mrs Brogan is still dressing, sir,' Annie informed him. 'Squire Passmore is in the grand salon, if you be wanting to pay your respects.'

For the sake of appearances he would make his observances to Cuthbert Passmore, but he had no more respect for the aged roué than he did for his equally degenerate daughter.

The wooden shutters were drawn across the sash windows of the panelled room. The inside of the house was as cumbersome and ungainly as its exterior. Not for the first Squire Passmore, the refined symmetry and delicacy of design of Robert Adam. Every room was panelled with walnut so that the interior resembled a beached galleon.

Four candles, thick as a man's wrist, stood at each corner of the open coffin and there was a wooden cross on a makeshift altar. Dan genuflected and lighting a candle said a prayer for the dead man's soul. It would take more than a few prayers to release that old devil's soul from Purgatory. There would be few people to weep over his grave and many glad to see him six foot under.

That duty done Dan ascended the stairs to his wife's bedroom. With luck she might still be sober enough to be civil to him.

Imelda was reclining on a day bed in front of a roaring log fire. Her maid Emma was kneeling at her feet as she finished applying scarlet varnish to her toenails. Imelda's cream silk wrap was open and underneath she wore matching camiknickers. Her small breasts had lost none of their firmness and her stomach was as flat as a young girl's.

In soft candlelight Imelda could still pass as the same age as Dan although she was ten years older. And she ruthlessly maintained the lie. A small lie for Imelda for whom deceit was as natural as breathing. Her thick sable hair was bobbed level with her jaw. Dispassionately, he noted her pallor and thick make-up masking an unhealthy complexion. Imelda might eat like a bird to keep slim, but the ravages of alcohol were not so easily kept at bay. Neither were the rigours of the disease which had closeted her within a Swiss clinic for the last month. The cure had taken its toll.

It shocked him that he could feel no pity. Once he had adored Imelda. He was awaiting his demob from the Flying Corps in 1919 when he first met her. The war was over and he was nineteen. He'd only been serving in France for the final eighteen months. Raised on an Irish farm, he was skilled at repairing broken machinery and had been trained as an aircraft engineer. He had no aspirations to be an aviator. All the aspects of war went against his spiritual principles of never wittingly causing another human harm. He had done his duty to his country and the horrors he had witnessed had reaffirmed his earlier beliefs that man was his own worst enemy.

Meeting Imelda was like radiant sunshine after a blizzard. He had been walking to the station with his kit bag when she drew up driving a sporty Bugatti. She offered him a lift and invited him to a party that evening. Captivated by her beauty and joy of life, he had not seen beyond to her evil. Imelda was a ravishing seductress who had set out to ensnare him. She made his girlfriends until then appear gauche and unsophisticated. She had no inhibitions. She lived and loved to the full and swore he was the only man she had ever loved.

He had been so enamoured that he had fallen for every lie which had swept him along through a whirlwind courtship to the altar. Within a month of marriage he realised that he had been tricked, his romantic ideals blasted to ashes.

He had wondered why she had married out of her class, but her declarations of love had bewitched him. The Squire, on safari in Kenya, did not attend the wedding and his telegram seemed content that he was a Catholic. The reason was soon obvious. A visit to the doctor had led to treatment of a venereal disease that he could only have contracted from his wife. Imelda had laughed in his face when he confronted her and he had not slept with her since. Five months after their wedding, the child she had told him was his was born prematurely – or so he believed. It was stillborn, having strangled on its cord. The baby was so dark skinned there was no way he could have fathered it. From its size it was a full-term child. He had learned since that Imelda liked her lovers varied. When he challenged her, she had boasted that the father was an Arab prince who had begged her to become his fourth wife.

'Even for all his wealth I wasn't going to share him with three others, all more senior than myself. And then there were his twenty concubines . . .' Imelda had given a mock shudder. Her eyes were cruel as she taunted him. 'Papa was tiresome. He threatened to disown me if I disgraced the family by bearing a bastard. Hypocrite! There must be half a dozen of his illegitimate brats around Chichester alone. There isn't a barmaid or servant safe from him. Then I met you. The rest is history. A romantic young Irish artist was easy to dupe.'

Once the blindness was stripped from Dan's eyes Imelda never manipulated him again. She hated him for that.

The marriage was over in all but name. Whenever they met they argued. Separate lives were easier to tolerate, but there could never be the freedom he craved. With each year of their marriage Imelda became more dissolute. She spent her life in giddy pursuit of pleasure with a fast set who travelled from one fashionable Continental resort to another.

She waved a manicured hand with red-polished talons to dismiss Emma before regarding Dan with a sneer.

'No greeting from my loving husband?'

'What would you have me say?' Dan returned laconically. 'Do you wish my condolences for the loss of a father you had no time or affection for?'

'He was a tyrant. I hated him. He was always lecturing me for my wild ways. And he had a string of whores. He swore to cut me out of his will if I didn't marry someone respectable before my bastard child was born. He thought marriage would make me settle down. But you weren't man enough to tame me.'

The insult failed to move him. He had heard them all before. He didn't bother to respond. His silence goaded her.

'You didn't do so badly. Papa's money has enabled you to waste your time dabbling upon canvases instead of working for a living.'

He didn't trouble to remind her that he never touched her father's money. It had only been used to settle her gambling debts or extravagant clothes bills. He'd rather starve than be further tainted by Passmore money.

'Still so puritanical,' she jeered. 'You jumped into bed with me fast enough before we were married. You even surprised me with your prowess. You weren't so innocent.'

'And I've paid dearly for that weak moment of lust,' Dan snapped. 'Now the squire is dead and his hold over you ended we can divorce.'

'Dan Brogan, always the noble martyr,' she sneered. 'I'd have divorced you years ago except Papa threatened to disinherit me. A Passmore doesn't air their failures in public. And for some reason he saw you as my saviour.'

'I didn't come here to continue old arguments. I'm leaving after the funeral tomorrow. Your solicitor insisted I was present at the reading of the will.'

'Got some little tart stashed away in London, have you?'

He marched out without replying.

Imelda seethed. Why did he still have the power to wind her in knots? She hurled her whisky glass at the door. Her hatred for her husband consumed her. She had never forgiven him for abandoning her bed a month after their marriage. It was all the fault of that bloody Arab. He'd not only got her pregnant, but given her a dose of the clap. The first of several doses since. Imelda scowled. She hadn't expected a penniless artist to have principles or morals. Dan had been easy to seduce. And so terribly handsome. She had never forgiven him for abandoning her bed just as she discovered that she had fallen in love with him.

In the early days of their marriage he had treated her with a consideration and tenderness no other man had shown her. But it had all fallen apart. He'd made such a fuss about a small dose of the pox. She had still reckoned that she could win him back after the baby was born. He had been so proud at the thought of becoming a father. It never occurred to her that it would be so dark skinned. On the night of the baby's birth Dan walked out of her life. That was ten years ago. He never lived with her again. That was when her love for him had twisted to hatred. She wanted to make him suffer as she had suffered in her unrequited love.

Dan stormed out of the house and walked to the sea shore. For two hours he paced the lapping water, the sharp wind buffeting the turbulence within his mind. As tiredness seeped into his limbs he became calmer. Reason replaced his anger. With Cuthbert Passmore dead, Imelda would inherit his wealth. There was no longer any reason why they should not divorce. He wanted nothing of the money, only his freedom.

He slowly retraced his steps. The mist parted around an old gnarled beech tree and in his imagination he saw a red-haired woman beckoning. Her glorious hair streamed in the wind, the mist swirling up around her knees. He ached to paint the vision. A thrill of excitement and anticipation coursed through his veins in a way he had not experienced in years.

'Sweet Faith,' he said softly, 'just as I thought I had reached the darkest pit, you have brought the light back into my life.'

Ruby spent an hour preparing herself for Tony's arrival. Fortunately her scarlet dress was her best one and Faith had been a darling to buy her some underwear and the coral dress. Guilt momentarily tugged at her conscience. She supposed she should have been more practical with the ten shillings she had nicked from Tony's wallet. Then again, with the right opportunity she could lift another pound tonight and treat herself to some perfume and shoes.

She emerged from the bathroom, her pale blonde hair falling in a shiny bob below her ears. She had borrowed the face powder and lipstick Faith had purchased and with a full stomach and a warm flat to sleep in, her spirits were restored.

Faith was curled up on the couch reading yesterday's paper left behind by Dan. The dishes had been washed and the room had been tidied. 'What you up to tonight, Faith?'

'A soak in the tub and an early night in a comfortable bed. You're seeing Tony, aren't you?'

'We're going to a nightclub.' She frowned. There was only the one bed, even if it was a double one, and one bedroom. It would cramp her style with Tony. He'd just have to take her to a hotel to round off the evening.

Faith yawned and stood up. 'I'm dead beat. I'll have my bath now.'

Ten minutes later there was a knock at the door and when Tony stepped inside Ruby threw her arms around his neck. His kiss was passionate, but as he lifted her up in his arms and began to carry her towards the bedroom, she dragged her mouth from his.

'Hey, ain't we going out?'

'Later, sweetheart. I've been thinking about your luscious body all day.'

She giggled. 'That's what I like to hear.' Then she noticed that beneath his overcoat he was wearing an ordinary suit and not evening dress. 'I thought we were going to a nightclub? You're not dressed for that.'

'I got held up at a meeting with the family solicitor.' He nuzzled her ear. 'I've missed you. Can't you feel how pleased I am to see you.'

He pulled her against him, rubbing his hips against hers. His eagerness excited her and she ardently returned his kiss. As his tongue explored her mouth desire flamed through her. With an ecstatic moan she pressed one hand down between them to close over his arousal. Once the bedroom door shut behind them he lowered her feet to the floor, the exploration of his hands playing havoc with her senses.

With expertise he unfastened the row of tiny satin-covered buttons down the length of her spine. His fingers were cool and competent, his thumb making seductive circles on her flesh which made her entire body tremble. Easing the straps of her dress down each arm, his lips caressed her exposed flesh and travelled across to the curves of her breasts. She moaned softly, her head rolling back as the dress slipped to her waist.

An enraged shriek behind them made Tony pull back from her.

'This is the limit, Ruby!' Faith exploded. 'I told you I wanted an early night. I've got work tomorrow. I had little sleep last night after you two pinched the bed.'

'I'm not adverse to a threesome,' Tony leered at her.

Faith glared at him. She had a towel draped around her figure and another around her head. As she clutched the towel protectively against her breasts, her furious stare burnt into the couple. Ruby had the grace to look sheepish and pulled her dress back over her breasts.

Faith's anger deflected towards Tony. 'Dan said we could use his flat, but I doubt he expected it would be turned into a knocking shop.'

Tony grinned. 'Bit high and mighty, aren't you? I've as much right here as you. I am Dan's friend.'

'And I am his guest!' Faith retorted. 'You didn't offer us accommodation last night, so don't think you can lord it over me now. What you and Ruby get up to is your affair, but I don't have to put up with it in what is temporarily my bed. So clear out.'

'Just who the hell do you think you are?' Tony took a step towards her, his face dark with menace. Faith did not flinch, the contempt in her eyes bright and dangerous. Ruby grabbed his arm.

'Faith is right,' she said. 'We ain't being fair on her. And we were supposed to be going out.'

Now that her initial ardour had cooled, Ruby wasn't happy with the way Tony had expected her to have sex with him, without taking her out first. 'Come on, Tony. We could go back to a hotel later,' she conceded.

He looked displeased. A typical man thwarted in getting his oats, she reasoned. Linking her arm through his, she smiled beguilingly. 'Faith has been out all day job hunting. She's whacked.' When he remained uncooperative, she stood on tiptoe and moulded her body to his. 'I'll make it up to you. But I got all dressed up for you, couldn't we go to a nightclub first? You said you were going to get me a job at your friend's club. I've got to pay my way when Ruby and I get our own place.'

Tony pouted. 'I said I'd see if Ernie will give you a job. Waitresses are always leaving.'

Ruby didn't tell him she intended to be a singer not a waitress. She just needed the introduction. It was as well Faith had interrupted them. She now had Tony tagged as a slippery bastard. But she knew how to handle his sort.

Faith stood her ground in the bedroom, the towel clutched to her body. There was a storm brewing in her eyes and although her friend was the sweetest creature alive, Ruby knew better than to push her too far. Faith wouldn't be taken advantage of. She was generous to a fault but there was also a strength in her which when she set a path, she could not be budged from.

The club was called the Gilded Lily. The air was musty as they walked down the wooden staircase devoid of carpet to the cellar. A bar was diagonal across one corner and thirty tables were grouped around a small dance floor. Several couples were dancing close together, the sequins or diamanté trimming on the women's dresses sparkling under the subdued electric light. On the stage a pianist, in his shirtsleeves and with a cigarette drooping from his mouth, was playing an unfamiliar rhythm. It seemed to reverberate through to Ruby's soul. It was haunting, primeval, stirring her blood, and the pianist played with an expertise which set her pulse racing.

There was a single spotlight on the musician. He was thirtyish, thin as only the very tall are thin, with hollowed cheekbones and a strong jaw. His dark blond hair was sleeked back with a side parting. One wayward lock fell attractively over his brow. As Faith followed Tony to a table her attention was again drawn to the talented musician. His eyes were half closed. He was absorbed in his playing and oblivious of the customers in the club.

Already a blue haze of tobacco smoke hung over the tables. Ruby took a cigarette from Tony's gold case and inhaled deeply. Her curious gaze surveyed the cellar. The tables with their flickering candles were bare of cloths, the floorboards unpolished. She was about to dismiss it as a dump when she realised that most of the customers were expensively dressed, precious gems glittering around the women's necks and wrists. The men were mostly in evening dress and bottles of champagne in ice buckets stood on the tables.

'That's not like any music I've ever heard,' she said as her body swayed to the slow seductive beat.

'It's called the blues,' Tony said. 'Mike Rivers, he's the pianist, is one of the best. You should hear him on the sax – it's sensational.'

Ruby nodded, the music palpitating through her, heightening her excitement. The music was sexual. It burrowed into her soul. Usually she liked the louder, faster big band sound where she could dance the Charleston or Black Bottom for hours without tiring. But this she wanted to lie back and listen to, let it play over her as languorously as a lover.

She shivered with pleasure and as she sipped the champagne Tony had ordered, she knew she had found the lifestyle she craved. She wanted to sing to this music and drink nothing but champagne. Gin and tonics were for the working girl she had left behind. Champagne was the drink of the wealthy and successful.

'If the musician is so good, why's he working here?'

'Jazz clubs aren't your local Palais de danse. Earnest Ernie only opened a few months ago. Mike is his brother. Half-brother actually. He plays here a couple of evenings to help draw the crowds. He's always in demand at other clubs. Got quite a following.

Earnest Ernie reckons this will be the first of several clubs he'll be running.'

'Earnest Ernie!' Ruby giggled. 'What sort of name is that?'

'Fancies himself as something of a hard case, does Earnest Ernie. Volatile too. It doesn't do to get on the wrong side of him.' Tony got up and pulled her out of her seat. 'What's all the interest in Mike and Ernie? Come and press that gorgeous body against mine. The great thing about the blues is it gives you a chance to cuddle up to your partner.'

Ruby discovered that Tony had roving hands on the dance floor as well as off it. 'Give over, Tony,' she snapped, removing his hands from her bottom for the fourth time. 'I don't like being mauled in public. Ain't you got no respect?'

The pianist was now playing a familiar love song and Ruby began to sing softly.

'You've got a good voice, sweetheart,' Tony murmured against her ear, 'but an even better body. It's eleven o clock. Let's get out of here and have some real fun.'

'I thought you were going to introduce me to this Earnest Ernie,' Ruby pouted. She wasn't going to let an opportunity to be introduced as Tony's friend slip by. It could give her a better chance at a job.

'I haven't seen him.'

'Then ask. He could be in his office or something.'

'Ernie likes to mingle, keep an eye on things.'

She drew back in his arms although her body continued to sway to the music. 'Wouldn't hurt just to ask, would it? I'd be *so* very grateful.' She moved closer to him in the dance and ground her hips against his before pulling away again.

Tony groaned. 'You sure know how to get a man all fired up. I'll ask.'

Ruby returned to their table and poured herself a glass of champagne. Mike was playing another soulful tune. She propped her chin on her palm to listen. It was pure magic. Her eyes half closed, her expression dreamy, she allowed the music to flow through her. When the number ended she opened her eyes and saw Mike staring at her. He lifted the whisky glass on the top of his piano and raised it in salute, before starting another number. She smiled. Mike could be a useful man to know if she was to get on as a singer.

'She's a looker all right,' she heard a man remark. 'Ain't usual for me brother to notice the punters.'

Ruby glanced over her shoulder and saw that Tony had returned with a stockily built, dark-eyed, dark-haired man with a pencil-line moustache.

'Sweetheart, let me introduce Ernie Durham, the club owner.'

'I'm delighted to meet you, Mr Durham.' Ruby held out her hand and stifled a giggle as the owner raised it to his lips. He couldn't be taller than five foot five and like most short men he had a swaggering style intended to create an impression. As he regarded her over the top of her fingers, the desire and interest in his eyes warmed her. Despite his lack of inches he was good looking. Apart from fancying himself a hard case as Tony had told her, from the way he was eyeing her he also reckoned himself a ladies' man.

'Tony says you want to work in a nightclub?' His cockney accent roughened a deep voice.

'I want to *sing* in a nightclub, Mr Durham,' she corrected.

He studied her with cool appraisal. Then fired out, 'You've got the looks for it. But can you deliver the goods?'

'What I deliver could be more than most men can handle.'

The innuendo sharpened his interest. 'So impress me. Go on stage and give us your best shot.'

She didn't need to be told twice. She saw Tony's frown and winked. 'Don't worry about me, I'll knock them dead.'

Her step was confident as she approached the piano. Mike looked at her quizzically then across at Ernie who nodded.

'Ernie wants me to sing. Could be he's gonna take me on.'

'Did he tell you we got a singer? It's her night off.'

'That's my good luck and her look out,' Ruby said throatily. 'How about "Lady Be Good" but make it slow and sexy.'

He played the opening chords and she posed provocatively by leaning against the upright piano. She began softly, the huskiness in her voice warm with invitation. She'd seen enough Greta Garbo films to know how to smoulder and exude sexuality.

The conversation at the tables continued and without an introduction she knew she had to put everything she had into the song to get the punters' attention. Running her hands down her body to her hips, she moved to the front of the platform and paraded slowly along its length until she knew that every man's gaze in the room was upon her. She wasn't interested in the women. They didn't pick up the bills.

She walked down the two steps to the front tables, selecting a middle-aged man seated with a brassy-looking mistress. Her voice lowered to throb with sultry promise as she ran her fingers through his hair before moving on. Slowly she sauntered from table to table and she wove a seductive web with every sensuous movement. Aware that her husky voice was not strong, Ruby used inflections to enhance nuances and innuendo, making the song uniquely her own.

As she came to the final chorus, her feline walk and the sultry promise in her eyes was directed solely at Ernie Durham. She could see the perspiration on his upper lip and the desire naked in his eyes. Leaning her back against his chest, she drew his arm around her waist and put her hand up to his cheek. His breathing was low and hard and when the song ended, she slunk a step away from him as the applause filled the cellar.

'More! More!' The demands were deafening.

Tony was glowering. He wasn't happy with the attention she was attracting. She winked at him. Then turning to Ernie her smile was assured. 'So what do you reckon?'

'Give them what they want. Sing to them.'

She sang two more numbers and the customers were still clamouring for another when she sat down beside Tony.

'What've you stopped for?' Ernie said. 'They love you.'

'That's just a taster. Whetting their appetite so that they'll come back for more.'

There was admiration in Ernie's stare as he nodded and smiled. 'You'll do. What's your name?'

'Ruby Starr,' she said, deciding that Simons wasn't grand enough for her new career. 'How much do I get a session?'

'You can start next Monday and also do Tuesdays and Thursdays, singing a dozen numbers at each session. If the punters are here in good numbers you get a pound a night, if not, ten shillings.'

'What about the weekends?' she asked. 'Seems like you'd get the punters packed in then. I'd earn more.'

Ernie's thick black brows drew together. 'Miriam Knight does those sessions. You'll have to pull more punters than she does to oust her from the popular nights.' He tipped her chin up with his finger, his eyes challenging. 'You're a woman who knows what she wants and how to get it. Your voice ain't as good as Miriam's. Give the punters more of what you were putting across tonight and they'll flock to see you. And get yourself togged out in something slinky and sexy.'

'How about an advance then?' she said sweetly.

'How about less lip,' his tone harshened. 'My singers supply their own wardrobe. And keep it sexy.'

He strutted away, clicking his fingers for two men to follow. Jumped-up little squirt, Ruby thought. He don't match up so big against his talented brother. She glanced at the stage. To her disappointment another pianist had replaced Mike. He didn't have his good looks or his expertise.

Tony ran his hand along Ruby's thigh. 'That was some performance. How about us finding an hotel?'

She was tempted to linger in the club, but Tony was getting impatient. His goodwill was still important. She wanted to come here at the weekend to see this Miriam who Ernie had raved about. Once she knew her opposition she could ensure that she gave the punters that extra special something. Also Tony was an exciting lover, she wasn't about to allow him to lose interest yet. Tonight she would give him the full treatment. If by the end of it he hadn't agreed to buy her a couple of gowns for the club, her name was not Ruby Simons – correction Ruby Starr.

Chapter Six

'Whatever made me think work in an art gallery was exciting,' Faith mumbled as she made Oliver Lincoln his fifth cup of tea that morning. In two days she had sold only one painting. Oliver never let her near a customer unless he was already serving. He waved her aside whenever a wealthy patron entered the showroom while guiding them to the most expensive exhibits.

His dancing attendance turned her stomach, but she had to admit when he began to speak of the paintings and artists he was a good salesman. Though it often stemmed from the reward to his pocket and not from the heart. It wasn't often Oliver allowed a customer to escape without making a purchase. Most of them he seemed to know personally.

She also discovered that an art gallery is not the busiest of shops and there were periods when she had nothing to do. Oliver spent his spare time on the telephone to friends or business partner, Charles Underwood, who Faith suspected was also Oliver's lover. It was obvious from the snatches of conversation she overheard that they argued a lot. Then Oliver would shut himself away in his office until he spied a wealthy customer in the gallery who enticed him out.

'Oliver, would you object to me reading an art book when there are no customers in the shop?' Faith showed him a volume on post-impressionists which she had borrowed from Dan's collection.

His eyes rounded in surprise and she rushed on, 'Until now I've only read about the classical artists. If you could recommend any books or suggest a library I could join, it would improve my knowledge and I'm sure would help sales.'

His stare was intense as he studied her serious expression. 'Dear girl, are you serious about this work?'

'I know you only employed me because Mr Devereux suggested it. Also my sales since then have been lamentable. But this job is a chance for me to make something of my life. The art world is so exciting,' she raced on in her enthusiasm. 'It's a world I never dreamed I could be part of. I want to be able to compare the techniques of the masters and know the prices they are currently fetching at auction.'

'Your enthusiasm overwhelms me. But a pretty thing like yourself will be married in a year or two and raising a gaggle of children. What will such knowledge benefit you then?'

'The Good Lord save all women from male prejudice.' Her eyes sparked with angry green lights. 'The appreciation of art is never wasted. Why should marriage and children rob me of something which gives me so much pleasure?'

'What a passionate creature you are. The young want everything these days. A woman's place is in the home.'

Faith threw him such a baleful glare he stepped back a pace. 'Now what have I said?'

'You've only consigned all women to enslavement. Do you think we don't have minds which need fulfilment? I'd prefer to stay a spinster if that's how men view a wife's role.'

When the telephone rang Oliver was relieved at the distraction. He waved a hand towards the art book. 'You may read that when we have no customers, providing your other work is not neglected. A cup of tea and one of those divine cakes from down the road would not go amiss at this moment.'

He picked up the trumpet-shaped receiver and announced grandly, 'Underwood and Lincoln Gallery.' Then, 'Dave, my darling boy. You cruel, cruel creature, you haven't rung me for a positive age.'

Faith sighed and fetched her coat from the back of the shop to buy the cakes he had requested. Oliver regarded her as an errand girl. She had to prove to him that her sale to Devereux had not been a fluke. She had to convince him that she was sincere in wanting to improve her knowledge.

When she placed Oliver's cake on his desk he looked up from the art catalogue he was reading. 'You're always studying those catalogues,' she remarked. 'Should I be reading them?'

He lifted a creamy brow. 'They are dry facts and figures.'

'But full of information needed about my work,' she persisted.

'Yes.'

'May I read them?'

He seemed about to protest but her determined expression stopped him. Instead he smiled. 'There's a pile in the bottom drawer of my office desk. Take them home.'

'Thank you, Oliver.' Until that moment she had felt that she was in the shop under sufferance. With this gesture Oliver had apparently accepted her.

After finishing another call he came over to her desk. 'Knowing about art is not enough. You have to understand the market. That expertise takes years to acquire.'

'But it isn't hard work if you love what you're doing.'

He smiled and beckoned her over to two new paintings purchased at a private sale by Mr Underwood yesterday. Oliver proceeded to tell her the history of the artist and the kind of prices his work was fetching. He also produced a catalogue to illustrate his comments. Faith drank in every word and when he tested her with questions, she answered easily and correctly.

Oliver nodded, satisfied at her aptitude. 'You have the making of an astute businesswoman. I shall enjoy working with such an enthusiastic colleague.'

She returned to her desk and wrote down everything she could remember that Oliver had told her about the paintings. Tomorrow she would buy a proper notebook and memorise the knowledge Oliver imparted. He saw her writing and nodded further approval. Faith couldn't wait to tell Dan Brogan all about her new career and its exciting challenges.

* * *

Faith used her lunch hour the next day to chase across the river to Southwark to view a flat. Dan was returning tonight and she had promised they would be out of his flat. So far every place she had viewed had been unacceptable, with poky rooms and the neighbours living in overcrowded conditions. She had been shocked at the prices in the heart of London. Ruby had wanted to live close to Soho and Ernie's club, but Faith insisted that they curb their expenditure until they had some savings behind them. The horror of her first days in the capital still haunted her. She never wanted to be in that situation again.

The flat was in a large four-storey town house on the top floor. The rooms were small. They had once been the servants' quarters but it was the view that enthralled Faith. Over the tops of the other dwellings and warehouses she could see the turrets of the Tower of London and the great dome of St Paul's. A half-hour walk across London bridge took them to the heart of the City. Twenty minutes on the underground tube and they were in the West End. The flat was cheap and practical. It had two bedrooms, a large sitting room and a small kitchenette. The bathroom they shared with three of the other residents was on the second floor and the toilet was across the hall.

It was agreed that they would move in tonight.

The shop bell tinkled and Faith recognised the plump, middle-aged woman who hobbled in. She was dressed in black, her coat shiny and her cartwheel hat was of a style popular in Edwardian times. Oliver gave the customer an assessing glance and sent Faith a silent warning not to encourage the woman. The woman had come in to the shop yesterday and Faith had spent an hour with her as they discussed the paintings. When Faith offered the woman a cup of tea, she had thought Oliver would explode with ire.

As soon as the woman left he had rounded on Faith. 'What do you think we are, a *tea-shop*? That old biddy came in out of the cold. Don't waste your time on such people.'

Faith did not agree with such a mercenary attitude. 'I didn't feel my time was wasted. She was knowledgeable about art. I liked her. You were dealing with the only other customer and he did not purchase anything either.'

'I was attending to General Bowshott. He *has* important contacts throughout the army. He *is* a valued customer.'

Obviously there was no point in arguing with him, but on recognising Mrs Naughton, she did not hesitate to make her feel welcome. 'Good morning, Mrs Naughton. How is your lumbago today? Better I hope.'

'Much better, my dear. It is kind of you to ask.'

From the corner of her eye, she saw Oliver put down the receiver and with a haughty glare advance towards them.

'May I assist, Madam? Did you have a particular purchase in mind after your visit yesterday?'

His scathing tone annoyed Faith and she saw the woman stiffen with affront. She favoured him with an equally haughty stare. 'I am being attended to by this young lady, who was kind enough to give me so much of her time yesterday. She will deal with the sale of some of the paintings at Old Charford Hall. With my husband and two eldest sons dying within ten years, the death duties are crippling us.'

'Old Charford Hall!' Oliver repeated in a shocked, reverent voice. He took her hand and bowed over it. 'Oliver Lincoln at your service, your Ladyship. Your pardon, I had no idea . . . Had you but introduced yourself yesterday, Lady Charford.'

'I used my maiden name. I had no wish to attract attention to myself while deciding which gallery was the most suitable. Miss Tempest impressed me with her patience and understanding.'

'Come into my office where we can discuss the matter in private,' Oliver fawned. 'Miss Tempest will bring us tea.'

Lady Charford subjected him to a freezing glare. 'You misunderstood me. My business will be dealt with by Miss Tempest.'

'But Miss Tempest has not the experience,' Oliver wailed.

'She is sympathetic and will not harangue me to part with paintings which have been part of our family for generations and are dearly loved. I expect her to come to Charford Hall this evening.'

Oliver's complexion was flushing alternately from red to white. He was sweating profusely and his elegant cravat had wilted.

Faith took pity on him. 'Mr Lincoln will serve your interests better than I. But I will attend with him if you wish.'

'The matter is most distressing.' She pickaxed Oliver with an assessing stare. 'Very well, but Miss Tempest will also attend.'

Oliver was beaming with false humility. 'Underwood and Lincoln are honoured to have been chosen to serve you, Lady Charford.'

'Stop grovelling, man. It's a trial on my nerves. Charford Hall is an hour's drive. My chauffeur will return for you both at five thirty. Is that convenient?'

'Perfectly, Lady Charford,' Oliver crooned.

At five thirty a Bentley drew up outside the shop, the driver's seat open to the elements. An hour later Faith stepped out on to the gravel drive of Charford Hall. She pinched her arm, unable to believe that this was happening to her. The Hall was like a rambling hotel in different styles of architecture ranging from Tudor redbrick and oak beams to a Georgian wing with huge sash windows. It must have fifty rooms. Oliver whistled softly.

'Looks like you've done all right for us. We'll make a killing if we can get our hands on an Old Master. And there will be a handsome bonus in it for you.'

Faith felt her loyalty torn between the customer who had placed so much trust in her and Oliver's expectations. She knew her loyalty must be to her employer, but it left an unpleasant taste in her mouth. Her euphoria drained away. This was a side of the art world which did not sit comfortably with her. The glitter of working in a gallery might have tarnished but it left a deeper ambition burning within her. What she really wanted was to be an artist. But that took money and in the meantime she had to work to save for her tuition fees.

Envy narrowed Ruby's eyes at her first sight of Miriam Knight. She sang like a nightingale. She was glamorous rather than beautiful with a tall willowy figure. Her brown hair was fashionably bobbed and Marcel-waved, but it was the dress that made her heart plummet. It was emerald tulle spangled with diamanté. Beside her Ruby's satin dress looked tacky and cheap.

At the end of each song the applause was rapturous. Or so Ruby initially thought. The applause was more enthusiastic from the women. Several couples were dancing while she sang. Ruby grinned. Miriam had a terrific voice but she had no life behind her delivery. She didn't sing to the punters, pout, wink or play the temptress as Ruby intended to captivate her audience.

'Now you know what the competition is like,' Tony smiled. 'Great voice. Not as sexy as you though.'

'She's got the right clothes to look the part. This red satin looks cheap compared to what she's wearing.'

'You'll knock them dead, sweetheart.' Tony grinned lasciviously.

'But I need a decent dress. Something sexy.' She wriggled closer to him rubbing her breast against his arm. 'Will you lend me the money to buy a couple of gowns? I'll pay you back. Honest.'

'It will take you months. Have you any idea how much a dress like that costs?'

'Ah c'mon, Tony. Don't be mean. What about your sister. Ain't she got a dress or two she don't wear? She's married to a banker and can't be short of a bob or two.'

'Dorinda is not in the habit of supplying gowns for my bits of fluff,' he said stiffly.

Ruby's eyes slanted dangerously. 'Bit of fluff! Is that all I am to you? You cheap bastard!' She lashed out, striking him in the chest with the handbag she had stolen from a shop earlier that day, before striding off.

'Ruby, you idiot.' Tony came after her. 'What's got into you, sweetheart?'

'Don't sweetheart me, you tight-fisted sod. Your bit of fluff indeed! I only wanted a loan for a couple of dresses. You want them to think I'm a waitress or something? You've been using me, Tony. And I ain't gonna be used, not by you, not by no one.'

She spun away from him. As she passed the bar her arm was caught by Ernie. 'Hey, babe, what's eating you? Competition with Miriam too tough for you, sweetheart?'

'I ain't your babe, or sweetheart,' she seethed, her hands on her hips and her breasts heaving in indignation. 'I'm Ruby. I've got a name, so damn well use it. And as for competition . . . Miriam can sing, but she's about as sexy as a landed fish. She draws a fair crowd, but there's empty tables. She ain't got what it takes to keep the punters coming back for more.'

Ernie looked over her head towards Tony. 'So it's boyfriend trouble then?' His eyes brightened with interest.

She played upon it. 'I hate men who are skinflints. I asked him to lend me some dough so that I could get a couple of decent dresses for when I sing here.'

'Maybe I could arrange a loan?' Ernie leaned forward to whisper. 'That's if Chalmers is no longer on the scene.'

Ruby didn't hesitate. By playing up to Ernie she could get to sing more often in the club.

'So what terms you offering on this loan, Mr Durham?'

'Just Ernie, babe. My terms could be negotiable. Come up to my office and we'll discuss it.'

Despite his lack of height he was a handsome man. There was a scar on his brow and his nose was broken. He looked what he was, a man of the world; tough, and with an element of danger surrounding him. An exciting combination. Danger and a raw sexuality emanated from him and she felt her stomach contract with desire. A slow self-assured smile taunted her. The scoundrel knew she was interested. And why not? Tony Chalmers had just lost his usefulness to her.

'Got any champagne in your office?' she queried.

'A bottle is already on ice.'

Tony barged in between them. 'C'mon, sweetheart. Let's get out of here.'

Her answering stare was contemptuous. 'I ain't your sweetheart, sunshine, so get lost. I've got business to discuss with Mr Durham. He knows how to treat a woman right.'

Linking her arm through Ernie's she flashed a seductive smile and allowed him to lead her into his office. A backward glance showed Tony rigid with anger. Out of devilment she blew him a goodbye kiss.

When the door closed behind them, Ruby drew back from Ernie to lean against it. 'I hope I was right about telling Tony that you know how to treat a woman right.'

'I ain't had no complaints, babe.'

She tensed. 'It's Ruby.' Her eyes blazed for a moment even as her body swayed against him. 'I'm not some nameless slut. I'm Ruby Starr and I'm going to be rich and famous.'

He threw back his head and laughed. 'Happen you'll go far, Ruby Starr.'

Still grinning he turned the key in the lock then lowered his mouth to hers. His hands slid round to grip her buttocks grinding her hips against him. The evidence of his desire rammed against her stomach. His technique may have lacked finesse, but its predatory hunger sparked Ruby's passion. She didn't need to be wooed and seduced. Her own needs were as basic as any man's. As his hand scooped up the hem of her dress and pushed between her thighs she moaned with pleasure. A pulse clamoured deep within her to find the release her body demanded. Her clothes were removed with effortless ease and Ernie lifted her on to the desk and thrust inside her.

'You're like a rampaging soldier,' she moaned in his ear. 'There ain't no need to rush.'

He ignored her, pushing into her with a vigour that left her gasping. When he withdrew she slid off the desk and found her legs were unsteady. Ernie had opened a bottle of champagne and was pouring two glasses.

'Wow! That was really something,' she said with a shaky laugh, her supple body stretching like a contented cat. 'Did I please you, Ernie? I ain't ever felt this good before.'

Ernie handed her a glass of champagne, his expression impassive. 'Cut the bullshit, Ruby. It was a good fuck but nothing sensational.'

She glowered at him. She was used to being praised for her ingenuity and insatiability and didn't like the criticism. Seeing her pout, he grinned. 'That don't mean to say it ain't gonna get better.'

She was still pouting as she downed the champagne and reached for her clothes. Her hand was taken and he drew her down on to the floor. When he tipped the chilled golden liquid over her breasts and stomach, she shrieked. 'Dammit, what the hell was that for? Waste of good champers.'

'I ain't wasting none.' Ernie was on his knees and began licking her breasts and lapping up the champagne as it ran down between her ribs to her navel. Ruby's cries of protest turned to moans of pleasure. She writhed as his tongue dipped inside the intimate heat of her.

She didn't return to the flat that night but stayed with Ernie. The next morning he took her to a dressmaker in the West End.

'Why aren't we going to one of the stores? I want dresses like Miriam – something with a bit of class.'

Ernie laughed. 'What you've got is worth more than class. You've got sex appeal and that's what the men will come to the club for. Don't go kidding yourself it's to hear your voice. Though that ain't bad.'

When they left the dressmaker, the woman had sworn that a gown would be sent to the club in time for Ruby's first appearance. Tony had ordered four gowns and also purchased a diamanté headband.

In the cab home she kissed him. 'Those gowns were sensational. I ain't never owned anything so grand.'

'It were your money, babe. My singers only wear the best. I thought I'd be generous and give you an ample loan. You can sign the agreement back at the office.'

Ruby paled. They had spent a fortune. About a year's wages. How the hell was she going to pay him back? She felt sick. She'd thought after last night that Ernie would have bought the gowns for her. Clearly not. This was another man to watch. She wasn't about to be used again. He'd really conned her this time. He was a bloody loan shark.

Ernie saw her unease and looked annoyed. 'You did say you wanted a loan for the dresses?'

Unwilling to antagonise him, she stretched her mouth into a smile. 'Of course. It's just that I hadn't realised how much they would cost. How am I going to be able to pay you back out of my wages at the club?'

'You're a classy babe. You can act as my hostess when I throw a party and earn a bit extra that way.'

His words were far from reassuring and something in his look warned her not to probe into his motives. She had an uncomfortable feeling that she was getting in deeper than she intended. Even so, she wanted one thing clear between them.

'Last night, Ernie. You and me hit it off right from the start. You're a good-looking guy. I don't go with just anyone. You ain't suggesting that I should go with other blokes, are you? Or these dresses go straight back.'

'Don't look so worried.' His voice lightened. 'You like parties don't you? You and me could make a good team. We'll need a singing contract drawn up with me as your manager. How does that suit you?'

Ruby relaxed. She liked the idea of being Ernie's hostess. She hadn't been wrong about him. He could help her career and introduce her to the right people, she was certain.

'About the dresses . . .'

His frown made her rush on. 'You didn't think that they were too revealing around the hips? Didn't you notice that they showed the line of my panties?'

Ernie laughed. 'You won't be wearing nothing under those dresses and every man in the audience will be aware of it and keep coming back to watch you perform.'

Ruby joined in his laughter. 'Now why didn't I think of that?'

Chapter Seven

Grateful for Dan's help Faith had left a bunch of primroses in a jam jar on the table in his studio with a note of her new address. Every evening after work she hoped that Dan would call round to contact her. There was no word from him and it had been over a week now. She saw little of Ruby who had dumped her things in the other bedroom and was out with Ernie every night.

Faith worked hard to make the flat into a home and pushed aside her disappointment that she had not heard from Dan. The blackened net curtains were washed and returned to a fresh cream colour, and at a jumble sale she had bought some green velvet curtains for the living room. From the same jumble sale she also purchased a lace tablecloth and a patchwork bedcover which she threw over the worn leather horsehair sofa. The brown linoleum and square of reddish and brown carpet were thick with grime and stank of cats where the previous owner had kept several of them. Unable to afford new floor coverings Faith decided to scrub the lino and carpet at the weekend. Clearly Dan had forgotten her. He had probably found someone else to paint.

When she returned from work Saturday evening she dragged all the furniture into the two bedrooms, eager to get the job done. Removing her good dress she pulled on a cheap wrapover apron to cover her petticoat and tied her long auburn hair up into a scarf. She didn't bother to eat. It would only take an hour to wash the floor and carpet and she could cook later.

Nearly three hours later the lino was revealed to be the colour of pale oak and the carpet had been returned to its original shade of vermilion with large beige roses. She hadn't realised that it had a pattern as it had been so dirty. Faith sat back on her heels and inspected her work. With a satisfied sigh she wiped the perspiration from her brow. Her back and shoulders ached but the results had been worth it. It was after nine o'clock. She would relax in a hot bath to ease her aches and then have an early night. Tomorrow if the dry weather held she would pack some sandwiches for lunch and go to one of the parks.

A knock on the door made her jump. Thinking it was the old woman who lived opposite, who had taken to borrowing a cup of sugar or tea of an evening, Faith groaned. The old girl would linger, obviously lonely and wanting to chat. She was hot and sticky from her work and the bath beckoned more enticingly than her neighbour's company.

When she opened the door Dan stared at her without recognition. 'Sorry, I thought Miss Tempest lived here. Which flat is hers?'

Embarrassed colour flooded Faith's cheeks. She snatched off the scarf and ducked behind the door to hide the ghastly wrapover pinny from him. As she leaned forward her hair fell each side of her blushing cheeks. She was mortified that he should see her looking such a mess. 'Dan! What a surprise. I've been cleaning the floor.'

Dan tipped his trilby back on his dark hair and stared at her in amusement. 'Don't I get asked in?'

'Yes, of course. No, just a minute . . . I look a wreck. Wait there until I'm decent . . .' she said, flustered.

From Dan's expression it was obvious he was not listening to her; he was staring at her face enrapt. It made her heart leap and a tingle of pleasure seep up through her toes to cover her entire body. When his expression did not change, her excitement was tinged with unease. She wasn't used to men affecting her this way. He had been in her thoughts constantly since that first night. Now the way he was staring at her was making her limbs feel weak. She did not feel in control and that made Dan dangerous.

'Get changed,' he commanded, stepping into the flat before she could stop him. 'I've my car outside.'

'I can't go out like this! And I'm not leaving the flat in the mess it's in. I've been at work today.'

There was a fervent light in his eyes which made her shiver. He was looking at her, but somehow was not seeing her.

'Keep your hair exactly as it is. That's how I want to sketch you.' His impatience was evident in his voice.

Her temper snapped. 'I beg your pardon. I haven't heard from you for over a week. How dare you demand that I drop everything and obey you!'

He looked startled, his eyes refocusing on her and his expression contrite. 'I didn't mean it to sound like an order. I've only been back in town a few hours.'

There were taut grooves around his mouth which hadn't been there last week and his eyes looked bruised from lack of sleep. Her manner softened. 'Didn't your trip go well?'

His cobalt eyes were guarded. 'No. And I see I've called at a bad time.'

It was clear he did not want to talk about his trip. When he stepped towards the door intending to leave, she capitulated. 'Don't rush off. I'm in rather a muddle here. And I look a positive fright. I know I said I'd pose for you but I expected a bit more notice.'

Dan checked his frustration. When he was gripped by the passion of his need to sketch, it was a hunger as potent as lust. And images of this woman had been haunting him throughout his disastrous visit to Passmore Grange. Nothing had worked out as he planned. Circumstances had forced him to honour obligations and stay on. He didn't want to dwell on these problems, they'd given him enough sleepless nights. He'd come here to forget his troubles – lose himself in the escape his painting offered. He kept his voice casual, hiding his craving to capture this entrancing woman on canvas.

'I see your friend has left you to do all the work,' he said gazing round the room. 'I came to ask you to pose for me tomorrow and got inspired when I saw your hair down. You look tired. Have you eaten?'

Faith realised that she was hungry and glancing at her wrist watch was shocked to see that it was nine thirty. 'Not since lunch. I thought this would only take an hour. I've got to get the furniture moved before I can get into my bedroom.'

'I'll give you a hand.' When he saw the heavy Victorian furniture he frowned. 'Did you move this lot yourself? You'll do yourself a mischief.'

'Not being brought up with servants I'm used to doing things for myself.' She moved to one end of the sagging sofa and bent down to lift it. When Dan didn't move she widened her eyes. 'You helping, or are you just going to stand there making the place look untidy?'

He took off his overcoat and jacket and rolled his shirtsleeves high over his forearms. Faith averted her gaze from the dark hairs on his arm, shocked at how profoundly the sight of them affected her. They were a reminder of his masculinity and strength and that she was alone and not decently dressed. They carried the sofa through to the sitting room. When Faith straightened she realised the front of the apron had gaped in her exertions. The outline of her breasts was visible beneath her cotton petticoat. Hastily she pulled the apron together.

'I'll move the rest of the stuff,' Dan announced, 'you go and get dressed. We'll eat out, or . . .' He smiled and drew her close to him, his voice warm with coercion. 'You are more beautiful than I remember.'

His gaze held hers. There was such tenderness in his eyes that her pulse began to race. As their gazes held, his stare lowered until it fixed upon her parted lips. He lifted an auburn tress, twirling it around his finger and studying it in the light from the gas mantle over the fireplace. Very slowly he bowed his head. The warmth of his breath caressed her cheek. Then his mouth was on hers, lighter than the brush of thistledown.

He drew back, his gaze intent, studying her reaction before his lips again descended. This time with a tenderness which made Faith melt against him. His tongue explored the softness of her mouth, causing spirals of pleasure to spread through her veins. A flame was kindled deep within her: expanding, all consuming, until she clung to him, her fingers locking about his neck. A feverish pressure began in her stomach and spread in white hot heat through her body to engulf her.

'Faith – oh Faith.'

The words sounded like a groan and a shiver of apprehension passed through her.

Self-conscious of the mess she looked and how her body was hot and sticky, she flinched away from him. He didn't release her. His lips moved to her hair. 'Which room is yours?'

It was like a dousing of cold water. She pushed him away. When he continued to hold her, she tensed and her eyes blazed. 'No, Dan. If that's why you came round then you can get out now.'

'Are you sure that's what you want?' He watched her with a predatory gaze. His closeness was a potent threat. All the angry, derogatory words she would have screamed at him remained locked in a throat suddenly parched.

She swallowed, rasping out, 'Let me go. Please . . .'

His arms opened. She nimbly vaulted the back of the sofa. With the barrier between them, she studied him. What she saw in his eyes was far from reassuring. He looked like a man who had just picked up the gauntlet. 'You've got to be light on your toes to catch me, Daniel Brogan,' she taunted. 'I was the best gymnast in our school.'

He vaulted the sofa with equal ease. His laughter pierced her composure. 'Don't issue challenges if you don't want them taken up.'

'It wasn't a challenge.' She snatched up a brass candlestick from a table, one of a pair she had bought in a junk shop yesterday. 'What does a woman have to do to prove her virtue? Don't come any closer.'

A lock of brown hair fell forward over his brow and his hands were jammed into the pockets of his grey slacks. Faith's heart lurched. He looked so handsome, so masculine. She must look fit to scare crows in the ghastly apron. That galled her more than anything, overriding her usual modesty.

He still didn't move, his gaze riveted to her face. 'You have exquisite bone structure. And that pose. If only I had my sketchpad. You'd make a marvellous warrior maid – Diana the huntress at bay – dangerous and seductive . . . You'll need a short tunic and your hair drawn high on your head to tumble like an auburn waterfall down between your bare shoulders!'

The man was insufferable! She was still shaken at the way she had reacted to his kiss. He had lost all interest in her as a woman. He saw her as no more than a fleshly statue to deck out as a mystical figure. A warrior maid! She'd give him warrior maid.

'I'll be posing for you decently clothed or not at all, Daniel Brogan. You can forget any funny business.' Her aquamarine eyes sparked with outrage and she brandished the candlestick in warning. 'And you're a bit too free with your kisses. I think you'd better go.' When he didn't move she lost her patience and hurled the candlestick at his chest. He caught it like an accomplished rugby player. When he took a step towards her, her heart jolted agonisingly.

'Stay back, Dan,' her voice quavered.

His gaze unwavering upon her face, he reached out to finger a lock of her hair. 'I'd never hurt you, Faith.' His voice was mesmerising, holding her transfixed. 'Stop pretending that my kisses don't affect you. You're a beautiful and exciting woman. I hate dining alone and I'm starving. Will you accompany me to a restaurant?' His fingers stroked through the copper strands and wound it around his hand. 'Magnificent,' he added softly.

Disappointment stapled her. It was her bloody hair he was praising, not herself. He was obsessed with it. She backed away from him. 'I think you should leave.'

'Now what have I done?' He looked genuinely puzzled. He held up his hands in submission. 'If you're so averse to me kissing you, then I won't. I'd not jeopardise losing you as a model. Go and get dressed. I'll take you out to dine and be the perfect gentleman. I promise.'

'And stop ordering me about. I need a bath after scrubbing the carpet. If you're too hungry to wait, then feel free to go.'

She had meant to sound cool and composed; instead her words were another challenge. Dan's eyes gleamed with amusement and he bowed to her and gave a rich laugh. 'I shall await madame's pleasure.'

How could she maintain her anger when he smiled at her so provocatively? Her step was light as she hurried to the bathroom. To her relief it was free and the water was hot.

Dan watched Faith leave. He hadn't come here to seduce her or take her out. He had intended merely to ask her to pose for him tomorrow and make arrangements to collect her. The female scent of her was still in his nostrils – haunting and tantalising. His frustration resurfaced. Women and their reasoning were a mystery to him. His eyes hardened. Hadn't he brought enough trouble on his head by once succumbing to a seductress's wiles?

How sweet had been the brief hours when he believed he would finally be free of Imelda. The blow of disillusion had been doubly hard to bear. In death Cuthbert Passmore had bound him even more securely to his daughter. Dan had not expected to be made chief executor and beneficiary of the old squire's estate. And he had been further horrified at the way the estate funds had been bound up in trusts so that it was impossible for Imelda to get her hands on the money. The old despot wanted a grandchild to inherit and this was his way of blackmailing Imelda into producing one. Only Passmore had not reckoned on Dan's disinterest in the money. The difficulty was that if Imelda and he divorced she would get nothing. The estate was to be sold and the money given to the Catholic church. Much as Dan despised Imelda, his sense of justice could not allow her to become penniless. There had to be another way to contest the will and win his freedom.

His thoughts became bitter and he refused to dwell upon them. Faith had made him forget his troubles when he arrived. He was surprised at how much he did want her. He spun on his heel to pace to the window and stare down at the traffic on the street below. This woman was not like the others who had modelled for him. He must tread carefully.

Her agile leap across the sofa had given him an enticing view of her thigh. He had already glimpsed the splendour of her breasts as she stooped over the sofa. His eyes sparkled as he visualised several poses for Faith to assume and the theme of his paintings. She would be perfect swathed in diaphanous material which drifted like a mist around her. He imagined her in an ethereal role. The Lady of the Lake rising from the waters. In his mind he saw her as Eve wandering naked in the Garden of Eden, her hand holding the forbidden apple.

He cupped his jaw with his fingers. She was perfect in form and her lovely face showed her innocence and unawakened sensuality. He had yet to overcome her modesty which he guessed would be no easy matter.

He turned towards the bedroom where, her bath finished, Faith was dressing. She had shown him an integrity and strength of will which surprised him considering her background. Experience had taught him to crush his romantic ideals. Now he had found his model, he was determined that nothing would prevent the paintings she had inspired from becoming a reality.

Briefly his conscience pricked him. He stamped it down. He had made too many sacrifices in his life for his art. In recent years it had been his work which had kept him sane. It was his mainstay – the only thing that was important to him.

When Faith returned to the sitting room Dan had moved the furniture and was standing by the window. He swung round at the sound of her footfall. His gaze was appreciative as it took in her smart appearance in a kingfisher dress which brought out the unusual colour of her eyes. She crossed to the mirror. Winding her hair into a coil she was about to place her cloche hat over it when he stopped her.

'Please, leave your hair free for me. It's a crime to hide such splendour under a hat.'

'Is it me or my hair you're taking out to dine, Dan Brogan?' she returned heatedly, remembering how her hair had attracted his interest outside the nightclub.

'Fortunately the two go together,' he responded with a grin as he helped her on with her coat. 'My car is outside. Do you want to eat up West or somewhere quieter?'

'You choose. It's been a long day and the West End is always so noisy.'

His car was a large maroon and black Daimler with beige leather upholstery. It must have cost a fortune. The obvious display of wealth made her uncomfortable. As on the previous occasion Dan's suit was of an expensive cut and material and his black overcoat was cashmere. Her pleasure in his company dulled. She didn't view his wealth as a means to an easy meal ticket like Ruby. What would a man like Dan be wanting with a poor orphan girl like herself? Only to paint her. She must remember that. There could be nothing else between them.

Dan kept to south of the river, driving through Bermondsey and into Greenwich to a restaurant on the edge of the park. It was small and intimate, the tables covered with red gingham cloths and candles in a bottle. Throughout the meal Dan fired questions at her.

'Now you have a job, you aren't going to back out of posing for me, are you? I had intended that we start tomorrow as it's Sunday.'

'I gave my word. Tomorrow is fine.'

He gave her a searching look before saying softly, 'And that means a lot to you, doesn't it?'

'Of course. Shouldn't it to everybody?'

'Sadly not. You'd never break your word, or let someone down. It is one of your strengths which makes you special.'

'I'm not special, Dan.'

He lifted her hand to his lips. 'Yes, you are. You have a rare warmth and honesty.'

The admiration in his eyes made her heart somersault and despite her reservations she knew that she was beginning to fall in love with him. Yet she knew nothing about him. Before she could ask any questions about his life, he spoke.

'So what is this job you've taken?'

Enthusiasm for her work made her forget her wish to question him. Dan would understand how she felt about working in an art gallery; Ruby had yawned and simply told her that she was 'doing great'.

'I had the most amazing stroke of good fortune,' she blurted out and proceeded to tell him all that happened. Dan kept asking her questions. When she finally ground to a halt they had finished eating and Dan had paid the bill.

'Why did you let me go on like that? I must have bored you.'

'It's interesting to listen to someone who is viewing the art world with fresh eyes. I'm delighted at your success. Underwood and Lincoln's has a good reputation.'

'Since they sell your paintings, I would expect such praise,' she teased. 'We've sold your two paintings of the moor. I thought they were superb. I loved the different aspects of night and day.'

They left the restaurant and Dan pulled her arm through his, saying, 'Shall we walk a while. It's not cold.'

She agreed, unwilling for the evening to end. They sauntered along the outside of Greenwich Park. Through the trees were visible the neoclassic colonnades of the Naval College and Inigo Jones's Queen's House. They paused to gaze up the green rise of ancient trees towards The Royal Observatory at the summit, the buildings spectral in the starlight.

Faith tried to conjure an image of the zero meridian line as though it should blaze like a comet through the heavens. It was awesome to consider that she was standing along a global reference on a par with the equator.

Dan's arm was around her shoulders. 'Are you cold?'

'A bit.' She could feel the heat of his body and his strength and didn't want him to move away. 'With the Royal Observatory and the meridian line here – and tonight the stars are so bright – I feel humbled and at the same time part of something momentous.' She laughed. 'That sounds absurd.'

'There is a kind of magic in the air around such places,' Dan said sincerely.

She nodded. 'This place is majestic. Like your paintings, Dan. I'm flattered that you wish to paint me.'

He turned her in the circle of his arm. The moonlight shadowed his handsome features and when he tipped her chin up to see her expression his touch stifled her breath.

'It will be my pleasure, I assure you,' he said softly, the husky timbre of his voice causing a shiver of anticipation to consume her. 'I'm glad my paintings please you and that you have found work more worthy of your talents.'

She strove to keep her voice composed as she answered, 'I'm not sure that I like the cut and thrust of selling art. But the pay is good. It will give me a chance to get some savings behind me so that I can become an art student.' Saying it out loud made it sound pretentious and she smiled self-consciously. 'It's an impossible dream I suppose,' she hastily amended. 'It takes a great deal of money and in the meantime I have to live. If it is meant to be, it will happen one day.'

'It's not an easy life,' Dan cautioned. 'Don't be taken in by the glamour.'

They walked back to the car. 'I'm under no illusions. And as for glamour; hard work and diligence never harmed anyone. Working in the gallery is a hundred times better than being a chamber-maid. Now that Ruby and I are working, anything is possible.' She shuddered. 'When I think of those first days in London, they now seem like a bad dream.'

Faith paused, hesitant at appearing too forward. In a breathless rush, she added, 'I wondered if you were free on Monday if you would escort me to the club so that I could hear her sing. I don't fancy going on my own.'

'I'd be delighted. What club is it?'

'The Gilded Lily.'

Dan frowned, his stare piercing and troubled. 'That's owned by Ernie Durham, isn't it?'

'Yes. Tony took Ruby there. Is there something wrong with the club?'

'Ernie Durham is trouble. I wouldn't say he's a villain, but he certainly lives on the shady side of the law.'

Faith's stomach clenched in alarm. 'But Ruby has been seeing Ernie. I'm afraid she ditched Tony after Ernie gave her the job.'

Dan rubbed his jaw. 'The fool. Not for ditching Tony, but for getting tied up with Durham. You've got to persuade Ruby to get out of there. And you mustn't have anything to do with Durham. He's an unscrupulous rogue and dangerous to be mixed up with.'

'Ruby will never give up singing at the club. She sees it as a chance to be famous.'

He answered gruffly, 'I don't know why you're so loyal to that woman. She's just a tart on the make.'

Faith shrugged away from his arm, anger flushing her cheeks. 'She is my friend. You don't know her. Ruby is wild because she's hurting inside that she was abandoned as a baby. Not that she would ever admit it. At least I was fortunate enough to know my parents before they died and I was sent to the orphanage.'

Regret deepened the grooves in his face. 'Your loyalty is commendable, if misguided. I doubt you had it easy.' He took her hand and drew her closer to him. 'Life hasn't hardened you like it has Ruby. And that's something precious. I hate to think that she may bring her troubles down on you. I don't want to see you hurt.'

Again his nearness was playing havoc with her breathing and the concern in his eyes made her anger fade. Her eyes were overbrilliant as she looked up at him. 'I can look after myself.'

'You've done well for yourself since you were penniless on the steps of Piccadilly. Just don't let that soft heart of yours be your downfall.'

'I know Ruby's faults. She is reckless and impetuous but not bad. Men often get the wrong idea about her. They take advantage of her. Inside she is vulnerable and is too stubborn to admit it.'

There was a starkness in his eyes which pierced her. 'She's not as vulnerable as you. You're an idealist. It would be too easy for a man to take advantage of your warmth and sincerity.' At his abrupt change of manner an icy finger touched Faith's spine. Was that a warning not to get emotionally entangled with him?

Chapter Eight

Ernie Durham watched Ruby launch into her opening number. It was Saturday night and Miriam had been taken ill. He was taking a risk putting Ruby on, but he wanted to see her perform before a large audience. She didn't disappoint him.

Ruby moved like a feline on heat, her eyes roving the depths of the club, seeking a mate. The black satin gown clung to her like a second skin. A languorous stretch of her arm lifted the swell of her breasts and revealed the slenderness of her ribcage. Each languid sway of her hips contoured their outline, her figure naked beneath the flimsy material. He had known scores of women and watched countless strippers perform their blatant sexuality; all had left him untouched. Ruby had that extra something; it filled his gut with a raw aching.

A survey of the men's enrapt faces at the tables showed that he was not the only man reacting to her sexuality. Ruby was going to make his fortune. The little fool had been too excited to even glance at the small print on the contract he had insisted she sign. He rubbed his hands together with satisfaction. He'd sewn that contract up so tight she couldn't even sneeze without asking him first.

Two burly men came through the door by the bar, standing on either side as a third man sauntered between them. Ernie pasted on an ingratiating smile as he went to greet Big Hugh Kavanagh and his younger brothers, Pete and Reg. Big Hugh was getting more muscle on this manor than old King George himself. A few months ago he'd wiped out the three leaders of a rival gang and taken over the razor-blade racket and prostitution ring.

'What you drinking, Mr Kavanagh?'

'I never drink until business is settled.' The dark eyes were lethal as a snake about to strike its prey. Ernie knew he had nothing to fear from this visit by Big Hugh, but you couldn't be too careful. Kavanagh had eyes and ears everywhere and Ernie had made several enemies in recent years.

He nodded and followed Big Hugh up the stairs to his office. Reg remained posted outside and Pete stood inside the door, ready to protect Hugh if there was trouble. Kavanagh didn't trust his own mother let alone an associate. Since his mother Lil was doing time in Holloway for beating her eldest daughter to death when she caught her in bed with Lil's lover, that wasn't surprising. Big Hugh's father, Fists Kavanagh, had been a hard-drinking navvy who became a bare-knuckle fighter on the circuit. He'd killed two men in the ring and reputedly another half dozen outside of it.

Kavanagh seated himself behind Ernie's desk and put his feet on the leather top. 'Got a job for you, Ernie. Jeweller's at Barking on Saturday night. The safe's the same as the Plaistow job.'

Ernie felt the usual rush of adrenaline at the prospect of cracking another safe. Kavanagh's gang were getting more ambitious as his own expertise grew. Many jewellers' still had old-fashioned safes which he'd learnt to crack a dozen years ago when he was banged up in Wormwood Scrubs doing a two-year stretch for beating up a Kraut Jew. Best favour the law ever did was putting him in a cell with Fingers Larkin.

Big Hugh took one of Ernie's fat cigars from its box and lit it. A cloud of blue smoke wreathed his bullet head as he continued, 'Set up a party in one of the plush hotels to provide us with an alibi. And bring that new singer of yours along. She ain't known to the law. Fix her drinks so she'll swear we were there all night. Pete will have the car out the back at two o'clock. Make sure the tart is out of her head by then.'

'You can rely on me, Mr Kavanagh.'

Those dark reptilian eyes stared through him and his cruel

100

mouth stretched into a parody of a smile. It set Ernie's teeth on edge. He knew the score with Kavanagh. One mistake and he was dead, as were others before him for botching a job.

When the Kavanagh brothers departed, Ernie wiped a hand across his face. It was slick with perspiration. Big Hugh was a mean bastard and was rising to be one of the foremost underworld leaders. He was fair enough in his dealings unless he suspected that someone had crossed him. Ernie respected him. Kavanagh had put a dozen bank and jewellers' jobs his way, each planned so meticulously that the police didn't even suspect they were the ones involved. That Big Hugh visited him instead of summoning him to his warehouse headquarters showed a change in their relationship and Ernie's importance within the gang. Kavanagh had put Ernie in charge of their gambling and protection rackets.

Ernie rubbed his hands. That would make him a man people didn't mess with. He'd have the power to even a few scores with those who had crossed him in the past.

On Sunday morning Dan called for Faith at eight thirty to drive her to his studio to pose for him. When they arrived at the studio Dan was impatient to begin sketching her. For two hours he instructed her to take up positions: holding a spear aloft, reclining, reading and standing with an urn resting on her hip. Taking up a fresh sketchpad, he commanded, 'Now sit by the window and look wistful as though you are thinking of your lover.'

'But I don't have a lover.'

'Then think of Valentino or Fairbanks, or whoever young women sigh over at the picture palace.'

Faith complied but her thoughts kept returning to the sensations he had aroused when he kissed her. She began to fidget, trying to concentrate on the filmstars instead.

Exasperated Dan put down the charcoal. 'What's wrong?'

'I feel silly.' She avoided looking at him.

'Then think of a happy memory with your parents.'

His businesslike manner was far removed from the teasing

friendship of the previous evening and it ruffled her. But hadn't she been the one to insist that their arrangement was a business one? She was being contrary and she disliked contrary women.

Pulling her thoughts together, she resolved to do justice to her role of model. She recalled her fifth birthday when her parents had taken her to a circus. Her expression became dreamy and she forgot her self-consciousness as Dan sketched her. Inevitably her thoughts moved on to learning of her father's death and the vicious attack on her mother which had killed her. The memories were painful.

Tears spilled on to her cheeks and with a sob she plucked her handkerchief from her pocket and wiped her eyes. 'I'm sorry, Dan.'

'What is it now?' His voice was abstracted as he continued his rapid sketching.

She sniffed, feeling awkward and embarrassed. 'I was thinking of my parents.'

'Ah well . . .' Again his distraction was obvious. 'Wonderful pose. Can you hold it for a few more minutes? And don't wipe away the tears. They're so poignant. So moving . . .'

A lump rose to her throat as she felt obliged to hold the pose. The strain was immense. She was hurt. Deeply hurt. How could Dan be so heartless? Did he feel nothing of her pain? Stricken by his callousness, she turned her tear-filled glare upon him. His expression was taut with concentration, his hand flying across the paper.

'No, don't move,' he commanded.

Damn him! She was not a machine. She jumped up and turned her back.

There was a clatter as his sketchpad was thrown to the floor and he was beside her. 'I'm sorry, Faith. You're grieving and I was selfish.' He looked genuinely contrite. 'Forgive me. The artist takes over when I see a striking pose. I was insensitive.'

'Yes, you were.' To her dismay she burst into fresh weeping. He took her into his arms, talking soothingly to calm her sobs.

As her tears subsided the heat of his body scorched her. Her breasts were pressed against his chest and with her head on his shoulder she smelt the male musk of his body. It was exciting and perturbing. As though he sensed her awareness of him he tensed, physically and mentally distancing himself from her.

'Time to get on. If you're feeling better.'

She broke away from him to sit on the windowsill and dabbed at her eyes. 'I feel so stupid. It's years since I've cried. Suddenly I missed Mum and Dad so much. Silly, isn't it?'

He moved to the far side of the studio and was examining a jar of paintbrushes. The tension remained in his body and it was some moments before he replied. 'It isn't silly. What with coming to London, finding a new demanding job and cleaning the flat, you've been pushing yourself too hard. And I've dragged you round here when you could have done with a lie-in.'

To talk of inconsequentials eased the atmosphere between them. She lightened her voice. 'I had no plans other than a sandwich lunch in one of the parks. I'd rather be here. I like watching you sketch. I envy your talent. How do you wish me to pose now?'

'I think you've done enough today. I didn't think about getting food in. Do you fancy going down to a pub on the river? We can get a bite there.'

She was tempted but she had a nagging feeling that he had asked her out of politeness. From the hard way her heart was pounding, she thought it better to decline. 'I'm sure you've got friends you'd rather visit. I've some chores to catch up on before work tomorrow. Are you sure you've got enough sketches to work on?'

'Plenty. Next weekend I'll start painting you. I've an exhibition in New York in the autumn and you're the perfect model for my ideas.' This time he looked unsure. 'That's if you agree. Of course, I shall pay you for your time.'

The thought of working with him over several months was exciting. She could learn a lot about the techniques of art just by watching him. This infatuation which was playing havoc with her senses was something she must learn to control. She would never again get the chance to learn from such an accomplished artist.

'I don't want payment. In return would you give me art lessons for a couple of hours a week?'

He subjected her to a thoughtful stare, his mouth tilting provocatively at the corner. 'I'd be an exacting and impatient teacher. But if you can stick me, it's a deal. How about every Wednesday since it's half-day closing at the gallery? You could pose for me for a couple of hours and then I'd work with you through the evening. We'll do the same on a Sunday.'

She was astonished. 'I didn't expect to take up so much of your time. You're an important artist.'

He grinned. 'And you're an exceptional model. You never complain at the time I keep you holding a pose. It would please me to help you. Take home one of my sketchpads and charcoal and bring some sketches with you on Wednesday. I want to see what inspires you.'

The radiance of her expression twisted his heart. To see such enthusiasm for life and how little it took to give her pleasure was a revelation. He cursed the cynicism which had overtaken him in recent years. An artist needed idealism to bring magic to his paintings. Faith was showing him that he need not have lost it entirely within himself. If Imelda was his *bête noire* then Faith was his redeeming angel.

On Monday, as promised, Dan took Faith to watch Ruby's performance. His eyes slitted at seeing Hugh Kavanagh and his two brothers enter the club and go up to Durham's office. He'd been suspected of a triple killing of some gangster leaders a few months ago, but had not been charged. There was no smoke without fire where Kavanagh was concerned. Big Hugh looked at home here. Was he a frequent visitor? Dan had brought Faith to the Gilded Lily to hear Ruby sing. It wasn't turning out to be the entertaining evening he expected.

Faith had quickly hidden her shock when Ruby began her act. He had seen the blush flare into her face and the sadness enter her eyes. Then she had sighed, accepting her friend for what she was, and in her loyalty refusing to judge her. Although Ruby was too obvious for his taste, he admitted that the woman oozed sex appeal. However, he didn't trust her. Nor could he shake the feeling that her friendship with Faith would draw her into danger.

Big Hugh's appearance added to his suspicions. Durham was a shifty rogue. Ruby was a fool to get involved with him. Fear for Faith roused a fierce need in him to protect her. The force of it shocked him. He didn't want to analyse his emotions for Faith. She was an exciting and stimulating woman. When they danced earlier he was aware of the chemistry sparking between them. Holding her in his arms, feeling the movement of her body against his, had incited his desire. She certainly deserved better than to be condemned to live as his mistress and never his wife. Shocked, he checked his thoughts. From her response to his kisses he knew it would be easy to seduce her. Yet when an artist and model became entangled art suffered. He couldn't risk that. And Faith deserved better from him.

Frustration darkened his mood which he directed at Ruby and Durham. If Kavanagh was here, then Durham was up to no good.

Ruby launched into a risqué and sultry rendition of 'Ma, he's making eyes at me'. When she finished the club erupted into applause and catcalls from the men.

Faith said proudly, 'They adore Ruby. I'm delighted for her. This is what she wants.'

Her loyalty touched Dan. It made him ashamed of the cynic he had become over the years. Once he would have been as uncondemning as herself, but women like Ruby could bleed a person dry of emotion. They were totally self-absorbed. Nothing mattered but their own pleasure and they did not care whom they hurt in the process. It struck him that perhaps in his need for Faith, he probably was no better himself.

He was aware that Faith was uncomfortable in the smoky atmosphere of the club and that the ribald comments directed at Ruby were upsetting her. Taking her hand, he squeezed it reassuringly. The concern for her friend which shone in her eyes touched a chord within him. This was a woman capable of unselfish love. An idealist, as once he had been an idealist. It was that quality of goodness and beauty which made her so special as a model. He was again impatient to capture that image on canvas. His disappointment was acute that he must wait until Wednesday when she would again come to the studio.

Ruby stepped off the stage and was immediately surrounded by men. Faith collected her bag and gloves from the table, saying, 'I must tell Ruby how terrific she was before we leave.'

Knowing that men in a club would see a lone woman as fair game, Dan remained at her side. He was surprised at the pleasure on Ruby's face as she hugged Faith and dismissed the men.

'Was I sensational, or was I sensational?' she said.

'You were sensational, Ruby. They adore you. Go back to your new friends. You won't mind if I leave now, I've work in the morning and it's gone midnight.'

'Must you leave? I'm on again in an hour.'

Faith's worries for her friend burst to the surface. 'This isn't you, Ruby. You're selling yourself too cheaply. You've talent as a singer. If you paid for lessons and had some real training . . .'

Ruby's expression hardened. 'What do I need to waste me money on lessons for! They love me. I'm gonna be a star.'

'Just be yourself,' Faith cautioned. 'This act you are putting on . . . you don't need to flaunt yourself. It's Ernie who is making you do this, isn't it?'

'I ain't doing nothing I don't want to.' Her chin jutted with defiance. 'I'm just using what I've got to get me where I want to go. There ain't nothing wrong in that.'

Faith knew it was hopeless to convince Ruby otherwise. 'You'll be a star, Ruby,' she said, hugging her again.

Ernie Durham had appeared at Ruby's side and with a proprietorial air took her arm. 'You were terrific, babe. But don't forget your job is also to keep the punters happy. Get them to order champagne and plenty of it.'

Ruby blew Faith a kiss before the men again swarmed around her.

Faith was silent as Dan drove her home. She had hated the way Ruby played up to the men. It shocked and saddened her. Ruby was changing and Ernie Durham was behind it. He was bringing out the wilder side of her friend. Ruby was insecure, so desperate to be loved, she couldn't see that those men were adoring her because of the fantasy she offered. She excited them sexually, but they didn't respect her.

She was frightened for her friend. Ernie Durham also made her uncomfortable. He had looked at Ruby as though she was his property. There was a cold calculation in his eyes which had made her blood freeze. She had to stop Ruby from getting further embroiled with Ernie. He was no good; she sensed the suppressed violence within the man and feared what could happen to Ruby.

'You're very quiet,' Dan said as he stopped the car outside her flat and switched off the engine. 'It wasn't what you expected, was it?'

She sighed. 'I'm worried about Ruby.' She turned to Dan, her eyes large with pleading. 'But it's not a bad place, is it? Tony wouldn't have taken her there if it was a bad place, would he?'

'Ruby knows how to take care of herself.'

'But she doesn't.' Faith groaned. 'She just thinks she does.'

Dan slid his arm along the back of her seat. Faith was everything that Ruby was not – everything that Imelda was not. Despite all his reservations he was captivated by her. 'Ruby will be fine. It's you I'm concerned about. You'll make yourself ill worrying about her.'

He lifted a lock of her hair and smiled. 'Are you going to invite me in for some tea? Ruby won't be back for hours.'

The temptation was strong. She knew he wanted her, not a drink. Her flesh burned for his touch and the enchantment he could weave upon her. Even so, an insidious voice inside her head cautioned. How many times had she warned Ruby about rushing headlong into relationships? And here she was tempted to do the same. What did she know of Dan or his life?

'I've had a lovely evening, but I'm tired. I have to get up early for work in the morning.'

Dan drew back without protest, but the lean lines of his face could have been sculpted from marble. It had been so hard to deny him when she wanted so much to be with him.

'How long you gonna be this time?' Ruby complained as Ernie's car drew up outside a warehouse owned by Big Hugh. She'd been seeing Ernie for a month and was beginning to feel he was taking liberties in the way he treated her. 'Last time you were over an hour. What am I supposed to do?'

'Stay here and stop bitching,' Ernie snarled. 'I've got business.'

He slammed the car door shut. Bloody nerve! Ruby thought as she stared at the bleak row of warehouses along the river. This was getting beyond a joke. Ernie was the type of man who always had to be seen with an attractive woman on his arm. Ruby was weary of being dragged out to these meetings and left in the back of beyond to entertain herself for hours on end.

Scowling, she laid her head back on the car seat and closed her eyes. Might as well catch up on some kip; Ernie would take his own sweet time and never mind how bored she was. At first she had been pleased that Ernie wanted her constantly at his side. The novelty soon wore off as she was dragged from one so-called business meeting to another. Then there were the card games which went on after the club shut until the small hours of the morning. She might have the grand title of hostess, but she spent all evening running to the beck and call of Kavanagh and others of his kind as they demanded drinks and snacks. She might just as well be a waitress. Watching men play poker was about as exciting as watching grass grow.

Often in the early hours of the morning she would doze in an armchair, vaguely aware that the conversation turned to business deals. The language was carefully couched to have an innocent front, but Big Hugh seemed to have his finger is several illegal pies.

A violent rocking made her wake with a start. A large man stood in front of the car.

'What the hell you doing?' she began. To her horror he brought an iron bar down on to the bonnet. It crumpled with a sickening screech of metal. She screamed. The man was a maniac. The bar was raised again. Her eyes widened with terror. It came smashing down towards the windscreen. Screaming, she put up her arms to protect her face and cowered in the seat.

The glass showered over her, needles of fire stinging her cut hands. She began to sob with fright. The door was jerked open and she glimpsed a bearded face and dark hostile eyes. Before she could fight him off, she was dragged out and thrown on to the ground into an oily puddle. Her shoes had come off and her dress was rucked around her thighs. Her heart was thudding painfully, pumping blood iced by fear round her shaking body. The man loomed over her with murderous intent.

'Don't hurt me. I ain't done nothing,' she wailed, scraping her heels as she edged back from him.

There was a shout from the warehouse and the sound of running feet. The man above her swore and backed away.

'You're Durham's tart. Tell 'im to stay off our manor. This is a friendly warning.'

He took to his heels. 'Pete, Reg, get after him,' Kavanagh yelled.

Ruby was shaking so violently she had trouble pushing herself upright. There was blood on her hands and her coat was ruined by the oil in the puddle. 'Bastard! What did he pick on me for?'

She was still swearing when Big Hugh crouched over her. 'You all right, babe?'

Ruby nodded.

Ernie was glaring at his ruined car and kicked the running-board with his foot. 'Fuck them,' he yelled. 'It's those bloody Greeks I bet.'

'They'll be sorted,' Kavanagh ground out. 'No one treats one of us like this and gets away with it.'

Ernie came round to Ruby and roughly jerked her to her feet. 'Did you see who it was?'

'I didn't see much at all. I just had time to cover my face before that maniac smashed in the windscreen. Then he dragged me out of the car and into this puddle.'

'Did he have a beard?'

'Yes.'

'It was the Greeks then. They'll bloody wish they'd never been born. This was a new car.'

'Sod the car!' Ruby's temper exploded. 'What about me? I could've been killed. If you hadn't come out when you did he was about to do me over. That man was capable of murder. I've never been so scared in my life. Look at me coat. It's ruined, and me dress.'

'Stop whining,' Ernie snapped. 'I'll get you a new coat and a dress.'

His derogatory tone was like a torch to a powder keg. Ruby flew at him, her nails raking at his face. 'I could've been killed! Don't you care? You're making more fuss over this car.'

He caught her wrists and dragged her arms behind her back, pinning her against his hard chest. 'Yeah, I'm sorry, babe. I'll make it up to you. Just calm down. Now this never happened. Understand me?'

'Ain't you gonna tell the police?' she raged. 'That maniac should be locked up.'

Big Hugh rapped out, 'Look, babe, the police ain't interested in the likes of what went on here. So just keep quiet. The Greek will be taken care of – our way.'

His words chilled her to the bone. This was gang warfare. The police would regard any deaths as a couple fewer villains for them to run in.

Ernie stared at her, his expression cruel. 'You've seen too much for your own good. Keep quiet and no harm will come to you.'

'I ain't seen nothing, Ernie.'

'That's my girl.' He turned to Kavanagh. 'Get someone to pick up the car and get it fixed by tomorrow. Can you give us a lift back to the club?'

Ruby was still shaken when they returned to the Gilded Lily. She was seated in Ernie's office with a large gin in her hand. Ernie was perched on the desk, his arms folded as he watched her.

'You did all right today, Ruby. I'm proud of you.' He took the drink from her fingers and drew her into his arms. 'You're a trooper. Happen you and me could go places. But you'll have to learn to turn a blind eye to what goes on when you're with me. No blabbing to no one. Especially Mike. Then happen we'll give you the Friday evening session to sing at the club. One good favour deserves another.'

She understood him perfectly. 'I ain't going to any more meetings, Ernie. But I won't talk. And I'll have that new coat you promised. One with a deep fur collar and don't try and say it's a loan. You owe me that at least.'

He ground his hips against hers. 'I'm sure you can show your gratitude in other ways. I won't place you in danger again.'

She complied to his demands. After her fight she needed to be held and loved. Sex was at least a substitute. A long night was ahead of her. Big Hugh and his men turned up as the club was closing. She was left drinking in the bar, waiting for Ernie to take her home. It was gone three in the morning and she jumped violently as the inner door from the street banged. She had been dozing with her head in her arms on the bar and for a second she relived the terror of the afternoon. Then a familiar voice reassured her that she was safe.

'Ernie keeping you up all hours?' Mike Rivers said as he poured himself a scotch. 'You look beat.'

'No rest for the wicked,' she joked, glad of his company.

Shouting broke out in the office. Big Hugh's voice drifted down. 'They'll pay up, or else. Get it sorted.'

Mike's face hardened. 'What's that scum doing here?'

Ruby shrugged.

Mike frowned and put his thumb and forefinger to her chin to turn her face to the light. 'You've got several cuts on your cheek and hands. What happened to you?'

'Nothing. A stone flew up off the road and smashed the car windscreen.'

'And Ernie dragged you down here. Then keeps you hanging about. You should be resting after a shock like that.'

The concern in his voice made her study him with deepening interest. Ernie had dismissed the danger to her. Mike was a nice

111

guy. And handsome. She couldn't resist flirting with him. 'You offering me a lift home?

'Not while you're Ernie's woman.'

'Who says I'm Ernie's woman?'

'I do. Why else you still here?'

Her lips drew back into a smile of pure enticement and she reached out to run her finger along his arm. 'You ain't scared of Ernie, are you?'

'I can handle my brother. I just don't share my women.'

Ruby didn't like what he was implying. He'd as good as said she played around.

She raised her blonde brows. 'How quaint.' Her sarcasm had a bitter edge. Strangely, she didn't like Mike having a low opinion of her.

Mike shoved himself away from the bar and took the stairs two at a time to the office and went in without knocking.

There was a burst of raised voices with Mike clearly giving the orders and not taking them. That surprised her. She had always thought that Ernie was the one very much in charge. Or that was the impression Ernie gave. Minutes later Mike stormed down the stairs and out of the club. It wasn't the first time she'd overheard the brothers arguing. Ernie had been insistent that Mike knew nothing of his meetings with Big Hugh. Did Mike truly not know what his brother was up to?

Ruby sighed and stared at the darkened stage. Was she mad to keep seeing Ernie after what happened this afternoon? Then she remembered how much she was in debt to him. The loan agreement he had drawn up bound her to work at the club until it was paid off. Her contract with Ernie was for three years, including singing at any future clubs he might open. At the time she had been thrilled at such a long-term prospect of singing. Now she was not so sure that the price had not been rather high.

Chapter Nine

Celibacy wasn't a virtue, it was a millstone round her neck, Faith decided.

She enjoyed modelling for Dan and absorbed her art lessons with enthusiasm, but Dan seemed to be deliberately keeping his distance. Perversely, that disgruntled her. With each meeting her attraction for him had grown, not diminished. Their meetings were confined to work in the studio and Faith tried to convince herself that it was for the best. Usually she failed.

Faith didn't mind not having much of a social life, keeping herself busy with reading and sketching in the evenings. Oliver also supplied her with art brochures and catalogues. She missed the company of Ruby who spent most evenings with Ernie. A night spent with Hardy, Galsworthy or D.H. Lawrence was not the same as a laugh and a giggle over the events of the day. Mind you, D.H. Lawrence's latest novel, *Lady Chatterley's Lover*, was rather an eye-opener and was causing a furore in the Courts.

Ruby kept at least one evening free for her and they would go to the palais de danse. Faith had met a couple of men who had asked her out. She saw them once then dropped them. She kept wishing they were Dan. Ruby loved going to the picture palaces and at least once a week she would meet Faith from work and they would catch an early viewing. They swooned over Valentino or Gary Cooper, laughed at the antics of Chaplin or Laurel and Hardy, or emerged red-eyed from a 'weepy'.

Work fulfilled Faith. The Charford paintings had been sold in private sales and Oliver had been generous with the bonus he gave her. It meant she could have afforded to pay for art lessons herself, but she was learning so much from Dan who was genuinely pleased with her progress. Instead she saved her extra money in a bank account. She never forgot the terror and insecurity of her first nights in London. She vowed never to be in that position again.

If the weather was dry, Faith took her sketchpad with her during her lunch break. She liked to visit the public monuments and sketch the people around Trafalgar Square, Marble Arch and Westminster Abbey. She hadn't gone back to Piccadilly Circus, still embarrassed at what had happened there. She enjoyed depicting street scenes. A protest march by crippled soldiers from the war, whose plight had been forgotten by the government, had particularly moved her. So did the numerous hunger marches of the unemployed which converged on Hyde Park. With over two million out of work many of the men were the family breadwinners. It made her appreciate her good fortune in working at the gallery. She was also intrigued by the colourful buskers with their accordions, marionettes or performing animals and the crowds they drew around them.

On a wet day she would take a bus to the National or Tate art galleries to view the paintings. Today was Friday and as it was fine she had asked Oliver if she could take an early lunch hour to go down to Buckingham Palace and sketch the changing of the guard. She had worked through her lunch hour yesterday so had two hours owing to her.

She was about to collect her things when Dan entered the shop carrying some wrapped paintings under his arm. All thoughts of her outing fled at his appearance. He had cancelled their usual Wednesday session this week as he been out of town on business. She had missed him and the week had dragged slowly. He winked at her, but Oliver was fussing around Dan before she had a chance to speak with him.

'Charles said you were coming in today,' Oliver declared. 'He saw some of your work in an exhibition in Southwark. He was quite put out that you hadn't offered any more to us. We sold the moorland scenes very quickly.'

'I've been tied up with work for an American exhibition.'

Oliver had carefully removed the wrappings and propped the paintings along the floor by his desk. Two were of Tower Bridge and the Houses of Parliament outlined against a river mist. The third was of Windsor Castle from the river at sunset.

'Are these recent works?' Oliver queried.

'They are the best of some pieces I did a couple of years ago.'

'Very impressive,' Oliver praised. 'Easier to sell than your more airy-fairy themes.'

Faith had come to look at the paintings which she hadn't seen before. They were of a different style to what she expected. They were superb landscapes but she felt rather disloyal at thinking that they lacked the special quality she had seen in the moorland paintings, or the first paintings Dan had completed of her. Those had made her blood quicken. Dan portrayed her as Diana the huntress and also as a woman gazing at her reflection in a woodland pool.

'May I introduce Miss Tempest,' Oliver announced belatedly.

'We are acquainted,' Dan returned enigmatically. When he did not expand, Oliver looked questioningly at Faith.

'We met at the Tate one lunchtime.' Faith didn't know why she lied, but Oliver was such a busybody and her relationship with Dan was special to her. She didn't want it speculated upon, or have it widely known that she was modelling for him.

'Oh, I see.' Oliver immediately lost interest. The phone rang and Oliver, who seemed to regard the instrument as his own personal possession, answered it.

'Charles. Yes. Yes. Brogan has just arrived. The paintings are splendid. Simply splendid.'

Faith had stooped to study the paintings and was aware of Dan watching her.

'You don't seem impressed,' he said softly.

She swung around horrified. 'I am. The mist is very evocative and the buildings expertly painted.'

'But . . .' He seemed to be enjoying taunting her.

'The moorland scenes had something extra special, an

115

intangible dimension which reached out to me. And it's in the paintings you did of me.'

He nodded. 'I wondered if you would notice. The moorland scenes were painted several years ago. I've been searching to rediscover that magical inspiration ever since. The spiritual essence at the heart of a painting which gives it a soul quality.' His voice dropped lower. 'You've given it back to me, Faith. These I painted last year. They are not my best work but an artist must sell his paintings to live.'

She blushed and glanced across at Oliver who was absorbed in his conversation with Charles Underwood.

'Are you free for lunch, Faith?'

'I had intended to . . .' She broke off. 'It was nothing important. I am free.'

'Good. There's an exhibition of Pre-Raphaelites at the National. I thought you would enjoy it.'

She had visited it two days ago. 'How wonderful. I'd like that very much. I'm about to go to lunch now and I've got an extra hour owing to me.'

His eyes sparkled with pleasure. 'I'll meet you outside when I've finished here. Best if Lincoln doesn't see us leave together. He may not approve of you fraternising.'

Why should Oliver care whom she spent her lunch hour with? But he could be such an Inquisitor about her private life that Dan had a valid point. But why was Dan taking pains to keep their relationship secret from Oliver? Was he ashamed of being seen out with a shop assistant? That stung her pride. She almost changed her mind. But spending two hours with Dan in the National Gallery was too wonderful an opportunity to miss. She was being oversensitive.

Oliver had finished his call. 'I'll write the cheque for you, Mr Brogan. I'm sure Miss Tempest will keep you occupied while I go into the office.'

'I'm sure she will,' Dan replied with a broad smile.

A quarter of an hour later they were dodging the scavenging

pigeons around the fountains of Trafalgar Square. Dan took her arm as they crossed the busy road to the steps of the National Gallery. To visit it with Dan was vastly different from seeing the paintings alone. He enthralled her as he spoke of the techniques used by the artists. She bombarded him with questions about the mixing of colours or voiced her own interpretation of the scenes which moved her most.

The two hours sped by. 'I'm going to be late back to the gallery.'

'Don't worry, Oliver won't sack you.'

'But I hate being late.'

'You never take advantage of anyone, do you, Faith?' His voice was admiring, making her heart swell with emotion.

'I would never intentionally do that.'

He had taken her hand and pressed his lips to it. 'Why can't more women be like you, my dear Faith?' For a long moment his gaze held hers. It echoed the yearning she knew to be in her eyes and which she was too deeply moved to hide. She saw him swallow and his eyes tinge with regret. Abruptly his mood changed. 'I'd better get you back to the shop. I'll pick you up as usual on Sunday.'

His mood swings always perplexed her. Since she began modelling for him he had made no attempt to kiss her again. She had never thought she would curse any man for treating her with gentlemanly respect.

Faith was about to leave for work the next morning when a key turned in the lock. She went into the hall. Ruby was tiptoeing across the carpet, her high-heeled silver dance shoes in her hand. She swayed with each step and the cigarette smoke from the club clung to her clothing. Ruby stubbed her toe on the corner of the table and swore in a slurred voice. She was drunk.

Catching sight of Faith, she started violently and cried out, 'Faith, you frightened me half to death! I thought you'd still be asleep.'

'Fine chance. I'm just off to work.'

'What a night, Faith.' She hiccuped and giggled. 'Oops, I'm a bit tiddly. Ernie got me a session at another club. Actually, I think Mike had more to do with it. He was playing there last week. Real swanky this club was. The customers loved me. I did two encores. I had them all in the palm of me hand. It were wonderful.' Ruby flopped down on to the arm of the settee and with a theatrical gesture appeared to embrace the world.

Faith acknowledged, 'It won't be long before Ernie realises that you are his star attraction. You should be singing every night. It's a pity he's got that contract so sewn up, otherwise you could work other clubs of your choice. Better venues. Is he letting you sing tonight?'

Ruby sat upright and pulled a face. 'Wouldn't you just know it. I've got the curse. Ernie told me not to come back to the club until it's finished. I can hardly give my usual performance padded up, can I?'

Faith hid her qualms that Ernie was only interested in Ruby for the sex appeal she exuded in her act. It cheapened her friend in a way she didn't like.

'It doesn't stop you singing. You've got something special, Ruby. You don't need to parade half-naked. Or flaunt yourself as you do.'

Ruby lifted a pencilled brow. 'Ernie says that Mae West made her name in America by her lewd comments and behaviour on the stage. It was in the papers. I could do the same in England.'

Faith was appalled. 'Greta Garbo doesn't even have to speak for men to idolise her. You don't have to be so obvious, Ruby,' Faith counselled with mounting concern. She knew how reckless Ruby was. Ernie was a selfish bastard who didn't appreciate Ruby's talent. He didn't care if Ruby discarded her self-respect. All he was interested in was making money out of her. Couldn't Ruby see that she was being used?

'Each to their own way,' Ruby said with a giggle. 'I'm gonna be a star, Faith. I've found what I'm good at and nothing, but nothing, is going to stand in me way.'

When Faith left, Ruby pressed a hand to her head. God, she'd had a skinful last night. She'd passed out at the party Ernie gave after the club closed. Ernie had been in a funny mood. Him and Kavanagh had been full of themselves when they came into the club in the early evening. She'd been piqued when Ernie disappeared for half of her act. Then at the party later, she hazily recalled that half the guests seemed to be missing. Then he'd been back, drinking heartily and in a buoyant mood.

She picked up the late edition of the *News Chronicle* that Faith had bought at the newsstand yesterday. Usually she was interested only in any news about film stars. Today, however, her attention was arrested by the front page headline. GREEK RESTAURATEUR FOUND BEHEADED IN ALLEY. ANOTHER GANGLAND KILLING ON THE STREETS OF LONDON.

Instinctively she knew that was why Ernie had been celebrating. The euphoria of her success at the club drained from her. Just what the hell had she got herself into by getting involved with Earnest Ernie Durham?

On Sunday the costume Dan had laid out for Faith was a long gown of white muslin with flowing floorlength sleeves in a medieval style. Its neckline plunged in a V to the seam under her bodice and its full skirt cut on the bias swirled about her legs as she moved. There was a circlet of white snowdrops and ivy to place over her hair.

The gown was sensuous against her bare flesh. When she returned to the studio, Dan was inspecting the sketches he had made earlier. When he saw her, his eyes widened with wonder. 'I knew that gown was right for you. It brings out the richness of your hair.'

If she had hoped to be praised for her beauty she was sadly disappointed. Dan's eyes were misty and his manner businesslike as he went on, 'Stand in front of that blue silk I've draped from the ceiling. That will represent a waterfall. I want you rising from the pool in the light of a full moon.'

He began to sketch her, then, with an impatient tut, rearranged the folds of her gown to better display the outline of her legs and brought her hair over one shoulder to fall in curls to her waist.

'That's it. Now lift up your head and spread your arms slightly behind you, like a figure-head embracing a ship's bow. I want you to look as if you and the waterfall are as one. Perfect. Hold that pose.'

Faith watched Dan outline the shape of her form and the waterfall on the canvas before he picked up a paintbrush and began to paint. His handsome face absorbed her and she was unaware of the time until an excruciating pain in her shoulders finally made her protest. 'Can we have a break, Dan?'

He looked at her startled, the misty light of inspiration fading from his eyes. He glanced at his wrist watch. 'That must be a difficult pose to hold. Drop your hands but keep your head as it is.'

Twenty minutes later she apologised, 'I have to move, Dan. I'm getting a dreadful crick in my neck.'

'Sorry, of course. The light has been so good I'd lost all track of time. Are you hungry? There's chicken casserole in the oven and the vegetables just need the gas lit under them. They'll be ready in twenty minutes.'

'All by your own fair hand?' Faith looked at him in amazement.

'A struggling art student couldn't afford to eat out. It was learn to cook or starve.'

'It sounds a wonderful meal.' She stretched and massaged the back of her neck and winced. Dan came behind her and gently brushed her hands away. 'Sit down. I never meant for you to pose for so long. But you're such a good model. I got carried away. Is your neck sore?' He tenderly rubbed his fingers across her shoulders, circling his hands in a way which eased the pain and sent ripples of pleasure through her stiff shoulders and down her spine.

'That feels wonderful,' Faith said, closing her eyes and enjoying the sensation of lightness flowing back into her limbs.

'What is the significance of the waterfall and the maiden?' she asked.

'Celtic mythology. Waterfalls were known as white ladies in

120

reference to the ancient goddess, the Earth Mother whose water succours the earth. The painting will have the elements of earth, water, fire – in the colour of your hair – and air – in the wind ruffling your gown. Few people will realise its true significance but they will be touched by the ancient beauty of woman and nature blended in harmony.'

As he spoke his hands continued to work their magic, moving under her hair to her neck where the muscles had knotted at the top of her spine. With a soft moan of pleasure she tipped her head forward. Dan lifted her hair away from her neck, his fingers kneading. Then the pressure in his fingers changed, becoming tender, circling slowly. In the wake of that all-pervading caress a flame flickered and grew within her.

The touch of his lips on the sensitive hollow of her neck created havoc with her senses. The warmth of his mouth traced a molten path across her shoulder. She knew she should stop him, but her body craved to feel more of his touch and those sweet kisses.

'You are so beautiful,' he said as he ran his long fingers through her hair. He raised its shining weight to bury his face amongst the russet curls. When he lifted his gaze, his blue eyes were darkened with desire and a thrill of anticipation fanned through her. She had tried so hard to stifle the infatuation which each meeting with him had nurtured. But watching him at work, the magnetism of his presence was impossible to ignore. She was enthralled by the expertise of so talented an artist. His handsome looks taut with concentration were capable of constricting her breathing. It was lunacy. It was irrational. It could only bring her heartache. But she had fallen head over heels in love with the artist.

Dan had not meant to kiss her. He had been entranced by her beauty as he painted her. She was Aphrodite. Venus. A goddess of love – a temptress and courtesan awaiting her lover. His need for her became a torment. Cupping her chin in his hands he turned her face towards him and savoured the taste of her mouth. When her lips warmed and parted beneath his, his kiss deepened, transporting him beyond caution, driving him to claim her freshness and innocence. To take a love unsullied by degradation. A love which could cleanse and heal ...

There was a moment of guilt too fleeting to take substance. Then he knelt beside her and took her into his arms. She smelt of lavender and the summer pastures of his youth. He felt reborn. When his hand moved to the fullness of her breast and discovered the hardened nipple proclaiming her desire, he knew she was conquered. Her arms were around him, her body pliant and yielding.

Faith was borne along by sensations too powerful to resist. He had painted her as a goddess, but she was mortal, with human failings and desires.

Her arms wound around his neck, her fingers delving into the silkiness of his hair and feeling the breadth of his shoulders. Thrills of delight throbbed through her veins, quickening her blood. She clung to him, tremors pulsing through her body. She wanted to drown in the essence of him, yield to the demands of her body. An illicit, scorching pleasure made her want to go beyond the barriers she had erected against other men. She wanted to feel his hands upon her naked flesh, his tongue licking and tasting her, making her forget propriety, inhibitions and moral servitude.

Where his lips touched with lingering tenderness, her skin tingled and glowed, rousing cravings she had not believed possible. There was no shyness as he eased the gown from her shoulders to reveal her breasts. She responded to his sensuality, her body moving sinuously as her remaining clothes were discarded.

His kisses became more ardent, rousing her to an uncontrollable passion. Clothes no longer formed an impediment to their fevered flesh. The sun was low in the sky and the studio was in twilight, the rosy glow from the gas fire reflecting over their bodies. Through heavy lids she glimpsed her alabaster limbs entwined with the pale amber of his darker skin. The fine hairs on his chest and legs were abrasive against her breasts and thighs and her body burned with a craving to be irrevocably his. Drugged by desire,

122

modesty and restraint were forgotten. His lips and tongue travelled across her breasts, waist and stomach until she was writhing with pleasure. Her willing body was initiated into an ecstasy unparalleled. Her own frenzy lifted her hips as he pressed inside her. There was a stab of pain. Inadvertently, she tensed. Her surprised cry was caught in Dan's mouth as he kissed her fears aside.

'Relax, my darling,' he whispered against her ear as his movements became slow and restrained until the pain passed.

Instinctively, she moved with him, encapsulated in a world of sensuality until it culminated in an explosion of passion which left her gasping, satiated and at peace.

Lethargic with contentment she opened her eyes. Dan was leaning on his elbows looking down at her. The adoration in his eyes as he kissed the slowing pulse at her throat was more potent than any words of love. She lifted her hand to his jaw.

'I'm glad you were the first. I didn't realise how wonderful it could be.'

He closed his eyes as though against an inner pain, and uncertainty smote her. 'Do you regret what happened?' She sat up, scooping the white gown from the floor to cover her nakedness.

'How could I regret the pleasure you have given me? It is I who should be ashamed for playing on your innocence.' He took her hand and kissed its palm. 'I adore you. You have brought a joy back into my life which I had thought lost for ever.' His voice was hoarse as he whispered, 'I don't want to lose you, Faith.'

When Faith eventually returned home she was floating on air. So this was what it was like to love and be loved in return. As she prepared for bed she stared into the bathroom mirror. Her face was still flushed and her lips were swollen from Dan's kisses, the memory of his lovemaking causing her heart to beat erratically and her breathing become shallow. Her body ached to again be clasped in Dan's arms. She clenched her fists and held them tight against her chest. Dan had spoken no words of love to her. Was he using her? No, she discounted that. The tenderness in his eyes and the reverent way he made love to her proved that he felt more than affection. Besides, she loved him too much to stop seeing him. Nothing could dim her love for him . . . except betrayal.

Chapter Ten

Dan had been summoned to the Savoy by an imperious telegram sent by Imelda. He would have ignored it had it not mentioned that their solicitor was attending. He had already advanced her enough on the agreed quarterly allowance to join friends on their yacht in the Mediterranean. If Imelda was demanding more money then she was going to be disappointed. His talks with the accountants had revealed the squire's finances to be in a shambles. He hated the thought of Imelda in London where she could happen across him when he was with Faith. Imelda might despise him but she could not bear to see him with another woman. Like a bitch in the manger, she would create an unholy scene at discovering herself to be the wronged wife.

Joseph Cowper, the family solicitor, was already in attendance and from his weary expression Imelda had been raving at him.

'I'm sorry to have kept you waiting, Mr Cowper,' Dan said. 'I thought we had dealt with everything after the funeral.'

'This is all most unfortunate. We have been in consultation with Cuthbert Passmore's accountants for weeks. It has come to light that the squire was dealing with two firms of accountants which has caused delay and confusion. Cuthbert Passmore's will was dated several years ago. There are simply no funds to meet the bequests in the will. Further, the estate and house are heavily mortgaged. This was done without our advice through a bank.'

Dan kept his expression impassive but he could feel the shackles of his marriage grow more constricting. Imelda issued a stream of invectives, shocking Mr Cowper.

125

'That's enough, Imelda,' Dan silenced her. 'Let Mr Cowper tell us the worst. I assume there is worse to come.'

The solicitor nodded. 'The payments have not been paid for six months and the bank is foreclosing on the mortgage. Unless you pay them five thousand pounds by the end of the month, the house and land will be sold to recover their debt.'

'I do not possess that much money, Mr Cowper,' Dan said heavily. His mind was racing. 'How the devil had Passmore got so heavily into debt?'

'If you leave your estate to the management of others . . .' Mr Cowper spread his hands. 'For years I have warned him that both he and his daughter lived beyond their means. The estate manager has been stealing from the estate and since the squire's death has disappeared. The home farm had been allowed to deteriorate and the stock cut back until it ran at a loss instead of a profit.'

'So my father left me penniless!' Imelda fumed. 'How am I supposed to continue to live as I do?'

'You cannot,' Mr Cowper informed her. 'You will be reliant on your husband to support you. Everything must be sold to meet your father's debts and the death duties.'

Imelda rounded on Dan. 'I cannot live on a smaller allowance.'

Dan mastered his anger at her selfish attitude and this further burden upon him. 'I'll honour my obligations to you, but on my terms. I can afford to buy you a modest house on the outskirts of London with one servant and an income of twenty pounds a month until your father's debts are cleared. After that I hope to increase your allowance.'

She laughed in his face. 'I can't possibly live on that.'

'You have no choice. Mr Cowper will draw up a settlement. Your extravagant lifestyle must end. You had better start by moving out of the Savoy to a cheaper hotel tonight.'

'Move out of the Savoy! You must be mad. I'll do no such thing. As my husband you must support me in the manner to which I'm accustomed. You can stop playing around with your stupid paintbrushes and get a proper job. I've friends in the city who can ensure you have a well-paid post in the Civil Service.'

Dan struggled to control his temper. 'You married an artist. I never promised you wealth or position. I'm already giving you more than I can afford. I've an exhibition in America in the autumn. If that goes well I shall be able to increase your allowance.' He turned to Mr Cowper. 'I'll call on you tomorrow to sign any necessary papers. I want you to draw up a Deed of Separation between my wife and myself which stipulates that over and above the stated sum I am not responsible for her debts.'

'I won't sign anything.' Imelda eyed him maliciously.

'Then I may forget that I am a gentleman and start divorce proceedings.' Dan regarded her coldly. 'If you want to continue your life as one of the idle rich, then find yourself another husband with the money to support you.'

'We are Catholics. The church does not recognise divorce!'

'Correction, *you* are a Catholic. I lapsed years ago. Do you think your sins can be wiped away by attending confession? I'll honour my obligations to you, providing you sign and abide by the agreement. Unlike you, Imelda, I don't fear hellfire. For Hell is here on earth and it is of our own making.'

Imelda watched him leave. Her eyes were blazing with fury. How dare he dictate terms to her? But deep down she was frightened. She could no longer control Dan. She needed him more than ever. She had been slow to recover from her last bout of illness.

Fear churned in her stomach at the unpleasant memories her illness evoked. She'd been in Paris for her thirty-ninth birthday, though she had celebrated it as her thirtieth. It followed a wild summer of debauchery which had made the lines around her eyes and mouth more difficult to hide under make-up. How long would it be before her looks no longer attracted young lovers? To chase away her fears of encroaching age she had roamed the Montmartre district and picked up a young gypsy when he had tried to steal her handbag. He was handsome and she'd never had a gypsy lover before. They had made love throughout the night until she had woken in the morning discovering both him, her jewels and purse gone. But he had left her with something – the most sinister reminder of her decadence. Syphilis.

The Harley Street doctor left her with no illusions. She must refrain from sex as she would contaminate others. The chances of a cure were remote and the disease would eventually kill her. She'd cursed him and stormed out. She'd been cured of the clap before and would be again. The rigours of the Swiss clinic had been punishing. She was drained of vitality. The arsenic they treated her with had left her unbalanced. For a fee the doctor had given her several months' supply of an opiate which induced euphoria, and to which she had become addicted. He had also assured her that another course of drugs would control the infection.

For twenty-five years sex had governed her life. In her frustration at being unable to hit back at the lover who had infected her, her rage was focused upon Dan. Her husband should never have denied her. It was his duty to satisfy her. In the first days of their marriage he had been an exciting lover. She chose to forget about the Arab prince's child, the lies and constant infidelities on her part. Like most self-centred people she remembered only a fictitious account of her life. Now her twisted mind blamed Dan's neglect for driving her into the arms of other men. Men who had never loved her. The only man who had loved her for herself was Dan. In a moment of self-pity she regretted the loss of his love. He had been a romantic fool placing her on a pedestal which had shattered when she had not lived up to his impossible ideals.

She smothered her maudlin thoughts. The stay in the clinic had frightened her, reminding her of her own mortality. Nursed by nuns, they had lectured her on the sins of the flesh and under the influence of the potent drugs she had believed herself the innocent corrupted by men. She repented her sins and poured out her confession and was promised salvation. Her religion had become a great comfort to her.

Imelda had returned to England for her father's funeral prepared to be reconciled with Dan. He was still an attractive man. The nuns had told her that she must be a good wife. Now just as she was prepared to forgive him for abandoning her bed, he was talking of divorce. She had believed she could rekindle Dan's love. He'd had no serious affairs or she would have heard of it through her numerous acquaintances. She had fantasised about their reunion. His rejection had been unforgivable. And now she was determined to make him suffer.

It was why she had agreed to Dan's conditions. She couldn't afford to be alone now. But Dan would pay dearly for his neglect and his threat to divorce her. If she couldn't have him – she could have vengeance.

Dan had walked the London streets for two hours after leaving Imelda and found himself across the road from the gallery where Faith worked. There was half an hour before closing time. It was already dark outside and he leaned against the wall of a bank to wait. The shop interior was lit up and he could see Faith moving inside. Just watching her made his throat tighten. She was so natural and unaffected. Guilt smote him that he was wrong to have taken her as his mistress without telling her that he was married. Faith would never have given herself to him unless she loved him.

Through the barren years of his marriage he'd had affairs only with married women and ended the relationship if he thought the woman was becoming too emotionally involved. He had cared for these women but none had touched his heart. With Faith he had broken all his self-imposed rules.

Because of Faith he was painting every day. When she was not there to model for him he had enough sketches to work from. Sometimes as he worked on a canvas he would find he had stopped and was staring into her face and that his spirit was uplifted.

Abruptly he swung away from the wall and walked briskly away from the gallery. He was angry at himself for the effect she had on him. He was even acting like a love-lorn youth gazing at her from afar. She fascinated him and that was dangerous. It was time he stopped seeing her for it would be all to easy to fall in love with her – and that wasn't in his plans at all.

Yet a half hour later Dan returned to the gallery and took Faith out to dine. It was Saturday night and they had gone on to a nightclub and danced until the small hours.

'Time to get you home,' he said finally, not wanting to leave her, his good intentions overridden by his need for her.

She smiled dreamily at him, her body swaying against his in time to the music. 'It's been a wonderful evening. It's too soon for it to end.'

'Then come back to the studio with me.' His lips were persuasive as they nuzzled her ear. 'Stay the night.'

He saw the pulse throbbing at the base of her throat. He searched her face to discover her feelings, seeing the trembling in her parted lips. He felt her answer in the quivering heat of her body, so lightly moving against his, and in the way her eyes darkened with echoing passion.

Faith was cocooned in the haven of his arms. Her senses were filled with the scent of his skin and cologne, her body glowing with the sensuality the movements of the dance aroused. Her body clamoured for him to make love to her, and to stay the whole night and to awake in his arms would be wonderful.

Yet a part of her held back. She fought the emotions which were surging through her like tidal waves. They had made love on several occasions after she posed for him, but it had stemmed from the magic of the moment: spontaneous, a chance touch sparking an undeniable flame. But to agree like this was somehow different.

'I don't know, Dan. It would be wonderful but . . .'

'You're letting your head rule your heart,' he coerced, drawing her fingers to his lips as they danced. 'I adore you. I want you . . .'

'And your heart, Dan? Does it rule you? Or am I just another woman to you?' She had to know. Her conscience troubled her that she had given herself to him without any word of commitment from him.

He laughed softly, teasing her, 'Are you worried that I won't respect you in the morning?'

The words scissored through her heart. She blinked rapidly to dispel the foolish tears which stung her eyes. She swallowed against her pain and pulled back from him. 'Take me home, Dan. I don't intend to be your light of love. And I don't need your mockery.'

His arms tightened around her and his face was fierce. 'I wasn't mocking you. My levity was misplaced. You are forcing me to analyse my feelings. Of course I respect you. More than any woman I know. And, yes, my heart rules me. It is yours. Does that satisfy you?'

There was a harshness to his voice which took away some of the joy of his words. It was hardly the passionate plea of love she would have liked, but it was sincere. The tenderness in his gaze told her that and she was satisfied.

As she melted against him, Dan closed his eyes. It was no good fighting it any longer. He was falling in love with Faith. But where could it end? Not happily for her . . .

That knowledge harrowed him. He didn't want to lose her, but how could he protect her from the pain she would feel once she learned that he was married?

Faith stirred from sleep with a contented sigh. Earlier she had been kissed awake by Dan and he had made love to her. She still glowed from the aftermath of their lovemaking. Her arm was flung back over her head and she had never felt so at peace or so happy. Still with her eyes closed she reached out with her other hand to touch Dan. She encountered the chill indent where his body had lain.

As her eyes flew open, she heard his sharp command. 'Stay like that. Don't move.'

Dan was propped on the end of the bed wearing a bath robe and across his lap was a sketchpad. The room was warm from the lighted gas fire but Faith felt the coolness of air against her naked flesh. She looked down to discover that the sheet had ridden low across her stomach in her sleep. It covered her as scantily as a loin cloth, revealing her breasts and legs.

'Dan, no!' She sat up, embarrassed. 'Tear that drawing up. I don't want pictures of me naked.'

'My darling, you look sensational.'

He turned the sketchbook around and Faith was startled at the image on the page. He had copied her pose. One hand was thrown back to lie on her hair which was fanned across her pillow, but the other hand rested palm upwards on the sheet as though beckoning a lover. Her expression was serene: that of a woman in love and fulfilled.

'Don't make me destroy it,' Dan said, taking the sketch from her and gathering her into his arms. 'That's how I want to always remember you. You're so lovely, so innocent and infinitely desirable.'

'But others may see it,' she protested. 'You have me. You don't need a sketch of me posing like that. I look wanton. Oh, Dan. You can see I've just been made love to.' She put her hands to her blushing cheeks.

He gently pushed them away and began kissing each finger in turn. 'You have a beautiful body. Don't be ashamed of it. I promise no one will see the sketch except me. It will be my greatest treasure.'

'So I am second best to a drawing of myself?' Her voice was sultry with provocation, her eyes slanting as she stared up at him. His robe had fallen away and she slid her hand across the taut muscles of his chest. The hard beat of his heart was vibrant beneath her hand. His body was lean, graceful and extremely masculine. The sight of it made her breath catch in her throat. 'Is the sketch then the fantasy woman you would have me become?'

With a groan he whisked the sheet from between them and caught her against him.

'You will never be second best. And you are no fantasy. You are the only reality I want.' The hoarse protest was torn from him. He eased her back on to the mattress and stared down at her. Her flame-red hair held all the glory of the setting sun. Her half-closed eyes were glazed with desire. When her lips parted with honeyed invitation, his mouth ravaged hers and his fingers

132

tangled in her hair as he kissed her fiercely and possessively. Passion and torment were a maelstrom driving him.

After a detailed phone call to Mrs Hedges the housekeeper in Sussex, Imelda had stormed out of the Savoy and driven to Chichester. Outside London she kept her foot on the accelerator, careless of the speed limit, and twice forced a car off the road. On her arrival, she noted that the servants had already begun to pack anything of value in cases. A van would arrive at midnight. She intended to be away from here long before dawn.

The van would deliver its contents to Harold Thorpe in Southampton. Imelda had met Harold some years ago at a party in London. He reckoned himself a ladies' man and an expert on antiques. She hadn't rated him much of a lover. He didn't have enough imagination to please her jaded appetite. But he'd had his uses. He had put several pieces of interesting jewellery her way at ridiculously low prices. She didn't doubt for a moment that they were stolen. He would get a better price for any valuables than the creditors would give her against her father's debts and the money would be all hers. Dan wouldn't get a penny of it.

She laughed maliciously. If the sale of the house and contents did not cover the debts, then Dan would just have to find the money. His name was becoming known as an artist. She'd seen the price people were prepared to pay for his work. He could afford it. And she wasn't finished with him yet.

Ruby wore her sexiest dress when she arrived at the Gilded Lily on Saturday night. It was ruby satin to complement her name. The neckline was cut in a sharp V to her waist showing her deep cleavage and moulded tantalisingly to the full outline of her breasts. The skirt was long with a slit up one side which revealed one shapely leg and thigh when she walked.

She was acting as hostess to a party for Ernie later. Squinty Watkins, a new employee, was standing by the stairs leading to Ernie's office. He had the same caveman bulky figure of most of the men now involved with Ernie.

'Get yourself a drink, darling.' Squinty barred her way. 'Ernie is busy. He says to keep the customers 'appy and make sure they buy plenty of booze.'

'Don't darling me. It's Miss Starr to you, Watkins.' It was on the tip of Ruby's tongue to tell Squinty what Ernie could do with his orders. She didn't fancy playing second fiddle to Miriam who would get all the limelight when she came on the stage. She had seen herself as hanging on Ernie's arm, staking her claim of possession over him. Then she realised the greater potential of the situation. She'd seen the hungry glances in the men's eyes as they watched her enter the club. What man in his right mind would be watching Miriam if Ruby Starr was holding court at the bar?

First though she had spotted Mike Rivers at a table in a shadowed corner. Mike never took much notice of her although she had seen him in the club on a couple of occasions she'd been singing. He'd been watching her then all right. Annoyed with Ernie for ordering her about, she went over to Mike.

'Mind if I join you? I'm waiting for Ernie.'

His gaze swept over her figure and he lifted a mocking brow. 'Lucky Ernie.'

She wasn't used to rebuffs. Mike was such a terrific musician, she admired him. Ruby decided to ignore his censure. She saw it as a challenge. Unaccountably, she was hurt by his coolness. She'd seen the way women sighed over his playing and gave him the come-on. He could have his pick of any one of them, yet he didn't seem interested. It fired her determination to make him desire her. Then she'd drop him like a hot potato just to put him in his place.

'You don't like me, do you, Mike?'

He lit a cigarette without offering her one, or ordering her a drink. Leaning forward in his chair he studied her for a long moment through the smoke of his cigarette. 'What gives you that idea? You're a talented kid, who's using what she's got to achieve what she wants. Each to their own.'

'You disapprove?' Ruby queried.

'No. But it's a rocky path and when you fall, you fall hard. I've seen it happen too often.'

Mike had been around the jazz scene more than a dozen years. He had seen many girls like Ruby come and go. Girls who dreamed of glory and ended up on the scrapheap, drinking too much, ending up on narcotics. They thought they were smart, but before they realised it they were in so deep, few escaped. It would be a shame to see this young beauty end up whoring to pay for her dope. And Ernie was flaunting her looks and body to give men a cheap thrill. The fool couldn't see that she was worth more than that. If handled right she could be big time. But for all Ernie's talk he was too eager for the easy quid to handle her with the finesse this woman needed. But why should he worry? Ruby was gathering a following around her and the club was full the nights she sang.

'Did it happen to someone you cared for?' Ruby said softly.

Mike hadn't reckoned she'd be so astute or sensitive. She wasn't the dumb blonde he'd taken her for. His opinion of her was revised. She was on the make, but he sensed that beneath her ambition there was still a vulnerability. The pity was Ernie would twist it into something vile. As Sylvie's manager had done to her.

He was unprepared for the shaft of pain which jabbed into his heart. After ten years the pain of losing his wife had not lessened in intensity. Sylvie had been his first love, his only love. She had a voice which was pure magic. Better than any female singer he had heard since. When he met her, he was twenty-two and she was two years older. Sylvie had been playing the London clubs since the end of the war. She'd been a nurse close to the front lines and the horrors she had seen had never left her. Jazz was her escape.

Having spent three years in the trenches, Mike knew that those memories were best locked away for ever. But Sylvie's greatest horror had been too personal to banish. She had been the nurse to attend Jacko, her twin brother. She hadn't recognised him at first when they brought him in. It was a long night and Jacko was among the wounded who had to wait several hours before a surgeon was free to deal with them. The surgeons only dealt first with those they thought had a chance of survival. The extent of Jacko's injuries from stepping on a land mine were horrific. Half his face was missing and both legs from the knees down. His tortured cries for water had drawn her to him. Belatedly recognising him, she had stayed with him through the night, holding him as he screamed in agony. There was no morphine, supplies had not reached them. Witnessing Jacko's agony and being unable to help him had haunted Sylvie to the end of her life.

When Mike met her she was already hooked on heroin. By then it was too late to help her. He'd begged her to stop and she'd promised him she would. To please him she'd agreed to a cure. Her body wracked with pain from withdrawing from the powerful drug, she was beset with the horrors she had seen in the war. Unable to endure it, she had escaped the surveillance of the staff in the hospital.

Mike closed his eyes to conquer the pain, his voice harsh. 'My wife was a singer.' The words were dragged from him. He never spoke of Sylvie and yet he found it easy to confide in Ruby. Perhaps because he wanted to warn her, before it was too late for her. 'Sylvie was the greatest singer I've ever heard. We were only married a few months. She was a heroin addict when I met her. Knowing it would destroy her, I made her come off it. She was almost through the cure when she couldn't take any more. She threw herself off the hospital roof.'

'Oh, Mike, I'm so very sorry. The poor woman. You must have been devastated.' Ruby reached for his hand as she spoke, all dissemblance gone from her manner. He saw behind the façade of the sex goddess she wanted to create for herself to the real woman beneath. Her voice made gruff with emotion, Ruby whispered, 'That was a terrible tragedy, especially as she was so close to being cured. There's sadness in your playing sometimes, that's why I asked. I never meant to pry.'

He shuttered his mind against the kaleidoscopic images of his wife. After Sylvie died he vowed never to get involved with a jazz singer again. He shrugged, his laconic drawl concealing his

136

emotions. 'It was a long time ago, kid. This is a cruel business and there can be a dark side to it. Don't get lured into the drug scene. There's always some bastard ready to persuade you they can give you a good time. All they do is destroy you. You've got talent and you're star-struck. Singing ain't everything. Get yourself to a drama school. In three years you could be in films.'

'Now that would be something, but Ernie says I can make it big as a singer.' Ruby wasn't prepared to wait three years for fame and fortune.

Mike stubbed his cigarette out and looked hard at her, 'Forget Ernie. You can do a whole lot better than him.'

Judging that as criticism rather than a warning, she responded with heat, 'So why do you stick round him? You're a great musician.'

'I see my half-brother has been sparing with the truth about our relationship. I'm his partner in the club. I put up three quarters of the cash.'

'Ernie acts as though he's in sole charge.'

'Usually I let him get on with it. I thought it would keep him out of trouble.'

Faith shook her head. 'You and Ernie are like chalk and cheese. What made you go into partnership with him?'

'It's a long story.' Mike stared into his drink and just as she thought he had clammed up, he added, 'My mam married Stan Durham after my father was killed in a traffic accident when I was two. Stan was no good. He spent most of their married life in prison. He was always on the thieve. Mam struggled to bring us up alone. She died when I was sixteen and Ernie twelve. I managed to keep us together until the war. Then Stan came out of prison and Ernie lived with him when I enlisted. Stan's inside again doing a twenty-year stretch for a bank robbery where the nightwatchman was killed.'

No wonder Mike was so different from Ernie. They didn't look like brothers. As she studied Mike with greater curiosity she saw that they had the same eyes and sensual mouth. Out of the two Mike was the better looking. He was several inches taller than

Ernie, slimmer and more wiry. His years as a soldier had given him a commanding presence, whereas Ernie was just a cocky bastard who thought he was tough.

Mike's expression hardened. 'Ernie likes to think he's the boss. And I'm not always here. I work other clubs. That way I'll get my own place sooner. Run on different lines to this.' He stood up. 'And talking of my brother I think I'll go tell him you're here.'

She realised that Mike didn't know how deeply Ernie was involved with Big Hugh. It was obvious Mike wouldn't tolerate any link between the club and villains.

'Squinty said he's busy,' she muttered. 'I heard voices from the office.'

He frowned and she sensed his suppressed anger. 'Is Kavanagh up there?'

'Could be!'

'Is Ernie seeing a lot of him?' Mike fired at her.

Ruby was torn by split loyalties. Ernie might be her boyfriend, but she liked Mike. He was a decent bloke. Evasively she shrugged. 'Ernie don't tell me nothing. He plays poker with Big Hugh a few times a week.'

He lit another cigarette, this time offering her one, and stated, 'I'll go and join them. It's time Kavanagh learned Ernie ain't the boss round here.'

Mike was troubled as he pushed passed Squinty to enter the office. Ernie was bringing some unsavoury men into the club lately. He didn't like the Gilded Lily being used by the likes of Kavanagh. Ernie had sworn there was nothing in it. Mike had promised their mam that he'd always be there for Ernie. But Ernie was too like Stan Durham. His brother was going to end up doing time again if he wasn't careful.

The conversation in the office halted abruptly as Mike entered. It wasn't Kavanagh with Ernie, but a man Mike didn't know. Ernie was sitting with his feet up on the desk and a thickset man with a scar across his brow was seated opposite him.

'Mike. I thought you weren't coming in until later,' Ernie said with a nervous smile.

'Aren't you going to introduce me to your friend?' Mike demanded.

'Bill Cooper. He were just leaving.'

Cooper stood up and Mike saw him thrust something into his pocket and was instantly suspicious. His hand snaked out and grabbed the man's wrist and pulled it out of his pocket. There was a wodge of tickets in his hand.

'What are these?' Mike growled. 'Some dodgy scheme you're up to, Ernie?'

'Nah, you got it wrong, mate,' Cooper blustered and for all his bulk Mike sensed the man was frightened. He didn't trust him. 'They're just some tickets for a fight next week. Thought me old mate here would jump at the chance to make some easy dough.'

'Out of town is it, this fight?' Mike grabbed Cooper by the lapels and began to push him towards the door. 'Bare knuckle, is it?'

'So what?' Cooper whined.

'It's illegal. That's what,' Mike gave him a hard shove which thudded him against the door. 'Now clear off out of here. And I don't want to see you in here again.'

The flick-knife was out of Cooper's pocket and swiped across Mike's throat in an instant, but not fast enough. With a soldier's reflexes Mike anticipated the cowardly move. He grabbed Cooper's wrist and twisted it. The knife fell to the floor seconds before the bones of the wrist snapped.

'Now get out. Or do you want more of the same?' Mike ordered.

Cooper scampered and Mike rounded on his brother. 'What the hell do you think you're up to?'

Ernie was pale. He had dragged his feet off the desk and now stood up. 'Making a bit of dough, that's all. The sooner I can get you off me back and in a club of your own the better. I'm sick of you interfering. I could be making some real dough if it weren't for you holding us back.'

'I warned you I wouldn't stand for nothing illegal. I don't want to see Kavanagh and his bullies here either. While I'm still your

139

partner in the Gilded Lily, you stay on the right side of the law. You could make a good living out of this place. If you don't like it you can get out. You're too greedy. And I'm done with nursemaiding you because Mam was afraid you'd end up like your old man.'

Mike glared at his brother. What he saw made his guts curl with disgust. They had nothing in common. Ever since he could remember Ernie had been nicking stuff from shops. He even bullied younger kids to hand over a penny or their sweets until he'd caught him at it. Outraged, he'd given him a beating.

'Pick on kids your own size if you want to throw your weight around,' he had raged.

Ernie had gone home whining to Stan that Mike had picked on him for no reason. Stan had laid into Mike and when his mother had tried to stop him, he'd laid her out cold on the kitchen floor. Ernie had smirked in the corner. Later Mike heard his brother bragging to Stan that he'd got sixpence out of the little kids by his bullying.

'That's my son,' Stan praised. 'A chip off the old block. Teach the little sods who's boss and make the blighters pay.'

Mike had been sickened. He hated Stan for the way he'd hit his mother. The only reason he stayed at home was to make sure he didn't do it again. The next time Stan took a swipe at her, it was Mike's fist which broke Stan's nose and blackened his eye. The old lag never touched his mother again whilst he was there to protect her.

Ernie thrust his hands into his pockets as he regarded Mike across the office. His lip curled back as he jeered, 'Do you think I want to spend me life in a poxy hole like this? I'm going places. You can keep this club. I'll have a string of them. There ain't no money in jazz alone. You're too chicken to take a few chances.'

'I've got more bloody sense,' Mike flared. 'Where's the pleasure or profit spending half your life banged up in prison?' He jabbed a finger into Ernie's chest, his eyes dark with warning. 'While we're still partners, you'd better keep your nose clean. You ain't dragging me down with you. If I catch another crook like

140

Cooper in the place then our deal's off, and you won't set foot in this place again. I'll buy out your share when I can. Then for all I care you can go hang.'

Ernie's eyes narrowed. He resented the way Mike took charge, but his brother didn't make idle threats. He wasn't in a position yet to deal with him. Mike was too good at taking care of himself. For the moment he needed the club as a front for other activities Mike knew nothing about. He might be Earnest Ernie Durham to his mates, but it was Good Old Reliable Mike that the police knew was above reproach. His brother gave the place respectability. The law knew he was against drugs and shady dealings because of his wife's death.

For months Ernie had been investing his takings from the robberies in dealings with Kavanagh. They had several lucrative rackets simmering. Big Hugh knew every shady deal going. He would make Ernie rich beyond his wildest dreams. He could already buy Mike out but as yet it didn't suit his purposes. Mike's respectability was good cover for him. Big Hugh reckoned they needed more coppers on their payroll to ensure they were safe from the law. In six months Ernie wouldn't need Mike. He was looking forward to watching Kavanagh's thugs beat him to a pulp.

Chapter Eleven

Ruby was angry at the way Ernie was treating her. He took her for granted. She wasn't one of his lapdogs he could order about. It was time he realised that she was a force to be reckoned with.

She sat at one corner of the bar on a high stool. Taking out a long cigarette holder, she glanced at a sandy-haired man in his twenties at the bar. He hurried over, offering her a cigarette from his gold case. She took it and as he held the flame from his lighter towards her, she cupped his hand in hers. The cigarette lit, she smiled at him.

'I'm thrilled to meet you, Miss Starr. I never miss your act. You're terrific. Could I buy you a drink?'

'Providing it's champers.'

'Of course.' He gestured to his companions. Six of them were seated at a table close to the stage. 'Would you like to join us, Miss Starr?'

'Bring your friends back here. We don't want Miriam's singing to stop us getting to know each other. Unless your friends prefer to ogle her.'

He was back in seconds with his friends who formed the core of a swarm of men around her. The champagne was flowing freely. When Miriam came on stage, Ruby kept the men distracted, her whispered comments making them laugh aloud. Over their heads she saw Miriam glaring at her and she enjoyed her triumph.

Later at the party in Ernie's flat, Ernie was furious. Miriam had been bitching about her. Big Hugh and his brothers were dancing with women who looked the worse for drink. She hid her anger at his criticism and retorted, 'Miriam's scared her days are numbered.' She was dancing with Ernie and rubbed her body against him in a way she knew would drive him crazy.

'I know what you're up to.' He regarded her fixedly. 'You ain't ready to do the weekend slots. I've fixed it so you have some singing lessons. You'll do the weekend when I think you're ready.' He pressed another glass of champagne into her hand.

She pulled a face. 'What do I need lessons for, I'm doing all right?'

His fingers twisted in the short hair at her nape and he tugged it cruelly. Jets of pain shot through her scalp and it took all her control not to cry out. 'I'm your manager and you'll do what I say.'

'All right, lay off the rough stuff. Ain't it more fun when we're nice to each other? Real nice.' Her hand slid down between them to rub against his crotch. She felt him swell beneath her fingers.

He laughed sardonically and pulled her into the bedroom. Another bottle of champagne was in the ice-bucket waiting for them. He made love to her with slow precision, engulfing her in a passion which destroyed coherent thought. When finally he rolled away from her she was exhausted. She was asleep before he could pour another glass of drugged champagne. Ernie dressed and left the room. She'd sleep until dawn and he'd be back long before then, with a solid alibi.

Ruby was dreaming she was back in the orphanage. She gave muffled cries as she tossed her head from side to side on the pillow. She was being punished as she had so often been as a child. First she'd been caned so hard she could not sit down, then locked in the dark cellar for a day without food. She was terrified of the rats which squeaked and nipped her flesh. It still caused nightmares and she always woke sweating and frightened, unable to face being alone.

With a sob Ruby sat up now, her heart was thudding painfully. She rolled over and reached for Ernie, needing to feel the strength and reassurance of his arms around her. The bed was empty. The room was in darkness – the darkness of her nightmare. She pulled the sheet around her and staggered to the door. There was a chink of light beneath it and the gramophone was still playing the Charleston.

She was relieved that the party was still going and the lounge was filled with people, though most of them were sleeping off the champagne. Ernie was not there. None of the men were. It was the women who were sprawled on chairs, some snoring through open mouths. Charlie, one of the club barmen, was keeping the music playing. He looked edgy as Ruby approached him.

'Where's Ernie and the others?'

'In the back room playing poker. Big Hugh said no one was to disturb them.'

Ruby knew he was lying. But still groggy she didn't pursue it. She tottered back to the bedroom and after drinking another glass of champagne fell into a dreamless sleep. She was awoken by Ernie shouting goodbye to his guests.

'Where have you been?' She peered at him blearily as he stripped off his clothes to get into bed.

'I ain't been nowhere.'

'Don't give me that. You've been out, ain't you? What you up to?'

For reply he slapped her face hard, sending her spread-eagled across the mattress. 'There ain't nothing going on. I don't like me women getting lippy. Understand?'

She wiped the blood from her mouth and nodded.

'That's more like it. I've been here all night. So have the others. Remember that!'

He fell on her then, excited by the violence and the robbery they had committed. He roughly grabbed her breasts and plunged into her, seeking his pleasure and ignoring hers.

Later in the day he tossed a velvet box in her lap. It contained a long rope of pearls. She licked her cut lip, her pleasure spoilt by it being a conscience present. 'Thanks.'

He stared at her nastily. The bitch tried his patience at times, but she had got beneath his skin. She just had to learn that he was boss.

Imelda returned to London on Sunday morning. The van with all the valuables she had taken from the house was safely in Southampton. She was exhausted and descended on her friends, the Clairmonts, who had a house in Kensington. She wasn't booking into a cheaper hotel or she'd lose status among her rich friends. She would enjoy their hospitality instead. What use were friends if you couldn't sponge off them? She ignored the cool reception from Moira Clairmont, having forgotten that she had stolen Moira's lover from her at Monte Carlo last Easter.

Once settled in her room, she was too angry at the way Dan had treated her to rest. She paced the room for an hour, growing more agitated by the minute. She was sick of him walking out on her. She was catching the train to Venice tomorrow and then joining friends on their yacht for a month, but she could not resist taunting Dan that she had bested him today. Quarrelling with Dan was a way of getting him to notice her. Anything was better than suffering his indifference. Telling the Clairmonts that she was lunching out, she drove to Dan's studio. As she turned the corner of Dan's square she saw him come out of the flat with a redhead.

She pulled over to the kerb and sat forward in her seat, watching Dan help the woman into his car. His manner was attentive in a way that he had not shown her in a decade. The woman's face was turned up to him and the radiance of her expression showed the depth of her love. Imelda's eyes narrowed as Dan slid into the driver's seat. Before driving off he leant across to kiss the woman long and passionately.

So that was why he was threatening divorce. He had a tart on the side. And from the looks of it he was in love with her.

Hatred gouged her. Dan Brogan had made a serious mistake in getting involved with another woman. He'd never have that tart. Never. They would both learn that Imelda Brogan was dangerous when crossed.

* * *

146

Spring had been a season of great happiness for Faith. On Wednesdays and Sundays she posed for Dan and afterwards he gave her art lessons, encouraging her to develop her own style. Every Saturday evening he took her out to dance, dine or to the theatre. Then she stayed overnight at his flat so that he began painting her early in the morning. Sometimes on a Tuesday or Friday evening he would unexpectedly call at her flat. She would cook a meal and they would talk for hours and then make love, but she never let him stay the night. And apart from a Saturday night she never stayed over at the studio.

The only marring of her pleasure was that Dan did not speak of love or marriage. Yet she knew that he must love her. He showed it in a dozen ways: meeting her unexpectedly of a lunch hour; or sending a posy of flowers to the flat on an evening she did not see him.

Although Ruby frequently spent the night with Ernie, to Faith's relief she did not move in with him. That relationship worried Faith. She didn't trust Ernie. Ruby could do so much better for herself.

In recent weeks Dan had been tense and his mood remote. This Sunday morning his lovemaking held a desperation to it. Afterwards he cradled her in his arms, his voice urgent. 'You know you mean the world to me, Faith. I don't want to lose you.'

'Why should you lose me?' Faith teased, quelling a moment's disquiet that while he was professing his devotion, he never mentioned marriage.

He spun away from the bed, his tension palpable. It gripped her with anguish and before she could stop herself she blurted out, 'I won't leave you. I love you, Dan.'

It was the first time she had spoken those words and she saw his shoulders tighten and he pushed his fingers through his hair. He pulled on a bathrobe and left the bedroom. 'I want to start early today. The light is perfect.'

His voice was clipped, businesslike and she felt chastened. It seemed Dan wanted her, but did not love her after all. He was taking her too much for granted. Painful as it would be, it was

147

time she stopped modelling for him. If he did not love her then their relationship must end.

She wrapped a sheet round herself and followed him into the studio. Her angry outburst was halted at seeing him studying some sketches. They were of her. He wasn't aware of her presence and his expression was tender. Her pain mellowed. His dark hair fell attractively over his brow. He was so handsome her heart ached with her love for him. She reminded herself that Dan was an artist. Weren't they given to temperamental moods? And artists were notorious for living unconventional lifestyles.

He looked up and saw her. It was as if a curtain was drawn across his face, shielding any emotion from her. Again hurt by his switching mood, she said tersely, 'What am I supposed to wear? Do you want the same pose and garment I wore on Wednesday to finish that painting?'

'No.' He paused, his manner unusually hesitant.

'What is it, Dan? You're in a strange mood this morning.'

His gaze slid from hers. 'You know I would never ask you to do anything you didn't want. But I'm haunted by this sketch. I have to paint it, Faith. Will you give me permission?'

She moved to his side and gasped as she saw the sketch he was holding. A militant gleam lightened her eyes to a turbulent turquoise. 'It's the one you drew when I was asleep. No, Dan. I don't want you to paint me naked. In fact I think it's time I stopped modelling for you.'

'Why?'

'Because I thought that you loved me even though you never said it. But you don't. I can't forget my upbringing. This is wrong. I feel cheap and used.'

'Good God, Faith, I do love you!' Dan's voice was husky. 'I adore you.'

He cast the drawing aside and put his hands on her shoulders. His stare searched her face, the expression in his eyes haggard. The warmth of his fingers circling the tense muscles across her back was spreading in expanding ripples of heat through her veins. His hands moving across her skin were a balm, anointing her, soothing away her reservations. She gave a soft moan of pleasure – or was it a cry of submission? The two were intertwined.

He pulled the sheet from her body. Her need for him supplanted reason, overthrowing her reservations. He spoke softly, beguilingly, subverting her will. 'I would have you for ever by my side, my darling. I want the painting to be a tribute to our love.'

Dan did love her. Of course he meant to marry her. 'You have me, why do you need such a painting?'

She already knew the answer. Her own experience as an artist might be limited, yet she had felt the consuming need to bring to life the images in her head.

'I should not have asked.' He forced a smile. 'I thought that you would understand. I wanted to create an image of you which was special.' Releasing her, he went into the kitchen and returned with a carving knife. Then went over to his stack of paintings on the floor and pulled one out. He held the painting and the knife towards her. 'I couldn't stop myself painting it from memory. Destroy what I've done. I should have asked you first.'

Dan turned the painting around and Faith saw her image staring back at her. Her hair was vibrant flames of amber, russet and burnished copper as it waved over the white satin pillow. One hand flung behind her head, the other reaching out beckoning to an unseen lover. It was the eyes which held her. They were incandescent aquamarine, filled with age-old wisdom and sensuality. Despite its erotic nature it was not salacious. It was an accolade to their love. It was also the finest portrait Dan had ever painted.

'It's a masterpiece, Dan. I can't ask you to destroy it.'

'Then it's yours. I couldn't rest until I painted it. I don't want others to see you as only I would see you. It is a tribute to our love and the joy you've given me.'

When Dan presented it to her, she shook her head.

'Keep it here. Hang it in the bedroom so long as no one else sees it. I'd be too embarrassed to hang it anywhere.'

'I shall treasure it always. Yet it is a sin to hide your beauty

149

away. Let me paint a duplicate but with your body covered by a diaphanous material which would merely hint at glorious secrets veiled.'

She agreed. Safe in the security of his love, she could deny him nothing.

He laughed and drew her into his arms. His kiss was as fiercely possessive as it was passionate. He lifted her up and she wound her legs around his waist. Desire flooded her as he carried her to the couch and discarded his bathrobe. Each touch and kiss was lingering, nurturing, transporting her to the bittersweet fulfilment of body and soul.

When he drove her home that evening his tension returned. 'I shall be out of town for a week dealing with business matters.'

Dan had been spending a lot of time with his solicitors and accountants lately. 'Is something wrong, Dan? Have you financial problems?'

His face was taut although he shrugged, answering in an off-hand manner, 'It's nothing for you to worry about.'

On the Friday evening when Dan was still away Faith returned to her flat from work and was delighted to find that Ruby had tidied it and cooked a meal. Ruby had been to the hairdresser's and had a Marcel wave which curled her blonde hair softly around her cheeks. When they finished eating, Ruby refused to allow her to wash the dishes.

'What's all this about? It isn't my birthday. Or are you after some money?'

'Charming, there's gratitude for you. I thought if you had a bit of a rest we could go up West. Me and Ernie had a row and he don't want me at the club tonight.'

'I wanted to do some sketching to show Dan when he gets back.'

Ruby stood in front of the fireplace mirror plucking her eyebrows into a narrow arc. 'You ain't going all soft over Dan, are you?'

'I'm in love with him,' Faith confided.

150

'You don't have to become a recluse. There ain't no use us living in London and staying in like a couple of dried-up spinsters,' Ruby wheedled. 'Let's go dancing. Ernie takes me too much for granted. Life's for having fun. You wouldn't get me moping around because Ernie ain't seeing me one evening. Sometimes I think I'm wasting my time with him. That he's just stringing me along. But that contract I signed means I can't sing nowhere else. He can be a right bastard at times.'

'Is the singing so important?'

'It's everything, Faith. Why else would I put up with that creep? I know I can make it big. It's all I want.' She applied blue eyeshadow to her lids and stood poised with her rouge brush in hand. Her expression was sullen. 'It ain't just the way he bosses me about me singing. He's so possessive. Wants me at his beck and call when he gives a party. That's why we rowed. I don't like who he mixes with.'

Ruby bit her lip, wondering how much she dare tell Faith about Ernie. She decided it was best to keep quiet. Ernie had warned her never to speak of matters which went on after hours at the club. Her arms were covered with bruises from the row which had ended up as a fight. Her mouth thinned mutinously. The bastard was too big for his boots. The police had called at the flat this afternoon. Thank God Faith had been at work. They'd wanted to know where Ernie was Wednesday night.

'He was with me all night, Inspector,' she lied. 'We were at a party at Hugh Kavanagh's house which went on until the early hours. Must have been forty people there. Why did you want to know, Inspector?'

'Just making enquiries.' His florid face was taut with contempt. 'A jeweller's was broken into at Ilford and the old Jew who lived upstairs disturbed them. He's in hospital. It's unlikely he'll regain consciousness.'

'So why do you want to speak with Ernie?' She hoped her voice showed only surprised innocence and not her own dark suspicions. The police wouldn't make enquiries unless they suspected that Ernie was involved.

She pushed the unpleasant thoughts to the back of her mind. If Ernie had been involved in the robbery, he wouldn't have been the one to hurt the old man. Or so she convinced herself.

She wasn't going to let the incident spoil her evening. Ernie was always finding ways to keep her at his side and she saw little enough of Faith and missed the warmth of their friendship.

'Let's do something exciting tonight, Faith. I'm bored. We ain't been dancing for weeks.'

Faith gave in. She would have been happy staying in and sketching. Dan praised her work but she was never satisfied with the images she produced. Inanimate scenes didn't work for her. The only time she felt she came close to her potential was when painting people at work or leisure. On her half day she'd gone down to the Embankment and sat on a bench watching the river traffic. Three young boys were playing football with an old cabbage and were pushing and shoving as they raced for possession of it.

She grinned as she watched them and opened her sketchbook and began to draw. Later she walked on to the Houses of Parliament and Westminster Abbey. First she sketched the buildings, then the people around her. It was the people who fascinated her: the portly roadsweeper with a fag dangling from his toothless mouth, the wiry draymen high above their beautiful shire horses, even the bustling office workers in bowler and pinstripe suits or the vagrant rummaging through dustbins. Wherever she looked London was charged with atmosphere. It had seeped into her bones. There was no place like it.

'So where are we going?' Faith asked as they waited at the bus stop.

'How about the Cocked Hat Club?'

'We can't go there unescorted. Let's go down the Palais.'

'Don't be a spoil sport, Faith. I can do with checking out the competition at the Cocked Hat. Mike says the new singer is terrific. She's black. Like Josephine Baker who is so popular in Paris.'

'Doesn't Josephine Baker parade half-naked at the Folies

Bergère? You're not going to start that, are you?'

'Of course not. This singer is modestly dressed. She's got a great voice.'

Faith wasn't convinced. 'What's this place like? If it's a dive I'm not going in.'

Ruby jumped on the bus and ran up to the top deck bursting with suppressed excitement. 'It isn't a dive. Mike plays there sometimes. It's the type of place a respectable man would bring his wife.'

As they approached the club, two sailors wolf-whistled at them. Faith ignored them. Ruby gave them a sidelong glance. 'Ooh, the blond one is a bit of all right. You can have the carrot-top. Though his freckles are rather cute.'

'You're incorrigible,' Faith laughed, but was determined not to get caught up with any men.

'You ladies alone?' A tall doorman with a military bearing stopped them at the door. 'Sorry, no unaccompanied ladies.'

'We're accompanying each other,' Ruby piped out.

'Very droll, madam,' the doorman observed. 'Off you go, ladies. I don't want no trouble.'

'They're with us.' The blond sailor strolled up and put his arm around Ruby's shoulders.

'That's right,' Ruby added. 'We were late and I thought they'd already gone inside.'

Faith was about to protest when the freckle-faced sailor smiled hesitantly at her. 'I'd be real honoured to escort you inside. This is my first time in London.' His voice was low with a country burr. He was of medium height and build with an attractive honest face. Even so she hesitated.

'My name's Bill Morgan,' he added. 'I'm married with a nipper on the way. Only got a twenty-four hour pass so I had no chance of getting home to Cornwall and back. Me other mates went off with a group of women and Harry and your friend seem to have hit it off. I don't fancy spending me first evening in London on me own.'

His unassuming manner softened Faith's wariness at being

153

picked up by strangers. 'I have work tomorrow. I can't stay late. And don't get ideas about dossing down at our place, because that's not on.'

'Stop finding excuses, Faith,' Ruby said impatiently. 'Let's have some fun.'

'I'll come if I pay my way,' Faith insisted. 'And I'm catching the ten-thirty bus home.'

'The night's just starting then,' Harry muttered.

'C'mon, Faith. Let's not waste any time, if you're gonna do a Cinderella on me.' Ruby took Harry's arm and with a smile at the doorman entered the club.

'Looks like we've been ditched,' Bill commented. 'I'll make sure you get back home safely.'

Faith deferred. Bill was nice enough. 'I insist on paying my own way. You need your money to send to your wife and baby.'

He was about to refuse but the warning light in her eye stopped him.

Once inside Ruby was soon dancing the Charleston with Harry. The club was better lit than the Gilded Lily and tastefully furnished with beige leather chairs and pink tablecloths. The walls were painted with dancing figures in the brightly coloured art deco style, reminding Faith of the hieroglyphics she had seen in a book about Egypt.

Bill led Faith out to join the dancers. After four dances she was breathless and Bill found them a seat at a table. The singer was announced and Ruby stayed on the dance floor, moulded to the sailor for the slower numbers.

The black singer's hair was cropped close to her head and she wore a demure silver beaded knee-length dress. She perched on a stool as she sang in a rich earthy voice. She sang from the soul, using none of Ruby's obvious tricks to gain attention. She used her arms and expression to act the joy or pain in her songs. Ruby, after an assessing look, ignored her, taking more notice of the sailor. That was typical of her, after claiming that the singer was the reason for coming here.

When the singer finished and the band resumed their playing

Faith looked at her watch. It was ten o'clock and nearly time for them to leave. There was an announcement which Faith did not catch and another musician walked on. He looked familiar. When he began to play the saxophone its haunting sound held her enthralled. When the number ended Faith rose to remind Ruby, who was still dancing, that it was time they left. Ruby left Harry's side and went up to the stage and blew the musician a kiss. Belatedly Faith recognised Mike Rivers. Mike lifted his saxophone in salute to Ruby.

'That was terrific, Mike,' Ruby said throatily. 'It gave me goosebumps down my spine.'

'You shouldn't be here,' Mike said. 'Ernie won't like it.'

Rebellion flashed in Ruby's eyes. 'He don't own me.'

Harry was at her side, his expression antagonistic and his body tense, ready for a fight. Ruby sighed. She didn't want to be the cause of trouble. 'This is Mike,' she introduced him. 'He plays at the club where I work. I thought it only polite to say hello.'

Mike had turned away, the opening bars of the next number had started and he closed his eyes as he lifted the saxophone to his lips. Ruby melted into Harry's arms. The music seeped into her bones and she swayed languorously. She saw Faith gesturing to her watch and she held up one finger indicating this was her final dance. She could have stayed and listened to Mike play all night. The seductive rhythm entranced Ruby and her attention kept returning to Mike as he played.

The music affected her and so unaccountably did Mike Rivers. Used to men fawning over her, Mike's uninterest needled her. Even when she appeared in a stunning and revealing gown, he did little more than acknowledge her existence with an inclination of his head. She thought she had seen regret in his eyes, but had paid no attention to it. Who was he to judge her?

Harry held her tight, nuzzling her neck. 'Give over,' she said, turning away. Again her glance strayed back to the stage. Mike had a charisma when he played. A quick scan of the room showed an interest in several women's eyes. It made her study him more closely. He must be ten years older than her but he had an athletic body. He was playing in a white dinner jacket and looked sensational.

'Fancy him, do you?' Harry said harshly.

'Don't be daft. He's a terrific musician, that's all.'

Harry pulled her closer, pressing his cheek against hers. Suddenly the sailor irritated her. She twisted from his arms. 'I've got to go.'

She was halfway towards Faith when her gaze settled on the stocky figure of Ernie Durham. He was staring at her, his eyes glittering with fury. Her stomach knotted with alarm. Harry, who had pursued her, was sandwiched between Squinty and Pete Kavanagh. Fear gripped her on noticing the glint of a gun in Pete's waistband.

'We're leaving,' Ernie demanded. 'Your sailor boy can go lose himself.'

Ruby's anger at his attitude surfaced over her fear. 'You don't own me,' she blustered. 'You're not me husband, are you? I'm just having a bit of fun. I'm with Faith. I was about to leave with her. Not you.'

'You're wrong. I do own you, according to your contract,' Ernie growled, his hand bruising her arm. 'Big girl, ain't she, your mate. Must know how to look after herself if she goes round with a tramp like you.' He jerked her towards the door. 'She can get home on her own.'

Ruby tore her arm from his and slapped his face. 'I ain't a tramp. And I ain't your property. So you can stick your bloody contract. I've had enough.'

The red mark of her fingers was livid on his face. His lips thinned ominously and his eyes were black and pitiless. Fear lanced her. God, what had she done! She'd gone too far this time. When he thrust his face close to hers, she barely managed to smother a yelp.

'One more word out of you and you'll regret it.' His voice was lethal. 'No one makes a fool of me.'

Her protest dried in her throat as terror gnawed through her. Ernie looked fit to kill her. An old bruise along her ribs was throbbing, painfully reminding her of the vicious turn his temper could take. As she was propelled towards the cloakroom, she shot a beseeching look at Faith who had started to follow her. Ernie's vice-like fingers gripped her wrist as they waited for her coat.

'What the devil were you up to in there?' he gritted.

'Just having fun. What you getting so riled up about?'

'Stupid tart!' His eyes were slits of rage. 'Ain't you got no sense? The Gilded Lily is your stomping ground. Nowhere else. Any punter who wants to dance with you only does so in my club where they can pay for the privilege.'

Ruby resented his possessiveness. She was a singer not a hired dancing partner. She belonged to no man. Ernie was a bully. He was also goading her too far. He might scare her, but she wasn't some mouse who was prepared to take it without retaliating. 'Who the hell do you think you are telling me where I can dance? It's a free world.'

'That's where you're wrong, sweetheart. You signed your freedom away when you put your signature on that contract.'

Ruby was dimly aware that the music had stopped and that the band was taking a break. Over Ernie's shoulder she saw a white-faced Faith approaching. 'Are you all right, Ruby?'

'Oh, I'm terrific,' she said sarcastically.

Bill and Harry had been accosted by Squinty and Pete and forced to back off.

'What's going on here?' Bill demanded.

'Nothing what concerns you,' Ernie replied. He glared at Faith and when Harry slunk into the gents, Squinty stopped her reaching Ruby. She saw Pete Kavanagh push Bill through the same door and stand in front of it to stop them coming out. A flush of anger coloured her cheeks and she shoved Squinty Watkins in the stomach. Not expecting such a move, he was caught off balance and fell against the wall. Faith rounded on Ernie.

'Your conduct is not that of a gentleman, Mr Durham. Take your hands off Ruby or I shall call the police.'

'This ain't your affair.' Ernie nodded to his companion. The man's ham-sized fist closed over Faith's arm.

Her eyes sparked with anger. 'Remove your hands, or I'll press charges of assault. I'm not intimidated by your bullying.' The fingers tightened punishingly and Faith felt the first dart of fear. There was cruelty in the man's eyes. He enjoyed inflicting pain.

'Miss Starr and her friend haven't done anything wrong,' Mike Rivers spoke from behind them.

Ruby felt a rush of gratitude and relief. She didn't want to admit how frightened she had been. She was appalled at the anger in Ernie's eyes and the way he had set his bodyguard on Faith who had defended her.

'This ain't your concern, Mike,' Ernie warned.

'I don't like the way you're treating Miss Starr. She wasn't doing any harm.'

'It's between Ruby and me,' Ernie returned. He jutted his head forward as though his shirt collar was too tight and puffed out his chest. With Squinty and Pete to act on his say-so, Mike didn't intimidate him.

'Anything which rebounds on the reputation of our club is my business,' Mike corrected.

The musician's eyes narrowed and the two men faced each other in silence for several moments. It was Ernie who looked away first. Ruby wasn't surprised. Mike didn't even need to get angry to make him back down and Ernie backed down from few men. The musician intrigued her. He was quite something to have tackled Ernie and won.

'I'll take you and your friend home.' Ernie's tone was less harsh. 'Do you think I want to come on heavy like this?'

She rubbed her injured wrist. 'You seem to like it.'

He lifted her hand and kissed the bluish thumb mark. 'Did I do that? I never meant to hurt you. But you can drive me wild. I was jealous seeing you making up to that creep.'

When she remained suspicious, he smiled. It was ingratiating but his eyes remained cold, unnerving her. 'Don't be mad at me, Ruby. I was just looking after your interests, if you weren't too dumb to see it.'

'How's that?' She felt bolder knowing that Mike was there to defend her.

'Exclusivity. Look, you want to rise to the top, you've gotta be selective. The punters ain't gonna pay if you spread yourself about. Be mysterious. Like Garbo. Carry on like this and you'll always be small-time. I can make you big. Give it a couple of years and you could even be starring at the London Palladium.'

Ruby's mouth gaped then shut with a snap. She had misjudged Ernie. He wasn't just playing the heavy.

'You really think so, Ernie?'

'Yeah, I've got contacts. We've gotta play our cards right. Start to get you a bit of publicity – but you've gotta be seen in the right places. And in the right company.'

'Do you really think I'm that good?'

'You're a natural. You could be in anything, sweetheart. But you've gotta play by the rules. I'm the pro in this game and you're the amateur.'

Faith kept her silence now that the situation was diffused. Faith was grateful to Mike Rivers for coming to their aid. He seemed a decent man. Unlike Ernie Durham. Earnest Ernie indeed! That man had a dark side which alarmed her. Sometimes it seemed that Ruby could not resist playing with fire. She attracted trouble like a magnet. Yet Faith could never desert her. Their friendship meant too much.

Chapter Twelve

When Dan learned that Imelda had taken anything of value from Passmore Manor he was furious. The house and the furniture that was left would not cover her father's debts. So far he had been unable to trace his wife either in England or on the Continent. She had vanished without signing the documents he had insisted upon. Legally he would be bound to honour any debts she ran up and knowing Imelda they would be substantial. He could feel the threat of bankruptcy looming.

Visions of Faith tormented him. She was his inspiration and his joy. Guilt assailed him that he had deceived her. He should have told her from the outset that he was married. He had never considered himself a coward but the thought of losing Faith devastated him.

And it wasn't as though he felt constrained by his religion. Apart from at his wedding and Squire Passmore's funeral he hadn't been inside a Catholic church in years. He knew he was deeply spiritual but the God he believed in would never deny a man happiness, or shackle him to a marriage which had its roots in hell not heaven.

He was determined to divorce Imelda. Her life was already scandalous; divorce would be the lesser of many sins she had committed in recent years. Unfortunately divorce was a long and messy business. It took years. Whatever happened he didn't want Faith involved; especially he did not want her cited as co-respondent as that would destroy her reputation. At all costs he would spare her that. But to divorce Imelda he first had to find her.

Ernie was considering plans for his future. The club was doing well and Ruby was now a bigger draw than Miriam. He decided to move Ruby to the weekend slots and if Miriam didn't like it then Ruby would sing every night. That suited him. It kept her under his control and where he could keep his eye on her. He had been livid with jealousy seeing her with that sailor. She could flirt and dance all she liked in his club but not elsewhere. She was known as his woman. He'd kill her before he let her make a fool of him.

Discovering Ruby had been an unexpected windfall. She had the face and figure men fantasised over and she knew how to exploit it. She was going to the top. He had already been approached to have her join a touring revue of theatres and halls in the country. Only the idiot had insisted that she cleaned up her act. There was no way he was going to allow that to happen. But she did need respectability to get to the top and stay there. The public were fickle. They'd never take anyone into their hearts if there was any hint of immorality.

He tapped his knuckles against his teeth. Ruby could be a gold mine in the future, if she was handled right . . .

The strains of Ruby's opening number drifted to the office and he sauntered outside to watch her. Her voice was lower and sexier since taking singing lessons. Just watching the way she prowled across the stage made him desire her. She was dynamite.

With satisfaction he scanned the crowded tables. Every one was full and there were men crammed around the bar. There wasn't a man in the club who didn't feel the same as he did. To his surprise the crowd also included Mike who was leaning against the corner of the bar. After the incident at the Cocked Hat Club, his brother had stopped playing here the nights that Ruby sang. Ernie thought it was because Mike disapproved of Ruby. Believing himself unobserved, Mike was watching her now. His eyes might not show his hunger, but Ernie knew him well. Mike fancied Ruby.

Ernie's gloating turned sour in his stomach. Mike was a threat he had not considered before. Ruby raved about his playing. He even suspected that she liked him more than she would admit. That didn't suit his purposes. Mike didn't take casual lovers, but women were always hanging around him eager for his attention. Ernie didn't like the thought that Ruby could be one of them.

A brittle gleam entered Ernie's eyes as he contemplated getting one over on Mike in a way that would most rile his brother.

When Ruby finished her last number, Ernie leapt on to the stage, putting his arm round her waist and kissing her cheek. 'Isn't she sensational, ladies and gentlemen? Take a note of her name. The lovely Ruby Starr. She's going to be a big star and you heard her first at the Gilded Lily.'

The applause was deafening as he hooked his hand beneath Ruby's elbow and escorted her off the stage. He waved aside the men who had begun to crowd around her. 'Miss Starr will be singing again later.'

He gestured to Squinty Watkins to clear a path for him and Ruby to the office steps.

'What's got into you, Ernie?' Ruby complained as she was hustled forward. 'The customers like me to mix with them.'

'Later. I've got something special lined up.'

'Kavanagh ain't having another party, is he?' She eyed him uneasily. 'I'm getting fed up with them. Most of the women he brings are whores. That ain't gonna help me image, is it?'

'This is between us,' Ernie said, kissing her cheek. The moment the office door shut behind them, he pulled her to him and lifting the hem of her gown ran his hands over her buttocks. 'You drive me wild, you know that, don't you, Ruby?'

Usually she was eager for the unconventional way he wanted sex from her. But she'd only sung one session and her dress would be creased for her second performance.

'Watch out for me dress, Ernie. I've got to go on stage again.'

'Take it off.'

'Someone could come in.'

He pulled a jewel case out of his pocket and handed it to her. 'Ain't I always good to you? Don't I always want my girl to have the best?'

Her eyes widened as she opened the jewel case. A pair of dangling diamond earrings gleamed back at her. 'Blimey, Ernie. Are these for real?'

'My woman don't wear nothing fake,' he said slipping the narrow dress straps from her shoulders. 'And that ain't all. We're gonna go far, Ruby. But we gotta do it right and do it together.'

A second box appeared and he snapped it open to reveal a ring with a large solitaire diamond. Both the earrings and ring had come from a jeweller's job they'd done a couple of months ago. 'I'm asking you to marry me. These are just the beginning.'

Ruby was stunned. 'Marry you! I didn't think you were the marrying kind?'

'I weren't, but you're something else. I can't live without you.'

His words pleased her and the diamonds were sensational. Who'd have thought a few months ago when she was slaving in that rotten hotel in Tilbury that she would ever possess such jewellery? But there was a catch. Nothing in life was free; she'd learnt that long ago.

'I thought we had an understanding, Ernie. I ain't got no plans to marry. What do I want to be tied down to one bloke for?' She spoke from bravado more than truth. With the right man she would be happy to marry and settle down. That man certainly wasn't Ernie Durham.

Ernie shrugged. 'We understand each other. I'm a broad-minded guy. And you've got your career to think of. It's time you reached a larger public in the old musical halls, theatres and palais. Your act is raunchy so your private life must be respectable. There ain't nothing more respectable than a married woman.'

Ruby wavered. The thought of marriage to Ernie had not occurred to her. And most of the time he treated her right. He took her to expensive restaurants. They always had the best seats at a show.

'Once we're married more doors will open to us,' Ernie tempted. 'We'll get in on the social scene. Mix with the toffs. We've gotta be seen in the right places. Ascot, film premières and the like.'

She turned the diamond earrings over in her hand. The gems sparkled, iridescent as moonbeams.

Ernie put his arms round her. 'Stick with me and those are just the beginning. I promise in a couple of years you'll be draped in mink and diamonds and be driven round in a Rolls Royce.'

The visions of wealth and extravagance were too much for Ruby to ignore. Ernie really wasn't so bad. Yet this was hardly the passionate proposal a woman dreamed of.

'When did you plan for us to get married?'

'There ain't no point in waiting.' He grinned, peeling her dress from her unresisting body. 'I'll announce it tonight and get a special licence so that we can get hitched the beginning of May. That will give me time to drum up plenty of press coverage. You ain't gonna be a star unless we get your name plastered across the papers.'

An hour later, with Ruby looking deliciously dishevelled, her lips swollen from his lovemaking, Ernie escorted her back to the stage. He scanned the room before speaking, wanting to see Mike's reaction when he made his announcement. Mike was at a table with two men and three women. Ernie looked directly at him as he called for silence. He nodded for the waitresses to bring out the champagne bottles he had previously ordered.

'Ladies and gentlemen, I know you will want to share my good fortune with me tonight. I'm honoured that Miss Ruby Starr has agreed to be my wife. Free champagne all round for you to drink a toast to my future bride.'

He saw Mike crush his half-finished cigarette into the ashtray with suppressed violence. That was his only reaction as the club room erupted into cheers and catcalls.

'You're going to *marry* Ernie Durham?' Faith asked, distraught. She had been getting ready for work when Ruby danced into the bedroom flashing her solitaire and earrings, after staying overnight with Ernie. 'Have you lost your mind? You know he's no good. He's already knocked you around.'

'He never meant to,' Ruby defended. 'He said it would never

happen again.' She twirled the large diamond ring on her finger so that it caught the light. 'And he's so generous. He's going to make me a star, Faith. Don't you want me to be happy?'

'That's what I want more than anything. But I don't trust Ernie. He's too smooth, too charming when it suits him. It's never sincere. And why does he need those cavemen trailing behind him if he's an honest citizen? There's more to him than he lets on and I doubt it's on the right side of the law.'

'So he does a bit of ducking and diving. Where's the harm in that? You've got too many middle-class hang-ups,' Ruby retorted. 'When did the law do us any favours? So what if Ernie bends it to suit his ends? How else is the likes of me and him gonna make it in this world? But he ain't bad. You don't know him like I do.' Ruby turned her head from side to side to admire the diamond earrings in the dressing-table mirror. 'He's gonna get me a matching necklace as a wedding present.'

'Beware of Greeks bearing gifts,' Faith declared ominously. 'Where's a bloke like Ernie going to get that sort of money? He won't be just bending the law, he'll be making it into a cork-screw.'

'Ernie ain't Greek. He's one quarter Italian though, on his Dad's side. And you know what they say about Italian lovers . . .' She winked. 'It's all true. He's insatiable.'

Faith clamped down her exasperation. Sex, money and a good time were all Ruby thought about. At least Ernie was giving her those. But for how long? When would it start to go bad on her, as she was sure that it would? Faith dragged a hairbrush through her long hair as though by assaulting the tangles she could make Ruby see sense. 'So he's a great lover. But do you have to marry him? And why so much of a rush?'

'It's to do with getting me on a revue tour of the country.'

'That would be wonderful.' Faith pushed enthusiasm into her voice, but she was gripping the hairbrush so hard its bristles dug into her palm. She wished she could shake off the feeling that Ruby was making the biggest mistake of her life. No matter what she said about Ernie, Ruby wouldn't listen. He had dangled the carrot of stardom before her and she had swallowed his tales of glory.

Seeing Faith's concern Ruby shrugged. 'Ernie has his faults but he wants what's best for me. He knows the people who can make me famous. Marriage is a small price to pay for that.'

'Then be happy, Ruby.' She concealed her reservations and kissed her friend's cheek. But she could not banish her fears. All she could do was be there when Ruby needed her. She had a foreboding that if Ruby married Ernie, she could land up in serious trouble.

'I can handle Ernie,' Ruby said with a wink. 'And me getting married ain't gonna stop us being friends. I'm sorry I'm leaving you in the lurch with the flat.'

'I can afford it. I get good money from the gallery and most months I get my bonus as well. Lady Charford recommended the gallery to her friends and they all insist I serve them. I have built up a large clientele list and know their tastes.'

'So cheer up,' Ruby laughed. 'And don't worry about me. I'm gonna have a big wedding and you will be my bridesmaid. I'll get you a dress that will knock Dan for six. You'll be the next one up the aisle.'

Faith prayed so. Ruby's news had diverted her mind from her own troubles. Dan had been away longer than he had anticipated and she'd received only one brief note, saying he missed her but hoped to return to London by the weekend. It was no longer just a case of loving Dan to distraction, she also suspected that she was carrying his child.

When Dan met Faith from work in his car the following Saturday, she noted that he looked drawn and he kept rubbing his brow as though it pained him.

'I hope you don't mind staying in tonight,' he said tiredly as he drove through the traffic. 'It's been a hell of a week. Nothing has gone right. Even the blessings have caused problems. They want more paintings for the American exhibition than I realised. I could do with the money, but the work involved is immense.

167

Plus an agent in Paris has got me an exhibition there this summer. That's not an opportunity I can afford to miss either. They'll want at least another dozen paintings.'

'That's wonderful news! It proves your fame is spreading. Isn't that what every artist wants?'

He nodded. 'It's just come at the wrong time. There's some legal matters which need my attention. It's not exactly conducive to freeing the mind for the creative muse.'

'Are you in trouble, Dan? The legal affairs, I mean . . .'

His smile was thin and not reassuring. 'I'll sort them out. The exhibitions are a godsend. It's just the pressure of getting enough paintings finished on time.'

It was obvious he did not want to talk about his problems and that hurt Faith. Dan was a private man. He never confided why he left London or where he was going. He simply said it was business.

'I thought I'd send to Paris the paintings you've modelled for. Fortunately I've dozens of sketches of you so I can work from them while you're at the gallery. You don't mind me using them, do you?'

There was an edge to his voice which increased her fears. 'Of course not, providing you make sure I'm decently clothed,' she warned.

He smiled but he still looked strained. 'Didn't I give my word?' He slowed at a crossroads and his gaze was abstracted as he concentrated on the traffic ahead. 'I'm leaving for Paris on Monday. I shouldn't be gone more than a few days.'

His smile broadened. 'I've missed you. You are my peace, Faith. You keep me sane.'

Faith bit her lip although she was bursting to tell him that she thought she was pregnant. Clearly this was not the time. She hoped that he would be delighted. But Dan looked so troubled she didn't want him to feel that he was having more pressure put on him. And she hadn't yet seen the doctor. It would be better to wait until she was certain.

Their weekend together fled by. They had picked up Faith's

sketches from the flat and after they had dined, Dan sat with his arm around her on the sofa as he studied them.

'These are good. You're beginning to find your own style.'

'You don't think they're too ordinary?' She tried not to get too excited by his praise. She had her own reservations about the street scenes. 'I wanted to convey the energy and atmosphere of the London streets.'

'They certainly do that.' He pulled out three sketches. One was of a dozen people around a stall in Petticoat Lane market haggling over the second-hand clothes. Another showed a tenement street in the East End, the children skipping or crouched over, playing five stones on the cracked pavement, their mothers seated outside their front doors peeling potatoes or white-stoning their step as they chatted to their neighbours. The last one was of a one-legged organ-grinder around whom several ragged children danced, their gaunt faces absorbed and ecstatic. 'You've captured the essence of your characters. What medium are you going to paint them in?'

'I hadn't thought that far. Probably watercolour. I wasn't sure they were good enough.'

His eyes brightened with pleasure. 'You have a natural talent. You're wasted in the gallery. This is what you should be doing. You must seriously consider taking proper lessons and devoting more time to it.'

She laughed self-consciously. 'I'm a working girl, don't forget.' She tried to make light of the matter, but guilt at the secret she was keeping from him made her look away.

He caught her chin in his fingers and tipped it round to meet his gaze. 'Is something wrong, Faith? I've been absorbed in my own problems and poor company.'

She shook her head; it would only take the slightest urging from him and she would blurt out about her possible pregnancy. The knowledge was buzzing in her brain like a fly against a window pane.

Dan began to kiss her. The touch of his lips and hands cruising over her body made her forget everything but the clamouring of her senses. He drew her down on to the rug in front of the gas fire. The room was warm and after they made love they remained locked in each other's arms. Her expression became dreamy as she visualised that this would be how their life would always be.

She found her mind kept wandering throughout the Sunday when Dan was painting her. Her expression was wistful as she thought of the baby and the three of them together.

'Faith, that's the second time I've asked you a question and you haven't answered.' Dan put down his brush and came over to the couch where she was reclining. He stooped to kiss her mouth, murmuring, 'Something has changed about you since I've been away. You're different. An incandescence radiates from you. I've captured it on canvas and it's fantastic. I've never seen you more lovely.'

'Oh, Dan,' she breathed softly, her hand sliding across his chest to hold him close. He was more relaxed than when he had met her from work yesterday. Should she tell him about the baby? Still something made her hold back.

With a secretive smile, she changed the subject before she forgot her resolution and blurted out her suspicions. She was startled that she hadn't yet told him about Ruby. During the last few days she had been preoccupied. 'We've been invited to a wedding. Ruby and Ernie. I'm to be bridesmaid.'

'That's a bit sudden. Pregnant is she?' His tone was so scathing her cheeks drained of colour.

'No. But would it have made any difference if she was?'

'It would be just like her to use that trick to get herself a meal-ticket for life. Too many couples get trapped into marriage that way.'

'Meal-ticket! Is that how you think women view marriage?' Faith choked and pushed him away. If that's what he thought of women who became pregnant before marriage, she prayed that her suspicions were wrong. 'A woman can't get pregnant on her own!' she snapped.

He was staring bleakly out of the window, too deep in thought to have heard her words. Her anger flared. 'Why do men see marriage as a trap? Isn't it the woman who bears the shame if she becomes pregnant before she's married?'

Without answering he crossed to the sideboard, poured himself a large whisky and drank it down. 'Ruby is a fool. She'll regret it.'

His last words echoed her own fears for her friend and diverted her anger. 'I'm worried about her. I've tried to talk with her. I'm sure she doesn't love Ernie. He's persuaded her that it's best for her career and that he's going to make her a star. There's no reasoning with her.'

Dan laughed derisively. 'Marriage isn't something which should be considered lightly. Durham is using it to harness her talent. He'll bring her more harm than glory.'

He sounded bitter. Faith's heart contracted with alarm. Was it anger at the way Durham was using Ruby, or something else? It was the something else which filled her with dread.

'Are you telling me you're not the marrying kind?'

His jaw clenched and he stepped towards her. She backed away, too incensed to want him near her. 'What if I should bear your child? Would I be angling for a meal-ticket for life?'

Tears streamed down her cheeks. She was inappropriately dressed in a flowing emerald chiffon gown Dan had asked her to pose in. It trailed on the floor behind her bare feet as she whirled and ran to get her coat. Her world had shattered like crystal. The shards were piercing her heart.

'What the hell has got into you, Faith?' Dan blocked her passage to the door.

'If you don't know then there's no point in me explaining. I love you, Dan. I know we are worlds apart. But women aren't all like that. I'm the one who's the fool. I let myself believe that you loved me enough . . . loved me enough not to use me.' She ground to a halt, sobbing so hard she was unable to go on.

He groaned and pulled her to him. 'Faith, my darling. I know you're not the same kind of woman as Ruby. I've upset you. But marriage . . . Damn it, Faith. I love you, but I can't marry you. Not for some time at least.'

171

She was rigid in his arms. 'Let me go, Dan. If you loved me you wouldn't make excuses. You're infatuated with the model and not the woman behind the fantasy you create.' Her anger soaring, she yanked a long tress of her hair. 'And you're obsessed with this. This is what attracted you, not me, not the woman. Just my bloody hair!'

'You're being ridiculous.'

Her eyes flashed dangerously. 'Am I? Don't worry, Dan. I won't trap you into marriage. I won't have you accusing me of tricking you . . . of taking your precious freedom from you.'

He shook her gently. 'Faith, I don't understand what's got into you. I've never lied to you. Never led you to believe . . .' His eyes widened and every vestige of colour drained from his face; even his lips were bloodless. 'My God, you're pregnant. I never meant that to happen.'

She wrenched herself from his arms, his words confirming her worst fears. He didn't want the child. He didn't want her. Pride lifted her chin and her eyes were glittering with ice as she regarded him. 'Whether I'm pregnant or not, I won't know until I've seen a doctor. But rest assured if I am, I'll bring my child up on my own. I shan't expect anything from you since you've made your feelings so clear. Get out of my way. I'm leaving.'

When he refused to release her she kicked out at his shin. He swore but held her tight. 'You're not going anywhere. Not until you've listened to what I've got to say.'

'You've said too much,' she seethed, finally managing to twist herself free.

'It's not that I don't want to marry you. I can't.' His eyes were grim with torment. 'I'm already married.'

The words crashed over her, robbing her of breath. She'd been the worst possible fool. She had trusted Dan and believed him honourable.

'My wife and I haven't lived together for several years,' Dan went on. 'But we are Catholics which is why we didn't divorce. After I met you, I decided I could no longer stay married to Imelda. But divorce takes years.'

She swayed and clutched at the wall for support. 'Why didn't you tell me you were married?' she accused.

'Because I never meant to fall in love with you. I never meant to hurt you. I thought I'd taken care of things so you wouldn't get pregnant.'

'The only certain way to avoid a pregnancy is to avoid sex.' She put her coat on, needing to get away before she broke down completely. Pain was lacerating her heart. Dan had betrayed her trust. 'I'm going home.'

'No, Faith. Please stay. We have to talk. I don't want us parting like this.'

Her injured pride made her stubborn. 'This is my problem, not yours.'

'Don't be foolish.'

'First I'm ridiculous. Now I'm foolish.' She struck out with her hands and pummelled his chest. 'Obviously I'm both of those for trusting you.'

He caught her wrists and gently pulled them against his heart. It was thumping as hard and painfully as her own. 'I love you, Faith. If you're pregnant, I'd never desert you. And I'll start divorce proceedings against Imelda. Her machinations have ruined my life and I don't want them ruining yours. You deserve better than what I can offer you.'

'I would never have slept with you if I had known you were married, Dan. I don't want to be a marriage breaker.'

'My marriage was over a long time before I met you.' His blue eyes were bleak as a winter sea. 'My words were unnecessarily harsh. I've wounded you unintentionally. I've become cynical but not without reason.'

He lifted a hand to touch her face. Still distrustful she flinched back and his eyes darkened with sadness.

'I deserve your censure. I wronged you. You've given me such joy and I was selfish. I didn't want to lose you. Come and sit down and let me tell you about my marriage. Perhaps then you won't judge me so harshly. I want you to understand that my condemnation was not aimed at you, but at another who deserves nothing but scorn.'

Her instinct was to break away. The sobs were stifled but inside they swelled, her heart aching in the clamp of a remorseless vice. She couldn't leave without Dan explaining. She didn't want excuses, but she was owed an explanation.

Holding herself stiffly she sat down. She wrapped her coat around her, her manner hunched and defensive. As he spoke of his marriage her antagonism wavered. No wonder he felt as he did with a woman like Imelda as his wife. When he told her of their last confrontation and of the house stripped of its treasures so that he could face bankruptcy, she was appalled.

'I understand. But I still wish you had told me first.'

He took her hands. 'Can you forgive me? I mean to stand by you. I won't let you face the shame of having a child alone. But I don't want your name dragged through the divorce courts either. It could take several days to track Imelda down. I'm sure for the right price – and Imelda will demand every penny I get from the exhibitions – she'll agree to a divorce.'

'I don't care about money, Dan. I just care about you.'

He held her close, murmuring reassurances and endearments. 'We will work this out, Faith. I promise. I'd ask you to move in with me once Ruby marries, but if Imelda learns of your existence . . . that I love you . . . she will unleash all her spite and vindictiveness. I don't want that to happen.'

She drew a shaky breath and laid her head against his shoulder. 'If I have your love, I can weather anything. Will you be back in England in time for Ruby's wedding?'

'I don't know. Imelda will take some persuading and I have to find her first.'

That evening Dan spent two hours on the phone trying to track Imelda down by contacting her wealthy friends on the Continent. No one had heard from her for a month.

'You want to keep that sexy wife of yours close,' Barney Halgrove tittered, his voice slurred with drink. Dan could hear a riotous party going on in the background of the Monte Carlo villa. 'Last week Imelda was at a masked ball in Venice. Some

174

Russian count was all over her. She left with him the next morning; they were joining his friends on their yacht to sail to the Greek Islands for a month.'

Dan left his Paris phone number. 'If you see or hear anything of her let us know at that number. There's some papers she has to sign to receive some jewellery found in a bank deposit box belonging to her father.' That lie was bound to get Imelda contacting him.

As Dan was making the calls Imelda was not in Greece. The Russian count was a self-opinionated bore. She was still festering from Dan's insults and wanted to revenge herself upon him. It was the only prospect which brought some excitement to her life. The morning after the masked ball she'd met an Englishman who could serve her interests better. He was in Venice with his insipid fiancée and her family. She travelled back to England with them. It had been a simple matter to seduce the Englishman. His fiancée wasn't allowing him into her frigid bed until after their marriage.

They had booked into the Ringside Hotel outside Richmond. Her lover extolled the virtues of the place and it was popular with other members of her class. Above all it was discreet. She didn't want Dan knowing her whereabouts until she had found a way of making him pay for wanting to discard her.

The Ringside served her purpose well. Her predatory gaze was drawn to the athletic-looking owner of the hotel who was mixing with the guests. Matthew Frost was a handsome man despite a limp from a war wound received when he had been a pilot. The touch of grey at his dark temples gave him a distinguished countenance. Imelda had weighed him up as a possible lover when they booked into the hotel, but within minutes she had seen his wife approach. The adoration in his gaze as he smiled at her figure, rounded by pregnancy, told Imelda that this was not a man who played around.

She was still tempted. A man like that was worth some extra effort.

175

Waiting for her present lover to arrive, she questioned the waiter who brought her champagne and learned that Matt Frost had been married for ten years and his wife Casey was expecting their fourth child. She had also learned that the hotel had been a convalescent home for officers after the war. Some still lived here. You couldn't miss them, they were the patrons with either an arm or a leg missing. They were dismissed as uninteresting in Imelda's eyes though her mind did conjure up some innovative images which would have livened up a one-legged man's sex life.

Her salacious thoughts were interrupted by a hard kiss planted on her cheek. 'Imelda, you look wonderful.'

She smiled at her lover, knowing that through him she could get back at Dan. Tony Chalmers had been after her for years. He was too immature for her taste, but now he had information that she wanted.

Tony was snoring drunkenly when she left the Ringside the next morning. She had learned that Dan was going to Paris and would be away for at least a week. She took a key out of her bag. One she'd had copied when Dan first took his studio. Letting herself into the flat she prowled around.

She moved from room to room, not sure what she was looking for – other than stirring up mischief. Her curiosity was roused at seeing a stack of paintings propped against the wall. She hoped they were good. They would bring in more money for her. There was no prestige in being the wife of an unknown artist. Flicking through them, she was unmoved by the mystical elements present in so many of the paintings.

Most of them were of the red-haired woman. Her interest in them was replaced by anger. He had never painted her. Hadn't she a better figure than that scrawny bitch? And as for that hair! How old-fashioned: a style fit for peasants.

Momentarily, she was tempted to slash the paintings. But without them Dan would lose his livelihood and could not pay her allowance. But the paintings were a means of hurting him most. It rankled that she had to hold back. Her mood dark, she wandered into the bedroom. There she halted, eyes narrowed, lips drawn back like a wolf about to rip apart its prey. Her hatred resurfaced with volcanic violence. Above the bed was another painting of the redhead. The slut was naked in this one. Naked and satiated from lovemaking. A seductress beckoning her lover. A woman in love and loved.

With a scream of rage she hurled the painting to the floor. She was about to grind her heel into the canvas when an idea stopped her. Her smile was evil. It was petty to destroy the painting and so much more satisfying to destroy the person instead.

Chapter Thirteen

There were blinding flashes from the press photographers as Ruby and Ernie came out of the Register Office. It was midweek and Faith had been given the day off work to be Ruby's bridesmaid. Ruby wore a knee-length ruby flapper dress which shimmered with thousands of sequins and a matching Cleopatra-style sequinned skullcap which framed her beautiful face to perfection. She looked like no bride Faith had ever seen, but she looked stunning. The pavement was thronged with people, mostly men, craning their necks to see the couple. They all pressed forward at once, crushing Faith who was jostled to one side.

Several wolf whistles had Ruby posing and blowing kisses in every direction.

'Wish it was me instead of Durham,' one man shouted.

'You ain't gonna give up singing now you're married? What we gonna do without our Ruby?' another groaned.

' 'Course I ain't gonna give up singing,' she called back as she twisted and turned, smiling at the men pushing to surround her.

Ernie took her arm. 'Next week she starts a three-month tour of the country in a revue.'

'Got a garter on for good luck, Ruby?' one cheeky lad asked with a grin.

'Two actually!' She demurely lifted the hem of her dress just above her knee and untied a ruby satin garter and tossed it into the crowd. Several men scrambled for it. 'Do you want to see the other one?'

'We'll see anything you've got to show us,' a burly man guffawed.

Ruby beckoned him closer and this time lifted her dress high enough to expose most of her shapely thigh. 'This were my special wedding present from Ernie. I thought it were more appropriate than the diamond necklace he promised me.' The sunlight sparkled off another garter set with large rubies. Cameras flashed like lightning bolts and the men surged forward for a better view. 'Ain't this something else?' she said giggling.

'You're something else, Ruby,' the crowd roared.

Faith, in a pale mint green dress, its jagged hem edged with silver sequins, watched the proceedings with growing unease. It wasn't a wedding celebration, it was a publicity stunt. Ruby was revelling in it. But she couldn't imagine anything worse than having so many people staring at her.

She looked across the mass of faces crowding the pavement, hoping that Dan had made it in time. She had not heard from him since he left for Paris ten days ago. She still didn't know if she was pregnant. After work tomorrow she must visit the doctor and find out. The rush of the wedding and Ruby's demands had taken up all her spare time. There was no sign of Dan. She inhaled deeply to banish a wave of faintness. The press of bodies was oppressive. A hand clutched at her elbow.

'Are you all right, Miss Tempest?' Mike Rivers was looking at her with concern. 'It's a circus not a wedding. Ernie's paid those men to whistle and shout to get better press coverage. As best man I'm supposed to look after the bridesmaid. Let's get out of here and leave them to it. We'll meet them back at the club for the reception.'

Mike cleared a way through the crowd and Faith was about to step into a waiting taxi cab when Ruby yelled her name.

'Faith! Here!'

Ruby's bouquet of white lilies shot through the air and Faith caught it.

'That's it, kiddo. You'll be next.'

Faith felt her face muscles creak as she forced a smile. She hadn't told Ruby that she could be pregnant, nor that Dan was married. With a wave she climbed into the back of the taxi next to Mike. As they drew away she realised that the musician was tense and was staring bleakly out of the window. Throughout the ceremony he had stood at Ernie's side, his back stiff and a muscle pumping along his jaw. Intuition made her heart ache for him. Mike was in love with Ruby.

Oh Ruby, what have you done! Mike is a hundred times the better man. Couldn't you see that he cared? Faith had begun to suspect that Ruby was attracted to the musician. Yet she was blinded by the promise of fame Ernie had offered to her.

The meal and afternoon passed in a blur. Faith felt out of place. She sipped her champagne when the couple were toasted. The rest of the guests were boisterous and tipsy. Hugh Kavanagh and his brothers were lording it in one corner. Everyone was enjoying themselves except for herself and Mike who sat quietly by the bar.

She missed Dan so much. Why hadn't he telephoned the shop or written? She hadn't eaten for worrying about a pregnancy and its consequences. No decent man would want anything to do with her. Loving Dan so fiercely, she could bear that, but the thought of the child bearing the brunt of children's cruel jeering was another matter. It destroyed her peace. A bastard child was always picked on by bullies. Protective mothers refused to allow their children to mix or play with them.

Doubts kept wriggling into her mind. What if Dan didn't love her? What if he really thought she had set out to trap him and wanted nothing more to do with her? She wouldn't be the first woman who, believing herself loved, had found herself pregnant and abandoned.

Dan rubbed a hand over his unshaven jaw and winced in agony as he stared into the blackness of a cellar which had become his prison. He had lost track of the number of days since he had been abducted.

When he arrived in Paris the French gallery were rapturous over the sketches he had shown them of Faith. They wanted a minimum of six paintings with her as the model and at least another ten of his other work to fill the exhibition planned for

July. The artist originally booked had died suddenly with only two paintings completed. Pierre Le Grand, the gallery owner, had seen Dan's work in London and been impressed by his fresh approach to the Pre-Raphaelite style.

'I like a woman to look mysterious and even unapproachable,' Pierre said, patting his goatee beard, his chubby face intense with his passion for art. 'We take pride that we can discover artists who will become famous for their unique styles. The popular style of today which gives us skinny women with flat chests and harsh lines does not appeal to everyone.'

Fortunately Dan had over a score of incomplete paintings he had started in recent years. He had lost enthusiasm for them long before he met Faith. That had all changed now. With six weeks' hard work he could complete them for the exhibition.

He had dined with Pierre that evening and concluded the financial arrangements and delivery dates for the exhibition. Pierre hailed a taxi, but troubled with thoughts of Imelda and Faith, Dan decided to walk back to his hotel. He shunned the company in cafés and bars, needing solitude to think. He sat on the steps of Sacré Coeur, the white sepulchre dominating the skyline. Before him was a panoramic view of the city, its street lamps twinkling like sequins.

Paris, after Venice, was the most romantic city in the world. He should be here with Faith, not brooding and alone. He would bring her here for the exhibition and show her Paris in July. He walked on and as he crossed a tree-lined square leading to his hotel a car drew up and two men leapt out behind him.

'Monsieur Brogan?' one queried.

'Yes.' As he turned to face them a cudgel struck the side of his head, felling him to his knees. They dragged him semi-conscious to the back of the car and sped away.

By the time Dan's stunned wits recovered, his arms were handcuffed behind him and he was lying face down on the back seat of the car. A revolver was pressed against his temple.

'What the hell is going on?' he demanded, though his heart was pounding with fear. 'There's got to be some mistake.'

'No mistake. You are wealthy Englishman, that is enough.'

'I'm not rich. I'm an artist. A poor man.'

'No more talk.'

A foul-tasting gag was rammed in his mouth and tied behind his head. He couldn't see where they were taking him. They must have driven for over half an hour before the car halted. Dan was dragged out and with the gun at his neck pushed into a building. He stumbled on a stone step and pitched forward into space, rolling and tumbling down a dozen concrete stairs. He lay at the bottom panting, his heart beating a frantic tattoo. Were they going to kill him? Why? His dazed mind tried to focus. He'd banged his head and bruised his ribs and shoulders in the fall. Thankfully no bones seemed to be broken. He pushed himself on to his knees and then stood up, his eyes blazing with the questions he could not ask with the gag in his mouth.

An oil lamp was carried down the steps by one of his attackers. He couldn't see their faces. The lower halves of them were covered in kerchiefs. Handcuffed he had no chance of fighting them to gain his freedom. The lamplight threw the cellar into stark relief. There was a single iron bed and a commode. Apart from that it was empty and smelt musty from long disuse. There was no window. When one of the men grabbed his arm he struggled to break free. A blow to his jaw sent him staggering back to land on the bed. With a knee placed in the centre of his back one wrist was freed from the handcuffs. The other arm was dragged up and the cuff snapped through the heavy links of a chain which was fixed to a ring in the wall. It was long enough for him to lie down on the bed, reach the water jug and commode.

Without a word the two men left, taking the oil lamp. He tore the gag from his mouth as they reached the door.

'You've made a mistake! I'm not a rich man!'

They laughed, one saying ominously, 'That's what they all say. If your rich wife does not pay our demands in three days, then we start to send her your fingers.'

Dan blanched. These men were insane demanding money from a man who was all but bankrupt. Trust the bloody French to get their information wrong. But that didn't help him. There was no money to pay them. What then? If they carried out their threat to cut off his fingers, he might never be able to paint again.

So far that threat had not materialised. He tried to work out how many days he had been here. Three or four, going by the meals brought in. In impotent anger he jerked at the chain. It held rigid and the metal of the handcuff bit into the flesh of his wrist, already rubbed raw from its constant chafing. He had a swelling the size of an egg where he had banged his head on the stairs and his ribs were tender and badly bruised. To take his mind off his suffering he thought of Faith. She must be distraught that he had not contacted her for so long.

He cursed himself for not writing or phoning, but he had been busy over the exhibition arrangements. That was a weak excuse. He was dreading that she would tell him that she was pregnant. Not because he didn't want a child. He loved children. He didn't want Faith to face the censure that would bring.

His free hand massaged the taut muscles at the back of his neck. His life was complicated enough without this injustice. He had been treated barbarically. Frustration and anger ground through him. He couldn't take his mind off Faith. What if she was pregnant and thought he had abandoned her? What fears was she facing alone? And he was powerless to help her. Powerless at this moment to help even himself.

Lost in thought, it was some time before Faith realised that the wedding guests had dwindled. Ruby was dancing with a man Faith did not know. There was no sign of Big Hugh Kavanagh and his brothers whom Ruby had introduced her to at the Register Office. Mike was playing the piano and she sat back to listen. There was a poignancy in his music which brought tears to her eyes. Was he feeling as bereft as herself? He'd lost the woman he loved to another man. Had she lost Dan? Had she in fact ever truly had him, since he was already married?

She stood up, deciding to leave. She was tired and it was obvious that Ruby did not need her. She went over to her friend.

184

Ruby smiled at her, her voice slurred by drink. 'This is the best friend a girl could ever have. You enjoying yourself? Didn't Dan come? Rotten sod, missing my wedding.'

'He's in Paris. I'm leaving now. I'm tired.'

Ruby waved the men away and put her arm around Faith's shoulders. 'You're missing Dan, that's all. 'Course you can't go. The fun is just beginning.'

'I have to go. Where's Ernie? I wanted to congratulate him. He's got himself a fine wife.'

Ruby scowled. 'He's disappeared on business. You'd think he'd give it a rest on his wedding day. You can't go until he gets back.'

Faith knew that Ernie had not been at the reception for nearly an hour. At that Ernie and the Kavanagh brothers sauntered in. All looked rolling drunk, but Faith sensed a falseness about their movements. They'd been up to something and whatever it was, it was no good.

Ernie kissed Ruby loudly on the lips and draped an arm around Faith's shoulders. It took all her willpower not to flinch away in disgust. Ruby rounded on her new husband, her voice a low snarl, 'Where the hell have you been?'

'Just outside. A bit of business.' His arm fell from Faith's shoulders and he turned to grip Ruby's wrist so hard that she saw her friend wince. 'I told you, you don't question where I've been, or what I do.' He dragged her into a secluded alcove and sat beside her. They were out of Faith's hearing but from their expressions it was obvious that they were arguing. Faith hung her head. How could Ruby have married that bully?

She turned away to see a grim-faced Mike Rivers behind her. He was watching the bride and groom. When he saw Ernie bend back Ruby's wrist anger twisted his mouth. Ruby's eyes narrowed and her foot kicked Ernie under the table. He gave a grimace of pain.

'There'll be a few battles there,' Faith said heavily.

Mike didn't answer but there was a dangerous light in his eyes when his gaze rested on his brother. A crowd of reporters had returned to the club and Faith picked up her handbag, preparing to leave. One reporter made a beeline for her, thrusting his grinning face close to hers. 'I thought I recognised you. Well, if this ain't a turn-up for the book.'

Faith frowned. 'I beg your pardon. I don't know you.'

He chuckled nastily and waved a newspaper under her nose. 'Don't act so prim and proper. Not with this plastered all over the city.'

Faith caught a glimpse of a woman's naked figure and the headline. NEW ARTIST DAN BROGAN BREAKS ALL AUCTION RECORDS WITH THE HOTTEST MODEL IN TOWN.

Her eyes rounded with shock as she stared at the photograph of Dan's painting. The painting he had vowed never to exhibit. The painting of herself naked.

Faith felt her knees buckle and Mike caught her before she could fall. She saw the shock on his face as he stared over her head at the newspaper.

Shame flooded her. The reporter was jubilant. A photographer appeared and his camera flashed.

'The painting is of you. What's your name? Are you Brogan's mistress?' The questions hit her like stones, humiliating and shaming.

She began to tremble and Mike stepped between her and the reporter. 'You've got it wrong. This lady isn't the one in the painting.'

'Give over, mate. I ain't blind. There ain't many women with hair like that. I noted it at the wedding and she's a looker. All we want is a few questions. The painting is the talk of London. It went for a phenomenal sum. It's made Brogan famous. Was he your lover?'

The torrent of questions ended as Mike punched the reporter on the jaw. He staggered back and crashed into a table which collapsed under his weight. Suddenly the club was ablaze with flashlights from the cameras. With an anguished sob Faith turned her head away. Mike shielded her with his body and, holding her against him, pushed his way though the reporters and photographers.

'She your mistress as well, Rivers?' the reporter spat. 'Gets around, don't the little lady?'

Somehow Mike got her through the press of leering faces with the cameras flashing around them. Baying voices screamed crude comments. Lecherous jeers bombarded her. It was a nightmare. A verbal tarring and feathering. Mike pushed her into a back room used by the musicians and slammed the door.

'Ernie's men will deal with those vermin. I'll take you home when it's quieter.'

Faith burned with shame. She felt degraded, violated and betrayed. She hugged her arms about her and sank down on to a rickety chair. Her translucent skin slowly bleached of all colour, her eyes were wide and wild like a trapped animal and her body shook uncontrollably.

Mike held a bottle of brandy under her nose. 'Drink some of that. It will help. There ain't no glasses.'

She waved it away, but he was insistent, pressing it to her quivering lips, compelling her to drink it. She took two gulps and coughed, pushing the bottle away.

He leaned against the door, his arms folded as he studied her. 'Don't let those sewer rats upset you. But surely you must have realised there'd be press interest over such a provocative painting.' His voice was gruff with condemnation. 'At least Brogan should have been here to support you.'

'Dan promised me the painting would never be sold,' she finally managed to force out in a small voice. 'How could he betray me like this? I trusted him.'

'I hadn't reckoned Brogan as a guy who took advantage of women. Did you pose for that painting? Or did he just use your face and hair?'

'No, it's me,' she groaned, unable to hold his stare. 'God, how I trusted him! I believed every word he said.'

She put her head in her hands, her magnificent hair falling over her face a fragile barrier concealing her humiliation. The door burst open and the newspaper with the front-page headlines and picture was flung on the table at Faith's side.

'Fine friend you are!' Ernie spat. 'I worked my arse off to get Ruby publicity in the papers and you overshadow her.'

'Do you think I did this on purpose?' Faith's head shot up, her eyes glittering with indignation.

Ernie was white-lipped with anger, his fists clenched as though ready to strike her. Faith was too upset to allow his rage to intimidate her. Where she had found it difficult to meet Mike's enquiring gaze, Ernie's anger roused her outrage. 'I've been betrayed by a man I trusted and you think I planned this débâcle.'

'You're a dark horse!' Ernie sneered.

'Leave it out, Ernie,' Ruby said from behind him. 'Faith wouldn't seek such publicity. Can't you see she's upset?'

Ernie rounded on her. 'What you defending her for? She's just stolen your limelight. Everyone wants to know who the mysterious woman of the painting is. The publicity I'd drummed up was supposed to put your name on everyone's lips, not hers. She's just jealous of your success.'

Faith stood up, her voice bitter. 'It would take a devious mind like yours to believe that. Don't judge me by the same low standards.'

'Who the hell do you think you're talking to?' Ernie leaned forward, his arm raised.

Mike grabbed it and shoved his brother aside. 'That's enough, Ernie.'

Faith stood her ground, but was appalled at the fury in Ernie's eyes. What kind of brute had Ruby married? He had no scruples and if Mike Rivers had not intervened he would have struck her. Fears for her friend tangled with the misery of Dan's betrayal.

Ruby appeared not to notice Ernie's menacing attitude. She was tipsy and swayed as she put her arms round Faith. 'I know this ain't your doing,' she slurred. 'But you gotta admit. It's sure made you famous.'

'Infamous don't you mean?' Faith corrected.

'Don't let that bastard Brogan get to you,' Ruby whispered and drew her away from the men. 'No man's worth getting cut up over.'

'Oh Ruby,' Faith stared at her in distress. 'How can you say that today of all days? You've just got married.'

'But I know what I'm letting meself in for. Ernie is using me like I'm using him. We deserve each other. That suits me for now. Whereas you and Dan . . .' She hugged Faith. 'I could see he was ambitious, but I had him down as caring for you.'

'Clearly his art was more important,' Faith groaned. 'Dan told me I was giving him something precious when I posed for him. I loved him. Trusted him. How could he do this to me? No wonder he didn't turn up today. He must be laughing at my naivety.'

'Then he's an idiot and doesn't know the treasure he's lost.'

'I'm so ashamed, Ruby.'

'Don't be. Personally I thought you looked terrific in the painting.' Seeing Faith's misery, she sighed. 'Perhaps I should have worn a transparent wedding gown then I could have made the front pages like Ernie wanted.'

Her flippancy didn't fool Faith. Worry for her friend was stark in Ruby's carefully made-up eyes. Faith felt guilty. This was Ruby's day and it had been spoilt by the incident.

She tacked on a brave smile. 'I'm sorry all this has ruined your day. I'll be all right. I've been such a fool. And I thought you'd made the mistake getting involved with Ernie. I may not approve of his tactics, but he does have your interests at heart.'

'Only because that'll make him a fortune. But he ain't so bad.' Ruby hid her own misgivings about her husband. She was angry at him for sneaking out this afternoon. He had waved a wad of fivers at her on his return but wouldn't tell her how he had acquired them. Protection money she reckoned. That was a dirty racket. Shopkeepers paid up or were beaten up and their shops wrecked.

Mike addressed Faith. 'It ain't gonna be easy for you for the next few days. Got any ideas how you're gonna tackle the press?'

Faith felt the walls of the room begin to close in around her. Panic welled. Decent folks would revile her. What respectable woman posed nude for a man to paint her? Her heart palpitated, stifling her. She drew a shaky breath, fighting to stay calm. Her world had been turned upside down, but she wasn't going to let it overwhelm her. Naivety might have been her downfall, but life in the orphanage had made her tough. She wasn't as vulnerable as people thought. When you have coped with the death of both your parents by the age of seven, anything else life has to throw at you is insignificant. She had a great deal of inner strength to draw upon.

'They'll want my resignation at the gallery,' she observed. 'The customers are bound to disapprove. But I've enough put by to keep me for a few months. And I'll get another job.'

She sounded more confident than she felt. Pregnancy was still her greatest concern, especially now Dan had so callously betrayed and abandoned her.

She thrust her pain and fears aside. See only trouble ahead and it will surely swamp you, she told herself. Be confident in your ability to triumph over adversity, and you will succeed.

Ernie was looking at the newspaper picture of Dan's painting. When he looked up he smirked at her. 'Kavanagh's got a couple of high-class strip joints. With a figure like yours and all this publicity, he'd make you the star attraction. You'd be the toast of the town.'

'Shut up, Ernie,' Ruby scolded. 'Faith's got class.'

Tension rippled across the room. Ruby out of friendship defended her, but her friend did not understand the pain and shame she was feeling. It emphasised the differences between them. Their friendship remained strong, but it was changing. Each had new responsibilities, fresh ambitions, different goals.

Faith said stiffly, 'If the reporters have gone I'll leave. You two have a honeymoon to enjoy.'

Mike moved to the door, 'I'll take you home, Miss Tempest. I've me motorcycle out the back. We can escape the reporters on that, or do you prefer a taxi?'

'Your motorcycle is fine. Thank you.'

Mike regarded her gravely. 'I never had Brogan tagged as a mercenary devil. But then he married money and that enabled him to continue his painting.'

190

Ruby gasped, 'Dan is married? I didn't know that!' She looked accusingly at Faith. 'Hell, Faith. Did you know?'

Faith nodded. The strain of the last hour was taking its toll on her and she was feeling ill. 'This isn't the time to talk of it. You're off on honeymoon tonight.' She kissed Ruby's cheek.

Ruby held her close. 'Ernie's booked us into the Ritz for one night. After that I don't leave for Blackpool to join the revue for a couple of days. I'll be at Ernie's house in Chelsea. Promise me you'll contact me if you need me.'

Faith nodded. They left the club. She clung to Mike's back as he wove through the London traffic. When she stepped on to the pavement outside her flat a severe cramp in her stomach made her gasp. Its familiarity should have been reassuring. Why then did she feel so devastated that she was not carrying Dan's child?

Chapter Fourteen

Imelda was pleased with herself. She lay in bed propped up on her pillows. The cocktail of opiates and alcohol she had taken induced a sense of well-being and invincibility. She sipped her second glass of champagne of the day.

It was midday, the curtains were still drawn and soon her maid would come and run her bath. The hotel was one of the most expensive in Paris and she was triumphant after the auction of the painting. Who would have thought Dan's strumpet would cause such a sensation or the portrait fetch so much? The money was a balm to her wounded pride and out of her husband's reach in her Swiss bank account. She had shown Dan that she could not be so easily dismissed. She'd come to Paris to ensure that Dan remained out of England for the auction.

She laughed maliciously. She had taught her husband a lesson he would not forget in a hurry. Those out-of-work actors had done their work well, abducting him and pretending to hold him for ransom. She'd got the idea from an Italian newspaper. She had also paid for his mistress to be hounded by some unscrupulous reporters. She'd learned enough about the Tempest woman from Tony to know that she would be shamed by the scandal of her posing nude being made public. Tony had been at the studio and walked into the bedroom and commented on the painting. Dan had been furious and told Tony that he'd promised it would never be sold. The Tempest woman would believe that Dan had broken her trust and would not forgive him. The damage was done. She'd get the actors to release Dan today. Just wait until he saw the

English newspaper she'd had delivered to him at his hotel. She laughed evilly.

Her eyes were wild as she stared around her hotel room. She hadn't slept for three nights she had been so charged up by wreaking her revenge upon Dan. Did he and his whore think she would allow herself to be cast aside, just so they could live happily ever after? Dan was her property. He was her husband and now he was becoming famous, he could afford to keep her in style. But he had to be made to toe the line. She tapped a long manicured nail against her teeth. Dan had never understood her. The cocktail of drugs and drink made her already unstable mind volatile. She plunged from euphoria to sudden depression.

A chasm of fear opened in her mind. She was no longer young. She knew the ravages of time and the life she led were beginning to show on her face. What was so galling was that the Tempest woman was half her age. That was the greatest insult Dan could throw at her.

She struck the bedclothes with her fists. Dan had taken her best years. A rush of tears stung her eyes. How could she face her friends if Dan divorced her for a younger woman? She would be laughed at behind her back.

Insecurity beset her. Dan had been a stabilising anchor through the turbulent years of their marriage. Now she felt threatened. Those paintings, especially the nude, had been done by a man in love.

She screamed and began to hit her pillow, each thud soaring her temper and reasoning out of control. She would make sure that her husband never found peace or love with another woman. She had paid an investigation agency to watch Dan and send reports to her. She knew where he was staying in Paris. She chuckled wickedly on learning that he was looking for her, when all the time she was so close, planning her revenge. The French actors had demanded double their fee when she gave them their final instructions. It was worth it. Dan had suffered, but not enough.

Her angry screams changed to diabolical laughter. Then her

194

long nails clawed through her hair and pulled at her lace nightgown until it was in shreds. Her hair was wild and her eyes bright when her maid, hearing her cries, came into the bedroom. Imelda was frightened now. Dan was no fool. What if he guessed it was she who had stolen the painting? He would never forgive her that. Divorce loomed inevitably. But she would not lose him. She needed him still.

The maid was alarmed by her mistress's cries. When she entered the bedroom the sight of Imelda shocked her. Her mistress's clothing was flecked with blood and her neck and chest scored with deep scratches. Her eyes were venomous slits. Every sinew of the woman's neurotically thin body was tensed as she flailed her arms, ripping at her nightgown and the sheets.

'I will never give him up for that woman!' Imelda screeched and reeled from the bed towards the bathroom.

The maid dared not move unless some missile was hurled at her. She knew from experience how accurate her mistress could be when she was in a temper. She listened with growing fear as Imelda banged about in the bathroom, smashing glass bottles and slamming cabinet doors.

'This will show him,' Imelda sobbed, her voice shrill with hysteria. 'This really will show him . . .'

The sounds stopped in the bathroom and an eerie quiet descended on the bedroom. The maid breathed deeply to still her thudding heart and started to tidy the room. It was some minutes before the unnatural silence alerted her that something was wrong.

'Madame?' she called and tapped on the bathroom door. There was no answer.

'Madame, what clothes shall I lay out for you?'

Again silence. A deeper fear gripped her. Imelda's moods were explosive and terrifying, but usually they ended with her sobbing hysterically in tears. This silence was frightening. Tapping once more on the door, she opened it. She screamed in horror. The white bathroom was splattered with arcs of blood. Her foot slipped in the pool on the floor. The remnants of Imelda's nightgown were scarlet as the blood pumped out of her lacerated wrists.

Sobbing, the maid grabbed a sheet, tore it into strips and began to bind Imelda's wrists. When she finished the weakened woman groaned, her voice lethal and evil, 'I've shown him. I'll kill myself if he divorces me.'

For Faith life became a living nightmare. If Dan had stood by her it would have been easier to bear. But his absence and silence confirmed his betrayal. He had used her to make his fortune and abandoned her to the wolves.

She was given no peace. The reporters were outside her flat from the first morning. How could they have got her address if not from Dan? She had run the gauntlet of them to go to work. More were outside the gallery.

'Drive on,' she ordered the cabbie, unable to face another ordeal of shoving, screaming reporters demanding her story. She instructed the driver to stop outside a hotel and wait for her. She used the hotel phone.

'Oliver, I can't come in today. I saw the reporters outside the gallery. I suppose you've seen what it is all about? I'm so dreadfully sorry. It's been awful.'

'*Seen*, my dear? I've been positively *grieved* by it all.' He sounded vexed. 'How could you have let Brogan auction that painting and not use our gallery? But you must come to work.'

He rushed on, heedless of her sob of pain at his mercenary attitude. 'We will make the most of having the mysterious model everyone is talking about working in our gallery. Of course the press are here. You're famous. So I shall forgive you this once. But any other paintings of you by Brogan must, simply *must*, be handled by ourselves. Have you no loyalty to your employer?'

Faith's anger bubbled over at Oliver's treachery. 'Keep your job! I thought you had more sensitivity. I won't be paraded like an exhibit in a freak show!'

'My dear, I can't believe you are taking this attitude. I'm just—'

She rammed the receiver back on its stand without listening further. It would have been easier to take Oliver's horror at such conduct from an employee, but his wanting to exploit her made him as bad as Dan.

She went to Ernie's house in Chelsea hoping to find Ruby there. Ernie opened the door and looked set to slam it in her face again.

'Ernie, I'm sorry about yesterday. It wasn't any of my doing. Is Ruby here?'

'She's busy. She's at the photographer's getting some shots done for her tour. Ruby don't need friends like you.'

Faith despised him. He was trying to control Ruby and she was not going to allow him to ruin their friendship. 'I can't go back to my flat, reporters are hanging around it. I was hoping she could pick up some things for me.'

'What! She's gonna be a star and you treat her like a bloody skivvy? Not to mention that this is supposed to be her honeymoon.'

Faith felt a stab of guilt. 'I wasn't intruding on her honeymoon. I'm sorry I've troubled you, Mr Durham. I had no one but Ruby to turn to for help. The reporters are even hanging round the gallery so I've had to quit my job.'

Ernie scowled. 'My, you are a celebrity, ain't you?'

'Notoriety is not something I welcome.' She turned to walk down the path. 'I didn't expect Ruby to do anything for me that I wouldn't do for her. She doesn't mind facing the press.'

'Hey, calm down.' Ernie came out of the house after her. 'Come inside. I've cut up rough because I wanted the best for Ruby. But she'd never forgive me if I turned you away when you need help.'

Faith was astounded. 'I wouldn't impose if I wasn't desperate. This is your honeymoon and I know Ruby has to prepare for her tour.'

'These things happen.' Ernie's truculence had turned to charm. He led her into the hall and picked up the telephone receiver. 'Talk to Ruby at the photographer's and tell her what you need from the flat. You can wait for her here.' He gave the photographer's number to the operator and handed the phone to Faith and walked into a room.

Ruby was delighted to help her and Faith gave her instructions. Ernie came into the hall when she finished the call.

'Thank you, Ernie. I do need to pick up a couple of things at the shops before Ruby gets back. I don't want to get in your way here.'

'I'm off to the club. I'll give you a spare key. Leave it on the table when you let yourself back in.'

She was surprised at his generosity. 'Thank you.'

'That's fine, sweetheart. Ruby will get her face in the papers again thanks to you. This is little enough I can do to repay you.'

She might have known Ernie was only helping her because it benefited his schemes. She just hoped Ruby wouldn't mention anything about Dan to the papers.

Ten minutes later she walked into a hairdresser's and without hesitation demanded, 'Cut it all off as short as possible.'

As her glorious hair fell around her feet, she felt no regrets. It wasn't she that Dan had loved, it was her hair. She hated it now. A half-hour later she stared into the mirror and would not have recognised herself. The cut was almost masculine in its severity. It was shaped into the nape of her neck at the back and layered so that it was flat to her scalp with a feathery fringe and flicked forward around her temples and ears. The effect was shockingly different, giving her high cheekbones and oval face a delicate elfin appearance. She rolled her head from side to side to see its effect and was amazed at how light her head felt without the weight of hair dragging at it. The image which stared back at her looked older, more resilient. The dreamer was gone, replaced by a woman determined to carve a new life for herself.

The late-edition papers were full of pictures of Ruby protecting her friend's reputation. She used Faith's need for privacy to her advantage, vowing she would never disclose her friend's whereabouts. Faith didn't begrudge Ruby her publicity.

They were in the living room of the Chelsea house after Ruby arrived home with the papers under her arm.

'Sorry to have been so long. I had to collect a couple of gowns from the dressmaker for the tour.

'Blimey! What have you done to your hair? I must say it suits you.'

'I felt like a change. And no one will recognise me this way.'

Faith didn't feel comfortable in Ernie's house. Every piece of furniture was in the latest art deco style. Most of the furnishings were showy and expensive rather than in good taste. Faith was unimpressed by the gaudy opulence. It was as impersonal as a furniture showroom and had none of the cosy comfort of a home. But Ruby liked it. She showed Faith round the house exclaiming with pleasure at all the latest styles.

'You mustn't go back to your flat,' Ruby insisted. 'Stay here as long as you like. Ernie and I are off the day after tomorrow. It will all blow over in a few days anyway.'

'Not in here it won't.' Faith touched her heart. 'My reputation is lost, but it's Dan's betrayal which hurts most. Thanks for the offer but I want to get away somewhere quiet where I can think and sort out my life.'

Ruby studied her shrewdly. 'This tour couldn't come at a worse time. I feel rotten leaving you to cope with this alone. Have you got enough dough to tide you over?'

'Yes, plenty.' Faith was curled up on an armchair, an unread copy of the *Tatler* open on her lap. It was all Ruby had for her to read. Not for her the housewife-orientated *Women's World* magazine or a novel.

'You look rough. I suppose you ain't been sleeping? I've got some tablets Ernie gave me. They knock you out like a light.'

'I won't take anything like that.'

Ruby was pacing the scarlet and gold lounge with such vigour the crystal lampshades jingled chaotically. She swung round, her hands on her hips. 'I could kill that bastard Dan with me own hands after the way he treated you. If he sets foot in London, Ernie will have his boys do him over.'

'I won't have talk like that.' Faith tossed the *Tatler* aside and got up to fetch her coat. 'I've only myself to blame for not being wiser. I still can't believe that Dan would betray me so cruelly. I'm catching a train in an hour. I've found a cottage to rent on the Isle of Sheppey for a month. It will be quiet there and no reporters. Here's the address.' She handed Ruby a piece of paper from her handbag. 'Don't give it to anyone, especially Dan. Not that he will dare show his face near me.'

At the pain in her voice, Ruby put her arm round Faith's shoulders. 'That's the ticket. Men! Life may be boring without them but I swear I'll swing for one yet.'

The door to the cellar opened and one of Dan's abductors entered.

'We go now. But I have to gag and blindfold you.'

'Where are you taking me?' Dan demanded.

A punch to his stomach doubled him over. 'No questions, or we kill you now.'

Both hands handcuffed and again blindfolded and gagged, he was led up the stairs and out into the street to a waiting car. The drive was interminable. The kidnappers did not speak. Eventually the car began to slow. His wrists were grabbed and he heard the click of the lock as the key turned in the handcuffs. Next Dan knew there was a rush of cold air as the car door was opened and he was shoved hard and fell with a thud on to a cobble street, grazing his knees and cheek as he landed. The car screamed away. Dan shook off the handcuffs and wrenched away the blindfold. It was daylight but the street was deserted. He staggered to the corner of the road and found himself on the embankment of the River Seine close to Notre Dame. The kidnappers had earlier taken his wallet but he had several francs in small change in his trouser pocket. He hailed a passing cab to drive him back to his hotel. The first thing he did on arrival in the hotel lobby was to phone Faith at the gallery.

'I don't know how you've got the gall to phone here,' Oliver screeched. 'Selling that painting of Faith at auction and not offering it to us. She's gone. We've had reporters sniffing round ever since that painting of yours hit the headlines.'

'What are you talking about? What painting? What auction? I've been in France for two weeks.'

'Huh! You may have pulled the wool over her eyes, poor girl, but you can't fool me. An auction like that and they would have got straight on to you with the news. Surely they have English papers in France. I don't like being used either, Brogan. My gallery was all right when you were trying to make a name for yourself. Now you've got international acclaim you go elsewhere.'

The phone went dead, burring like a wasp against his ear. Dan's head was whirling. None of Oliver Lincoln's words made sense. Except that Faith was no longer working at the gallery. Fear twisted his gut. Something serious had happened and it affected Faith. She wouldn't give up her job which she enjoyed so much without reason.

Dealing with practicalities first, he rang his English bank to transfer some money to a French bank for him to draw upon. It meant a further delay before he could leave Paris.

Then crossing to the reception desk he asked for his key and was also handed an English newspaper.

'This was delivered for you, Monsieur Brogan.'

When Dan saw his painting of Faith staring back at him anger dried his throat. The paper was dated the day after his abduction. How the hell had the painting been auctioned? Who had stolen it? The amount it had sold for staggered him. His mind reeled. Imelda was behind this. Somehow she'd got hold of the painting. That accounted for his being kidnapped and locked in a basement for four days. They spoke of ransom but it couldn't have been paid. Why then had they let him go free? And Faith? How had this affected her? Dear God, what must she be thinking?

'Who delivered this?' he asked the man behind the desk.

'I don't remember, Monsieur. I think an errand boy.'

As he turned away a priest in a long black cassock approached him.

'It is Mr Brogan, isn't it?' When Dan nodded, he went on, 'I fear I have bad news, Mr Brogan.'

Dan eyed him warily. What now? 'Your wife lies close to death. She tried to kill herself – a mortal sin. Mrs Brogan keeps repeating that you want to divorce her. Devil's deeds which will imperil your soul and hers.'

Dan took a moment to compose himself. How did Imelda know he was here? Was she behind his imprisonment as some form of twisted punishment? His wife's mental state was unhinged. It wasn't her first attempt at suicide. She had taken an overdose when he first left her to live a separate life. Of course, her maid had been close at hand to save her, she didn't intend to die, just emotionally blackmail him. He suspected that she had staged another suicide to prevent their divorce.

The priest was still speaking, making it impossible for him to think clearly. Dan's expression was bleak as he listened to the accusations.

'You have taken vows before God to love, honour and cherish your wife. You duty is to her above all else.'

All Dan wanted to do was find Faith and tell her that he loved her. Yet how in honour could he do that? He could imagine the pain and humiliation Faith was suffering.

'I will pay for my wife's medical treatment. The bills can be sent to my solicitor in London.'

'You cannot shirk your duty.' The priest's voice was low but it flayed him with its contempt. 'Your wife could be dying. She has been sinned against by you.'

'Suicide is also a sin, father. One of many my wife commits without conscience.'

'She is a wretched and unfortunate woman. She repents of her past life. She wants to be a good wife to you and you will not let her. She has asked for you. You have a duty before God to attend her.'

His conscience roped him to the Inquisition rack. Responsibilities held him tortured as the screw turned.

'I need to send a telegram before I go to my wife.'

His tread was as weary as an old man's as he returned to the reception desk. He wrote out a form to be delivered to the telegram office and forwarded to Faith's flat.

Imelda, without make-up, cheeks and eyes sunken, her lips bloodless and with a blood transfusion tube into her arm, failed to move his compassion. Her thin arms were outside the covers and the bandages around her wrists were white manacles tying him to a marriage and woman abhorrent to him. She was using her threat to manipulate him.

'This emotional blackmail won't work, Imelda.'

'Then my death will be on your conscience. I would rather die than face the shame of a divorce.'

'Don't be melodramatic. We both know you won't kill yourself. You enjoy life too much.'

She regarded him scathingly. 'What life would I have? I will live in penury and obscurity, while you become famous and live blissfully with your whore. I will not be mocked and set aside for a younger woman.'

There was a fanatical gleam in Imelda's eyes. She had always been unstable, believed herself above the law. But now there was also fear in her eyes. She looked old. He saw a line of grey along her scalp. Her black hair was dyed. Dan wasn't going to let her manipulate him again. 'Divorce me and I'll see that you have a generous settlement.'

Her gargoyle's smile was vindictive. 'But as my husband it is your duty to provide that anyway. Your mistress has abandoned you. She's gone into hiding after being hounded by reporters. Your career can only be enhanced by scandal. They expect it from artists. But what of her? I can ensure that her life becomes unbearable.'

She knew how to twist the knife. How to wield it to destroy.

Chapter Fifteen

Ruby was worried about Faith. She knew her friend was hurting although she was putting on a courageous face. Guilt pricked her that she was leaving to join the revue tour when Faith needed her.

'What is it with you two?' Ernie grumbled when she mentioned the subject. 'You ain't joined at the bloody hip. You're big girls now. You've got your own lives to lead.'

She didn't argue with him. Ernie wouldn't listen to anything which interfered with his plans. They were in his office at the club and he was restless after another call from the police. At the last minute he'd decided to accompany her on the tour. She suspected that he felt it better to get out of London for a while.

It was her last performance at the club before the tour. Every table was full and the place was crowded. When Ruby went on stage Ernie left the premises. She hid her disappointment. Before they married he always had a table reserved at the side of the stage to watch her. Ernie was turning out to be a jerk. An overheard phone call had told her more than she wanted to know about some of Ernie's deals. He was into money lending and when his clients didn't pay up she heard Ernie order Knuckles Stoker, the latest bar-room heavy, to do them over.

Ruby noticed Big Hugh seated at a reserved table at the front. Ernie had told her to play up to this man. Kavanagh liked to feel important. Dutifully, although she detested him, she sang her last two songs to him.

With her routine finished she moved amongst the tables, flirting and encouraging the men to buy champagne and drink her health. Aware that Ernie had not returned to the club, she decided to call it a night and go home. They were leaving early in the morning for Blackpool. She went up to the office for her coat. The door opened and Big Hugh entered. For once his two brothers weren't with him.

'Ernie ain't here,' Ruby declared.

'I wasn't looking for Ernie.' Hugh leered at her in a way which made her stomach heave. 'That was some performance.'

Ruby shrugged, feeling a prickle of unease at the way he was gazing at her breasts. 'So how about you showing me what that come-on was all about?'

She stitched on a smile, pretending a levity she wasn't feeling. This man gave her the creeps. 'It's all part of the act. I always flirt with the punters, it don't mean nothing. I'm a married woman.'

'Marriage wouldn't stop a woman like you having a bit of fun.'

'I think you had better leave, Mr Kavanagh.'

He shook his head. 'Not before I get what I came for.'

As he advanced towards her Ruby ran for the door. He caught her arm and spun her round and slammed her against the wall. 'Don't play hard to get. All I want is what you were promising me out there.'

His hand jammed down between them, painfully grabbing her crotch, probing deeper through the satin of her gown. 'That was just an act. And what about Ernie? He don't allow me to fool around.'

'I can deal with Ernie. Besides it can be our secret.'

Ruby tried to bring up her knee but his thighs were like clamps preventing her. She struggled to pull away and the narrow strap of her gown broke, the material sliding down to reveal one breast.

Ruby yelled and lashed out at him, her high heel striking down on his toe. He yelped liked a whipped dog, his grip loosening. A hard push released her and she snatched up her coat, pressing it against her to hide her ruined dress and ran from the office.

Pete Kavanagh was already halfway up the stairs at hearing his brother's cry. Ruby whispered, 'It's all right, Pete. I inadvertently stepped back on Hugh's toe.'

Knuckles Stoker, built like a tank with lank hair falling over his collar, grinned up at her as she walked down the stairs. She was shaking so violently, she almost tripped. But she knew better than to show Kavanagh up in public. 'Mr Kavanagh is just leaving, Knuckles. Ernie says he's to have a bottle of champagne on the house. And call me a cab. I'm going home. Let Ernie know if he comes back here, will you?'

She followed Knuckles outside and was relieved that an empty taxi was passing. She didn't fancy having Big Hugh coming after her.

Once inside her home she poured herself a stiff drink. It was then she heard a noise from the bedroom. Ernie must have come home early. She smiled. After Hugh's sordid attack, she wanted to be cuddled and made love to by Ernie.

With a soft giggle she pulled her gown over her head and tossed it aside. She could already picture the ardour with which Ernie would pounce on her naked body. It made her breathing ragged with anticipation. Wearing only her stockings, ruby garter and high-heeled shoes, she pushed open the bedroom door and flung her arms wide.

'Hi there, darling! Look what I've got waiting for you.'

Her invitation froze on her lips. Two feet with scarlet-painted toenails were wrapped around Ernie's neck and his naked buttocks were pumping into the woman's writhing body.

'You bastard!' Ruby screamed. She picked up the ice bucket holding the empty champagne bottle and tipped the ice over the two bodies. The woman squealed and Ernie swore.

She swung the bucket, aiming it at Ernie's head. He deflected the blow. She turned on the woman, grabbing her bleached hair with its line of dark roots. Her long nails were hooked into talons as she dragged the woman from the bed and began lashing into her. The woman swore obscenely, revealing she was a common prostitute off the streets. That was more humiliating than if she had been a high-class whore.

Rolling across the floor, they kicked and scratched, tearing at hair, biting at any piece of flesh which came into the range of

207

their teeth. Sweat poured off Ruby as she reared up, her breasts swinging as she slapped the prostitute across the face, gouging her cheek with her diamond engagement ring. Ruby was an accomplished fighter. Life in the orphanage had taught her to defend herself at an early age.

The prostitute was no match for her and coiled into a ball. 'Leave off. I was only doing what he paid me for.'

Breathing heavily Ruby turned on Ernie. He was standing over them, his eyes glazed, his erection like a truncheon at watching two naked women fight.

'What are you doing home?' he rasped. 'You were supposed to do another session at the club. But that show was something else,' he added, falling on her. 'A real turn-on having me missus fighting for me like that.'

The prostitute was edging towards the door. 'Get back here,' Ernie demanded. 'I've got enough for the two of you.'

Even Ruby's fury could not regenerate her energy. She was exhausted from fighting the whore. She had no strength left to ward off Ernie's assault. He rammed into her, his body stinking of the whore's scent and sex. Unable to fight him, she lay perfectly still as he raped her. With each thrust her heart turned colder. She had not expected her marriage to be all roses and heavenly choruses. Neither had she expected it to plunge her so quickly into a living hell.

Chapter Sixteen

On his return to England Dan went straight to his studio. It was obvious it had not been burgled. Nothing but the painting had been taken. It smacked of Imelda's greed and vindictiveness. His abduction had been an elaborate charade to keep him in Paris. Imelda had paid those apes to keep him imprisoned until the painting was sold and she had worked her evil to destroy all that was precious between Faith and himself. God willing, in that she had failed.

The staggering figure the painting had sold for meant nothing to Dan. He'd never see a penny of it. Nor would he want to. It was Judas silver. The fame he had craved left a rancid taste in his throat. Acclaim was hollow. A tinsel crown when he feared how much Faith had suffered. He would have given it all up and been content as a penniless street painter to have Faith as his wife and safe from harm.

Armed with the truth, he drove to Faith's flat. He was desperate to placate her, to shield her from further pain.

After several rings of the door bell, it looked as if Imelda was right and that Faith had gone into hiding. Her heart must be breaking at what she would see as his treachery. Did she hate him now?

The hollowness enclosing his heart increased. His need to reassure her and tell her that he had not betrayed her trust was overwhelming.

''Ere, ain't you Brogan?' A disembodied voice emerged from the shadowed doorway opposite and a scruffy man in a greasy raincoat and battered Derby hat stepped into the daylight. 'Ain't you the artist fella who painted the tart who lives here? Bit of all right she was. Wouldn't mind having a taste of that meself.'

Dan's temper snapped. He spun on his toes and rammed his fist into the man's jaw. 'Miss Tempest is a lady.'

The reporter rubbed his unshaven chin. 'Come off it, mate.' He chuckled and pulled out his notepad, rattling out questions like machine-gun fire. 'She were your mistress then? I thought so. Got any other paintings of her posing nude that you gonna sell? Funny you ain't been about while all the fuss was going on. Married though ain't yer? The missus must have caused a stink when she saw the painting. Society woman weren't she – your missus?'

Dan turned away sickened. If this was a taste of what Faith had endured, how could he possibly make it up to her?

He rang the ground-floor bell and a disgruntled landlady opened the door a crack. Her chin-length hair hung down flat each side of her sallow cheeks and a smudge of scarlet lipstick weaved across her thin lips. 'I ain't talking to no reporters so piss off.'

'I'm Dan Brogan. A friend of Miss Tempest. You must recognise me. I wondered if you knew when Miss Tempest would be back.'

'Never would be too soon,' the landlady grimaced. 'Disgusting business. She's not been here all week. She scarpered and left me with a mob of reporters hanging round. Six weeks' rent she paid in advance. This is a respectable house. Her kind ain't wanted here. Dirty little tramp, posing like that. I want her room cleared. She can find herself somewhere else to live.'

Her attitude filled Dan with misgivings. Faced with so much hostility and censure it was small wonder that Faith had taken flight. But where would she go? And for how long?

Anxiety lacerated him. He had to find her. Explain. Ease her pain. His thoughts were fragmented by his anguish for the woman he loved.

With Imelda being so unstable their immediate future was uncertain, but having tasted the joy Faith could bring to his life, he didn't want to lose her. Why in heaven's name had he painted that blasted portrait? Faith hadn't wanted him to. He, idealistic idiot that he was, had insisted. In her love she could deny him nothing. His arrogance had believed them inviolate – now that precious love was desecrated.

Dan went to the Gilded Lily seeking Ernie or Ruby who must know where Faith had fled. Neither was there. He'd forgotten the wedding and Ruby's tour. Mike Rivers was unwelcoming and antagonistic as soon as he walked in the door.

'You ain't welcome here, Brogan.' Mike faced him with clenched knuckles, his eyes glinting with anger. 'That were a dirty trick you played on Faith. I hope you're happy now that you've got your fame and fortune at the expense of her reputation.'

His frustration exploded. 'I had nothing to do with the sale of the painting. I've got to see Faith. Let her know I never betrayed her trust.'

'Why, you lying . . .' Mike stepped forward, his fist lifted. Then as he stared into Dan's stricken face, his arm fell to his side. 'So out with it. How come the painting got sold if you had nothing to do with it?'

Dan was tempted to tell Rivers to mind his own business and just tell him where Faith was. But he realised that Rivers was protecting her. And God knows she needed loyal friends.

'I love Faith,' Dan said softly. 'I would never harm her. The painting was stolen by my wife. She saw it as means to get back at me for caring for another woman.'

'Conveniently for you, it also made you rich and famous.'

'Is that how Faith sees it?'

'What do you expect? That she should applaud your treachery!' Mike was again antagonistic.

Dan tipped back his trilby, his stare haggard as he regarded the musician. 'I've got to see Faith. I must know that she's all right.' His eyes pleaded more eloquently than his words. Dan was not a man to beg, but for Faith he would humble himself if he had to.

'Do you intend to divorce your wife?' Mike challenged. 'I

heard she was worth a mint. Kept you in style for years by all accounts. Weren't you a penniless artist when you married her?'

'I've never touched her money,' Dan rapped out, but baulked at explaining his marriage to a stranger. Yet Mike wasn't going to tell him where Faith was, unless he did. Dan would be the same if the roles were reversed. He must appear the lowest scum on earth; little more than a gigolo in the musician's eyes. And he hadn't lived with Imelda in years. 'Are things ever as cut and dried as they appear? My wife is mentally unstable. She's in a Paris institution after attempting suicide because I wanted a divorce.'

He broke off, his stare bleak as he added wearily, 'I know Faith must be hurting. I can't put back the clock. Though I'd give everything I own to do so. I need to speak with her. Are you going to deny her the satisfaction of slapping my face and telling me what a no good bastard I am?'

'Putting it like that, I reckon not.' Mike's expression no longer judged him. 'I never reckoned you a man who'd treat someone as fine as Faith like dirt. She's left London. Wanted to go where no one knew her. Chose the Isle of Sheppey in Kent of all places. Ain't nothing there hardly. Takes you hours to get there by train. I suppose she wanted isolation.'

'Have you got her address?'

Mike shook his head. 'Ruby's doing a tour of old music halls. They left this morning to drive to Blackpool. I'll ring their digs tonight. I doubt she'd take a call from you. Give me your number and I'll contact you.'

'I'll go to Sheppey. I spent a week painting there one autumn.'

'Bit of a backwoods place for you, ain't it?'

At Mike's incredulous stare, he explained, 'It's sparsely populated but its isolation appealed. The mist rising off the marshes gave the passing ships a haunting quality. I believe I spoke of it to Faith once. I'll telephone you from Sheerness when I arrive and let you have my number.'

When he called Mike he learned that Faith had taken a rented cottage the other side of the island on the cliffs at Warden Bay. The track leading to the cottage on the cliff was unsuitable for traffic. He abandoned his car and walked the last half-mile on foot.

There was a bracing wind despite the bright sun which beat down. Sheppey in June was very different from when he had visited it in October. The sky was cobalt with pennant-thin clouds trailing out to sea. The sea was a deep jade spangled by white-crested waves.

The single-storey cottage stood some distance from its nearest neighbour, about two hundred yards from the edge of the cliff, and there was a wood close by. It was a tranquil setting for someone needing the healing that nature can give. He stared at the lion-head door-knocker for several moments, willing Faith to be inside. He knocked. There was no answer. He knocked twice more, loud and insistent. Still no answer.

Frustration ground through him. Refusing to walk away, he went round the side of the cottage and opened the tall wrought-iron gate. At first the garden appeared empty. There was a raised herb garden outside the kitchen door and beyond that an oval bed of roses, the first blooms just opening to perfume the air. An expanse of lawn was edged by shrubs and at the far end was an orchard. Trees of hazel, beech and rowan framed the far boundary which led into the wood.

There was no sign of Faith. Yet the tranquillity of the garden penetrated his morose mood. The sound of the waves breaking on to the base of the cliffs was soothing. A pair of collared doves flew out of a beech tree on the edge of the wood. It was then that he heard the persistent creaking. Moving towards the sound, he paused to stare in wonder. Faith was on a swing hanging from a sturdy branch. She wore a large straw sun hat. Her head was thrown back as she stretched out her legs and then bending them behind her made the swing rise higher. The full skirt of her cream summer dress trailed behind her. He was mesmerised. It was a vision which would be carved in his memory for the rest of his life.

Slowly he walked towards her. She did not notice him. She was lost in the soothing rhythm of the swing. She kept her head tilted back and legs together and outstretched as the swing gradually lost its momentum.

He waited for it to halt before he softly called her name. Since leaving Paris he had planned what he would say to her. But as her head jerked up, her hat fell to the ground and his rehearsed speech dissipated with the onset of shock.

'Your glorious hair! What have you done to your hair?'

She was off the swing and running towards him like an arrow from a bow, her aquamarine eyes flashing with a light which struck straight at his soul. He stood rigid as her fists hammered against his chest.

'My hair! Is that all you can say? You were always obsessed with it. I'm glad I cut it. I hate it. It wasn't me you loved, it was my hair. Get out. Leave me alone. I don't know how you dare show your face here.'

He didn't even try to stop her attack, painful as it was. Neither did he touch her. His thoughtless words had been a catalyst channelling her anger. She looked more beautiful to him than ever. There was no hatred in her eyes as they glinted up at him. The shadows of disillusion were in their depths and the fire of resolution wounded him more powerfully than her blows.

In a voice gruff with torment, he said, 'My darling, I am so dreadfully sorry about what happened. I never sold that painting. It was my greatest treasure. It was taken from my flat while I was in Paris. I never learned about the auction until a few days ago.'

'Lies. All lies!' Her fists struck him with every word, her breathing laboured from her exertions. 'Like everything else you told me. Or rather didn't tell me . . . Such as being married. Even our love was a lie.'

'I never lied about loving you.' He gripped her arms, staring at her with fierce intensity. 'I was wrong not to tell you about my marriage, but I told you my reasons for that.'

She shoved herself away from him, holding her hands against her chest as though any contact with him was now repulsive to her. 'Yes. You were worried you might lose your prize model.'

The pain in her voice smote him. 'I was only worried I would lose the woman I love.'

'But your art was still more important, wasn't it?'

He sighed, wanting to crush her in his arms and kiss her pain away. But that would be an insult to her. She deserved her time for accusations. They were part of the healing.

'Once I would have said that art was the only thing worthwhile in my life. That was before I met you. Imelda stole the painting. She sold it because she knew it would drive a wedge between us. I swear I knew nothing about it.'

'Strange, it also happened to be your best work and sold for more money than I'm likely to earn in a lifetime. It made you rich. And don't try and tell me there are no English papers in Paris.'

'Not where I was. You were not the only one to fall prey to Imelda's schemes.' He battled to keep his own anger at the injustice he had suffered from his voice. He spoke to her softly, cajoling as a horse breeder gaining the trust of a wild mare. He told her of his experiences in Paris and finished by saying, 'It was Imelda's malicious way of ensuring that I knew nothing about the auction until it was too late.'

Faith hugged her arms tighter about her. She stared at him, torn by wanting him and retaining the anger roused by his betrayal. How could she trust him? Dare she trust him? There was a shadow of beard along his jaw and dark circles under his eyes. She wavered, wishing her heart was not thudding so violently. Wishing he was not so handsome that even now she could not look at him without wanting him. She remained firm, her body still. If she moved all resolve would crumple.

He went on heavily, 'I don't deserve your forgiveness after what you've gone through. But I need to know that you do not believe I could betray your trust. I was an idealistic fool to paint you as I did. The artist and romantic are damning traits in my Irish blood.'

She digested this, seeking to remain aloof despite the thunderous clamouring of her heart. It meant a great deal that he had not betrayed her.

'Did you speak with your wife about a divorce?' She flung it out like another accusation, still too raw and distrustful to lower the defences she had so carefully built against him.

'Yes. She refused to consider it. She attempted to take her life. Her mind is too unstable to discuss it reasonably with her at present.'

Faith hung her head, weighing these words, not trusting herself to speak, nor wanting to make it easier for Dan. She wasn't going to build false hopes, she had already accepted the path of her future life.

There was a nasty bruise on his temple and a cut on his cheek which gave weight to his incredible story. No sane woman would pay men to treat her husband like that.

'If I go ahead with the divorce,' Dan continued, 'Imelda has threatened to create a scandal which will destroy you. I love you too much to see that happen. There is no end to the evil of which she is capable. I have to wait until she is in a more stable frame of mind. It's not even as though the woman loves me. She never loved me.'

'Perhaps you underestimate yourself, Dan. From what you have told me of your wife, she cannot bear a man to slight her. She believes herself irresistible. Yet you no longer find her attractive. She cannot forgive you that. Her behaviour is hardly that of a rational woman. All the time that she's unhappy with an unfulfilled relationship, she will begrudge you the chance to find happiness with another.'

Slowly he reached out, placing his hands on her shoulders. When she did not pull away he drew her closer, his thumbs caressing her jaw. 'I'd ask you to wait until I am free of her, but . . .'

Faith closed her eyes. 'Dan, I would wait an eternity for you.'

His finger traced the seam of her lips, his eyes dark with the force of his emotion. 'I love you too much to bring you harm. Imelda would create a scandal making you appear the scarlet woman and her the wronged wife. I won't risk that.' His control broke. His arms slid around her, holding her against him. The warmth of his breath fanned through her short hair.

'Damn Imelda,' he grated out. 'Say you forgive me. Tell me you know I didn't betray you.' His embrace tightened. 'I love you. If there was any way on earth that we could honourably be together . . .'

'And Imelda's threat to kill herself?' Faith asked fearfully.

'A bluff to control me. She tried it before when I first left her. There was a maid close by to come to her aid. But enough of those problems. What of yours? Are you carrying my child?'

She shook her head. 'It was a false alarm.'

The pain of her loss was in her eyes and he took her face in his hands. 'My darling. Perhaps it is for the best, but I cannot rejoice.'

'I would have been proud to have borne your child, Dan.'

His hungry lips answered hers. 'Oh, Faith, I missed you so much. I thought I had lost you.'

There was no restraining the fiery trail of kisses which caressed her face. Mouths parted, tongues touching, seeking unity. Their breaths mingled, the force of their passion stronger than reason, stronger than sensibilities.

His kisses took her by storm, at once bruising in their intensity, then instantly cherishing, rendering her incapable of resistance. The sunlight became their only clothing as they sank on to the warm grass. When she saw the yellowing bruises on Dan's body it was further evidence of all he had suffered. She knew he had not betrayed her. It made her passion stronger. The scent of bluebells and early roses was in the air, a blackbird and cooing doves serenaded them.

As Faith drifted on a sea of passion she was convinced that Imelda was bluffing. A beautiful woman like her could have any man she chose for a husband. Any man but Dan.

Both Dan and Faith had not bargained on how unstable Imelda's mental condition was. Two days after her discharge from hospital, she turned up at Dan's studio.

A demonic argument ensued. She raged. She screamed abuse. She uttered threats and curses. When those failed, she flung herself at his feet, clinging to him and sobbing. 'You can't abandon me. I need you. I will never divorce you. We can start again. I've changed, Dan.'

Carefully he prised her fingers from his legs. Her outburst was too melodramatic and ten years too late. 'For once in your life, accept the inevitable gracefully, Imelda. Our marriage is over.'

She left the studio cursing him, her mind seething as she opened the bottle of gin lying on the front seat of the car.

An hour later a policeman rang Dan's door bell. Still angry after the scene with Imelda, Dan eyed him balefully.

'Mr Brogan?' the policeman enquired.

'Yes.'

'I regret that your wife was involved in an accident at Epping. She ran her car off the road into a tree.'

Dan stared at him dumbly. Was this another trick of Imelda's? Another faked suicide?

'It is unlikely your wife will live,' the constable informed him gravely. 'She's unconscious and has suffered severe spinal injuries and broken both her legs. She's gone straight into surgery.'

Dan closed his eyes but nothing could shut out the nightmare he was locked in to.

He spent the night in the hospital waiting room. He had been allowed to see Imelda briefly as she lay unconscious. Her head was swathed in bandages and both her legs were in plaster. At three in the morning the doctor approached him.

'Your wife has recovered consciousness, Mr Brogan,' he announced gruffly. 'She was lucky to escape with her life. But I have to tell you she may never walk again. Her spine has been damaged.'

'How long before you can tell whether she will walk?'

'Your wife needs special care. It could be months before we know for certain. I noticed there are marks on her wrists . . . ?'

'My wife tried to kill herself recently.'

'And she nearly succeeded again today. She needs psychiatric help. Why should she be trying to kill herself?'

Dan turned away to look out of the window at the overcast

night. Imelda had won. He was trapped. Her insanity and evil had destroyed her body and with it his life. How could he divorce her now that she was a cripple and totally dependent on his support?

Fate has its way of mocking worthy intentions. Faith conceived in the garden on the Isle of Sheppey. It was also the last time she had seen Dan. With Imelda so ill, her conscience would not permit her to be his mistress. When she went back to Underwood & Lincoln to collect her things, she was surprised when Oliver rushed to greet her.

'My dear Faith, forgive me. I was wrong to berate you as I did. But I'd had this awful row with Charles and the reporters were such a trial. I took on a new assistant.' He rolled his eyes to the ceiling. 'He was handsome, debonair, but, my dear, I can't tell you how unsuitable. He could have been selling kitchen pots instead of fine art. I've had Mr Devereux and several other regular customers asking after you. They were most put out you were not here to serve them.'

'Was it me they wanted or the woman in the painting?' she answered waspishly.

'I can understand that you're upset. And I was insensitive. Your job is open if you still want it.'

She was still angry at Oliver's attitude. But she needed work and she would never better Oliver's offer. She accepted it graciously.

It was to prove a blessing when she discovered that she was pregnant. The fuss in the papers over the mysterious model in Dan's painting proved a seven-day wonder. Some customers commented on her change of hairstyle, and although one or two looked at her slyly, to her relief none mentioned the subject of the painting. The memory of her humiliation at the hands of the reporters was not so easily brushed aside. She never wanted to be in that position again.

She didn't tell Oliver that she was pregnant until the fifth month when it was beginning to show.

'I was starting to wonder,' he observed. 'Some of the customers will be offended. Stick a ring on your finger and you

219

can stay on until you cannot hide your condition any more. That's the best I can offer, I'm afraid.'

He had been considerate and eager to make amends since she came back. She was lucky he was being so understanding; many employers would have dismissed her.

She had also started to look for somewhere else to live. She'd left her original flat after an unpleasant scene with the landlady and had taken a cheaper place. Now she was thinking of moving further afield where no one knew her. She would have to pass herself off as a young widow when her child was born. She needed to be accepted as that from the start.

She was in the back of the gallery filing invoices when she became aware of a presence behind her. She turned, her heart leaping. Dan was in the doorway, staring at her.

'Oliver told me you were here. I dropped in a couple of paintings Charles Underwood bought from me.'

She stood with her hand on the filing cabinet, fighting against the impulse to throw herself into his arms. He was thinner and the strain of the past months was etched around his eyes and the hollows of his cheeks.

'How have you been, Faith? You look well.' His gaze slid from her face to rest upon her swelling stomach. The contours of his face sharpened. 'Oh my darling, why didn't you tell me?'

'You had problems enough.'

'You're so stubborn!' His anger surfaced. 'Did you think I'd abandon you?'

She shook her head. 'I'm coping.'

'I'm sure you are.' His voice remained crisp. 'Didn't it occur to you that I would want the best for you and our child? I've been denied enough. Don't stop me doing this.'

His words made her feel ashamed. 'I always meant to tell you. I just kept putting it off. And I was managing. I'm going to have to leave work in another month.'

His restraint broke and he moved towards her. She stepped back and held up her hand. 'Please, Dan. If you touch me I'll break down. I shall realise all that might have been . . .'

'Get your coat. We've things to discuss. Oliver will understand. It was he who told me you were out here.'

Dan took charge, refusing to listen to her protests.

In the following month he brought her a three-bedroom Victorian house at the end of a terrace, which overlooked the common land of Wanstead Flats. The front garden was small with a black and white diamond-patterned path and rosebeds. Although most of the houses were rented, it was a respectable neighbourhood. It was furnished and redecorated throughout and an inside bathroom, toilet and electricity were installed before he allowed her to move in.

He had helped her with the move and as they sat in the front room at the end of an exhausting day, she refused to accept his offer of a monthly allowance.

'You've done enough, Dan. And I am grateful. Don't make me feel like a kept woman.' They were sitting in armchairs on opposite sides of the sitting room. Since their reunion at the gallery Dan had not attempted to kiss her or hold her. But his yearning for her was stark in his eyes. It echoed the restraint she had put upon her own emotions. Faith kept her hands tightly clasped together. Being in the same room as Dan and not giving in to the need to hold him was torture. Dan looked gaunt. He had lost weight since Imelda's accident. He was working through the night often without sleep to finish his paintings for the exhibition. By throwing himself into his work he was able to find some peace from the torment of his own anxieties.

She remained obstinate. 'I can support myself and my child.'

'I have the right as its father.'

'I would never deny you those rights,' she said, her heart aching at the pain in his eyes.

'But you would deny our love?'

'I have never denied that. But while Imelda is an invalid, I could never reconcile my conscience to being your mistress. And you can't divorce her in the circumstances. We have to accept that we cannot be together. You also have your career as an artist to consider.'

'I would give it up for you.'

At his sincerity, her resolve crumbled. She knelt at his side and took his hands. 'You would come to hate me. Painting is more than a way of earning a living for you. It's a vocation. Things are at their darkest now, but we are fighters, Dan. We will survive and so will our love. You cannot fight your destiny. If we are meant to be together we will be, but not at the expense of ruining other lives.'

'Why is it that what I love most in you – your sense of right and loyalty – is what now keeps us apart?' He lifted her hands to his lips and kissed them. 'Imelda is recovering. I have not given up hope that she will walk again. There are specialists in America. I've written to them. I'm over there for a second exhibition in May. This time in Los Angeles.' He leaned forward. 'When Imelda is cured . . .'

Faith put her hand across his mouth. 'Let's take each day at a time. I'm delighted you've got the success you deserve as an artist.'

'It's lost its appeal without you. I'm still working from the sketches I did of you. But it's more important to me that you have everything you need. Don't add to your burden by being too stubborn and independent. I shall set up a bank account for you with five hundred pounds in it.' He tried again to persuade Faith to accept an allowance.

'No, Dan.'

His stare was piercing. 'I can afford it. My paintings are selling for good prices now. I've paid off Squire Passmore's debts and there's enough to meet Imelda's medical bills. It will be there if you have need of it. I need to know that you have that security while I am away in America. And I want you to use it to continue your art lessons. You have talent. How can I pursue my career if you have sacrificed yours?'

'Very well.' Faith agreed to ease his conscience although she had no intention of touching the money. It was a matter of pride that she could support her child and herself on her own.

PART TWO

Neither do I condemn thee: go, and sin no more
Bible

Chapter Seventeen

'You're a fool not to see Dan, if you still love him,' Ruby told her for the hundredth time. 'Especially as the baby is due. It's not as though Imelda is a proper wife to him. Or has been for years. Your independence is foolish. Why should you shoulder all the responsibility? For heaven's sake, he's wealthy. Make him pay . . .'

'He's not rich. His paintings sold well in America but not for the high prices of my portrait. And he never got a penny from that. Imelda has the money stashed away somewhere for her own benefit after she's bled Dan dry. He bought me this house, that's enough.' Faith rubbed the small of her back to ease the ache which had been troubling her on and off all day. They were in the garden in the mild Spring sunshine with Faith insisting on planting some herbs and summer bulbs.

'A woman has got to provide for her future,' Ruby continued.

Faith barely heard her; she was visualising how the garden would look next year when the baby would see it. She held up a hand to halt her friend's lecture. 'My child will want for nothing. We've been over all this before. I love this house. I can walk across the common every day. The people are friendly and have accepted me. Madge next door has been a good friend. My only regret is that they believe I am a young widow. I hate lies and deceptions.'

'I suppose you think I've not been the friend I should have been.' Ruby stopped Faith digging a hole for more bulbs and did it for her. She was defensive, resenting the ease with which Faith had made women friends. Other women were too suspicious of

Ruby's looks and predatory manner to befriend her. Silly cows. Except for Faith she'd rather have the company of men any day. In the last year Mike Rivers had often turned up when she had needed a friend. He could handle Ernie.

She mentally shuddered. Marriage had showed her the real bastard her husband could be. The revue tour had been exciting and she had been popular but was far below the star attraction. Fame had eluded her yet again. No other work had been offered since. One council had banned her act and she had been charged for performing indecently and had to appear in court next month.

'Good bit of publicity!' With this Ernie had brushed aside her fears that she could go to prison. 'It'll be a godsend, see if it isn't. Your name will be splashed across every paper in the country. You'll be hailed as a Sex Goddess. Ain't that what you want?'

Ruby wanted fame more than she wanted riches. She would never understand how Faith could be happy slaving to pay the rent by taking a mundane job in the corner bakery until a few weeks ago. Faith had scrimped and saved throughout her pregnancy. She never spent a penny on herself except for food or to pay for those daft art lessons she was always going on about.

As Ruby stared at her friend, she had to admit that though Faith's life had nothing in it to recommend it, she did looked radiant. There was a self-possession about her, a maturity which had not been there a year ago.

'If you don't get money from Dan,' Ruby pursued, 'how you gonna cope when the nipper's born?'

'Madge has two children at school and a six-month-old baby. She's agreed to look after mine so that I can work. The money will help her out. Her Dave is a bit too fond of stopping off at the pub after work, and she has trouble making his wages stretch.'

Faith had made her plans carefully. She was determined that her child would want for nothing when it was born. Every evening for months she had been hand-sewing baby linen. Madge had taught her how to knit and she had made several layettes all in white. Seeing Ruby's frown Faith assured her, 'I intend to go back to working in an art gallery. That's what I'm good at. And I've

226

continued studying and have been visiting auctions when I could.'

'It's still all work and no play. For Gawd's sake, don't be so stubborn. Brogan can set you up proper. Pay for a char to do the housework, even a nanny for the kid.'

Faith was about to protest when a knife-sharp pain stabbed low in her back. 'Could you ask Madge to pop in, Ruby? I think it may be the baby coming.'

Ruby paled. 'Gawd!' She panicked, darting to the door, back again for no reason, and then to the door again. 'Ain't it early? I can't leave you. Hell! Don't you need a doctor? A midwife?'

'Just get Madge,' Faith insisted as another pain struck with a severity which made her gasp. 'She knows what to do.'

Ruby returned with Madge. Her neighbour was six inches taller than Ruby's petite frame and well endowed with the ample curves of a motherly hen which suited her easy-going nature. Her short curly brown hair was partially hidden under a green paisley scarf knotted on top of her head. A navy-spotted cross-over apron covered her white blouse and calf-length black serge skirt.

She smiled encouragingly at Faith. 'I've sent Dave to fetch Mother Dawkins. She'll check out how far gone you are. Have you been having the pains long?'

'They could have started in the night. I thought I was in for a gyppy tummy.' Faith sat back in the chair as another pain swept over her. When it receded she said, 'That's the third in about ten minutes.'

Madge turned to Ruby who had lit a cigarette and was poised on the padded leather arm of a chair. 'You gonna sit there like a stuffed doll, or are you 'ere to be useful? 'Cos Mother Dawkins will be wanting hot water and lots of it.'

Ruby went out into the scullery and there was the sound of running water and banging of enamel saucepans. She carried two back and stared helplessly at the kitchen range. 'How do you use that contraption?'

'I'll do it,' Madge complied. 'You're more decoration than use. Sit with Faith.'

Ruby perched on the chair arm looking ill at ease.

'You don't have to stay, Ruby. I know you don't like illness and babies aren't really your style are they? Why not come back tomorrow when it's all over? I've been told I shall need a few days in bed, though I don't intend to stay there the fortnight the doctor was talking about.'

'I won't leave you,' Ruby insisted. 'I'll pop down the corner shop and call Ernie. He can get Miriam to cover for me. Now she's married she's happy to fill in now and again for some extra cash. Ernie can bring me over a change of clothes. I'll stay here while you need me.'

Faith reached out to take Ruby's hand but a contraction made her grip it so hard that Ruby winced. When it faded Faith said, 'Thanks, Ruby. I appreciate that. Madge is a brick but she has her own family to look after.'

Mother Dawkins, a stick-thin woman in a long black coat and black straw hat, arrived to examine Faith. Ruby left to make her phone call. Ernie was displeased at the news.

'How am I gonna get a singer at such short notice? You get yourself down here tonight, or else.'

'Don't start with the "or elses", Ernie. Miriam will fill in. Faith needs me. She's having her baby. She ain't got no one else. Tonight ain't one of our busy nights. Can you bring me some overnight things and another dress?'

'What do you think I am, your bloody servant? I'll send one of the boys over with your stuff,' Ernie bellowed down the line. 'And mind you're at the club tomorrow night. We'll be busy then.'

Ruby knew he would make her pay for defying him tonight. But what was one more beating? She could give him almost as good as he gave her. Trouble was, the fights were getting more frequent. Ernie got turned on by the way she paraded on the stage, but straight sex was becoming a thing of the past. Ruby didn't like many of his 'games' as he called them. After Ernie had been unfaithful to her, she had taken a lover. When her husband found out, the man was run down in a traffic accident the next day. Squinty Watkins was driving. Ernie had beaten her so badly that she'd spent two weeks in hospital. She hadn't taken another lover and regularly drank herself senseless to forget her troubles.

Ernie had never liked her friendship with Faith. It was through Faith that Ruby was aware of her own failings. That the good-time life she craved could be hollow. Unhappy in her marriage, it made her hunger for stardom more acute.

Nathaniel Tempest was born as the soft apricot hues of dawn filtered through the branches of the sycamore tree outside Faith's window. A blackbird trilled the first notes to be accompanied by a full dawn chorus. There could be no sweeter music to accompany Faith's son's arrival in the world. He was wrapped in his night-gown and shawl and placed in her arms, the pains of his birth forgotten as she stared down at his tightly shut eyes and dark halo of hair. Love swelled her heart until it felt it would burst. Tears of happiness blurred her vision.

'He's so tiny. So precious,' she breathed.

'Looks a bit like a skinned rabbit to me,' Ruby announced.

'He's a darling,' Madge crooned. She had returned with an uncanny sixth sense just as the head had appeared and the baby was born.

Faith smiled at her friends. 'Thank you for being here. I want you both to be godmother to him.'

Ruby, who was never moved by children, stared at the infant and experienced a glow of happiness. She had sat on the side of the bed all night holding Faith's hands, talking softly and urging her on when the pains became bad. It had reaffirmed her belief that child-bearing was not for her, but there was a lump of pride in her throat that Faith had chosen her to be Nathaniel's godmother.

'My godson must have the best pram money can buy. It will be my special gift to him.'

Madge saw that Faith was looking exhausted although her eyes were bright with excitement. Gently, she took the baby from his mother's arms and laid him in the dark oak cradle which she had loaned Faith. Its carved wooden sides and steeple hood had been made by Madge's great-grandfather. 'Sleep now, Faith. I'll call back later and do what I can.'

When Madge left Faith gazed at her son as he slept. Ruby sat on the side of the bed and held her hand. 'You've a fine son. But it ain't right that you bring him up all on your own. He needs a father. Imelda Brogan is a scheming bitch. She'd ditch Dan soon enough if it suited her purposes.'

'That's hardly likely while she is still in hospital undergoing treatment. It looks like she'll be confined to a wheelchair. For months she was in a psychiatric hospital until the doctors were convinced that she would not try and harm herself again.'

'Like I said, the woman's a lunatic,' Ruby jeered.

Faith pressed a hand to her brow; she wasn't up to this argument with Ruby. 'You're right about Nathaniel not being deprived of a father. Will you phone Dan and tell him of the birth? He should see his son. He goes to America again in two weeks. He's got a second exhibition there as the first in New York was so popular.'

'I'll ring him. I don't know why you haven't got a phone installed. Brogan can afford to pay for it.'

Faith shook her head. Ruby would never understand that she was content to live simply. And a telephone would make it too easy to contact Dan. As it was they limited themselves to an exchange of letters once a week.

Ruby was unsettled as she sat in the dressing room of the Gilded Lily putting the final touches to her make-up. The mirror told her that she had never looked more gorgeous. She had grown her hair longer and the Marcel waves framed her face and fell to her shoulders in a silver-gold cloud. This wasn't the fame Ernie had promised would be hers. The court case for indecency had resulted in a fine, but the revue had not re-engaged her. Nothing in her life was as Ernie had promised. He was proving a liability. But Ernie would never allow her to leave him.

'No one walks out on me,' he had warned her. 'I ain't finished with you yet. You didn't think I married you for love, did you? I've spent a fortune on you and I expect a return for my money with interest. You're me wife and you'll do as I say. Make a fool of me and you'll regret it.'

He hadn't been joking. Knuckles Stoker had been nicking money from the till. He was found floating in the Thames with both his hands cut off. Ernie owned her. He even creamed off ninety per cent of her earnings, leaving her with a pittance.

Ruby refused to let Ernie get it all his own way. He only got ninety per cent of the money he knew about. Any trinket or money she received from an admirer was hidden away in a box she kept at Faith's house.

She was packing the punters in at the Gilded Lily, so much so that Ernie was buying out Mike's share of the club. Kavanagh was putting up a half-share to open a second club. Mike had got himself a club by the river in Chelsea. That had started this latest row with Ernie. He was scowling across from her now. All she had done was agree to sing in Mike's club for a few evenings until it became established. Ernie had hit the roof and slapped her across the room, until she had reminded him she had to sing in an hour.

'I ain't going out there with a fat lip. So just leave it out, Ernie.' She countered by biting his wrist which had wound around her throat.

He'd pushed her away. And poured himself another drink as he watched her cover a darkening bruise on her cheek with more powder. He'd been drinking heavily all evening and Ruby's manner angered him. She was too fond of nagging him for not being more like Mike.

His eyes narrowed with resentment. Mike was getting above himself. Always lecturing him about what he could, or couldn't, do with the club. He'd also given Ernie the beating of his life after Ruby had ended up in hospital. Mike had warned him to lay off hitting Ruby or he'd get the same treatment from him again. Mike saw himself as Ruby's champion because he fancied her. Ernie gloried in that power over his brother. And as for Mike's threats . . . he'd been biding his time. One day every insult, every warning, every bit of action Mike had spiked, was going to be accounted for – with a vengeance.

He glared at Ruby now as she preened in front of the mirror. Her looks could still make him desire her, the way she moved driving him beyond reason. But he'd be damned if he let her be aware of it. His indifference kept the power in his court and not hers.

'What you trying to do, yer stupid bitch, cut our throats?' he growled at her. 'Let Mike find his own singer.'

'But that's not fair,' Ruby defended. 'Mike's talent as a musician made this club successful before I came along. The least you can do is repay him.'

'Repay him! He's held me back. I could've made something of this place. Built it up with gambling out the back: Black Jack, Roulette. You name it. I've got enough coppers on my payroll for them to turn a blind eye.'

Ruby went cold. Drink was making Ernie's tongue run away with itself. She knew he had always resented Mike's interference in the running of the club. He wasn't usually this indiscreet as to blab about the secret side of his life.

'But the police do come round,' Ruby persisted. 'What about those jewellers' robberies they thought you'd done?'

'That's just it. They were bought off. Nothing came of it. Kavanagh made sure they got their cut and they made sure their investigations drew a blank.'

He was strutting back and forth across the room, his swagger more exaggerated than usual.

'Not all the police are corrupt. It don't do to get cocky, Ernie. What do you want to go pushing your luck for? We don't do bad here. We'd make more if you got me some decent dates and followed up on that music hall tour.'

'That's in hand. I've got big plans for you.'

Ruby was no longer convinced he could give her the success she craved. Ernie would be the one to get rich, not her. She was becoming embroiled in a life which had lost its glitter.

The rigours of the birth caught up with Faith the following day. She had slept little, her mind whirling around thoughts of Dan and their baby. It was late afternoon and there had been no word from Dan. Ruby had been unable to get through to him at the studio by phone and had sent him a telegram. Each hour dragged. She realised with alarm that she hadn't received a letter from Dan that week. Could something have happened to him and no one had let her know? Was he ill? The uncertainty of their relationship was highlighted by her worries. It was a hellish way to live, not having the right to know if he was well or ill. She pitchforked her fears aside. They had decided on the course their future must take. She must not allow a moment's weakness to ruin it.

Nathaniel snuffled in his sleep. She was more fortunate than many women. She had experienced a profound love and she had her memories and now Nathaniel. There was no room for regrets. She settled down, trying to compose her mind. She must sleep to recover quickly from the birth. Ruby had left to sing at the club and had promised to return in the early hours of the morning. Madge frequently came in to check Faith had everything she needed.

Eventually Faith dozed. It was dark when a sound made her open her eyes. She could just make out Nathaniel's dark head above the white blankets in the cradle. Then her heart jolted with fear. Above him a dark figure loomed into her vision, holding a candle high over the baby and a hand outstretched as though to snatch him from his crib.

'No!' she cried, and heedless of the pain swung her legs over the side of the bed.

'Don't move!' a deep voice commanded. 'It's all right. I didn't mean to startle you. Madge let me in.'

'Oh Dan,' she answered inadequately, too full of emotion to say more.

He put the candle down on the bedside table so that it threw its light over both mother and child and sat down on the edge of the bed, taking her hand in his. 'I didn't put the light on. Madge said you needed to sleep. How are you? You look radiant.'

'I'm fine. But how did you explain your arrival to Madge? She thinks I'm a widow.'

'I said I was a friend. But from the look she gave me, I think she guessed I was the father.'

Guilt at having lied to Madge furrowed through her, but it was fleeting, she was so overjoyed to see Dan. There was a single cry from the cradle and Faith saw that Nathaniel had opened his eyes.

'Pick him up if you wish,' she prompted softly. 'He is your son. His name is Nathaniel. Nathan for short.'

Daniel looked dumbfounded. 'We never spoke of names. I had a twin brother Nathaniel. He died at birth. You could not have known that.'

'I was going to call a boy Henry after my father, but when he was born and I looked at him, the name Nathaniel came into my mind and I knew it was right for him.'

Dan picked up his son, holding his own body stiff and awkward as he carried him to the bed. The love Faith saw shining in his eyes almost destroyed her resolve. Her own love for Dan had not abated.

'How is Imelda?' she finally asked.

'She's out of hospital, but goes back twice a week for treatment. The doctors say that she has a manic nature. Naturally she blames me for her condition. They've given her electric shock treatment, ice baths and all manner of ghastly remedies. I've engaged a full-time nurse who watches over her night and day. The specialist in America has agreed to treat her. She will travel with me when I leave in a fortnight.'

'Will you be living together?' Jealousy choked her.

Dan shook his head. 'No. I've made her sign a Deed of Separation. But I'll continue to support her.'

Guilt attacked Faith that she was responsible for Dan's wife's condition. If they had not become lovers, Imelda would not have attempted suicide. Her self-inflicted injuries were horrific, the more so for a woman who had pursued pleasure as Imelda had done. 'I pity Imelda. She had so much and now she has so little.'

'Save your pity. She was trying to bring me back to heel and her plans went wrong. It wasn't love which made her drive into that tree. It was spite. And God forgive me, but I've no pity left for her. She has taken too much that was precious from me.'

'Dan, it's not like you to talk that way.'

He hung his head. 'I know. And I hate myself for it. But seeing you and Nathan . . .'

Overcome with love for him, Faith took his hand. He smiled wearily. 'Imelda was a hedonist caring only that her own insatiable whims were satisfied. A sane person would not have manipulated people as she did.' He reached out to cup her cheek in his hand. 'I've missed you so much, my darling.'

She turned her face to kiss his palm. 'And I you. But Nathaniel's birth changes nothing between us. It cannot. But you may see Nathan whenever you're in England.'

'I shall be in America for several months. I'll write with my address.'

His love for her was in his eyes but when he leaned forward to kiss her, she drew back, her voice cracked with pain. 'Don't make this harder than it is, Dan. For Nathaniel's sake we must be friends, nothing more.'

'You're a courageous woman, Faith Tempest. I love and admire you.' He placed Nathaniel in her arms. 'He couldn't have a more worthy mother. Be happy, my darling.' Dan stooped to kiss her cheek and left the room without a backward glance. She heard his deep voice as he spoke to Madge and then the door closed behind him as he left.

Sadness washed over Faith. She held Nathaniel tenderly, her eyes filling with tears and splashing down on to his hair as she kissed his temple.

Madge appeared with a cup of tea, her voice kindly as she took the baby from Faith and laid him in the crib. 'Go on, weep all you want. It's better out than bottled up inside.'

Her capable arms enfolded Faith and she rocked her gently as though she were her child.

Eventually the tears stopped and Faith smiled wanly at Madge. 'You've guessed he's Nathaniel's father, haven't you? He's married. Do you hate me now? I wish I'd never lied to you. You've always been so kind.'

'Get on with you,' Madge answered. 'Wasn't my eldest born just six months after I married Dave? And isn't that young man

235

of yours handsome enough to make any woman fall for his charms? He loves you, that's also obvious. And don't go thinking that I'll gossip about what went on here tonight. I wouldn't be much of a friend if I did, would I?'

'I don't know how I would have coped without you, Madge.'

'Think nothing of it. That's what friends are for.' Her expression was drawn with sadness as she regarded Faith. 'Married men are trouble. More so when they are as handsome as your Mr Brogan. He ain't gonna be an easy man to forget.'

'I'll never forget him, or stop loving him,' Faith replied softly. 'But I have a new life now. And there's no point hankering for what might have been. My life was the richer for loving Dan. And I was blessed to bear his son. I have no regrets. Only a future to build.'

Chapter Eighteen

'You said you'd make me famous,' Ruby screamed at Ernie when he was pushing her to be hostess at yet another party. 'One lousy revue tour and that was it. Fine manager you are. I ain't working the Gilded Lily the rest of me life.'

'You'll do as I say,' Ernie flared back. 'So quit complaining. I've me own interests to sort out.'

'I'd never have married you if I'd known it would be like this. Mike says if I took acting lessons I could be in a West End musical.'

'Mike will say anything to get into your bed.' Ernie grabbed her and shook her hard. 'And you know what will happen to the two of you if I ever find out that he has.'

He slapped her cheek and stormed out of the house. Ruby was proving a liability. She wasn't getting the breaks he'd expected. He'd had offers from other clubs but why should he lose her as a draw to the Gilded Lily? Her act went down better in small clubs rather than the large halls. He was sick of her moaning. He made more money from a single jeweller's job than he had out of her tour last year.

He closed his ears to her complaining. Now that he was a partner with Kavanagh they would soon have a string of nightclubs, all catering for gambling in private rooms. Ruby would be an asset to draw the punters. She was worth more to him in the club than touring the country. Ruby was popular with the rich young men who came to the club, men with money to throw around and Ernie was determined that it would all be thrown in his direction.

A month after Nathaniel's birth Faith began looking for a job. She was determined to work in an art gallery and was also continuing her lessons. The spare bedroom of the house in Wanstead had been turned into a studio where she spent any spare time painting.

It was soon apparent that many art dealers were prejudiced against hiring women. And with so many men still out of work, it made it even harder. Her lack of qualifications also made it difficult even though Oliver Lincoln had given her a good reference.

She paused outside Hornsey Brothers, a double-fronted jewellers window in Walthamstow High Street. One of the windows contained several paintings which were for sale on the first floor of the shop. The shop had advertised for a temporary assistant for their art showroom. Two of the paintings in the window were good examples of a popular Victorian artist. A third she suspected was undervalued. It was by a little-known Edwardian artist whose work was now being sought by the big auction houses. The window was poorly lit and there were too many paintings on display to show any to their best advantage.

The bell tinkled rustily as she opened the door and stepped into the shop. Glass cabinets lined the walls, the largest containing large items of silverware and another antique clocks, all ticking noisily. Four glass counters displayed jewellery and watches. A tall, thin man appeared from the back room. His ascetic face was lined, and he regarded her through a pince-nez perched on the end of his hooked nose. 'How may I help you, Madam?'

He wore a black frock coat and pinstriped trousers and a red velvet smoking cap covered his bald head. His age was indeterminate and on first glance she judged him at close to sixty. On seeing his thick black eyebrows, however, she guessed he was only in his late forties. 'I'm Mrs Tempest. I'm enquiring about the post as sales assistant.'

He studied her over the top of his pince-nez. 'You look rather young to have had much experience as an art dealer. But it is my brother Gerald who will interview you. Please come this way, Mrs Tempest.'

She followed him into a back room which held a large black safe and also served as a parlour. It was cluttered with heavy Victorian furniture. Every surface was covered with porcelain and bronze figurines and tall antique vases. The room was like a treasure trove. A phonograph with its huge trumpet was playing a crackling Caruso recording. Gerald Hornsey was seated in a bathchair, a tartan blanket over his legs. He was as short and stout as his brother was tall and thin. He also wore a formal morning suit with an old-fashioned frock coat. A triple chin rested on a high-winged collar with a bright paisley cravat tied in elaborate folds and held in place by a huge gold pin. He had thick brown hair peppered with grey which curled over his ears and collar and he looked younger than his brother. They were an incongruous pair, but when Gerald Hornsey smiled at her, two dimples appearing in his florid cheeks, she instantly liked him.

For half an hour Gerald Hornsey fired questions at her. He studied her reference and nodded appreciatively. 'What was your impression of our window display?' he ended by asking.

She lowered her eyes, unwilling to appear rude, but feeling that honesty was the best policy. It was obvious that Gerald Hornsey was not as up to date on current art trends as Oliver Lincoln or herself.

'The display is cluttered. The paintings detract from each other. And the Edwardian artist is undervalued. One of his works sold last month for three times that price.'

He lifted a fleecy grey eyebrow and glanced across at his brother who had left the room twice during the interview to attend upon a customer. 'The position is temporary not permanent,' he informed her. 'That is why we have been unable to engage a man. They are after a permanent position. I feel for the families of all the men out of work. The situation is getting worse but most of the unemployed are labourers. They have not the expertise needed. No one we interviewed saw anything wrong with the window display. You have a point. Sometimes a woman has an eye for such things. You were previously employed as a sales assistant with Underwood and Lincoln. Why did you leave?'

'I was expecting my son. Now I prefer to work closer to home with shorter hours.'

He nodded. 'Would you accept a temporary position? You are a widow, I understand?'

'Yes, but I would like to know why it is only temporary.'

'I broke my hip three months ago. It's not healing as it should. We are a small business. We cannot afford to lose the art sales. Neither would it be practical to keep on another employee once I am up and about again. At present I cannot get up to the showroom. I had hoped for a man to take the post so that he could drive me to auctions or out to visit customers. Can you drive, Mrs Tempest?'

'No, but I would be willing to learn. It has never looked very difficult.'

He laughed. 'I like your pluck. You're not frightened of taking on what is considered a man's role.'

'The government have finally given all women the vote now, Mr Hornsey. I am the breadwinner, a widow with a baby to bring up. My knowledge of art is as good as any man's. I am a good saleswoman and I would enjoy learning to drive.'

'Then the job is yours, Mrs Tempest. It is six days a week.'

Faith's initial pleasure died. She hadn't wanted to leave Nathaniel for so long. But since the post was temporary she had little choice and the extra money would come in handy.

It was now obvious to Ruby that Ernie wasn't bothering to promote her as a singer. He was too embroiled with Kavanagh and his villains. At least while she worked at Mike's club, the River Boat, it introduced her to a wider audience. It was her first night there tonight. Ernie had insisted that she return to the Gilded Lily at one in the morning for a final session there.

'At least you keep the late-night punters happy that way. If you insist on doing Mike a favour by singing for him for a few weeks, it don't mean you can neglect my club. You'll have to work all three clubs at once when my new club opens next month.'

Ruby would be exhausted by the time she finished at the Lily at four in the morning. Ernie was pushing her too hard. She paused inside the bar of the River Boat. The club's name was a play on Mike's name and the fact that it was by the Thames, close to Vauxhall Bridge. It was superior to the Gilded Lily. The decor was more subtly lit with triangular painted glass wall lights. The walls were panelled with walnut and mahogany in geometric designs and photographs of the great jazz musicians decorated the walls. There was a cleared space for dancing and twenty tables ringed the dance floor. Behind these was a raised area of thirty more tables where customers could also dine.

It was the opening night and Ruby was shown out the back to a dressing room by the doorman in evening dress.

'Mr Rivers will be with you directly, Miss Starr. The accountant is with him at the moment.'

'I'm early. We have to run though some numbers before the club opens.'

She scanned the room when the doorman left. There was an armchair and even a divan bed. She grinned. Now that had possibilities, but not for resting. There was a bottle of French perfume on the dressing table. She lifted the top and sniffed its fragrance. It was heavenly, more exotic than the overpowering perfume which Ernie always bought her. She dabbed it behind her ears and on her wrists. She was not so impressed at discovering two evening dresses hanging behind the door. It looked as if Mike had engaged another singer as well as herself. It took the edge off her excitement. The singer had put her stamp of possession on the dressing room. They must be her perfume and dresses.

When Mike appeared, she regarded him with pleasure and surprise. He was in evening dress and bow tie, his brown hair still unrestrained by brilliantine flopping forward over his brow. It was a drastic change from the open-necked shirt and trilby which Mike usually favoured at the Lily.

'You look terrific, Mike.'

'New club. New image. There's nothing seedy about the River

Boat. Top class jazz, by the best musicians.'

'Is this how you wanted the Gilded Lily to be? I can see why you got irritated with Ernie. The place is very stylish.'

'Style attracts people with style. I've seen too many seedy joints and the corruption which lingers just below the surface to want any part of that.'

Ruby leaned back against the dressing-table and smiled enticingly. She had fancied Mike for months, her attraction to him heightened by not taking other lovers. For him she was prepared to face Ernie's anger. Mike was a match for his brother's bullying. Hadn't he done Ernie over last time he'd beaten her so bad she'd ended up in hospital? Trouble was, Mike might flirt with her, but he never went further than that.

'How many numbers do you want me to sing? Ernie's being difficult. He insists I'm back at the Lily by one to do a turn there.'

Mike frowned. 'He's working you too hard. I shouldn't have asked you to sing here.'

She pushed herself away from the dressing-table and ran a finger along the lapel of his dinner jacket. 'I'd do anything for you, Mike. I know how you've kept Ernie in line. Stopped him hitting me like he used to.' She could feel his heartbeat pounding hard beneath her fingers and tipped her face up to smile into his. 'I must've been mad to marry Ernie.'

'Is he treating you all right now?' He took her hands and held them in his, preventing her sliding her fingers inside his jacket and over his chest. He was tense, holding his emotions in restraint.

Ruby knew that Mike was not as immune to her as he made out. She wanted him so badly. No man had held out on her wiles as Mike had done. Why did he continue to refuse her? It made him even more attractive and an irresistible challenge.

Ruby sighed. 'He's all right.' She looked up at him through her lashes. 'He ain't a good man. Not like you, Mike. You know how to treat a woman right.'

She moved against him so that her breasts caressed his chest. 'You've got style, Mike. This place says it all. All Ernie sees is the fast buck.'

Mike stepped back so that their bodies didn't touch. 'I wanted to go over the numbers you'll be singing tonight. I thought we'd go for the slow songs. And I don't want you parading on the stage. I want you seated on a stool by the piano as I play.'

'But my act is the way I move,' Ruby said aghast.

'Not in this club. You're a beautiful woman. You don't have to come on so strong to the customers. You're a singer. You ain't out there to sell yourself. Give them an illusion of seduction, and they will love you all the more.'

Ruby voiced her hurt. 'You saying I'm cheap?'

'I'm saying that Ernie has misguided you. You've got class, Ruby. Use it. You move like a Goddess of love without resorting to blatant sexuality.'

She was mollified by his compliments. Mike's opinion was important to her.

'We've got two hours before we open. Let's run through some numbers.'

He led her out to the grand piano where a high stool had been placed beside it. Perched on it, she leaned against the piano. He played a couple of love songs but she didn't feel right as she sang them. Her body was too constrained. When he began the opening bars of the third number she grinned at him and hitching up her skirt used the stool to climb onto the top of the piano and perched more decorously with the skirt falling back to reveal her crossed legs from the knee down. Now as she sang she leaned back to sing the more romantic lines, her eyes teasing and flirting with Mike.

'This is more like it,' she said as the number ended.

'As long as you don't fall off,' Mike countered. 'It is certainly different.'

'Couldn't I come on stage when it is blacked out and the lights go up with me reclining on the piano lid? I could swivel round for the second number and sing sitting upright.'

'It could work. We'll try it if you like. And I want you to change your image and the way you dress here. There's a couple of gowns hanging up behind the dressing-room door.'

'I ain't wearing someone else's dresses.'

Mike grinned. 'They're yours. So is the perfume. I bought them for you.'

'You did!' Her initial joy quickly withered as suspicion struck. That was how Ernie first got her embroiled in owing him money. Look where that had led? She worked for peanuts.

'Ernie's got me money all tied up in that damned contract. I can't repay you and I ain't gonna work for you for nothing as well.'

'You mean Ernie doesn't hand over the money you earn?' His surprise was genuine. 'He had your contract drawn up without my knowledge. What's he up to, Ruby?'

'Screwing me in every sense of the word,' she snapped back bitterly.

Mike looked furious. 'And you think I'm out to do the same?'

'You're his brother. I thought you were different. But blood will out in the end, as they say.'

'Dammit, Ruby. Those dresses were a gift. A thank-you for singing here. And I'll pay you a fair wage and make sure it doesn't get into Ernie's greedy hands.'

'You mean that, Mike?' Ruby's eyes shone with pleasure. 'You bought me the dresses with no strings attached?' She slid from the piano to kiss his cheek.

His arm slid around her waist and for a moment she thought he was going to kiss her. He stood back, his smile wry. 'I insist you wear the dresses here. They're better for your image. Go and try them on.'

Ruby frowned when she held the first dress against her figure. It was a narrow sheath of white satin which covered her breasts and was split from the floor to the knee. Over this was a tulle overdress which glistened with silver sequins that fanned out from beneath the bust in a spray to the hem. It had a high neck which circled her throat and the transparent material also covered her arms with tight-fitting sleeves. It was both modest and elegant.

The second dress was of a similar design but in black with jet beads covering the tulle in a different pattern. She decided on the black. It fitted her to perfection. To complete the outfit there was a black sequinned cap which sat on the crown of her head with her blonde hair fluffed around it. As she stared at her reflection in the long mirror behind the door, she was amazed at the difference. She looked sensual, glamorous and sophisticated. She looked like a film star.

There was a tap on the door and she was ushered out to take her place on stage. Throughout her performance she was aware of Mike's eyes on her. She sang for him. There was a deeper resonance in her voice as she concentrated on the romantic inflections needed for the song, instead of acting out the role Ernie insisted that she play before his customers.

When her final song ended, the applause was deafening. Mike was smiling broadly as he came round to put his hands on her waist and lift her down from the piano. There were calls for more, but none of the usual lewd catcalls which followed her performance at the Gilded Lily. Mike stepped back for her to take her bow and when they finally allowed her to leave the stage, he led her back to the dressing room.

'Don't you want me to mix with the punters?'

'No,' he said emphatically. 'They are here to enjoy your singing. Be a woman of mystery and they will adore you all the more.' He turned to go and she put a hand on his arm.

'You're not going to leave me alone. I'm all buzzing after my performance.'

'As the owner I should be mixing with the customers. The house is only half full and I need their goodwill to spread the word that this is the place for a good time. I've got you to thank for making it a success tonight.'

'And is that all I get? Just a thank-you?' She had moved so that she was between him and the door. 'I felt like a star tonight. Someone special.'

'You are special, Ruby.'

'Am I, Mike?' She slid her arms around his neck and pressed herself against him. 'We make a good team.'

Her eyes were heavy with desire and every pore of her body

was aware of him as a handsome, virile man. Yet she was aware of his tension, of him fighting to resist her. She smiled and leaned her head on his shoulder, her body swaying against him. 'The band is playing. Stay a few minutes. Dance one dance with me. Ease the loneliness, Mike. For I am lonely. You know Ernie doesn't love me. Nor I him.'

'He's your husband, and my brother,' Mike said heavily. His fingers enclosed hers, gently drawing them from around his neck. She stood on tiptoe and with their hands still linked together, she kissed him on the mouth, her lips moving persuasively, hungrily. There was a moment of resistance, then with a groan, he was returning her kisses, with a fierceness which exhilarated her.

He buried his face against her neck, kissing the sensitive flesh behind her ear as he unfastened the back of her gown. It slid over her shoulders as she moved slightly so that it fell unhindered to the floor. She removed Mike's jacket. Ruby scarcely breathed when Mike picked her up and carried her to the divan. He laid her tenderly on the cover and stood back to strip off his clothes, revealing a hard muscular body. His shoulders were broad and his waist narrow and stomach flat. He lowered himself to her side, his body half covering hers, his hands reverently caressing her breasts and stomach in a way which made her glow with an urgent and glorious rapture. The heat spread through her, expanding, soaring, and with a sigh she curved against him, her arms pulling him down to her.

It was she who was impatient to experience his complete possession of her. 'Take me, Mike. Make me yours.'

He kissed her throat, his lips tantalisingly travelling over her breasts and ribcage, making her cry out, making her want him with an intensity with which she had never wanted a man before. Still he did not enter her. His kisses were endless. They roused her to greater heights. He paused every few moments to gaze down at her with desire and love; smiling as he gauged her reactions. He was gentle, considerate, her own pleasure more important than his own. Never before had she experienced the deeper joy of true loving. Lust was different. It was the mindless coupling

246

enslaving the body without harmony, without the oneness she felt now.

He was taking her to the edge of a precipice then skilfully maintaining the fine balance between blossoming ecstasy and frustration. His unhurried lovemaking was poignant and more fulfilling than she had dreamed possible. She was writhing, desperate to be his. 'Now, Mike. Please.'

Mike needed to keep his mind detached or he would fail Ruby. Like every man who had seen her perform he had wanted her. But he wanted the real woman, not the sensuous shell which a quick tumble could satisfy. To control his passion he watched her lovely face moving from side to side with the pleasure he evoked. Her nails scoured his back, her body glistening with perspiration as she reared up, her legs binding him closer. As her release exploded through her, she called out his name. Only then did he increase his pace, moving inside her, so that her moans of ecstasy rekindled, her mouth curving and throat arching, her cries muffled by his kisses as he brought her again to fulfilment.

Ruby felt she was floating on a cloud of contentment. Her body had never been so replete. Mike was gazing at her without speaking. He swallowed convulsively. Then with a groan he sat up, sinking his head into his hands.

'I've wanted you for so long, Ruby. But I never meant this to happen. Hell, you're my brother's wife!'

'Then I'll leave him.' She knew she would never have a more perfect lover than Mike. She'd known enough men to know when love hit her and she was reeling with the heady sensation of it now. And crazily, now that she had found love, she didn't want to lose it.

'Then you mustn't return to him tonight.' Mike cradled her against him. 'I can handle Ernie.'

Her eyes widened with fear and she threw her arms around him, holding him tight. 'I ain't never felt this good, Mike. And I'm scared. Ernie is mean. He ain't gonna take this lying down. He'll kill us both.'

Mike kissed away her fears, but in his heart, he knew Ernie was

247

capable of anything. But he couldn't give Ruby up. He'd fight his brother with all the means in his power.

Chapter Nineteen

'I've got to go back to Ernie, tonight,' Ruby said after they had dressed. 'I must have been mad to sign that contract. If I leave him I won't be able to sing again.'

Mike pulled her to him. There was such tenderness in his eyes, emotion tightened her throat.

'I'll look after you,' Mike promised. 'You don't need to work. But he can't stop you singing here. It's my club. You'll be here as a customer and called on to the stage by popular demand by the diners. You'd be singing as a favour to them. As far as Ernie is concerned money won't come into it.'

'Ernie will sue me for breach of contract and loss of earnings.' She realised that although Mike had few illusions about Ernie's ruthlessness, he still saw him as his kid brother. Her husband had not shown his brother his darker side. The violence. The perverted sex. The inflated belief in himself that he was a big-time villain immune from the law.

She sighed, gauging how little she could tell Mike while warning him of the danger. 'Ernie will never let me leave him. I know too much about him and Kavanagh.'

Mike's hazel eyes glittered with protective anger. A vein was pulsing in his temple but he kept his voice reassuring as he caressed her cheek. 'We'll convince him you won't say anything. It don't do my reputation any good having a villain for a brother. That's what he is, isn't he?'

'Ernie is bad news. And I'm gonna leave him. But if he gets wind that there is anyone else, especially you, he'll go berserk.

He ain't above setting Kavanagh's gorillas on you, or wrecking this place.'

'I can't let you go back to him. You'll be in danger.'

She smiled grimly. 'I can handle Ernie. I ain't taking any risks. I know things about him which can get him put away for a long time. That's the only way we'll be safe, Mike. I need time to make sure I've got proof. I'm pretty sure he's turned over those jewellers' which the police were investigating. He reckons he's got the law paid off, but all coppers ain't bent.'

Mike clenched his fist and his body was tense with suppressed anger. 'I knew he was up to no good, but he always denied involvement with Kavanagh.'

'Ernie was always sparing with the truth. Him and Big Hugh are partners.'

Mike paced the room. 'You've got to protect yourself from Ernie. Write down any proof you have of his illegal activities. Discredit his alibis on the days of the robberies. It will go in a sealed envelope and be left with a reputable solicitor and will be opened if anything happens to you. Even if Ernie tries to rough you up again, the solicitor will pass the letter straight to the police.'

'Ernie ain't gonna like that.'

'We both know you won't use the information unless he tries to harm you. It's your safeguard. Use my solicitor and address it to Inspector Terry Armitage. He's been after Kavanagh for years and he's not on Ernie's payroll.'

Mike kissed her brow, his voice gruff with frustration and anger. His eyes were troubled as they gazed deeply into hers. 'I had me suspicions about Ernie and Kavanagh. I should have done something about it.'

'What could you do? Don't blame yourself, Mike.'

He looked defeated. 'His old man was a crook. He's spent most of his life in the nick. Ernie's gone the same way. That's why I wanted out of the partnership. At first I thought owning a club would keep Ernie straight and give him a decent living. He weren't interested in jazz, he wanted to use the club as a cover for a gambling den and he'd have been peddling drugs if I hadn't come down on him hard.'

Ruby twined her arms around his neck. 'Don't spoil this moment by talking of Ernie. This is our time, Mike. And it's too short to be spoilt. Love me, my darling. Make me forget the bad things.'

Mike responded to her kisses, but his conscience was uneasy. He was in love with his brother's wife and the only way he could safely claim her as his own would be if Ernie was locked away in prison. And hadn't he promised his mother that he would do everything in his power to prevent that?

Hatred for her husband was all that kept Imelda alive in the months following her accident. Her plan to teach Dan a lesson had gone disastrously wrong. She had intended to crash the car into the tree and then pretend that she was seriously wounded. Fate had mocked her. She'd drunk so much gin that she misjudged the speed and the angle of the corner.

Now she was a prisoner in this damned wheelchair. With daily muscle massage and exercises she had been tied to the Los Angeles hospital. It might be the best that money could buy, but it gave her no satisfaction. If she was going to screw Dan for every penny she could, she at least wanted to be enjoying herself.

Yesterday Paulo Santiago had been recommended to treat her. His treatment was described as unorthodox, but his success rate was high. And he was selective about the patients he worked with. She was waiting for him now. As soon as she saw him, she knew he was the right specialist for her. He was in his late twenties with olive skin and smouldering dark eyes and thick black hair. He was more exotically handsome than Rudolph Valentino had been. Just looking at him and imagining his hands on her was a therapy in itself.

'Mrs Brogan, your accident was eleven months ago and you have been here for five months now. Still there is no improvement.' He examined her solemnly. 'You are a beautiful woman, a tender hot-house bloom. These austere walls are not the place for such a delicate creature to heal. You need a house with an all-weather swimming pool set in beautiful grounds.'

'You are so right, Mr Santiago,' Imelda answered, devouring him with her eyes. 'I am unhappy in here. Everything about hospitals is so depressing. All you suggest will be done. No expense will be spared.' She held out her hand to him and he took it and raised it to his lips.

'If you have faith in me I will make you walk again.'

Discharging herself from the hospital she persuaded Dan to rent a house with a pool and a full-time nurse and maid in attendance. Paulo attended her twice a day to massage and exercise her legs and back. Swimming was one of the exercises that she was encouraged to do and she also engaged an ex-lifeguard called Ricky Leighson to carry her to and from the pool and attend her in the water. He was as fair as Paulo was dark. Having two handsome men dancing attendance pandered to her vanity, making her feel like a pampered queen and the men her devoted slaves. Her body might be numb from the waist down, but it didn't stop her enjoying the sight of Ricky's muscled half-naked body when they swam together. After her swim, Ricky carried her to the table where Paulo would massage her. He also worked stripped to the waist.

This morning her pleasure in having Paulo attend her was marred by anger. The newspapers had shown a photograph of Dan and had praised his paintings. The Americans adored his work. She scowled at the memory. As his wife, she should have been there at Dan's side instead of shut away in this house. Only one of the papers had mentioned her name. And that showed Dan as the considerate husband. It heaped praise on him for the expensive treatment he provided for the recovery of his estranged and crippled wife.

'Saint Daniel Brogan,' she muttered. 'I could tell the papers a few things about him.'

'Did Madam speak?' Paulo enquired.

She clamped her jaw tight as his competent oiled fingers paused in kneading the muscles of her thighs. Too often she spoke aloud. It wouldn't do to give the servants food for gossip. She might threaten to expose Dan as an adulterer to the papers, but she had too much in her own past to hide to risk any exposure being turned upon herself.

'It was nothing, Paulo. But I could do with a glass of champagne. Be an angel and summon Marie.'

'No need to trouble Marie. I will do it.' He always acted the gentleman. There was always champagne nearby kept constantly on ice. She lay on the table wearing nothing but a towel draped across her hips. She took the drink, sipped it and smiled over her shoulder at Paulo as he continued to work on her thighs and calves. 'Will you join me? I hate to drink alone.'

'Not while I am treating you. Perhaps later.' He regarded her with a mixture of respect and admiration. Imelda thrived under such attention. He was worth every dollar of his extortionate fees. There was no feeling in her legs but when he moved up to her spine, his thumbs circling across her waist, the faintest sensation like warm water on sunheated skin was detectable. It was like the first drop of rain after a long drought to Imelda. She closed her eyes, savouring even this minute response.

'Work lower, Paulo. You have magic in your fingers. Sometimes I imagine that I can feel pleasure in a man's touch again.' She reached back and snatched off the towel. 'My body is so useless. Is it ugly to you?'

'Madam knows she is beautiful.' Paulo began his professional patter, adept at pandering to older women's vanities. It was second nature to him. It had enabled him to pay for his medical training and still live reasonably well. He came from a large, poor family. At seventeen he became a gigolo to bored and wealthy women. Until then he had picked up what odd jobs he could. But he was ambitious. He wanted big cars and expensive clothes and the lifestyle of the rich. The older women had bought him the cars and clothes he craved. When he realised how much money there was to be earned treating the rich, he had decided on his future profession. His natural charm and appreciation of women had done the rest. Two years ago he had qualified.

'A woman of twenty would be proud to have your figure,' he answered as his hands slid over her buttocks. Knowing that she could not feel his touch he could indulge his own sensuality. He could never get enough of women, even the older ones. The touch of female flesh excited him and this one was a born tease. He'd seen her swimming naked with that muscle-bound ape Ricky. She never hid her figure from him and watched his reaction as his hands moved over her.

'Madam is more relaxed today,' he said.

'I wish you would call me Imelda.'

He smiled. 'A beautiful, exotic name like its owner.'

Imelda soaked up his compliments as her numb body soaked up the perfumed massage oil.

His eyes narrowed and his fingers kneaded harder, cruelly, into the unresponsive flesh. They slid into the cleft of her buttocks, diving deeper, probing the core of her. It made him grow hard and before his breathing betrayed him, he removed his fingers from her heat and began pummelling her flesh, back over her buttocks to her waist.

'What are you doing?' Imelda murmured, raising herself on to her elbows and half twisting so that he could see her breasts with their dusky aureoles. 'Come round here. Are you misbehaving, Paulo?'

'Imelda, I have too much respect for you. It is part of the treatment.'

He could have kicked himself for being so stupid. He had thought he could get away with anything with this one. Her expression revealed nothing.

'How long have you been treating me, Paulo?'

'Six weeks.'

'Come round here.' She pointed to the front of the couch. 'I want to see you.'

He did as he was told, aware that he was still aroused. She laughed throatily at seeing the bulge of his erection and licked her lips. 'So you *do* like my body.'

'How could I not? And you are so perfect in many ways. I

254

admire your courage. You still take pleasure in life. If only you were not my patient, I . . .' He sighed regretfully.

'But a body to heal needs sustenance, does it not?'

Her hand touched his groin, her fingers walking along the tumescence, her tongue protruding provocatively between her teeth. 'I am but half-alive. It's been so long since a man touched me as a woman should be touched. Passion is as much a mental stimulant as a bodily one.'

'Sometimes the patient is wiser than the healer. You're more attuned to the needs of your body. You must tell me your needs.'

She giggled throatily and undid his fly and her lips fastened over him, sucking and licking until he groaned. He bent over her, his hands sliding over the perfumed oil sleeking her back. As his body jerked in orgasm, his hands clenched, his nails digging into her. She moaned softly, her torso and hips shifting just perceptibly.

Paulo gasped. 'Imelda, you moved. Your hips moved.'

She sighed languorously. 'Your hands feel divine. Has any woman given you as much pleasure as I just did?'

'No, Imelda. I have never met a woman as exciting as you. But you misunderstand. Your hips moved. It means that with time you will be walking again.'

'Paulo, is that true?'

He moved round her to run his hands over her waist and spine, squeezing, pinching until she groaned. 'It's like a feather skimming my flesh. I can feel the warmth and more . . .' Her hips gyrated stiffly. 'I can feel it. Oh, Paulo. Thank you. Thank you.'

She pushed herself upright and he swung her still useless legs round so that she was sitting facing him. Taking his hand she put it on her naked breast. 'Kiss me, Paulo. Make me feel alive. Make me feel desirable again.'

'You will always be desirable to me, Imelda,' he lied, mentally calculating just how much money he could make out of this rich, spoilt woman.

Life settled into a routine for Faith. She worked five and a half days a week. On Sundays if the weather was fine she would rush through her housework and spend an hour putting the garden in some kind of order. Then taking a packed lunch and a prepared bottle for Nathaniel she would set off to walk over Wanstead Flats or Victoria Park. They were popular places at the weekend. On hot days families would picnic or spend time on the boating lake. She would sit under the shade of a tree and happily sketch the people relaxing and at play for hours.

On Wednesday afternoons she would visit the markets or places of local interest. Sometimes she sketched factory workers leaving work, or costers selling their wares. She was interested in people, how they lived and worked. She had developed her own style when she transferred these scenes on to canvas. She was best at painting people and focused most attention on the expressions of her subjects and their actions, making the scene come alive. The backgrounds were more indistinct, giving the impression and shape of a building.

On a Tuesday evening from seven until nine Ruby came over to look after Nathaniel while Faith attended her art lessons. John Milner, the tutor, applauded her talent, echoing Dan's words that originality was what got you noticed. At the end of November the tutor was putting on an art show and wanted a selection from Faith to choose from. The prospect excited and terrified her. Was John Milner only being kind? What if no one liked her work? She set herself a target of completing one painting a week from the numerous sketches she had made throughout the summer.

Aware that Gerald Hornsey's mobility was rapidly improving and that he was now able to walk slowly up the stairs to the art showroom, Faith knew that her job would soon come to an end. With so many men out of work, she doubted it would be easy to find another which was so convenient and interesting. In the three months she had been at Hornsey Brothers she had catalogued all their paintings. Several had been undervalued and had been repriced. She had also learnt to drive their large Austin and taken Gerald to several auctions. Twice she advised him not to bid higher when he was inclined to do so. She realised then that his eyesight was failing and when she looked closely at his eyes saw a filmy grey thread growing across his pupils.

Since she would soon be out of a job and because both Gerald and Cyril Hornsey had been so accommodating, she risked taking three of her paintings into the shop.

'Would you consider hanging these in the gallery?' she asked Gerald hesitantly. 'I know they are not what you usually sell, but the artist is a friend of mine and . . .'

'Let me see them,' he replied.

She held each one up. At first he frowned and pulled at his chin. 'They have depth and the scenes are interesting but my customers usually prefer less populated scenes – landscapes or still life.'

She hid her disappointment, her confidence crushed. She had been foolish to bring them. She'd had so few lessons. Compared to Dan's paintings they were primitive.

'Good quality frames,' Gerald went on. 'Makes a lot of difference that. I hate to see a good painting in a cheap frame. Not bad at all. Especially the boating lake scene. But this fairground and street scene may not be so easy to sell.' He looked closer. 'Is that pub the Green Man? I like the Morris Men dancing outside. I'll put it in the window.'

'The artist isn't expecting you to purchase them. Just hang them in the gallery. If any customers should be interested Hornsey Brothers would get twenty per cent on the sale price. Is that fair?'

He took the painting from her and moved to the window to study it closer. 'Good grief, it's signed Tempest. That wouldn't be a relative of yours, would it?'

'Sort of.' She held her breath.

His expression cleared. 'But you're an orphan. Did you paint these?'

Faith blushed. 'I know it's an imposition to ask you. But my work here is only temporary. I was hoping if I could sell a few paintings I . . .'

He put up a hand to stop her. 'My brother and I are considering

257

taking you on permanently. But only for two days a week. And it is only right that we support you as an artist. You do have talent. We'll put a notice next to the painting in the window promoting you as a local artist. What price did you expect for them?'

'I thought twelve guineas. They are quite large and the frames are carved ebony. They cost me a half a guinea each. Gilt frames didn't look right.'

'Twelve guineas! I've never heard anything so ridiculous. My dear, they will be priced at twenty-one guineas and you will be heralded as a bright new talent. I shall contact the editor of the *Gazette*. He will send a reporter to interview you and your photograph . . .'

Faith shuddered at the mention of a photographer. What if she was recognised? All the old speculation would be dragged up about herself and Dan. She had just made a new life for herself.

'My paintings are nothing special. I would feel a fraud if they were over-publicised.'

'Nonsense, you have talent. You mustn't be shy about it. My neighbour works at the museum. They often hold exhibitions of London artists. Your paintings are most appropriate as they depict local people at work and leisure. I shall speak with him about your work.'

'I had not expected so much.' Faith was overwhelmed. 'I had hoped that by selling a few paintings it would mean I did not have to work such long hours away from Nathaniel.'

'Publicity is the key to success, Mrs Tempest.'

'I'm not ready for an exhibition of that scale. My art teacher is displaying some of my work at a students' annual exhibition in November.' Inwardly Faith quaked at the thought of any publicity. It was too close to her humiliating experience with the press. And must be avoided at all costs.

Ernie Durham had been too busy promoting his own interests to take much heed of Ruby in recent weeks. As long as she was at the club for the late sessions and continued to draw the punters he was happy. She'd been more difficult about agreeing to hostess his after-hours parties. She was becoming a liability. All she did was whine about him not getting her the singing venues he'd promised. She'd no enthusiasm for the sex games he liked unless he slipped something in her drink. A couple of the punters had complained that her act was tepid compared to the raw sexuality she used to portray. He hadn't bothered to watch it for weeks. When he did he was appalled.

After her performance he dragged her into the dressing room. 'What sort of an act do you call that? It was bloody pathetic.'

He lashed out, striking her cheek and sending her staggering back against the make-up table. 'You were like some prissy schoolmarm. That's not what the punters want.'

'I'm sick of parading like a whore. I'm your wife. You should respect me more.'

He laughed wickedly. 'You ain't been much of a wife lately. Always too damned tired to be of any use to me.'

'You mean I'm sick of your perverted sex games. I'm sick of never having any money,' she threw back at him. Being with Mike was making her realise how cheaply Ernie regarded her. It made her present life seem tawdry and unbearable.

'You were nothing but a cheap tramp when I gave you a job. You owe everything to me.' Again he struck her, knocking her to the floor this time.

She shuffled away from him, raising an arm to protect her face. 'You ain't got the guts to fight a man, that's why you pick on women. If you want someone sorted you'd send your thugs round to do it.'

'You don't keep a dog and bark yourself.' He lunged at her. 'And you use a bitch on heat in the way she deserves.'

Furious at his crude comparisons she clawed at his face, screeching her loathing, 'You're just small-time, Ernie Durham. Biggest mistake I made was marrying you.'

He kicked her thigh, then snatched at her hair, sending pincers of fire through her scalp. She sobbed at the pain. Unheeding, he hauled her face up towards him, his mouth curling back in a cruel snarl. 'You do as you're told, or you'll regret it.'

Her foot caught his knee. His face mottled with blotches of purple and red as his rage exploded. He fell on her, fumbling at his trousers. 'Bitch, I'll teach you!'

Instantly Ruby froze. His touch repelled her and sensing it, he was all the more sadistic in his assault. The more she fought him, the more excited he became. To resist only hurt her further. She lay unmoving beneath him as he drove inside her. With each thrust her disgust rose. She had to get out of this marriage. She couldn't take any more of this. She had to get away.

So help her God, before she allowed Ernie to hit or rape her again, she'd kill him.

Another exhibition was behind him and Dan could relax. He had taken a few weeks off to visit his sisters who had emigrated from Ireland some years ago. They were overjoyed to see him, but their large broods of children made him hunger for sight of Nathan and Faith. Promising to visit them again before he left America he hired an isolated cabin surrounded by woodland and overlooking a lake. Here he could breathe and escape Imelda's incessant telephone complaints and demands. There was not a telephone at the cabin but he had left his address with his lawyer in case of an emergency.

Until now he had settled all Imelda's demands for treatment. This Paulo Santiago was charging ridiculously high fees. But she claimed that feeling was slowly returning to her legs under his care. He continued to pay the bills without complaint. The sacrifices he had made meant nothing to his self-centred wife. He had done his best for her, but Imelda never saw it as enough. He had only just avoided bankruptcy and her medical expenses were taking most of the money he earned.

The Los Angeles exhibition had been another success. Every painting had sold. But it had made Imelda greedier than ever. Having settled Squire Passmore's debts, he'd even managed to save the house which would be settled on Imelda once he divorced her. Unfortunately that day seemed remote. Even with the feeling returning to her lower body it could still take a year before she was walking with crutches.

Imelda on crutches would remain a yoke around his neck. She would continue to play the invalid and wronged wife in a divorce. He walked round the lake. His thoughts were bleak, shuttering his artistic eye to the beauty of the rolling hills, or the sun's rays dancing on the water.

Galleries were clamouring for more paintings but without Faith his inspiration had left him. The spiritual fire she had kindled had been severed by the aggravation of contending with Imelda's demands. He had hoped to reclaim some of it by spending a month in the country. It was not enough. His isolation had only increased his restlessness.

He was sat on a boulder overlooking the lake, his mind seeking solutions. Lost in contemplation, he did not notice the heat begin to fade from the day and the blood red sun as it drifted down behind the tall spruces and hills. Birdsong was as haunting as panpipes and the lake turned crimson. Still Dan sat motionless. His breathing was shallow, his mind floating in a semi-trance, finally at peace and at one with nature.

A stone rolling into the water broke through his reflections. As his eyes refocused on his surroundings he found himself staring at the raised head of a mature stag, the antlers majestic as they curved back over his neck. It was a beast in its prime. Dan was awed. Evening mist was rising from the ground, tendrils spiralling upwards in the twilight. The Celtic heritage of his Irish ancestors quickened in his blood. It was an image he must capture on canvas.

Before his mind's eye the stag transmuted. Its outline became amorphous, seeming to rear up into human form: an image of an ancient horned God. Mischievous Pan. The druid Cerrunos. Herne, Lord of the forests and beasts. All gods of protection, good harvest and of the spirit of nature; the consorts of the Earth Mother. Their horns were a sign of their divinity before the Christian church corrupted those horns as a symbol of Satan and all things evil.

The vision of the horned figure wavered in the mist and again there was just the stag drinking. But another veil was lifted from Dan's mind. He visualised the native American Indians who had once roamed these woods when centuries ago they were thick forests. He knew then that he had to visit the ancient lands, their holy places and speak with the ancestors of that noble race. He'd always felt an empathy for the native Indians as a child, choosing to be Geronimo and not a cowboy when playing with his brothers or friends. He wanted to paint the Indians as they hunted and bring alive some of their folklore.

For the first time in months he felt recharged. He would travel simply with just a rucksack and his artist materials. He would be out of communication with Imelda's demands. Perhaps then he could find some measure of peace.

He'd write and tell Faith his plans and send her some form of address to contact him. If only she had installed the telephone as he had insisted. Faith could be so stubborn. None of her neighbours had a telephone in their house. She didn't want to appear to be above them. She had also refused to allow him to buy her a small car when she wrote telling him that she had learnt to drive. How different she was from Imelda! It made him love her all the more. It made their separation even harder to bear.

When Ernie got back to his flat with Kavanagh he was furious to find Ruby not there. He'd told her that she was needed to hostess a party that night. He made his excuses to Big Hugh.

'Women! They can be a handful at times,' Big Hugh sneered.

'I can handle Ruby,' Ernie responded, infuriated by the ridicule in Kavanagh's voice. Ruby had got above herself. She needed to be taught a lesson. She had disobeyed him and made him look a fool. He scanned the scribbled note she had left on the mantelpiece.

I'm sick of being your punchbag. Get yourself another singer. And if you don't treat me with respect you can get yourself another wife. I ain't putting up with the way you treat me no more. When you've had a couple of days to see reason, I'll be in touch.

She'd be in touch! Ernie raged. Who did the tart think she was? No one dictated terms to Ernie Durham. She'd gone too far this time.

Summoning two of his heavies he went to Mike's club. His brother had stood up for Ruby in the past because he fancied her. Not that Mike would do anything about it. Ernie grinned. Mike was a fool in his estimation. Ernie had not hesitated to get Mike's wife Sylvie into bed when she'd wanted some drugs. He was the one who kept her supplied with heroin, and Sylvie would do anything to keep her supply. But he'd kept that to himself. Mike would have torn Ernie apart if he'd learned that he had been her supplier.

The River Boat was closed. Ernie glared at the darkened windows. There was a crack of light behind the curtains in the office. He rapped on the door. If Ruby was there alone with Mike, he'd have the excuse he needed for his heavies to beat the daylights out of his brother. To his annoyance Mike was not alone. There were five musicians in his office having an impromptu jam session.

'This is an unexpected surprise, Ernie,' Mike announced, putting his saxophone aside. 'What brings you here?'

It was obvious Ruby was not at the River Boat. And Ernie wasn't about to tell Mike that she had scarpered. Even so his humiliation fired his anger.

'Ain't a crime to want to see how your brother is getting on. How's the club doing? Ruby says it's popular. You won't be needing her singing here no more then?'

'I wouldn't say that,' Mike said easily. 'Ruby seems to enjoy the atmosphere. It's a different venue and clientele for her. There was a man in yesterday who was interested in Ruby singing in a new musical he's trying to get backers for. It will open in the West End.'

'I'm her manager, not you. Why ain't I heard nothing of this?'

'Early days.' Mike shrugged. 'Nothing definite yet. I didn't tell Ruby either. Didn't want to raise her hopes in case he doesn't get the cash he needs. I knew you'd want what's best for Ruby though. I'd intended to discuss it when things were more certain.'

Ernie scowled. He was torn between jealousy that Mike could get Ruby the break he'd been striving unsuccessfully for, and greed at what it could be worth.

'Nothing can be agreed without my say-so,' he reminded his brother in a cold voice. He looked round at the musicians. Most of them were large men who knew how to look after themselves. Some of the jazz clubs were rough joints. No point in making something out of this tonight. It added to his anger that he couldn't justify Ruby not singing here, unless he came up with a better deal for her. At present that was unlikely.

'Good to see things are going so well for you,' he said as he gestured for his men to follow him out.

Inside the car his temper soared. What was Ruby up to? He wouldn't put anything past her. And where the hell was she? If he couldn't work off his bad mood on Mike then he'd find Ruby and teach her a lesson she wouldn't forget in a long time. The only other place she could be was Wanstead with that prissy friend of hers.

Chapter Twenty

Ernie bashed on the door of the house until Faith opened it a crack. He shoved his weight against the wood, throwing Faith back against the wall as he strode inside.

'Get Ruby,' Ernie demanded. 'She's coming back with me.'

Faith recovered from the shock of his rough entry into her home. She pulled her dressing-gown tighter around her and rubbed the sleep from her eyes. Nathaniel was screaming in his cot at having been so rudely awoken by the banging.

'What are you talking about?' Faith stood her ground, her body trembling with indignation. 'How dare you burst in here! You've woken Nathaniel. It's three thirty in the morning.'

'Get her!' Ernie bellowed.

'Ruby is not here.' Faith strove to check her own temper. 'And can you please keep your voice down? You're frightening Nathan and as for the neighbours . . .'

'Stuff the neighbours.' Ernie rounded on her. 'Where's my wife?'

Faith closed the front door. 'I've told you she's not here. I'm going to fetch Nathan to calm him down.' She turned her back and her arm was gripped in a bruising hold and she was spun round.

'Don't turn your back on me.' He thrust his face threateningly close to hers, his breath reeking of whisky. 'Or act so high and mighty. You ain't no better than you should be. That's Brogan's bastard crying, ain't it?'

Faith drew a steadying breath, her eyes flashing with disdain. 'If you've come here asking after Ruby, you must be worried about her. When did you last see her? Has something happened to her?' She punched out questions to confound him, while she strove to master the situation. She was relieved her voice was steady. Aware of her vulnerability and that Ernie had a reputation for violence, she was uneasy. If she showed it, Ernie would be merciless. 'Let me get Nathaniel. Go in the front room and help yourself to a whisky. There's some in the sideboard cupboard. If Ruby isn't here and she's not with you, I'm as worried as you about her whereabouts.'

That appeared to throw him. He'd been so sure she was here. Faith spoke with concern, 'I can't think with Nathan crying. Get yourself a whisky and we'll talk when I come back down.'

Ernie didn't move. He was breathing heavily. 'She's here. You're covering up for her.'

Pushing Faith aside he bounded up the stairs, crashing open the bedroom doors as he searched them. Faith hurried after him. Her heart was racing with panic. The man emanated menace. He exuded violence with every door he banged open. She rushed into Nathan's room, lifted her crying son out of his cot and held him protectively against her. It gave her the courage she needed to face Ernie as he came into the bedroom glaring round.

'I told you, Ruby isn't here.'

He gave a guttural growl and stomped back downstairs. This time Faith followed more slowly, holding Nathaniel tight, her legs shaky and her heart clattering against her ribcage. Nathaniel had quietened, snuggling against her neck as he sucked on his knuckle. She met Ernie in the hall after he had searched every room.

'Have you and Ruby quarrelled?' she accused.

He didn't answer. There was a wildness in his eyes and a mean twist to his lips. Suddenly his hand shot out and his fingers squeezed her throat. 'I want to know the minute you hear from her. Understand?'

Unable to breathe or swallow, Faith nodded. Nausea and fear were churning in her stomach. He remained holding her throat, his head cocked to one side listening for any sound of movement. 'If you know what's good for you, you let me know when you hear from Ruby.'

Faith nodded. His lips curved cruelly as his hand moved from her throat down inside her nightdress to close over her breast. Holding Nathaniel, Faith was powerless to fight him.

'Get out of my house or I'll press charges of indecent assault against you.'

'You ain't in a position to do that. Not with a bastard kid. And what would your neighbours say, if it got round you ain't the respectable widow woman you claim to be?'

'Get out, Ernie!' Her voice rose.

'What you gonna do to make me leave?' He grinned evilly at her. Lust darkened his eyes and his fingers squeezed her breast. She bit her lip to stop her cry of revulsion. When his hand moved lower across her ribcage and down to her stomach, it felt like maggots crawling across her flesh. She was outraged at what he was subjecting her to because she was holding her baby and couldn't retaliate. 'You're disgusting. I'm not surprised Ruby left you. Get out! Get out!'

Her voice was again rising and she struggled to control it. She didn't want him sensing her rising fear. He would use it as a weapon against her. In a lower tone she warned, 'If you touch me and I tell Ruby, she'll never come back to you. And the police will take my word against yours. They've been round here a couple of times asking what I know about the club or you.'

He withdrew his hand to again close it round her throat. 'What did you tell them?' he shouted and Nathaniel's tiny body jerked and he began to cry.

'Nothing. What was there I could tell them?' Her stare was cold and his gaze slid from hers. 'I reckon the police have got more on you than you think.'

His fingers tightened. 'Just you keep your opinion about me and me business to yourself. Or else . . .'

There was the sound of footsteps on the path and a loud rap on the door.

'Mrs Tempest,' Dave Taylor called. 'Are you all right? We heard shouting. Madge said I was to check on you.'

Thank God for Madge, Faith thought with relief. The pressure

267

on her neck loosened and Ernie thrust her from him.

'You think you're bloody clever, don't you?' he blazed. 'Well you ain't. Don't mess with me. Just make sure you tell me where Ruby is when you hear from her.'

Faith swung round and opened the door to find Madge in her dressing-gown with her hair in curling rags and Dave with his trousers over his striped pyjamas. Madge was holding a rolled-up umbrella and Dave a poker.

'I'm fine,' she said. 'Mr Durham was just leaving. He thought Ruby was here. He became rather upset when she was not. We're worried about her. She went out without telling him. Sorry if we disturbed you.'

Madge was glaring at Ernie Durham. It was clear from her expression that Faith's explanation had not fooled her. Another light went on across the road and the curtains twitched.

Ernie pushed past her, his face white with fury. 'Just you let me know when you hear from Ruby.'

He marched down the garden path and slammed the gate, causing yet another curtain at a bedroom window to move and a pale face to appear at the pane.

Faith sighed with relief. 'Thanks, Dave. Thanks, Madge. He was getting nasty. I'm sorry your sleep was disturbed.'

'Only too glad to be of help,' Dave stated. 'Pretty young widow on her own is at risk. I wouldn't like to see anything happen to you. There's some funny blokes about. That one's a nasty piece of work. I've heard some right stories about him down the pub. Word gets round who the villains are in the East End. He's got a nasty reputation.'

'He's my friend's husband.'

'He's gone now,' Madge announced. 'And fortunately no harm done. Or was there?'

Faith shook her head. 'I don't mind admitting I was relieved to hear Dave's voice. I'll get a chain put on the door in future.'

'Anything untoward happens, you just bang on the wall,' Dave said, moving off.

She thanked them again and managed a reassuring smile for

Madge before she shut the door. Her knees suddenly gave way and she sank down on to the bottom stair holding Nathaniel close. There had been a moment when she had seen the lust in Ernie's eyes, that she knew he was capable of raping her. That he would have enjoyed forcing his will over her. It wasn't just the threat to herself which unnerved her. How would Nathaniel have fared if she had fought Ernie? Her child was her most precious possession and her mind conjured horrors at the consequences to him if Ernie had become vicious.

There was a faint noise from the cupboard door under the stairs. 'Has the bastard gone?'

'Yes, Ruby. You can come out now.' Faith moved the pram which hid the door from sight.

'Gawd! That was close.' Ruby squeezed through the small door and straightened. She put the small suitcase she was holding on the floor and, pulling a face, dusted the coal dust off her coat and dress. There were several smears across her face. She was white and shaken. Knowing that Ruby had a fear of dark places, her heart went out to her.

'Are you all right?'

Ruby managed a shaky smile and nodded.

'You look like the urchin I remember when we first met,' Faith said to lighten the mood. 'You were always playing in the dirtiest places.'

'I'll have that drink you offered Ernie.' Ruby darted for the sideboard. 'I bought a bottle of gin last time I came. You still got it? What made you offer Ernie a drink? What if he'd stayed? I could have been in there all night.'

'Since he forced himself in here I thought it best to bluff him and act as though I was worried something had happened to you.'

Ruby helped herself to a large gin and carried the bottle back to the kitchen. 'It was a good job we was talking in here and hadn't gone to bed or he would have seen my stuff in the bedroom.'

'And just as fortunate that I had planned an early night and was reading in bed when you arrived earlier. I looked the part.'

'I never thought he'd come here,' Ruby said. 'Not tonight anyway. I'm sorry, Faith. It weren't fair to put you through that. I'll find somewhere else to stay in the morning.'

'No, you won't. I'll let Mike know you're here and you can decide how you're going to tackle Ernie. He won't let you go easily, Ruby.'

'I'll sort something. I wouldn't put Ernie past having this place watched. I won't have you in danger.'

Faith was still shaken by Ernie's threats and abuse.

'I'll put Nathan back to bed,' she said. 'He's asleep now. Don't put any lights on just in case Ernie has left one of his heavies to spy on the house.'

When she returned from putting Nathaniel in his cot, she poured herself a gin and downed half of it. 'I needed that. I don't mind admitting I was frightened. So what are you going to do?'

Ruby took several puffs on her cigarette and stabbed it out in the ashtray. She drank another gin before answering. 'Mike would protect me but that will only cause trouble for him. Ernie's always been jealous of his brother. The only way I can be free of Ernie is by getting him put away for a long time. For that I've got to find out more about what he's been up to.'

'I never liked Ernie. But shopping your own husband doesn't seem right?' Faith protested.

'You got any better ideas? That bastard is capable of having Mike and me killed and the bodies never found.'

'I don't think he'd go that far! You and Mike are too well known. Police would ask too many questions.'

'Not if instead of hiding our bodies, he made it look like an accident. We wouldn't be the first burnt corpses found in a car accident and fire.'

Faith shuddered, fear channelling through her at the images Ruby was creating. 'Don't talk that way. Is Ernie really that evil?'

'Kavanagh's men are.' Ruby poured herself another drink. 'I'll have to go back to Ernie. Act the penitent. I can string him along until I get the information I need. Then I'll tip off the law.'

'It's still so dangerous,' Faith cautioned.

Ruby shrugged and stood up to pace the kitchen. In the grey dawn light her face was strained and her shoulders hunched. 'I've taken precautions so that Ernie won't dare hurt me. So don't worry.'

Faith watched her friend with concern. Ruby was drinking too heavily. She'd put away half a bottle of gin and it didn't appear to have had any effect on her except for a slight slurring of her words.

'You want to chat up any reporters you've had contact with,' Faith advised. 'Be seen in the places the columnists cover. You were always good at getting publicity. Ernie can't complain at that.'

Ruby's eyes sparkled. 'That's a great idea to cover me tracks for tonight. I'll go to one of those spa towns for a week. I could do with losing a few pounds and laying off the booze.' She eyed her empty glass and with a shrug refilled it. 'If I ain't gonna get no booze at the spa, I might as well enjoy it now. And I know the perfect publicity. You get word to a couple of reporters who know me. Let them know that I've gone missing. That will give Ernie something to think about and teach him a lesson as well.'

'What will that serve except to make Ernie angrier?'

Ruby smiled. 'I'll go to this spa in disguise. Wear a dark wig. Then after a few days when I ain't showed up, you tip off the papers where I am. I'll say I sort of blanked out, needed to get away. After all, I haven't had a break from singing every night for four months.'

Despite her fears for Ruby, Faith laughed. 'You certainly don't go for half measures, do you?'

Ruby winked at her. 'And when Ernie gets nabbed, I'll be really famous. The wife of a jewel robber doing time. People will flock to hear me sing. I'll be a star.'

'I don't think that was the way Ernie planned for it to happen,' Faith remonstrated.

'Then that's his look-out.'

Faith shook her head. 'Don't tempt fate, Ruby. You know what they say about getting what you wish for? It doesn't always happen the way you expect it.'

* * *

Ruby's disappearance made headlines in three national newspapers and they resurrected the scandal of her being fined for indecency. One carried a photograph of her in a revealing dress which made her smile with satisfaction. Faith had done everything that she'd asked. Ruby had made only one phone call since her arrival in the modest hotel and that was to Mike.

'What the hell's happening, Ruby?' he demanded. 'I've been out of my mind with worry.'

Aware that a nosy operator could listen in, she was evasive. 'I'm fine. I can't speak on the phone. Go and see Faith, she'll tell you everything. I'm safe where I am. And I'm making plans for the future. I'll deal with Ernie. This is for the best. I know what I'm doing.'

Mike groaned. 'Leave it to me, Ruby. I don't want you hurt. Ernie's furious. He's been round here twice. I think one of his men followed me home last night and stayed outside my house all night.'

Ruby giggled. 'That will prove we ain't together. I don't want to risk him learning of us. Not yet. That's the only danger I'll face. Tomorrow Faith is putting out word to the papers that I've gone missing. The publicity will be to my advantage.'

'Are you sure you're all right?' Mike's voice softened with tenderness.

'Fine. I'll ring you soon. Don't worry about me.'

'But I do, Ruby. I should be with you. Protecting you.'

'This is the best way.' She was adamant. 'And the only way we can continue to see each other without Ernie suspecting anything.' She hung up quickly before the need to see Mike and be held in his arms overruled her caution.

She spent the next three days quietly, visiting the baths and sampling the waters. She'd rather have a gin and tonic any day, but was determined to lay off the booze, keep away from rich food and get plenty of rest. She'd need all her strength when she had to face her husband again.

After a morning shopping in the town for a dress which would create the effect she was now aiming for, she returned to the hotel and picked up the morning papers to peruse over her coffee. She was delighted to read the way Ernie was playing up to the reporters. It was what she had expected from him in order to save face.

'Ruby Starr is a true professional', he was reported as saying. 'She'll be back in London and singing at the opening of my new club, the Silver Bird, in a couple of weeks.'

Good old Ernie, Ruby thought. Never one to miss a trick. She frowned as she read on: 'My wife has been under great strain since the court case. It was naturally distressing for her. She's an artist and to have her performance reviled that way upset her. I'm sure that she has not done anything foolish and that she is safe and well.'

That statement made Ruby uneasy. Until then she'd enjoyed feeding false trails to the papers and revelling in the attention focused on her disappearance. But Ernie's statement was ominous. It had a sinister ring. What if Ernie preferred a dead wife to a live one? He could use her disappearance as a means of tracking her down and making her death look like a suicide. She shuddered. Would Ernie go that far? She wasn't prepared to put it to the test. It was time to end the ruse.

She phoned Derek Shipley, a reporter on the *Daily Herald* and promised him an exclusive story. Then she phoned Mike. The relief at hearing his voice almost made her break down. She had missed him so much. Quickly she outlined her plans and asked his advice on how to handle it. It took all her persuasion to stop him coming to collect her himself.

An hour later she phoned Ernie from the foyer of the hotel, making her voice sound tearful.

'Ernie, I'm so sorry about everything. I sort of flipped. I didn't know what I was doing. Come and take me home. I'm in Tunbridge Wells.'

'Who you been with?' he shouted.

'No one, Ernie. I swear it. I was upset when you hit me and started going on at me. I was crazy mad at you. Then I found myself on a train. Didn't even know where I was going. I saw a poster for Tunbridge Wells on a station.' Realising that she was babbling, she concentrated on making him believe her story. 'I couldn't think straight. I needed time to myself. I ain't been feeling meself lately. You can ask at the hotel. They'll tell you I've been here alone all this time.'

'It's been four days, you stupid tart. You must have seen the papers. I've been made to look a right berk, not knowing where me own wife is.'

'I ain't been in no state to read papers. I've been taking the baths here and resting. I thought you didn't love me no more. That you wouldn't care that I went off for a few days. Today's the first day I've seen the papers. Wow, all that publicity, Ernie! I'm real sorry if I caused a fuss. Should I let the police know where I am?'

'I'll handle that. Just get back here.'

She held the earpiece away from her ear as he swore violently. From the corner of her eye she saw Derek Shipley stroll into the hotel with a photographer behind him. Ruby gasped dramatically, 'Oh no! Derek Shipley of the *Daily Herald* has just come into the hotel. He's seen me. What will I do?'

Ernie swore again. 'Tell him you blanked out from strain and overwork. Instinct brought you to Tunbridge Wells. Though God knows why you should have chosen such a place. It ain't your style at all. Tell him all you could think of was getting peace and rest so that you wouldn't disappoint your fans when my new club opens. And keep him talking until I get there. He can have an exclusive photo of a loving couple reunited. It will be great publicity for the new club. At least something useful has come out of this charade. I'll deal with you later.'

Ruby smiled to herself as she put down the phone. She had heard the excitement overlaying Ernie's exasperation and anger. She could handle him.

The receptionist looked startled at seeing her without the black wig for the first time. 'You look just like someone I saw in the paper this morning, Miss Simons.' Then her mouth gaped. 'Well,

I'm blowed. You *are* her: Ruby Starr. The cabaret singer that's been missing.'

Ruby smiled and patted her blonde hair. 'So it appears.'

The camera flashed and Ruby, in a straight wine red cashmere dress which reached demurely to her slender calves, posed again for the photographer, elegantly holding her long cigarette holder.

'So what's your story?' Derek Shipley urged, whipping out his notepad and hustling Ruby to a corner seat in the lounge.

Ruby strung out the interview for three hours by flirting outrageously with the reporter. Shipley fancied himself as something of a ladies' man. And was aware that if he telephoned this scoop in to the paper, it would make the evening edition. They could use an old photo of Ruby. Then if he hung round until Durham turned up he could get another exclusive of the husband and wife reunited, which would make the morning edition.

When Faith collected Nathaniel from Madge after work the day following Ernie's visit, the first stories about Ruby's disappearance had hit the London evening papers.

Madge was full of it. 'Your friend's all over the papers. Gone missing, has she? Didn't I see her leaving your house the morning after that incident with her husband? I thought you said he'd come looking for her. Not that I'm one to pry.'

Faith nodded. 'You saw Ruby. She hid in the coal hole. He'd hit her during a quarrel.'

Madge's lips thinned with disgust. 'I knew that bloke was no good. Durham's a scoundrel. Dave reckons Durham's linked with all those jewellers' which have been robbed recently. Durham's done time for robbery and for kicking an old German Jew to death.'

Faith had grown pale. She hadn't realised that Ernie had such a reputation. 'Are you sure those stories are true and not just exaggeration?'

'You get a lot of ducking and diving goes on round here. Especially with so many men out of work. Some ain't above nicking something if the chance comes their way. Usually it's

pretty harmless and they have nothing to do with violence.'
Madge busied herself wiping down an already spotless table top
– a sign she was troubled – and went on heavily. 'I ain't telling
you this to upset you. But I reckon you should know what
Durham's like.'

'I've never known you spread gossip, Madge.' Faith smiled
affectionately.

'Me Dad always said if you ain't got nothing good to say about
someone keep your trap shut. And I ain't gossiping now. It's more
like a warning.' She folded her arms across her large breasts.
'Don't get involved with Durham. If your friend is married to him
she must've known what he was like.'

'Ruby only saw what she wanted to see,' Faith defended.

'Then she has only herself to blame.'

'We go back a long way, Madge. I'd never abandon Ruby if she
needed my help.'

'At least be warned,' Madge repeated sorrowfully. 'Durham is
bad news. A mate of Dave's went to school with him. Says he was
a bully. Always demanding money from the smaller kids and
giving them a good thumping if they didn't give it to him. His
brother was always bailing him out of trouble until he went off to
the war.'

'Thanks for the warning, Madge. I know you mean well. But
Ruby will always be my friend.'

Madge remained troubled when Faith left. If Faith stayed loyal
to Ruby Starr there were bound to be repercussions. She didn't
much like the singer. Too showy for her own good. And hard as
nails. She was a user, a chancer – too interested in the good time.
Nothing was for free in this life, Madge reckoned. Everything had
its price. She only hoped that Faith would be spared from paying
it along with Ruby Starr.

Chapter Twenty-One

Ruby saw Squinty Watkins through the hotel window. Her heart sank. It didn't bode well for her that Ernie hadn't come alone. At least with Derek Shipley there Ernie couldn't cut up rough. Any sign of that and she was staying put.

Her first sight of Ernie didn't put her mind at rest. In a homburg and with a black cashmere overcoat draped over his shoulders he looked imposing. His expression was murderous. She sank back in the chair out of his range of vision. Shipley was busy boasting of an interview he'd done with Margaret Bondfield, the first woman cabinet minister in Ramsay MacDonald's labour government.

'Sweetheart!' Ernie boomed across the foyer. 'Have you any idea how worried I've been?'

Ernie had obviously seen Derek Shipley and this show of concern was for his benefit. Ruby knew her only chance of winning Ernie round was to play the penitent wife.

'Ernie, darling!' She rose gracefully and ran into his crushing embrace, the camera flashing wildly. 'I've been so silly. I didn't know what I was doing.'

'It was all that worry and upset over that stupid court case,' Ernie crooned, kissing her passionately, but she could feel the tension in his body. 'As long as you are safe and well that's all that matters.'

He turned to Derek Shipley. 'Ruby is a trouper. She's so popular she never stops working. She does too much. I'm gonna have to take more care of her in future. We can't have this happening again.'

Only Ruby seemed aware of the double edge of his words, Shipley was frantically scribbling notes of every word between them.

Ernie kissed her cheek, playing the adoring husband. He hadn't looked at her that way since their wedding, and it was as false now as it was then. He produced two tickets from his jacket and handed them to Shipley. 'Complimentary tickets for the opening of the Silver Bird. We've got some celebrities coming along.'

'I'll be there, Mr Durham.' Shipley waved his notebook. 'And this will be in the morning papers. You take care of Ruby now. She's some woman.'

As soon as Shipley left Ernie's lip curled back. 'Get your things. Just what the hell did you think you were playing at?'

'I told you, I was mixed up,' Ruby blustered. 'You getting mad at me was the last straw.' She made an effort to make peace between them. To succeed in her plan to find out all she could about the robberies Ernie had done with Kavanagh, she'd need to keep Ernie sweet so that he didn't get suspicious. Summoning a bright smile she put her arm through his. 'I don't know what got into me going off like that. I wouldn't do such a thing again. I missed you.'

He glared at her. 'I suppose it got some publicity for the club,' he said, grudgingly. 'I've got tickets for a fancy dress charity do at the Café Royal tonight. I hired a Cleopatra costume for you. There ain't much to it and it should give the photographers a field day. May as well get what publicity we can out of it.'

She curbed her protest at appearing half-naked in public. Under Mike's guidance she had begun to tone down her image. She had changed from overt seductress to a mysterious temptress; alluring but unapproachable. Ernie wanted her to look cheap. Mike was giving her style and class. At the moment Ernie didn't look in a frame of mind to be argued with. She'd have to grin and bear his tacky exploits to get her noticed. With luck it wouldn't be for much longer. Mike wouldn't like it though. She hoped he would understand.

By the middle of October Imelda was managing a few shaky steps on crutches. Paulo attended her twice a day and often stayed all night, leaving her only to attend his other patients. He had insisted that she dismiss Ricky. Imelda saw this as a sign of jealousy and her growing power over him. Paulo was possessive and swam with her as part of the exercise programme he had devised. They always swam naked and he would massage her legs and back underwater which led to them making love. She hated him leaving her to visit other female patients, although he declared that none of them was important to him.

Over the weeks she had not realised that their relationship was changing. Now she was the one who was making jealous scenes whenever he left her. She was like a teenager in love for the first time and could deny him nothing. Paulo was always tender and apologetic on his return. His ardour proved his adoration and how much he had missed her. Such devotion was an elixir. She was besotted with him. Her legs were getting stronger and with each progress she showered him with expensive presents.

The money she had received from selling her father's treasures and Dan's painting was dwindling fast. Dan had refused to increase her monthly advance. The house was paid for separately as were the food and medical bills and servants' wages. She constantly raged about what she considered Dan's meanness. But secretly gloated that it was his money which enabled Paulo to continue as her therapist and lover.

'Why do you bother with him?' Paulo resented any mention of her husband. 'You're a rich woman. He does not care for you as I do. Divorce is easy in this country. You should get rid of him.'

Imelda allowed him to believe that it was her money which paid for everything. Money was power in America. Without it you were nothing. Paulo adored her. She thrived on that adoration more than ever now she was disabled. It proved to her that her looks were still her greatest asset. But for how long? Panic smote her. This could be her last chance to keep the love of a young and exciting lover who was also rich. He drove an expensive car, lived in a large house in the most prestigious part of town. From the fees he charged, she knew that his income must be several times greater than Dan's. And an artist's income was sporadic and could rise or plummet on the whims of the public.

Also she had lost her control over Dan and she resented that. She couldn't even reach him since he had taken off to live like a native. Her last demands for money to his solicitor had met with a curt refusal. She was beginning to wonder if it would have been better to have divorced when he wanted it. Where had her desire for vengeance got her? It had almost destroyed her. Yet all was not lost. She could still triumph over Dan.

Since her return Ruby couldn't go anywhere without one of Ernie's men accompanying her. If she went to Wanstead, Squinty drove her there and sat outside in the car until she came out. The nights she sang at the River Boat, he sat at the bar. At least she managed to get a few moments with Mike alone, though with Squinty capable of bursting in on them at any moment, sex was impossible.

An uneasy truce sprang up between Ruby and Ernie. Sometimes she felt like she was walking barefoot on hot cinders not to rouse his anger. Providing he allowed her to keep singing at the River Boat and she could get to see Mike, she was prepared to act the caring wife.

Her session finished at the River Boat, she returned to the Gilded Lily. She heard Kavanagh's voice as she paused on the steps leading to the office.

'We're gonna have to lay off any jobs for a while. Bloody Armitage is proving difficult since that night watchman snuffed it. We might as well wait until Christmas now. That's when the shops have more cash in their safes. We'll do a triple hit one after the other. The cops won't know what's hit them with so many alarm bells ringing.'

Ruby was tempted to linger outside the door to learn more. Although neither of Kavanagh's brothers had been guarding the stairs, her figure in the white satin evening dress was clearly visible from the floor below. She didn't want to look as though she was eavesdropping.

Her eyes narrowed. Her dislike for Big Hugh mounted with each meeting. Without knocking she entered and the conversation stopped. Ernie scowled at her.

'Am I interrupting something?'

Hugh waved her into the room, smiling lecherously. 'You can interrupt any day, babe.'

Ernie smirked behind his hand. He loved seeing Big Hugh get turned on by her. It gave him a sense of power over the larger man. Ruby also knew that if it suited Ernie's purposes, he'd throw her into Hugh's arms without a qualm. The thought alone made the bile rise in her stomach.

It was ten weeks to Christmas. She was stuck with Ernie until then. Impatience ground through her. Ten weeks! She couldn't go so long without meeting Mike in secret. They'd have to find a way. Her blood tingled in anticipation. The danger of a lovers' tryst made the prospect even more exciting.

Faith was downstairs in the jeweller's shop. Both Cyril and Gerald were serving customers and there were two others awaiting attention. It had been a busy Saturday morning as the shop also took in clock and jewellery repairs which were done by the brothers in the back workroom. They also bought jewellery and silver ornaments and for larger items of silver would act as pawnbrokers. After Faith dealt with a woman who needed a gold chain repaired on her bracelet, her attention turned on a slim, blond-haired man with a darker goatee beard. He asked to see the tray of ladies' gold watches in the window. He was a regular customer who often came in to buy jewellery for his family.

'Another birthday present, Dr Jarvis?' she said with a smile as she placed the tray on the counter. Up close she guessed that he was only a few years older than herself. The beard suited him. It hadn't been grown to hide a weak chin, for he had a strong line to his jaw. 'Your sisters and cousins are lucky women. You always buy them beautiful presents.'

'Ours is a large family.' His direct grey gaze was brief but disconcerting. He had a commanding presence and the Hornsey brothers had told her that he was their own doctor and was highly thought of by all his patients.

'Actually it is for my nurse and receptionist. She's been with the family practice for forty years and is retiring. I don't know how I could have managed without her when my father died two years ago. Even now she will be difficult to replace.'

'A gold watch is a very generous gift. I'm sure she will be delighted with it.' The sincerity in her voice was real and not the usual bland sales patter.

He shrugged. 'Which one would you suggest?'

She considered the contents of the tray. 'This one. I expect your nurse is a practical woman. She will not want anything too ornate.'

He nodded and smiled. 'It's exactly right. I'll take it.'

The smile showed his white teeth. She hadn't realised how striking his features were. His dark brows and lashes in contrast to his blond hair were attractive and the goatee beard added distinction to his aquiline nose and smooth cheeks.

'I was also interested in one of the paintings in the window,' he added.

Faith's stomach tightened with anticipation. Her painting was still in the window. It had been there a month and not sold. None of them had. She was beginning to despair that Gerald Hornsey had placed it there out of kindness and that no one else liked her work.

'Which one?' she croaked and cleared her throat self-consciously.

'The scene outside the Green Man with the Morris dancers. I thought I'd put it in the surgery waiting room for my patients to enjoy.'

'That's wonderful.' She was blushing like a schoolgirl. To her further mortification he looked amused.

'I'm pleased you so heartily approve of my choice. May I ask why?'

The heat in her cheeks raced to the roots of her hair. She shook

282

her head and murmured, 'I'll get it from the window.'

When she returned with the painting Dr Jarvis was talking to Cyril Hornsey. Self-consciously, Faith laid the painting on the polished mahogany counter.

'So that's why our Mrs Tempest was blushing,' Cyril said with a chuckle. 'That's her painting you've chosen. Talented, isn't she? She's got an exhibition over Wanstead way next month. I wish her every success. It isn't easy for a young widow with a baby to bring up.'

The doctor studied Faith with deepening interest. 'You have other paintings on display here?'

'Yes, there are two upstairs in the gallery.'

'Then I must see them. Will you show me them, Mrs Tempest?'

He followed her up the stairs and before she could point out her two paintings, he moved straight to them.

'Your style is very individual. I like it. The fairground scene with the young men trying to impress their girlfriends on the coconut shy, and the strong man parading on his podium is realistic. It also has a humorous side in the way you have depicted the characters.'

'Thank you. I painted several of the fairground when it was over Wanstead Flats during the Empire Day celebrations. There was so much material to use.'

He moved across to a painting of the boating lake in Victoria Park. It was of an idyllic summer's day. Women in their summer dresses and parasols reclined in boats as the men rowed them, and a family was picnicking under a tree. The father and his three young sons were playing cricket.

'I'll take that one as well.'

Faith gasped. Then suspecting that he was buying it out of kindness, she said stiffly, 'Really there is no need, Dr Jarvis. I'm delighted that you have chosen one of them.'

'What do you mean there is no need? The boating lake is perfect for my study. My sisters are always telling me I never stop working. That painting will remind me to get out to the parks more often on a Sunday.'

She smiled and blinked rapidly to dispel a rush of emotional tears. 'They are the first paintings I've sold.'

'The first of many I am sure.' His gaze was full of admiration. 'Where is this exhibition next month?'

'It's hardly an exhibition as such. My art teacher is showing the work of several of his students the last Saturday in November. It's in the church hall next to his studio in the High Street.'

'Have you many paintings on display?' he asked as he stepped forward to lift the painting from the wall before Faith could do so.

'My tutor asked for a dozen so he could choose the best. I expect there'll be three or four.'

'There should be more if these are anything to go by.'

She paused in wrapping the picture in brown paper. 'That's very kind of you to say so, Dr Jarvis.'

When the paintings were paid for, he tipped his hat to her. 'It's been a pleasure talking to you, Mrs Tempest, and meeting such a talented artist.'

She was flattered by his praise but was not so sure she deserved it. Dr Jarvis was a kind and generous man. It was like him to buy the paintings because she was a widow with a child to support. Guilt furrowed her brow. Would he have been so charitable if he had known that she was an unmarried mother? She felt as if she had taken his money under false pretences and that sat uneasily upon her. If it had been anyone but the kind Dr Jarvis buying her paintings, she didn't think she would have felt so bad.

When Gerald Hornsey handed her the money for the sale of the paintings less the shop's commission, she was again assailed by guilt.

'You must bring four more paintings in for us to sell. Dr Jarvis is a discerning man.'

'What if he just bought them out of kindness?' Faith observed uncomfortably.

'Didn't he choose the picture of Morris dancers before he knew that you were the artist?'

She nodded.

Gerald Hornsey patted her hand fondly. 'There you are then.

He knows a good artist when he sees one.'

She could not convince herself that she had been right to accept Dr Jarvis's money under false pretences. It played on her mind all evening.

'I won't agree to shopping my own brother.' Mike was adamant.

They were in Ruby's dressing room at the River Boat, stealing a few precious minutes together. Ernie's watchmonkey was at the bar waiting to drive her back to the Silver Bird for another two-hour session.

'Are you content with stolen moments like this? I'm not.' She moved into his arms and laid her head against his chest. 'I'm always spied on. What chance have we of meeting somewhere in private and having the freedom to make love?'

Mike groaned and held her close. 'I love you, Ruby. I want you as my wife. But how could I live with myself if our happiness came from putting Ernie in prison for years?'

'How do you propose we deal with him?' Ruby was exasperated she could not sever Mike's family ties. He knew Ernie was no good, but he couldn't shake his guilt that he was in love with his brother's wife.

She dropped her antagonistic approach. It never worked with Mike. 'I can't take much more,' her voice quavered. 'And if I leave him . . .' She broke off and then blurted out tearfully, 'He ain't never gonna accept that. He'll find me. He'll make me pay for deserting him. And you know what that means.'

'I'll be there to protect you.'

Ruby wrenched away from his hold, her frustration overspilling. She clawed her hands through her short hair, holding it back from her face. Her eyes were large with fear. 'And who will protect *you*? You could give Ernie the pasting he deserves, but you ain't no match for his heavies. Ernie's always been jealous of you. If he thought I loved you . . .'

Mike gave her a cynical glance. 'We've got to take things one step at a time. I'll talk to Ernie. See if he'd agree to a separation. You could get a flat somewhere.'

'Then we could see more of each other!' Her arms slid around him. 'That would be wonderful.'

Mike shook his head. 'To protect you I'd have to stay away. For a time at least. Ernie will have the place watched.'

'Ernie ain't gonna agree to that.' Anger pumped through her veins. She'd made such a mess of her life by marrying Ernie. At least she had found a career which would give her the fame she craved.

'Why not go to stay with your friend at Wanstead?'

Ruby was tempted. 'I'd like that, but again it's Ernie. What if he caused trouble? It wouldn't be fair on Faith. And she's got a kid now to consider.'

'Ernie can't fault Faith as a suitable companion. She doesn't have men friends and works hard. I'd have thought Ernie would prefer you to stay with her than be on your own.'

'It would be nice to stay with Faith. Though she's not much fun these days with a baby tying her to the house every night. But then I've got me singing . . .'

Mike's expression was apologetic. 'To keep Ernie sweet you may have to give up singing for a while.'

Ruby gasped, her agitation making her pace the room. 'How will I make my name as a singer if no one gets to hear me?'

'If you leave Ernie, the break must be complete. And if you don't sing in his clubs, how can you elsewhere? He'd sue you for breach of contract.'

'You mean I can't even sing here?'

'Not for a time. But it will be worth it in the end.' Mike smiled. 'First we'll get you away from him. Then we can start to plan our future.'

'I don't think you should speak to Ernie,' Ruby warned. 'It will only get him riled. I'll leave him but I'll handle it.'

Without warning the door burst open. Squinty glared at Ruby. 'You ready? We should have left here by now.'

'How dare you burst in here without knocking!' Ruby rounded on him.

'Weren't interrupting nothing, was I?' he leered at her. 'Didn't reckon you'd be stripping off in front of Rivers.'

Ruby realised her error in accusing him. Her skin was clammy with ice. What if he'd burst in and found her and Mike kissing? Or had that been his ploy? Ernie would want to know if anything was going on between Mike and her. Thank God they had not been in each other's arms. But the feeling of being smothered by watching eyes was unendurable. Ernie had her trapped. She couldn't leave him without sacrificing her singing career. That went against the grain.

'There's such a thing as manners,' she clipped out. 'Obviously I would not be changing in front of Mike. But how could you be certain that he had not left?'

'I'm paid to know things,' Squinty said insolently.

'It's my fault for keeping Ruby late,' Mike intervened, his manner cool and detached. 'We were talking about some new numbers I wanted her to try next week. We were arranging days for rehearsals.'

'I had only planned to visit Faith on Wednesday afternoon,' Ruby improvised. 'The rest of the week I'm free. Best to get started on Monday.'

'Tuesday,' Mike corrected, his eyes warning her to play it cool. 'I've got some business to sort out on Monday.'

Ruby picked up her astrakhan coat. With a mischievous smile she kissed Mike's cheek before leaving. Devilment made her eyes sparkle as she added, hoping Mike would appreciate the double meaning behind her words, 'Those new numbers will stir up a sensation, I shouldn't wonder.'

It was half an hour before the jeweller's opened and Dr Jarvis began his surgery. Faith stood beside the brick gate post with the brass plate engraved with Dr Joseph Jarvis's name. Madge had taken Nathaniel earlier than usual so that she could make this visit before work. Her hands were clammy with nervousness. In her handbag was an envelope containing the money for the paintings. The house was a double-fronted Victorian building and a curved gravel path led from the gate to the porch. It was impressive. A house befitting a doctor. A gardener was sweeping the last of the autumn leaves from the lawn and the flower beds were neatly dug over and planted with wallflowers to bloom in the spring. The doctor's car was parked in the drive.

Madge had said she was a fool to take on so about the sale of the paintings. She had established herself as a widow. Why allow her conscience to ruin that?

Perhaps she was being foolish. But she hated lies. It was to protect Nathaniel that she had said that she was widowed. It certainly wasn't to gain sympathy from kind men like Dr Jarvis.

But it wasn't easy. She tilted her head and squared her shoulders. She wasn't ashamed of loving Daniel or of bearing his son. Her knock was firm upon the door. A plump maid answered.

'Is Dr Jarvis at home? I'm Mrs Tempest. He does know me.'

'Surgery don't start for another half-hour. There's already a queue in there. Mornings are always busy.'

'It is a private matter not medical,' Faith persisted. 'It's important or I would not trouble him so early.'

The maid looked her up and down and finding her smart attire acceptable, opened the door wider. 'Please wait here. I'll enquire if Dr Jarvis is available.'

The maid entered a room further down the long hall. Moments later Dr Jarvis stepped into the hall buttoning his dark grey suit jacket. He looked puzzled but also pleased to see her.

'Mrs Tempest, this is an unexpected pleasure. I trust neither you nor your son is ill.'

'No.' She found it hard to hold his quizzing stare. 'I wanted a word if it's possible. I know you're busy and I start work in half an hour.'

'Come into my study. Mama and my sisters are still at breakfast. We will not be disturbed there.'

'Please finish eating. I can wait.'

He shook his head and opened a door towards the back of the house. 'Please sit down, Mrs Tempest. How can I be of service to you? You look very grave. Is something wrong?'

She took the only seat by the desk. There was a skeleton

wearing a bowler hat in a corner and one wall was taken up by a bookcase filled with medical books. He stood by the bookcase waiting for her to speak.

'This isn't easy. I was very flattered when you purchased my paintings.'

'One of which is behind you so that I can see it every time I raise my head.'

She turned and blushed at seeing the painting displayed so prominently. It was the park scene. 'I'm not sure you didn't buy the paintings under false pretences.'

He laughed, regarding her with amusement and interest. 'I can assure you, Mrs Tempest . . .'

'That is the false pretence, Dr Jarvis,' she interrupted quickly. 'I'm not a widow. Although I told the Hornsey brothers that I was. I was desperate for work at the time and have never been proud of the deception. I'm not married to my son's father.' She put the envelope of money on the desk and stood up. 'This is the money you paid for the paintings. You may have thought you were helping a struggling widow. And would be less inclined to have purchased the work of an unmarried mother. I hadn't expected anyone to buy two paintings. I felt that you had been misled . . .' She broke off, then rushed on breathlessly, 'I'm sorry.'

She stood up, moving quickly to the door. He reached it before her. She kept her head lowered, unable to look at him.

'I purchased the paintings for the enjoyment of myself and my patients,' he said gently. 'Already several have commented on the pub scene. Here, take back the money.'

When she hesitated, he took her hand and pressed the envelope into it. 'It took courage to come here today. There was no need to tell me this.'

He released her hand and feeling emotionally vulnerable she opened the door and hurried out. She was relieved and confused by his gesture. Had Madge been right and she had been mad to come here? Now she had placed her reputation in jeopardy. If Dr Jarvis spoke to her employers she could lose her job. Somehow she didn't think that he would.

Chapter Twenty-Two

Faith was nervous. Today her paintings were on show to the public and she had been given the day off work to attend. Madge was accompanying her and Dave had taken the older children to visit Santa's Grotto in Vernon's Emporium at Marble Arch. The grottoes for all Vernon's Emporiums scattered throughout London had been designed for the last twenty years by Tanya Hawkes and had won international acclaim for the designer and were the most popular in London. For many families visiting them they had become a Christmas tradition.

Faith and Madge walked to the church hall. Nathaniel was in his pram and Madge pushed Annie, her youngest, in her pushchair. Fog distorted the outline of houses and showed no sign of lifting as the morning wore on.

'I hate these grey months,' Madge groaned. 'From now to February seems like London's never free of fog for more than a few hours at a time.'

'We could have a white Christmas. The kids will love that.'

Madge chuckled. 'You're always looking on the bright side. Have you heard from your young man recently?'

Faith stamped down a rush of longing. 'He hopes to be back in England in the New Year. And he's not my young man, nor can he be. He's still married.'

'To a self-centred rich bitch, from what you told me. Ain't fair a man like that gets saddled with such a cow.'

'Don't spoil today by talking about it,' Faith said forcefully.

'Ay, I'm so thrilled to be going to see your paintings.

291

A real celebrity that's what you are!'

'Hardly that,' Faith said with a laugh. 'This is a minor exhibition by an art tutor.'

Faith had deliberately waited until the afternoon before visiting the exhibition. When she was painting she always felt closer to Dan. Having been inspired to paint scenes depicting how everyday people worked and spent their leisure in the East End, she hoped that they might be regarded as a social statement. Perhaps even bring awareness of the poverty and hardship faced by the poor to the more affluent who could do something about it.

Half a dozen people were browsing round the exhibition when they entered. Leaving the pram in the entrance hall, Faith carried the sleeping Nathaniel inside and Madge kept hold of Annie's hand so that she did not toddle away. There were over sixty paintings around the walls. Her tutor, John Milner, had told Faith he was displaying several of hers.

John was engrossed in conversation with two men so Faith walked slowly round the exhibits, appraising the still lifes and chocolate-box landscapes. There were some portraits of exceptional quality by Ben Soloman, a middle-aged builder who had lost three fingers from his left hand when a hod of bricks fell on him. Another set of landscapes were by a retired architect, Thomas Cruickshank; the clever use of light was superb. How would her own work fare against two such talented men? Several of the paintings already had small green flags stuck on to the frame indicating that they had been sold.

She found that her knees were shaking as she caught sight of her paintings hanging from a central partition. She gasped in astonishment at seeing that John had put all of the dozen on display.

Her heart did a country reel as she approached. Three people were standing in front of them blocking most from her sight. Then her hand went to her mouth and tears of joy sprang into her eyes. Three of the paintings had green flags attached.

'I've sold some, Madge! I've actually sold some.'

Madge beamed at her and pushed her way forward. 'They are beautiful, Faith.' She then turned to a woman with a cloche hat and a fox-fur around her shoulders. 'Ain't they marvellous? And that's the artist over there. A mate of mine, she is.'

Faith blushed with embarrassment at Madge's enthusiasm. The woman turned to give Faith a cool stare and sniffed. Clearly she was unimpressed by her work. The elderly woman with them dressed in black also turned. She leaned heavily on a walking stick. She wore a cartwheel hat popular in Edwardian times and her grey hair was pulled into a bun at the nape of her neck. She smiled at Faith.

'You have shown exactly how the working class live. Yet you have also portrayed the strength in the faces of the people and their camaraderie. I like that. Too often today the emphasis is on the poverty, the rags and misery on faces. These people are survivors. They band together in adversity. Always there to help out a friend.'

'Mam!' the younger woman protested.

The older woman glared at her. 'I'm not ashamed of my roots. Neither should you be. We were lucky that we had some breaks and managed to set up a business which made us a fortune during the war.'

'Papa worked hard,' the daughter declared haughtily. 'If the men I see lounging on street corners weren't afraid to work for a living they could make something of their lives. They are dirty and live like rats in a midden.'

'Be quiet, Celia!' the mother raged. 'Those men are desperate for work. Thousands of them have no jobs. Even the docks are laying off men.'

The older woman turned away from her daughter and addressed Faith. 'You've captured the spirit of the people. I get cross when they are patronised or dismissed as the great "unwashed" as my daughter's contemporaries mock them. Your work has moved me.'

'It's very kind of you to say so, Madam.' Faith was touched by her kind words.

'These are good.' The woman nodded at the street scenes.

'Especially this pub scene. It's the Crooked Billet, isn't it? You've got the piano being played and some old bawd singing her heart out. And this one: with the kids huddled round the hot-chestnut brazier outside another corner pub, brings back memories that does.'

The woman studied Faith thoughtfully and added, 'My second husband owns a chain of small hotels throughout the West End which are popular with the middle-class visitors to the City. Your paintings in the reception and dining rooms would be a tactful reminder that not everyone is so fortunate as themselves. Do you undertake commissions?'

'Yes,' Faith said, never having done one before but she was certainly not going to refuse outright. 'What did you have in mind?'

'Street scenes like these for the bar and some scenes from our own hotels; inside the restaurants and lounges. I assume you would give us a discount for such a large number.'

Faith swallowed, unable to believe her good fortune. 'Of course. How many hotels does your husband own?'

'Eleven. Do you live locally? I'd like to call and see your other work. I'm Mrs Thomas.'

Faith gave her address. 'I'm free on Wednesday afternoon.'

'I shall arrive at two thirty.'

At that moment John Milner came up. He was stocky and wore baggy olive-green corduroy trousers, a Fair Isle jumper and paisley cravat. The dome of his head was bald and he had a bushy grey beard.

'I didn't see you arrive, Faith,' he apologised.

She introduced Madge and Mrs Thomas and thought it politic to move away while Mrs Thomas and John settled the cost of the paintings. Faith was surprised to see that John had priced her paintings between fifteen and twenty-five guineas depending on size. She had expected them to be much cheaper. Most in the show were around five to ten guineas.

Mrs Thomas waved at Faith as they left and John was grinning as he returned to her side. 'Mrs Thomas bought five paintings and you've sold another three. One to the Council to hang in the library.'

'You've made a fortune!' Madge gasped. 'It's more than some men earn in a year. Not that they ain't nice and if folks 'ave the money,' she hastily amended, looking worried lest she had offended Faith.

'Miss Tempest is a very talented artist,' John said, stiffly.

Faith interrupted, 'I'm staggered by my sales.'

'You deserve it,' John replied. 'The exhibition has been a success. Tom Cruickshank and Ben Soloman have also sold well. The local paper is sending a reporter round. He should be here soon. I'm sure he'd like to interview you. Cruickshank is coming in to meet him.'

'I'd rather not,' Faith said quickly. 'It's getting late and it's rather damp with the fog to keep the children out too long. I can't thank you enough for supporting me.'

'It's been my pleasure, Faith. Seeing raw talent blossom into something special is what makes tutoring worthwhile. And despite your family and work commitments, you've worked hard to improve your painting. You'll get your money for the paintings at the next class.'

A man in a large cap and overcoat with a camera over his shoulder stood inside the door surveying the hall. Guessing he was the reporter, Faith couldn't get away fast enough. She kept her face averted from him and pulled a protesting Madge outside.

In her haste she did not see Nathaniel toss his favourite teddy out of the pram or that Dr Jarvis had just arrived. He stooped to pick it up when she was halfway down the street.

He was disappointed at missing Faith at the exhibition. And was about to run after her then stopped. He had been thinking about her often since she had called on him at the surgery. He regarded her as an extraordinary woman. Looking at the teddy, he smiled. It was the perfect excuse to call on her and return it. He would get her address from her tutor and visit her after his evening surgery.

Faith had walked a mile before she realised that Nathaniel had lost his teddy.

'It was the one Dan brought him and was his favourite.' Inwardly she chided herself for being so stupid at running away from that reporter. As if he would have remembered one painting of her so many months ago. Even so the memory of the reporters hounding her made her shiver. She didn't want to take any chances, life was going so well for her at the moment. Unwanted publicity could ruin all she had set out to build.

Ruby rehearsed new songs at the River Boat two afternoons a week. Mike had taught her to pitch her voice deeper and shown her how to move and act during her songs. He also encouraged her to take dancing lessons. They had given her a graceful poise and her performance was now stylish. The customers loved it. Ernie hated it. But she refused to change her new image.

Life with Ernie was stormy and her unhappiness grew. His moods were erratic. He constantly criticised her, so that most evenings ended in a row. Then Ernie would force himself on her, using sex as a weapon to dominate her. She couldn't take much more of it, but suffered in silence. She daren't risk Mike confronting Ernie. She couldn't forget that he'd had her last lover mown down by a car.

The afternoons with Mike were treasured because of the contrast between them and her home life. Her greatest frustration was that they were never alone.

'It's better this way,' Mike told her with a grin when Squinty had gone to the gents. 'How could I resist you?'

'I don't want to be resisted,' she returned with a pout.

'Be patient, Ruby. It's not any easier for me. And when I think of you and Ernie together . . .'

Ruby looked over her shoulder to ensure that Squinty had not returned and winked. 'I'm getting rid of that gorilla for the rest of the afternoon.'

She hurried across to his pint of brown ale and taking a twist of paper from her pocket sprinkled its powder into the drink. She gave it a stir with a spoon she had also put into her pocket. Satisfied that all the powder had dissolved she hurried back to Mike. He was frowning.

'What have you done?'

She grinned. 'It ain't nothing. Just a dose of senna pods. Give him half an hour after drinking that an' he'll be too busy squatting on the throne to care what we're up to. Just as well the lavs are far enough away so that he can't hear the music anyway.'

'Ruby, I can't allow. . .' Mike stopped as Squinty returned and scowled at them. He was typical of the men Ernie employed and Mike didn't like the way he was insolent to Ruby. Mike lowered his voice. 'The dose ain't gonna harm him, is it?'

Ruby shook her head. 'It will keep him from spying on us for an hour.' Raising her voice she added, 'Let's go over that last number again.'

She winked at Mike as Squinty lifted the glass to his mouth and downed half of it in one go.

Twenty minutes later Squinty clutched his stomach and belted out of the club room. Ruby grabbed Mike's hand and drew him towards his office. She leaned back against the solid door and slowly unfastened the tie of her wrapover dress. The two sides fell away and underneath, in anticipation of this moment, she wore nothing but her stockings held in place by ruby garters. 'Now tell me you can still resist me?'

'You're so beautiful,' Mike moaned as he gathered her into his arms. 'You're a temptress, Ruby.'

He ran one hand reverently over her breast. His touch was cherishing, light as thistledown as it traced the fullness of her breast and down over her ribcage to the voluptuous swelling of her hips. Then his lips crushed hers.

'Oh Mike, it's been so long,' she moaned between kisses. 'I've wanted you so much.'

Their breathing became laboured. His mouth trailed along her throat to fasten over each breast in turn, his tongue circling, gently sucking, until she was writhing. Her fingers were impatient upon his trousers. When her hand closed over him, she felt the throb of demanding flesh like iron wrapped in silk. With his hands supporting her buttocks, she wrapped her legs around his waist. With a sigh of pleasure she was impaled upon him.

'I don't want to hurt you, my love,' Mike murmured.

'You could never hurt me. Don't stop.'

His strong arms supported her whilst she moved her hips to sink deeper on to him. He moved with precision, slowly tantalising. The ebb and flow of motion was cataclysmic. It was a mixture of torture and joy. Her legs clamped like a vice around his waist. She could feel his urgency building as he carried her to the polar-bearskin rug and laid her on it. He held back his own gratification, allowing her to surrender to the frenzy which was consuming her. Only when she cried out in release, the sound stifled as she nipped the side of his neck, did Mike seek his own fulfilment. Her inner muscles were like a fist clenching and unclenching, her cries a sob of bitter-sweet rapture as she climaxed when he erupted within her.

Hearts pounding in unison, their bodies slick with sweat, they kissed each other with deepening intensity. They moved sinuously, murmuring endearments until their breathing slowed.

Ruby said huskily, 'My love, my only love.'

'I love you, Ruby.' His lips were passionate against her hair. 'I want you. But not furtively like this as though our love is wrong. You're worth more than a quick tumble against my office door.'

She smiled irrepressibly. 'A quick tumble is better than nothing, my darling. I ain't cut out to be a nun. But you're the only man I want.'

Mike kissed her again then pulled away to adjust his clothing. 'Squinty will be in the bar again soon.' He handed her a hand towel from the drawer of his desk. 'You got me so fired up, I never used nothing.'

Ruby shrugged. 'A girl's entitled to one slip-up and get away with it. Or there ain't no justice in the world.'

Ruby walked through the club room into the ladies and saw Squinty looking pale and shaky emerging from the lavatory.

'You all right? You look rather peaky.'

He grunted and whirled round to dash back inside the gents. Serve the slimy toad right. He'd been too lippy to her in the past. Thought he was the bees-knees and could order her about because

Ernie had told him to spy on her. Unfortunately, a ruse like that wouldn't work again, or Squinty would become suspicious. But with her body still glowing from the pleasure Mike had given her, she was not about to be denied a lover. She wanted Mike too badly to be patient. She wanted free of Ernie and was no longer prepared to play Mike's cautious game.

A bottle of sherry was open on the parlour table in Madge's house. Faith had purchased it on the way back from the exhibition to share with her friends and celebrate the success of her afternoon. Madge had once said that she thought a glass of sherry was very posh and she always treated herself to a bottle on her birthday. Faith wanted something special for her now as a way of saying thank-you for being such a good friend. She had also treated Madge's family to fish and chips from the corner chippie. Nathaniel was lying in his pram placed in the corner of the room, playing with his silver and ivory rattle which Ruby had brought him. Madge was at the piano vamping out 'Roll out the barrel' and Dave, Faith and the children were singing.

As the song came to an end there was a knock at the door which Dave went to answer.

'Now, kids, up to bed with you,' Madge ordered.

'Aw, Mum, can't we stay up a bit as Aunty Faith's here?'

'Bed!' Madge repeated, shooing them out of the room. 'Mind you go out back to the lav first. I don't want no excuses for coming downstairs. Faith will come up in ten minutes. And if you're in bed she might tell you a story.'

It was a routine Faith enjoyed whenever the Taylors invited her into their home of an evening.

Jostling, pinching and egging each other on two older children scrabbled for the back of the house just as Dave returned with a visitor. To Faith's amazement she saw it was Dr Jarvis. He wore a camel overcoat and held his brown Derby hat in his hand.

'I knocked next door and when there was no answer I was going to ask your neighbours to take in this.' He held out the bear. 'I thought your son might have trouble sleeping without it. Mr

299

Taylor said you were here, Mrs Tempest.'

Faith rose from the chair and took the bear from him. 'That was very kind of you to go to so much trouble. How did you know it was Nathaniel's?'

'I arrived at the exhibition just as you were leaving and saw it fall out of the pram. By the time I picked it up you were far down the road. Mr Milner gave me your address.'

Quickly recovering her manners, Faith introduced the doctor to Madge. Her neighbour smiled at him and then at Faith. 'We're celebrating Faith's success this afternoon. She got a commission from the wife of a hotelier to paint scenes from their hotels. Did you see how well her paintings sold?'

Faith interrupted Madge's boasting. 'Would you like some sherry, Dr Jarvis?'

'That would be most acceptable.' He put his hat on the top of the piano, obviously at ease amongst the large family.

Dave had gone to stop the children squabbling in the scullery. With a smile at Faith, Madge added, 'I'll just get a clean glass from the kitchen. Hope you'll excuse a tumbler, doctor. Usually mine and Dave's tipple is a glass of stout.'

When she was alone with the doctor Faith said, 'I'm sorry to have put you to so much trouble. I didn't notice that Nathaniel had lost his bear until we were almost home.'

As though in protest, Nathaniel began to cry. Faith picked him up and he stopped. His tiny hand reached up to touch his mother's mouth.

'How old is he?' Dr Jarvis held out a finger for Nathaniel to grasp. He smiled as the tiny fist closed over it and the baby gurgled with contentment at so much attention. 'He's a bonny lad.'

'Nine months.'

'Do you still see his father?' As soon as he spoke, he shook his head and put up his hand. 'I'm sorry. I should not have asked that. It isn't any of my business.'

'No, it isn't.' She held his gaze and saw no condemnation in his eyes. He didn't deserve her rudeness. 'You've been very

300

understanding. Others would have simply judged me as immoral – a woman beneath contempt.'

Madge cleared her throat, announcing her presence before she walked into the room. Her gaze was speculative as it took in the couple. She handed the doctor the glass and poured him a sherry.

'I'd best sort those kids of mine out,' Madge excused herself again. 'It sounds like they're having a pillow fight now, the little rascals.'

The doctor regarded Faith seriously. 'A toast to your success. You're a very talented woman.' He sipped the sherry and put the glass down on the table. 'I'll not intrude upon your celebrations with your friends any longer.'

Nathaniel had fallen asleep and Faith laid him in his pram. Dr Jarvis had retrieved his hat and she walked with him to the front door. When she held out her hand she was surprised at the warmth and strength of his handshake. In the dim hall light she saw him hesitate. To break the awkwardness, she said, 'I hope your nurse liked her watch.'

'She burst into tears but I think she was pleased.'

'I'm sure that she was. Thank you for returning the bear. You could have dropped it in to the shop on Monday.'

'I had other motives. I was wondering if you'd like to go dancing?'

Faith was startled. 'I have my son to look after.'

'I'd be happy to baby-sit, if you want to go out, Faith,' Madge called down from upstairs.

Faith knew that her friend was matchmaking. It made her uneasy. 'I'm sorry, but I've walked miles today. It was very kind of you to invite me, Dr Jarvis.'

'Perhaps some other time?'

She didn't know what to say. She liked the doctor, but she didn't want to get involved with another man.

'Thank you again for bringing the teddy.'

He accepted her dismissal with a steady appraisal. 'Goodnight, Mrs Tempest.'

When the door closed Faith turned to discover Madge standing

301

in the hall with her hands on her hips. 'What did you refuse him for? You need your head examined! A proper gentleman he were. And he's interested in you.'

'Which is why it wouldn't be right to go out with him. I love Dan.'

'Nathan needs a proper father. Forget Dan. There ain't no use pining for what can't be.'

When Faith returned to her house later Madge's words still rang in her mind. She was a realist. Was she holding on to false hopes that she and Dan had a future? She sank into an armchair. His image was clear before her. Her arms ached to enfold him. 'Oh, Dan, my love. My love.'

She brushed a tear away impatiently. She would always love him, but with his wife crippled how could they find happiness together? And she had Nathaniel to consider. Being orphaned so young she knew the need for the security and love of two parents. Was she being fair to her son to deny him a father figure in his life? A man who could be a real father to him, rather than the shadowy figure of Dan, who could only visit on occasions.

Chapter Twenty-Three

For days Ruby had been puzzling how to get away from Ernie. She'd hoped to shop him to Inspector Armitage when she discovered the locations of the three Christmas jobs they were planning. But try as she might, she had heard nothing further of them. Frustration gnawed at her. Christmas was looming closer and she had promised herself the present of seeing Ernie locked away for good.

She was working the Gilded Lily that night. The atmosphere in the club had changed since Mike had pulled out of the partnership. There were few wealthy customers, except for a group of eight men in evening suits who were already drunk when they arrived. They were rowdy and ill disciplined.

The other customers were dressed in wide-lapelled suits with baggy trousers. They all had that cold calculating stare Ruby now associated with villains. Hugh and his brothers were there. Kavanagh sat at the largest table by the stage. As usual he was loud-voiced and constantly demanded the attention of the waitresses in the new uniform designed by Ernie. They wore low-cut black satin dresses, which were so short that they showed the tops of their stockings and coloured garters every time they bent over a table. Payment for the drinks was either stuffed into their cleavages or slid inside the garters by the customers. The men thought it entertaining. Ruby thought it was sleazy. Ernie had no taste and was bringing the club into disrepute.

When she'd challenged him, he had laughed derisively, 'We're making more money than ever.'

'The waitresses are seen leaving with the customers.'

'So what? As long as they pay me half of anything they earn.'

'That makes the Gilded Lily little better than a knocking shop. I don't want no part of it.'

Ernie grabbed her wrist and wrenched it up behind her back. 'You'll do as you're told. It wouldn't hurt you to be a bit more accommodating to the customers: police inspectors, a judge, council officers. Men who I can then control. They'd pay a fortune to be alone with you for an hour.'

'I ain't whoring for you.'

He shrugged. 'Then how yer gonna buy all the expensive clothes you've taken such a fancy to? I ain't doling out any more on you.'

'You've changed your attitude,' she said, but the knowledge contracted her stomach with panic. Ernie's possessiveness may have been a nuisance but it showed he cared. If he now expected her to whore for him, then his feelings had changed. 'Go to hell. I ain't cheapening myself that way.'

Ernie stared at her spitefully. 'Madam Hoity-Toity, ain't you, all of a sudden. Mike's been giving you grand ideas. And what's this I hear that Squinty was taken queer at the River Boat?'

'Touch of the gyppy tummy, weren't it? He knocks back the drink a fair bit.'

'You and Mike ain't up to no funny business?' His face contorted with hatred, spittle spraying from his mouth.

Ruby rounded her eyes in surprise. 'Me and Mike? You gotta be kidding. He's a bit long in the tooth for me.'

He yanked at her hair, jerking her head back so violently she thought her neck would snap. 'Don't play the innocent with me. Mike fancies you. If you and 'im . . .'

Fear spiked her. 'There ain't nothing like that between us. He's a mate. For Gawd's sake, he's your brother!'

Hearing the fear in her voice, Ernie pulled harder on her hair. Ruby was getting too big for her boots. She needed reminding who was boss; who had made her what she was. He drew back his fist to slam into her gut.

Her eyes blazed with a lethal light. 'Go on, hit me! Then I can't sing, you great oaf. I ain't going out there if there's a mark on me.'

She held back from telling him about the statement already with Mike's solicitors about his activities and alibis. This treatment was mild to what she had suffered before. There wasn't any point in getting him riled when she could handle him.

Ernie felt his body stir. On occasion this wildcat still had the power to drive him to a sexual frenzy. He got a thrill out of subduing her. The ache in his groin increased. He was tempted to fling her across his desk and take her there and then, just to teach her a lesson. There were more ways than a beating to bring her into line.

Immediately she went limp in his hold, a glazed look of contempt replacing her fear. 'Is that the only way you can get it up, by bullying me? You're pathetic.'

His desire for her shrivelled. She was poison. If it weren't that Mike was so hot for her, he'd throw the tramp out on the street. His thoughts were brutal. Mike needed bringing into line. He was giving Ruby ideas. He thought himself so superior to Ernie. There was the faintest stirring of conscience. Mike had stood by him in his youth and bailed him out of trouble. Then any feeling of guilt was sharply smothered. Perhaps he'd allow his brother his moment of glory at the River Boat. He grinned to himself. The higher they climbed the harder they fell. Him and Ruby both.

Ernie shoved Ruby away from him so hard that she crashed into the table. 'Then get out there and sing. It's about time you pulled your weight around here. You're spending too much time at the River Boat.'

'Perhaps that's because Mike's doing more for my career than you ever could.'

'What career?' Ernie laughed cruelly. 'They say dung finds its own level.'

She bit back the retort that he was the level she had sunk to. Her husband's moods were unpredictable. Once she would have used sex to gain the upper hand over Ernie. But now sex with him nauseated her. Each day she was finding it harder even to be civil with him. To hide her disgust, she lit a cigarette and held the long holder away from her in a nonchalant pose. 'You coming back to the house tonight? Or you gambling all the profits away with Kavanagh?'

'What's it to you?'

She shrugged. 'Don't expect me to stay behind and play hostess. I'm a singer.'

'You're what I made you, Ruby Starr, and don't you forget it.' Ernie moved to the door. 'If you weren't married to me you wouldn't even have a job here. Mike's just stringing you along, 'cos he fancies you. For all his talk nothing ain't come of that stage musical, has it?'

'The producer couldn't get sufficient backers.' Ruby wouldn't believe that Mike would use her as Ernie had done. She was tired. The gin she'd been drinking all evening was making it harder to be rational. Mike would never betray her. He would rescue her from Ernie's clutches. The River Boat was prospering. They would have a wonderful life together.

Her elation faded as she came down the office stairs. The contrasts between Mike's loving and Ernie's cruelty and also the brothers' two clubs were extreme. The Gilded Lily had gone to seed and the Silver Bird wasn't much better. The River Boat already had a reputation for some of the finest jazz in London and Mike had employed a high-class chef to encourage his customers to dine and dance.

Seeing two men disappear through a door to the gambling rooms at the back of the club, Ruby frowned. There was a poker game going on tonight. Ernie only allowed them in after midnight if the stakes were high.

There was a short man in a brown suit hunched over a drink in an unlit corner. He'd been there several times recently. He gave her the shivers. There was a shiftiness about him she didn't trust. From his build and rougher speech she surmised that he worked in the docks. Customers often stopped by his table. Later in the evening those customers behaved strangely. Some were charged with excess energy, laughing foolishly. Others became lethargic and stupefied. She'd never been into drugs, although she suspected that Ernie had slipped something into her drink on occasion to make her more compliant to his demands. When she'd confronted him, he'd laughed. 'You were drunk, babe. That was all.'

If the man in the brown suit was a drug pedlar, he wouldn't be allowed in the club unless Ernie knew what was happening and was profiting from it.

She felt no pleasure as she took her place on stage. The pianist accompanying her was a lush. At least tonight he looked partially sober. How had she ever thought that this was the route to fame and fortune? She had no more money now than when she worked as a chambermaid. Ernie bought everything for her, but getting cash out of him was as difficult as castrating an adult bull. And with the same bovine response.

It was two thirty in the morning and she was worn out. The club never shut before five. The blue haze of tobacco smoke which hung over the room stung her eyes and irritated her throat. She had a headache from the chatter and bawdy comments shouted at the waitresses. Halfway through her second number a waitress with breasts bigger than her brain was leaning over a table. Her tits were pressed into an ogling punter's face. Her dress had ridden so high it showed the flesh above her stockings and her frilly drawers. As Ruby proceeded with her song the man slid his hand under the leg of the waitress's knickers. His drunken companions whistled encouragement, drowning Ruby's song.

Ruby lost her temper. This lot didn't want class, they wanted sex. She realised how much she had changed since meeting Mike. Why should she cheapen herself for jerks like them? She stopped singing and stormed from the stage. She didn't even bother to get her coat but strode out into the night. It was drizzling with icy rain when Squinty caught up with her.

'Ernie wants you back inside to finish yer numbers.'

'You can tell Ernie, he can go to the devil. I ain't singing in that bordello again until he gets rid of the tarts who work the tables.'

Squinty's expression was nasty as he reached out to grab her. 'Get back inside and do as you're told. Ernie's the boss.'

'He's my husband and don't you forget it. If I told him you've got wandering hands when you're driving me, you could find you ain't got a hand to drive with.'

His eyes slitted. 'I ain't never touched you.'

She smiled coldly. 'I'm Ernie's property. He acts first and asks questions after. So be a good puppy dog and tell your master I've a headache and I've gone home.'

A taxi was approaching. Ruby gave a piercing whistle to attract the driver's attention. It wasn't until the taxi pulled away that she realised tears were streaming down her face, mingling with the rain. She checked her self-pity. It never served any purpose and only weakened you. And she wasn't weak. She'd been struggling all her life to get what she wanted. Sometimes, like her marriage to Ernie, the end results had not been all she'd desired.

Ernie might frighten her, but that gave her a deeper resilience to escape him. There wasn't much that she hadn't striven for and not achieved. Ernie was a loser. She'd ditch him. Life with Mike would be happy and rewarding. He would give her the fame that she craved. The producer of the musical was still interested in her. He'd get the money for the show sooner or later, but there was no need for Ernie to know that. Mike would make her a star where Ernie had failed.

Her plans were formulated quickly. These she would keep to herself. Mike was too cautious. She was used to getting what she wanted by her own means. Patience wasn't her way.

On entering her house, Ruby saw none of the expensive furnishings she had been so proud of when she came here as a bride. For all its luxury it was a cage, a prison, just like her marriage.

She picked up the telephone. 'Get me Inspector Terry Armitage's home at Forest Gate,' she instructed the operator.

The male voice on the other end was sleepy to begin with. She disguised her voice. 'The waitresses at the Gilded Lily are all on

the game. Durham's their pimp. There's drugs there. A man –
docker type – brown suit, stocky, sits in a dark corner. He's a
dealer. Tonight there's also an illegal poker game going on.'

'Who is this?' the suddenly authoritative voice demanded.

She put down the phone without answering. It was a quarter to
three; would he bother to act tonight? A raid on the club by
Armitage's men would add more incriminating evidence against
Ernie. She never wanted to work in the the Gilded Lily again. If
it got closed down for a few months all the better for her. Ernie
was so slimy he'd wriggle out of any charges brought against him.
However, it would all go on his file. When he eventually appeared
in court every police fact would go against him. He'd get a long
sentence.

The insistent ringing of the telephone woke Ruby. She peered
blearily at the bedroom clock. It was gone noon. When she lifted
the receiver, Ernie's angry voice blasted her eardrums. 'This
bloody phone has been ringing for five minutes!'

'I was asleep. And where are you? You didn't come home
again. Fine husband you are.'

'I'm in Bow Street nick.'

Ruby smiled. Ernie must never suspect that she had grassed on
him. He'd kill her for sure.

'In the nick? What the hell for?'

'The club got raided. Can't pin nothing on me though. They're
closing it down until the court case comes up in the New Year.
They reckon I'm living off immoral earnings.'

'Oh, Ernie. That's rubbish of course. Isn't it?'

'Too right! I'm innocent,' he yelled, his voice cocky with
bravado. 'Nothing bent about Earnest Ernie Durham. I need a
hundred-quid bail. It's disgusting. An innocent man has to find a
hundred quid so he don't get slammed up with criminals.'

From his tirade Ruby guessed the call was being overheard by
a policeman. 'So pay the bail and come home.'

'Ain't got it on me, have I? You'll have to get hold of the
dough.'

'Where am I supposed to get a hundred quid? You never give me any money. I ain't got nothing. Can't get nothing out the bank neither. You wouldn't let me have a joint bank account.'

'Shut yer mouth and listen,' Ernie ground out. 'Get the money off Mike. And do it fast. Do you think I like cooling me heels in a bloody police cell?'

'Charming as ever, Ernie darling.'

The line went dead. Typical of Ernie. He never had a good word to say for his brother but he'd expect Mike to cough up a hundred-quid bail. And Mike would do it out of loyalty.

She padded into the bathroom to run a bath. She relished the excuse to see Mike but she wasn't rushing herself for Ernie's benefit. It would do the arrogant sod good to spend some time in police custody. She'd always despised the men who lived off immoral earnings. She could no longer delude herself. If Ernie was in so thick with Kavanagh it was obvious he was part of the protection rackets and organised crime that villain was involved in. It wasn't a bit of petty pilfering. It was nightwatchmen getting beaten up and guns being used to kill people. She hated violence. And now Ernie was also running prostitutes and drugs. Drugs ruined people's lives and ended up killing them. Why should she feel sorry for Ernie?

'I warned Ernie not all the police could be bought.' Mike stared at Ruby and rubbed his brow. 'What are they charging him with?'

'He didn't say. But things have got bad lately. It could be for running a gaming house. Even pimping. From the way the waitresses act they're all on the game.' She kept quiet about the drugs. Mike would never forgive Ernie for that after how his wife had died. She had grassed on Ernie to teach him a lesson and get her own back for the way he treated her. If Mike didn't pay the fine, Ernie would find someone else to. And he would settle the score with Mike in the most unpleasant way he could devise. Her triumph lost its edge. Had her anger last night been foolish? Ernie wouldn't rest until he found out who grassed on him. She feared that even if Ernie went down for a long stretch, she would never

310

escape him. He would have contacts outside the prison. They would get her and Mike once he learned they were together.

She strove to master her panic. There had to be a way to get free of Ernie without spending the rest of her life awaiting his vengeful attack.

Mike continued to rage, 'Ernie's a bloody idiot. There's an honest living to be made out of his clubs. But that's not enough for him. He always wants easy money. There ain't no such thing.'

'Don't go upsetting yourself, Mike.' She ran her hands over his chest trying to pacify him. She loved him so much. Being apart from him was crucifying her. 'Just be thankful you're out of it.'

'Am I? The police know I was his partner in the Lily. There'll be sniffing round the River Boat now. Anything Ernie does will reflect on me.'

'But you've got nothing to hide.'

'It won't do the club's reputation any good though. It will hit the papers. They'll drag in my name with Ernie's, especially if I'm seen at Bow Street bailing him out.'

'I'll take the money. Don't be seen getting involved.' His face was a rigid mask of disapproval. Her mind was racing with thoughts of the publicity she would attract. 'What's the point of ruining the reputation of the River Boat?' she insisted. 'You've put in so much hard work. Don't let this spoil it for you.'

Mike subjected her to an exasperated stare. 'I don't like the idea of you going to Bow Street on your own.'

She laughed. 'It's a cop shop. I'm hardly gonna get done over. But I love it when you worry about me.'

'I never stop worrying about you, Ruby. Ernie must be in deeper with Kavanagh than I realised. I doubt that *he* spent the night in a cell.'

'He probably had enough dough on him to pay his own bail,' she replied, waspishly. 'Ernie loses hundreds to him each week at poker.'

Mike went to the office safe. 'Just as well I hadn't banked this before you arrived.' He held out a wad of large white five-pound notes.

Her fingers curled around them and over Mike's hand. 'I hope Ernie appreciates what you've done for him.' She stood on tiptoe and kissed him.

He returned it with passion and after a long moment reluctantly pulled away. 'You'd best get going. Didn't you say Ernie telephoned at midday? It's almost four. There ain't no point in making his temper worse. He's gonna be in a foul mood after last night. Tell him I'll be round the Gilded Lily tomorrow for him to repay me.'

Ruby took a cab to Bow Street. Travelling by motor car or taxi cab was the normal now. Not so long ago she'd have been so broke, she'd have used the trams or walked. Quite the Lady Muck, she mused. Lady Muck was right. Married to Lord Muck and Filth. She stared out of the window despondently. But not for much longer.

The taxi turned into Bow Street. She smiled at seeing reporters and photographers outside the police court. This was more the ticket. She hadn't had her name in the papers for months. She pulled out her powder compact and lipstick. Her make-up replenished, she winked at her reflection in the mirror. Unbuttoning her coat she hoisted her skirt above her knees to give the reporters a flash of her slender legs as she got out and asked the cabbie to wait.

'Who's the tart?' one reporter asked another.

'Dunno.'

Ruby hid her annoyance. By now her name should be on the lips of every reporter eager for a scoop. It was Ernie's fault she was still a nobody. Even her publicity at her wedding and later disappearance had been forgotten.

She produced her most ravishing smile, putting a hand on her hip to hold her coat open and display her figure. 'I'm Ruby Starr, gentlemen. Wife to Earnest Ernie Durham. His club the Gilded Lily was raided last night. I sing there. And at the Silver Bird. Also the River Boat.'

'Were you at the club when it was raided?' One reporter

breathed whisky fumes over her. He'd obviously enjoyed a liquid lunch.

Her expression portrayed injured innocence. 'Gentleman, I'm a respectable woman. I've no idea why the police should raid my husband's club. I'm sure it's been a terrible mistake.'

'Why are you here?'

'To pay his bail.'

'Then he must've been charged.'

She looked bemused. 'I don't understand police procedure. The first I'd heard of the raid was when my husband telephoned me this morning.'

Ruby entered the police station, but not so fast that the photographers didn't get a chance to use their cameras.

Ernie looked thunderous when he was finally brought up from the cells. 'Took your bleeding time, didn't you? Where's Mike?'

'He's busy. You can't expect him to keep nursemaiding his little brother every time you get into trouble,' she couldn't resist taunting.

Ernie shot her a venomous glare and grabbing her arm frogmarched her outside. There was a clamour of demanding voices from the reporters and the cameras again flashed.

'Shit! What the hell's all this about?' He propelled her roughly into the waiting cab and slammed the door behind them.

'That's charming after I've spent the afternoon running round after you!' she blazed. 'I want some answers, Ernie.'

'It's none of your damned business. But I was grassed up last night. I found out from a friend at the nick that it were a woman.'

Ruby's heart stopped. When Ernie turned to her, his eyes were shards of malignant evil. 'When I find out who grassed me up they're gonna wish they'd never been born.'

'What charges were brought against you?' Mike demanded as he stormed into his brother's office. Kavanagh was lounging back in a chair, his feet on Ernie's desk.

'What's it to do with you?' Ernie sneered. 'You ain't me bleeding keeper.'

Before answering him he turned to Hugh. 'I'd like a private word with my brother.'

The gangleader shrugged. 'Ernie calls the shots in this club now, you, Rivers. Want me to get the boys to throw him out, Ernie?'

Ernie's lips curled back as though the idea amused him. He lit a fat Havana cigar and tossed one to Mike who instinctively caught it. 'Give us five minutes, Hugh. I don't need no one to deal with me own brother.'

Mike put the cigar back in the box, his body tense as he watched Ernie trim and light his. The suit his brother was wearing was a loud pin-stripe with wide lapels and wide trousers. The hang of the jacket could easily conceal a short cudgel or handgun. There were lines scored about Ernie's mouth which hadn't been there two years ago and heavy pouches puffed his eyes. He'd put on a couple of stone since marrying Ruby. Outwardly his brother had done well for himself, but there was a coldness in his eyes which he'd seen in all of Kavanagh's bullies. He'd learnt how to inflict pain and he enjoyed it.

'Mum would turn in her grave to see you now, Ernie,' he said heavily. 'She never saw the bad in you.'

'Leave Mum out of this. And don't try and kid me this is about the police raid. It's about Ruby. You fancy her.'

'Ruby's a great woman. She's me sister-in-law.' Mike felt he was walking on quicksand. How had Ernie sussed that? Was it so obvious that he cared for Ruby? Even so, he doubted that Ernie had proof that he and Ruby were lovers. 'You and me never shared our women.'

'And we ain't gonna either.'

'Don't go getting crazy ideas, Ernie.' Mike kept his voice level; he never raised it when he made threats. He saw the slight shaking of Ernie's hand as he took the cigar from his lips and blew a smoke ring. 'Ruby is a great singer,' he went on flatly. 'I'd like to help her career. It don't seem like you've come up with much for her.'

'Maybe I don't want me wife traipsing round the country. I've got enough to do running the clubs.' Ernie rocked on his heels, his expression smug.

314

Mike itched to punch him. That would solve nothing except to make him feel better. If he wasn't careful, he'd make things worse for Ruby. Fighting to control his temper, he added, 'I don't like some of the rumours I've heard. It turns my gut to see you going the same rotten way as your old man.'

'He were a loser. I ain't. I've got more in the bank than he thieved in all his life. A smart house and two clubs. I ain't the loser out of us two.' Ernie's voice was rising as his spite burst forth. He was sneering now, puffing out his chest in self-importance. 'What savings have you got? Or rather how much do you owe the bank for the loan you got to do up the River Boat? You don't even own the flat you rent.'

'My money's clean.'

'Is that all you've got to say? I was in a business meeting. You ain't a partner in this club no more. You ain't welcome here either. Here's your hundred quid.' He took it from his wallet and threw it at Mike who caught it deftly. 'Ruby won't be singing at the River Boat no more.'

'You may find Ruby has her own opinions about that.'

'Ruby does as she's told.'

Mike could feel the hatred emanating from his brother. There never had been any love lost between them. The only reason he'd looked out for Ernie was because their mother had asked him. They studied each other in silence. Mike was taller by several inches and a trained soldier but Ernie was three stone heavier. They both knew that in any fight Mike would be the victor, as he had been in the past. Ernie's brawn was no match for Mike's speed and skill.

Mike lost control of his temper and grabbed his brother by the tie. 'If you lay a hand on Ruby, I'll give you triple what you give her. Lay off her!'

'I knew you fancied her.'

'Don't talk rot. I won't tolerate any woman in my family getting slapped round.'

Ernie recalled the last time Mike had turned on him. He'd vowed then that Mike would pay for that beating. He'd held off until now. He had wanted to make Mike mentally suffer. Big brother Mike was about to learn that it didn't pay to threaten him.

The black car was parked in shadow, its lights and engine switched off. For an hour Ernie had been watching the River Boat. He'd arrived when Ruby was due to finish her performance.

The bitch had ignored his orders not to sing here. That was Ruby's first mistake. Her second was not leaving as soon as she had finished. Even the last of the customers had left quarter of an hour ago. Was his bitch of a wife playing around with his brother? Damn them both!

Tonight he had meant to teach Mike a lesson. To show him that Ernie made a powerful enemy. That had changed now.

His diabolical temper formed a red mist before his eyes. No one put one over on Ernie Durham. His brother had thought he'd got away with it for years. Ernie didn't admit that until he'd got in so thick with the Kavanagh gang, Mike had the power to scare him witless. But Hugh had shown him how to create fear in others. You didn't need to do the dirty work yourself, you paid others to do that.

As for Ruby, she had lost her value to him. Subservient she had some worth. She was too independent now, too determined to have her own way. Ruby was obsessed with her singing career. She'd made her third mistake by slagging him off in front of Hugh earlier that evening. Kavanagh had turned nasty. He'd intimated that if Ernie couldn't control his own wife, how could he instil terror into others?

'Get on with it,' he snapped at the two heavies in the back.

'There's lights on. Ain't Ruby still in there?'

'Just do it, unless you want to join 'em?'

They slunk out of the car without a sound. Like the sewer rats they were, they blended into the shadows.

The main lights had been turned off. Ruby and Mike sat on a padded seat by the bar drinking a brandy. It wasn't often Ruby stayed this late. She'd been strung up when she arrived, cursing

Ernie. She was near the end of her tether.

'I ain't taking no more, Mike. Who does Ernie think he is, telling me where I can and can't sing? I'm still working his club, ain't I?'

'You must leave him. Book into a hotel for a few weeks. That should give you some protection.'

'But I want to be with you, darling.' She ran her fingers along his jaw.

'We've got to do what's best for your safety—'

A splintering of glass from the back halted his words. Mike sprang up. 'What the—'

An explosion ripped through the door, its hot blast lighting the club like daylight. Then its force knocked him several feet across the floor. Its brightness momentarily blinded him. Splinters of wood and glass showered over them. Ruby began screaming. A second explosion followed from the direction of the office. The air was thick with choking dust. When plasterwork from the ceiling and debris finished falling, Mike heard the low roar of flames.

'Christ! The place has been torched,' he yelled. 'That's a fire bomb.'

Ruby was still screaming.

'Are you hurt?' he shouted

He staggered upright. The side of his head ached like hell and so did his right shoulder. Some debris must have hit him. The explosion had knocked out all the lights. The orange glow from the flames cast a sinister illumination into the bar. It was filling with lethal smoke. The seat where Ruby had been sitting was empty. Her screams directed his gaze to where her legs were sticking out from under the table. There was blood on them.

His own pain was forgotten. They had seconds to get out before the smoke overcame them. He flung the table across the room and scooped Ruby over his shoulder.

'I'll get us out of here,' he managed before the smoke made him cough and stagger.

The nearest exit was a fire door across the room. He weaved

drunkenly towards it. The heat was intense, his eyes were streaming and throat raw. Smoke stifled him, robbing his lungs of air. His senses were swirling. Ruby's slight form felt like a concrete slab, weighing him down. His knees buckled. Only another dozen paces to the door . . .

Ruby's terrified screams goaded him on. He plunged forward. Then his foot caught against a table leg and they crashed headlong to the floor. Ruby was no longer screaming. She was making strange half-choking, half-sobbing sounds. Mike felt his head would burst. Black smoke was a wall before him, flames a barrier behind them, their heat searing his neck.

Each terrified second stretched like a tortuous minute as he struggled to remain conscious. Panting heavily, he summoned the last of his strength and reared up on his knees. His outstretched hand groped for the bar of the fire door. He encountered bare wall. He'd miscalculated, misjudged the angle of the door. One arm remained clamped around Ruby's waist. Her figure was limp. She was unconscious. His own senses were deserting him.

Trusting upon instinct, he veered to the left, hauling Ruby with him. He groped his way along the wall. His lungs felt as if they would explode. Dizziness from lack of oxygen was about to engulf him. He touched the door frame. Another step and his hand was on the hot metal rod of the fire door.

Outside the River Boat Ernie's hostile eyes reflected the spreading flames. The first explosion had blown out the back of the building, shattering every window. The second had ripped through the office where his tart of a wife and treacherous brother were.

His expression was impassive as the two men clambered back into the car. They had done their job well. Already the fire had spread to the second floor and tongues of flame were licking through the roof. In the distance he heard the bell of a fire-engine. Some nosy-parker must have alerted the fire brigade. Time to get out of here. A final glance at the burning club convinced him that it was a raging inferno – an apt tomb. Word would now get round that Ernie Durham was a man to be reckoned with. He laughed evilly and murmured to himself, 'So long, Ruby. How do you like singing with the angels?'

Chapter Twenty-Four

Mike was on his hands and knees, his body partially over Ruby's inert form as he gasped to draw air into his lungs.

A bell was clanging nearby. The sound of stamping boots resounded like an army on the run towards the front of the club. He tried to call out but his voice was no more than a hoarse croak. The effort sent him into paroxysms of coughing.

'Someone's over there.' A gruff voice rose in command. 'Alert the ambulancemen. Get the fire hoses working. Don't look like there's much 'ope of saving it though.'

Mike heard the words as though from a great distance. Every sense was tuned to Ruby who was lying so still. Her beautiful face and pale blonde hair were blackened by the smoke. Her arms and legs glistened from the rivulets of blood streaming from scores of cuts. The white tulle of her gown was speckled with burn holes from the explosion blast. He gathered her into his arms, willing some of his own returning strength to seep into her. He rocked her gently, his lips caressing her blackened hair. 'Don't die, Ruby. Don't die on me, my love.'

He took her wrist, searching for a pulse. It was faint. Gently he stroked her face. There were globules of blood reflected in the light from the flames. Unaware of the tears streaking down his cheeks, he kept repeating, 'C'mon, Ruby love. We're safe now. Open your eyes. C'mon, my love.'

'All right mate, we'll see to her,' the gruff voice commanded. 'We'll get yer both to the hospital.'

Strong hands were lifting him up but he fought them off. 'I ain't leaving Ruby.'

They sat him up on the wet ground and suddenly his stomach rebelled and he vomited. His hands were shaking as he raised them to his mouth.

'That's the shock, mate.' A man hunkered beside him and placed a blanket over his shoulders. 'What's yer name?'

'Mike Rivers. I'm the owner of the club.' He put a hand to his aching head. 'There were two explosions. The woman is the singer here, Ruby Starr. I'm her brother-in-law. We'd better get word to her husband.'

Even as he said it another wave of nausea rose to his throat. He countered it. The fire was no accident; not with two explosions. Firebombs! But who? In his shocked state disjointed thoughts buzzed like flies around a rotting carcase. It could be any club owner who had muscle with the gangsters. Prostitution, gambling, drugs were just a few of the rackets revolving around the club scene. He'd steered clear of that. He'd had no choice but to pay protection money to a rival gang to Kavanagh's. No club could escape those dues. He'd accepted it because he couldn't do anything about it. That gang was big-time. It was pay up or be blown up. He'd paid so it wasn't them. And those gangsters would be down on whoever did this like a ton of bricks. So who was responsible? Ernie? Why did his name keep jumping into his mind?

He shook his head and winced at the nails of pain being riveted into his skull. He wished he could be certain that his brother was innocent. Ernie couldn't have known that he and Ruby were in there. Even Ernie had not yet stooped to murder. Or had he? Some recent robberies had put one night watchman into hospital and another had died. Mike had to admit he no longer knew his half-brother.

He kept his stare fixed on Ruby as two men worked over her. They lifted and strapped her on to a stretcher. Mike took her hand as he was helped to the ambulance.

'How is she?'

'I reckon she'll pull through,' the shorter of the ambulancemen replied. He had a thick bushy moustache and a hooked nose. 'You can't always tell if the smoke has damaged the lungs. She's got some nasty cuts on her shoulders from glass. Looks like there's a splinter still embedded.' The man assessed him in the light from a naphtha lamp hanging on the ambulance door. 'You've got some deep cuts yourself. Reckon you'll 'ave two shiners in the morning from being clobbered on the 'ead. That cut on your brow needs stitches.'

Bemused Mike put a hand to his temple and it came away sticky with blood. His fingers were blackened with smoke.

The ambulanceman went on, 'The pair of you were lucky to get out of that. Looks like it went up like a bonfire.'

The next afternoon Faith was taking a late lunch break. She had picked up some shopping from the market and was walking back along the High Street when a one-armed newsseller waved the paper and cried out, 'London club fire-bombed. Singer injured.'

There were scores of London clubs yet Faith felt a dart of fear that the singer was Ruby. It was irrational but she couldn't rest until she knew. Buying the paper she scanned it hurriedly. The words punched out at her. She sobbed aloud, 'My God, it *is* Ruby!'

She stood in the middle of the pavement oblivious to the mutterings and shovings of the pedestrians around her. There was a glamorous picture of Ruby used by the papers when she'd disappeared. She read the article quickly, talking to herself in her anxiety. 'Thank God, she's alive. Not seriously wounded. But the River Boat has been burnt to the ground. Oh, poor Mike.'

'Mrs Tempest, are you all right?'

The words were repeated twice more before Faith's shocked brain realised that she was being spoken to. She dragged her gaze from the paper and met Dr Jarvis's concerned stare.

She nodded and held the paper out to him. 'Ruby Starr is an old friend of mine. They say she's in hospital. I must find out how badly she was hurt.'

323

'I've finished my rounds. Let me take you to the hospital. My car is parked over the road.'

'That's kind of you. But I couldn't impose. You're a busy man. I can get a bus. Where is this hospital?'

'That settles it,' he said firmly. 'I'll take you. You're too upset to be travelling by public transport.'

'I must let Mr Hornsey know. I can't just leave work.' She put a hand to her head, her thoughts whirling in confusion. 'Oh dear, perhaps I should telephone the hospital and visit when the shop closes.'

'You'll be in no state to work if you're worried about your friend,' Dr Jarvis advised. 'We'll stop off at Hornsey's on the way and I'll tell them what has happened. They'll understand.'

Faith smiled with gratitude. 'I'm not usually so dizzy-witted. But realising that Ruby could have been killed . . .'

She allowed him to take her arm. His presence was a comfort as they stopped off at the jeweller's then drove on to the hospital. They climbed the stairs to the women's ward. Halfway along the corridor they were stopped by a stout, dark-haired ward sister. 'No visitors until two o'clock. You must come back then.'

'I'm Dr Jarvis, Miss Starr's GP,' he improvised. 'I will take responsibility, Sister. Which doctor is treating her? I'd like a word with him if that could be arranged.'

'Come into my office, Dr Jarvis.' The ward sister eyed Faith suspiciously. 'Miss Starr can receive relatives only.'

'This is Miss Starr's sister,' Dr Jarvis declared.

'We were not informed of a sister. Her name is not down as the next of kin.'

'I have a surgery this afternoon which is why I brought Mrs Tempest to see her sister now. She just learned of the fire and is worried about her,' Dr Jarvis said pointedly.

The ward sister demurred. 'Of course. Come with me. A nurse will escort Mrs Tempest to the ward. We can't have visitors wandering alone around the hospital.'

A few minutes later a young nurse bustled in and asked Faith to follow her. In the waiting room at the end of the corridor she

324

recognised Mike Rivers pacing the room. There was a bandage around his head. He looked across as she passed and she waved. His expression cleared. With the nurse ahead of her, she did not stop. She clutched at the bouquet of flowers that she had purchased outside the hospital gates, her gaze scanning the ward for a sign of Ruby.

'Miss Starr has the screen round her bed,' the nurse said. 'We had a reporter burst in earlier and start to interview her before sister could stop him. Just five minutes, if you please. We can't have the other patients upset that their visitors must stick to the times on the board.' She nodded to the notice with the visiting hours painted in large black letters.

When Faith stepped behind the screen she was shocked by Ruby's appearance. There were dozens of tiny cuts across her beautiful face. Her eyes were closed and her bloodless lips were compressed with pain. A long tube ran from her arm to a bottle of blood on a stand beside the bed. Faith blinked back a rush of tears.

'Lord, Ruby, you gave me a turn when I read the papers,' she said softly.

Ruby opened her eyes. 'Yeah, I only made the second page. But I was in them again, weren't I? Just wish Mike hadn't lost the club.'

'How can you think of the publicity when you could have been killed?'

Ruby looked at her in astonishment. 'I weren't gonna lose a heaven-sent opportunity like that, were I? Made Mike promise to get the story to Derek Shipley who covered me disappearance in Tunbridge Wells. Good old Derek came up trumps, didn't he?'

Faith shook her head. Ruby would never change. 'Thank God, you're alive! How badly hurt were you?'

'It looks worse than it is, so they tell me.' Ruby managed a feeble smile. 'They want to keep me in for a couple of days. I was concussed and lost a lot of blood. They had to operate to remove a wide sliver of glass from my shoulder.'

'It won't be long then before you can go home.'

'Home is the last place I want to be.'

The vehemence of her tone appalled Faith.

Ruby went on sourly, 'I ain't going back to Ernie. The explosion showed me how easily death can strike. I'm not wasting my life by living with a man I despise.'

Faith took her friend's hand. 'If you're that unhappy you could stay with me. I'm only working two days a week. I could go in for half days and ask Madge to look in on you.'

'I won't need looking after. But I'd love to stay with you. I ain't going back to Ernie. Our marriage is over.'

'How will Ernie take it? I wouldn't like a repeat of his last visit. I've got Nathaniel to consider.'

'Mike will sort out Ernie.'

The nurse appeared, telling Faith that her five minutes were up.

She kissed Ruby's cheek. 'I'll come again later.'

She left the ward to seek out Mike in the waiting room. He was talking earnestly to Dr Jarvis. Their conversation broke off as Faith appeared. Both men looked serious.

'Ruby is going to be all right, isn't she?' Faith asked with sudden fear.

Dr Jarvis answered, 'Her wounds are mostly superficial. She'll be out in a couple of days.'

'How are you, Mike?' she turned to the musician. 'I'm so sorry about the club.'

'Thanks. At least the club was insured. I'm fine. It's Ruby I'm worried about. Any chance of her staying with you?'

'I've already suggested it. Though I'm not sure Ernie will like it.' She frowned, remembering the last time Ernie had come to her house. Something of her alarm must have shown in her eyes for Mike put his hand on her shoulder.

'Ruby told me what happened during Ernie's last visit. I've spoken to the police. They've said that a man will keep an eye on your house. Ernie's under too much suspicion from the law to cause any trouble over Ruby staying with you,' he reassured. 'But there's no point in taking risks.'

326

There was a noise in the corridor and they heard the ward sister demand stridently, 'I have told you that you cannot go in there, Mr Durham. Miss Starr must rest.'

'She's my wife. And you ain't gonna stop me seeing her.'

Mike went to the door. 'Leave it out, Ernie. The sister is only doing her job.'

Over Mike's shoulder Faith saw that Ernie was accompanied by one of his men. The heavyset man was carrying a basket of flowers so large that it hid half his body.

Mike dropped his voice so that the people in the waiting room could not hear him. But there was menace in his stance as he spoke swiftly to his brother. Ernie's face set with anger. He snatched the flowers from his companion and rammed them into the ward sister's arms. 'Give them to my wife. Tell her that she's always on my mind.'

He spun on his heel and marched away. The tone of his voice filled Faith with dread. It had been a threat, not an endearment.

'Don't pay no mind to Ernie,' Mike said. 'I told him the police would be watching your street. You won't get no trouble from him. That was just bluster to scare Ruby.'

'Do you want a lift home, Mr Rivers?' Dr Jarvis asked. 'You should be resting. Miss Starr is out of danger. They'll let her home tomorrow.'

'I'll grab a cab,' Mike replied. 'I said I'd give the police a full report and I have to get on to the insurance people as well.' His glance slid past them to the ward where Ruby lay.

It was obvious that Mike was in love with Ruby and Faith knew that her friend loved him. On impulse she hugged him. 'Look after yourself, Mike. You're a good man. I'll take care of Ruby. You're always welcome at my house.'

He smiled wryly. 'I appreciate that. But Ernie may have his goons watching the place. Ernie will never let Ruby go if he guesses there's anything between us.'

At the hospital gate Ernie was pushing himself through a crowd of reporters.

'Who do you think was responsible for the fire at your

brother's club, Mr Durham?' a journalist shouted.

'I've no idea.'

'And your wife, Mr Durham? How is she?'

'Recovering,' Ernie snapped.

His bodyguard elbowed the reporters aside and Ernie stepped into his car and was driven away. He turned towards Faith as the car sped past. The hatred she saw in his eyes made her blood curdle. No matter what Mike said, she couldn't believe that they had heard the last from Ernie Durham.

As Faith walked to the doctor's car, she was silent. Ruby had married the wrong brother. Were Mike and Ruby as ill fated as Dan and herself, never to find true happiness with each other?

Living with and painting the North American Indians had spiritually revived Dan. Never a day went by without thinking of Faith or wanting to hold her and his son in his arms.

Riding out to the ancient sacred sites he had felt the presence of the Great Spirit and the hallowedness of the land. He empathised with the Indians who regarded themselves as the earth's custodians and not its possessors to plunder its bounty at will. Nights under the stars were times of deep reflection. Here nature was the dominant force, Mother Earth the lifeblood of the people. It called to the spirit of his Celtic ancestors. The Catholicism which had held him bound in restraint no longer shackled him. The artist was a free spirit. As free as the wind and the running water.

Always he had striven to live his life without harming others. His conscience dictated that he must do what was right. It was why he had married Imelda when she told him she was pregnant with his child. That had been a lie. He had paid for his slide from grace. He had paid more dearly than most men. Faith was the wronged one, not Imelda.

His illicit love had tormented him. He could not bear to dwell upon the harm his love had brought Faith. She had given him her love unreservedly. Her reward had been to bear his child in shame. Imelda had lied and cheated for her own ends. Having

328

learnt how powerful and self-sacrificing true love can be, he knew that he had never loved Imelda. Lust and infatuation had blinded him to her true evil. Now it was time to pay his dues. The doctor's latest report had said that Imelda was slowly regaining the use of her legs. He wouldn't shirk his financial obligation to her, but he would no longer remain married to her. Here in the wild he had come to terms with his failings and had made his own peace with his God.

Dan was prepared for a scene and the inevitable power struggle with Imelda. He arrived at her house accompanied by his lawyer. He wanted everything legally explained to Imelda. The maid looked flustered at his arrival.

'But, sir, Madam is . . . Madam is . . .'

'Is my wife at home?'

The maid's olive face had turned the colour of oatmeal as she nodded, 'But, sir, I think . . .'

Dan ignored her. 'Go about your work. I don't need to be announced.'

The maid put her apron to her face and ran to the back of the house. Her manner told him much. He had seen it before when Imelda was up to her tricks. He could hear his wife's laughter from the direction of the pool. He strode outside, the lawyer a step behind him. He heard the man's cries of sexual pleasure at the same time as he saw the couple in the water. They were naked. The young man who was Imelda's physiotherapist was standing in the shallow end of the pool and Imelda's body was wrapped around him. Her head was thrown back as he continued to thrust into her and her moan rose into sexual frenzy. Dan turned away. He had seen enough.

'Imelda!' he rapped out. 'My lawyer is here. With such a witness I shall have no trouble divorcing you.'

'Dan!' Her voice was a screech followed by a violent splashing of water.

He walked away, angered at himself for allowing his conscience to bind him to Imelda for so long. Finally fate had

329

smiled on him and Imelda had condemned herself by her own wanton and selfish actions.

Imelda continued to scream after him, 'Dan, come back!'

Paulo dragged her back into his arms. 'Hush, my love. Why are you so angry?' For weeks Imelda had spoken of her love for him. She had bought him expensive presents. She was the heiress of a British squire. In Paulo's ignorance he thought that made her related to royalty. Imelda would also get a hefty divorce settlement from her famous artist husband. He was growing tired of playing the gigolo. Imelda needed him. Her legs were getting stronger but it would be a year or so before she could walk properly. They had so much to offer each other. He could give her all the sex she craved and she could make him a very rich man. And he intended to take her for every penny she had.

'My darling,' Paulo kissed her. 'What do you need Brogan for? You have me. I adore you. I can love you all night. Let Brogan divorce you. Then we shall marry.'

Her pride wounded, Imelda let her body float against him. He was so handsome, virile and caring. How her friends would envy her such a young husband. And Paulo was not a poor man. He had told her he made as much as the doctors here. He was a specialist. And the Americans paid through the nose for medical specialists. Living in America she would not have to face the censure of being a divorced woman. It wasn't looked on as a disgrace here as it was in England.

And there was also the problem with her other illness: the one she never spoke of. It was still being treated by a discreet doctor. Her year of enforced celibacy had kept signs of it at bay. So far she had responded well to the treatment. But it could flare up again at any time. There was no cure. When it struck it could be as debilitating as her spinal injuries and would eventually kill her.

But she would not think of that. Life was for the fun to be had today and must be lived to the full. Let Dan divorce her. Why should she now care? The Tempest woman would have found someone else by now. Dan would have lost her. Whilst she had a wealthy young lover who worshipped her. Besides, there were far more millionaires in America than in Europe. After all, if a woman had been divorced once, she could easily be so again, especially when a young man's youth, energy and wealth were gone.

'Yes, I'll marry you, Paulo. We have so much to give each other.'

Both smiled into the distance as they embraced, their eyes calculating as they visualised what was in it for them.

An hour later in the lawyer's office, Dan asked, 'So how long will it be before my divorce comes through?'

'I don't think your wife will be foolish enough to contest it. Especially since you are prepared to be so generous if she does not. Go down to Reno in Nevada. It's renowned for its quick divorces.'

Dan held out his hand and shook the lawyer's vigorously. 'I can think of no better New Year gift.'

He wrote to Faith telling her of his plans, but did not mention the divorce. He wanted it to be his special surprise for her when he returned to England in the New Year.

Chapter Twenty-Five

Faith took a week off work when Ruby came out of hospital. Gerald and Cyril Hornsey had been very sympathetic. She promised to return for the two-week rush of customers before Christmas.

Ruby was an exacting guest but after the trauma she had been through Faith tried to be patient. For the first time since she had known her Ruby was depressed and prone to bursting into tears.

'Look at my face,' Ruby wailed for the umpteenth time that morning. 'I've lost my looks.'

'The doctor said that in a month or so the scars would have healed and under a thin layer of powder won't even be noticed,' Faith again reassured her.

'Nothing will hide the scar on my shoulder. I've got ten stitches in that.'

'So you can't wear low-backed dresses any more. Is that such a loss? Mike isn't going to stop loving you because you have a scar on your shoulder.'

The tears began running down her cheeks again as she rocked back and forth in the armchair by the fire. 'I miss Mike. He hasn't been near me. He doesn't love me any more.'

Faith knelt at her side and put her arms around Ruby. 'You know that isn't true. It isn't wise for Mike to come here. He doesn't want to stir up trouble between you and Ernie until you have fully recovered. If you're going to divorce Ernie then it is best if Mike is not involved. From what you've told me Ernie has always resented Mike's success.'

'Hates him more like,' Ruby groaned. 'Mike's everything that he isn't. Why did I marry that sadistic runt?'

Faith held her tight as she sobbed against her shoulder. 'Everything will come right. You'll see. You're a fighter, Ruby. After Christmas when you've rested you'll bounce back. You and Mike will be together.'

'Like you and Dan,' she said bitterly. She sank her head into her hands. 'What a mess we've made of our lives. Both of us fell in love with the wrong man.'

'Dan is the right man for me. And Mike is the right man for you. It's the circumstances that are wrong.' She felt her own heartache threaten to overtake her. To fight against it she spoke lightly, 'I got another letter from Dan today. He'll be back in England for the New Year.'

Ruby lifted her head from her hands. 'I hope you're gonna take him back. Don't waste your life. If you love Dan don't risk losing him.'

'But how can we be lovers while he is married?'

'Same way as you'd be lovers if he wasn't.' Ruby grinned weakly, but seeing that her attempt to joke had fallen flat she advised, 'Forget what's right. Follow your heart. What's that Imelda ever done but made Dan miserable? Loyalty made him stick by her. What's important is that you love Dan and he loves you. Seize your happiness while you can. There's precious little of it in this life.'

Faith sat back on her heels. 'I wish it was that simple. If it was just Dan and I, I wouldn't care that people gossiped about us. It's Nathaniel. He doesn't deserve to be reviled by the community for being a love-child. I couldn't be so selfish as to condemn him to that.'

'So go somewhere where no one knows you or Dan. Set up house as man and wife.'

'Dan has won acclaim as an artist. He's a man in the public eye. You know reporters. They never rest until they ferret out every juicy bit of scandal. How can I risk that?'

'You worry too much. A bit of scandal would make you famous in your own right as an artist. You've got talent. But to be famous you need luck as well. Artists are accepted as being Bohemian in their way of life.'

'I don't want fame.'

'That's where you and me are different. I'd give anything to be famous. I want to be adored by millions – well, thousands at least. I want to show the world that a foundling child no one wanted made it good.'

'Oh, Ruby,' Faith said, hearing the pain in her friend's voice. The pain which had driven her and been bottled up for so many years. 'Mike loves you. I love you. You don't have to prove anything.'

Ruby's eyes were like polished flint. 'I have everything to prove. Not least that my existence has some meaning . . .'

Nothing had been heard from Ernie for a fortnight and Faith was due back at work the next day. Ruby was edgy because she had learned nothing of the robberies Ernie had planned for Christmas Eve. All she could do was put through an anonymous call to Inspector Armitage saying that they were going to hit three jewellers' within a mile or so of each other. It wasn't enough information for him to be able to catch them red-handed, but at least they would know the culprits and pull them in for questioning.

Faith didn't like leaving her friend alone in the house. Ruby was still subjected to bouts of depression and was complaining that she wanted to see Mike.

'We'll invite Mike over for Christmas,' Faith suggested in the evening. They were seated in front of a roaring coal fire, roasting chestnuts in the grate.

'But that's two weeks away. I ain't seen him for ages.' Ruby was fidgeting with the skein of blue wool she was supposed to be holding for Faith to wind into a ball.

'Hold the wool still,' Faith said remonstrating. 'Mike has been busy. He's sorting out new premises for the new River Boat. He's hoping to open soon after the New Year.'

'If he loved me he would see me,' Ruby moaned.

'You know that isn't safe.'

Ruby dropped the skein of wool into her lap, tangling it. Her expression was mutinous. 'I ain't scared of that runt Ernie. I'm not hiding away because of him. I can take care of myself.'

'Not against Ernie and his bully boys, you can't. Let Ernie cool down. He's got a dangerous temper.'

'And I can be just as dangerous,' Ruby said defiantly. 'He ain't so tough. Like all bullies you have to call their bluff. And I've got the means to stop him in his tracks.'

Faith didn't like the look in Ruby's eyes. She was being irrational.

Ruby laughed at her puzzled expression. 'I ain't stupid. I ain't gonna take on Ernie on me own.' She picked up her handbag which was on the floor by her chair. It had never left her side since she came out of hospital. Ruby burrowed into it and drew out a revolver.

'My God, Ruby! Have you gone mad? Where did you get that?'

'Mike insisted I carried it for protection.'

'I won't have a gun in the house with Nathaniel,' Faith said, becoming frightened.

Ruby turned a haunted gaze upon her. She no longer had any faith that the document with Mike's solicitor would stop Ernie getting at her. 'How else am I gonna protect myself from Ernie?'

Faith shuddered. She'd had a nasty feeling that Ernie was behind the fire at the River Boat . . . She could never abandon Ruby, but she was uneasy with her in the house. And now a gun! She was terrified that something could happen to Nathaniel. Then she remembered the policeman on duty in the street. Mike had insisted that there was nothing to worry about. So why had he given the revolver to Ruby and insisted on the policeman's presence? Did he suspect that his brother was responsible?

After Faith had gone to work the next morning, Ruby applied a thick layer of make-up and left the house. Madge was wheeling Nathaniel's pram up her garden path.

336

'Feeling better, luv?' Madge asked on seeing her.

'Yes, thanks. Thought I'd get a bit of fresh air.'

Ruby grimaced as she opened the gate, aware that Madge was watching her. She would tell Faith what time she'd left and when she arrived back. Ruby squashed her flash of guilt. She wasn't doing Faith any harm. Why was she feeling guilty?

As she walked along the pavement, she detected the squeak of worn shoes following behind her. It caused the hairs at the nape of her neck to prickle. Damn Ernie! Was that one of his spies? She didn't turn. There was no point in letting on that she had rumbled him. She kept to the main streets, pausing several times to look in windows. When she walked on the squeak of shoe leather followed. She jumped on a tram as it was about to pull away from the stop. It was going in the opposite direction she was heading. Three stops on she alighted and ran down into the underground station. She glanced around her as she waited for the train to arrive. There was no squeak of leather and no one she recognised on the platform. Had she been mistaken? She became cross with herself for allowing the incident to frighten her. Still, it didn't do to be too cocky. If she had been followed she'd given them the slip. She chuckled to herself. She was smarter than any of Ernie's goons.

The train pulled away and in the adjoining carriage a pair of shoes creaked as their owner walked to a seat. In the heavy traffic the tram had travelled at a pace he'd had no trouble keeping up with. Billy Bowles cursed the creaking shoe leather which must have given him away. They hadn't been squeaking when he set out this morning. Even so he was too experienced to let a woman make a monkey out of him. Thought she was clever, did she? Ernie had been right to have her watched. She was up to no good. Why else had she double-backed on her tracks and was now taking the tube train up the West End? Durham would pay handsomely for this information.

Billy Bowles smirked when an hour later Ruby disappeared into Mike Rivers's flat. She had thrown herself into Rivers's arms when he opened the street door. He had the information Durham wanted.

Billy Bowles strutted with self-importance into Ernie's office. 'It's as you thought. There's something going on between your wife and Rivers. She were with him for four hours. All over each other like a rash they were.' Billy waited expectantly. He'd been little more than a runner and odd job man for the Kavanagh gang for years. Durham was Kavanagh's right-hand man. If Durham was pleased with his work, he'd be given more prominence in the gang.

Ernie stubbed out his cigarette. He'd never liked Bowles. He was too oily and eager to please. He was always grovelling to Kavanagh. Now the squirt was smirking that he'd discovered Ruby was having it off with Mike. It would be common knowledge amongst the other men within the hour.

He kept his face rigid, showing no emotion. Inside he was like a time-bomb with its clock ticking. He eyed Bowles dispassionately. There was a twitch to the older man's lips.

Bowles looked at him expectantly. 'So what's the information worth?'

'What sort of payment you thinking of? You've been paid to watch that house.'

'I could be useful, Mr Durham. More useful than I have been. I reckon me talents 'ave been wasted, so ter speak.'

Ernie stared over his head. Bowles stopped his bluster and started to shift uneasily. There was slyness in the man's eyes. Ernie had been a fool to trust him. He put a hand inside his jacket, straightening the line of his tie. With his other hand he beckoned Bowles closer. 'I like to reward a man for his talents.'

Billy Bowles grinned. It turned to a sickly grimace as Ernie removed his hand from his jacket. Between his fingers was a hunting knife. He jabbed it into Bowles's stomach with an upward ripping motion.

'What the—' Bowles gasped, his eyes starting.

Twice more the knife slashed. Bowles fell to his knees.

'You've always had a big mouth.' Ernie gave a cruel laugh. Again the knife slid into unresisting gut, making a soft sucking sound when it was yanked out. Bowles toppled over, his eyes glazing as the life ebbed from them.

Ernie wiped the blade on the lapel of Bowles's jacket and flipped the corner of the rug over his body. Decent rug that had been. Bloke down the market said it was Chinese. Still, there were plenty more rugs and plenty more men like Bowles to do his bidding. Ernie stared down at the corpse. It should have been Mike. Next time it would be.

Returning the knife to its sheath in his waistband, he stared out of the office window. The streets were filled with Christmas shoppers. A pity Mike would have to wait. Bowles was scum. His men would dump his body in the flooded ground of a disused sandpit in Essex. It would be dark in a few hours and then that problem would be solved.

Not so Mike. Not yet at any rate. Be a bit too suspicious if anything happened to his brother so soon after the River Boat had been fired. Inspector Armitage had been sniffing around. He intimated that it wasn't a secret there was no love lost between Ernie and Mike. The last thing Ernie needed was the law hard on his tail. Not with those three robberies planned on Christmas Eve.

His expression cleared. Their plan was audacious. Three raids in broad daylight all within a couple of miles of each other. Everything had been planned to the last detail by Hugh, with cars being switched four times to put the police off the scent. Then it was back to Kavanagh's place. Their alibi was watertight. Hugh's mistress was the daughter of a cabinet minister. He'd got her and her younger sister hooked on heroin and the two would do anything for their supply. If the police broke in on Hugh and him, they'd find them in bed with the two daughters of the minister. The women would swear they had been with them all day and would be too stoned to know otherwise. Hugh was counting on the threat of a scandal making the police accept their alibi. It was perfect.

Adrenalin pumped through his veins as he anticipated the thrill of a hold-up. He'd missed the excitement and danger in recent weeks. And it was time to show the larger criminal gangs that their outfit was now a force to be reckoned with.

The perfect robbery on Christmas Eve and as a special present to himself on Christmas Day he'd get rid of his brother for good and also that scheming tart Ruby.

On Christmas Eve Faith had been dealing with two customers at once, the shop was so crowded. At lunchtime Faith was about to fetch her coat when the bell over the door rang again. She glanced at the clock and saw it was just gone a quarter past one. Both Gerald and Cyril were serving and she returned to the counter. Dr Jarvis smiled at her.

'Rushed off your feet are you?'

'You could say that,' Ruby replied. 'How may I help you?'

'A brooch for each of my five sisters. Something that's a bit unusual but all of a similar design. I'm in the doghouse if one thinks theirs is not as pretty as another's.'

'Phew!' Faith laughed. 'That's a tall order.'

He chuckled. 'I know you won't disappoint me.'

There was a softer note in his voice as he regarded her. Since he had taken her to the hospital he had called into the shop a couple of times to enquire how Ruby was recovering. Faith began to wonder if that was just an excuse to speak with her. Each time before he left he had asked her out. She had refused. Since receiving Dan's letter she knew it would not be right to encourage another man. But the doctor's persistence was flattering and she was finding that she looked forward to his coming into the shop.

'We have some pretty gold brooches set with semi-precious stones in the shape of exotic birds. Is that the kind of thing?'

'Sounds admirable.'

Faith fetched the tray from beneath the counter and set it out in front of him. The brooches were two inches long and the long tails of the birds were set in amethysts, topazes, pearls, garnets and other stones.

'They are exquisite but who will have which? That's the headache,' he said with a mock groan.

340

'Simple. Why not chose the stone relating to each sister's birth sign? It will bring them luck.'

'A charming idea. Now which stone is Pisces . . .'

Faith had lifted the amethyst peacock into her hands when the door burst open and three men wearing kerchiefs over their lower faces burst in. One had a revolver. Another pulled a shotgun out from under his overcoat.

'Don't make a sound! Get down on the floor and no one will get hurt.'

Two women customers screamed and fell to the floor and huddled together. When one continued to scream she was slapped across the face by the man with the shotgun. 'Shut it. Or next time you get a bullet.'

The woman's screams subsided into sobs. An elderly man backed against the wall cabinet holding the silver. The shotgun was pointed at him and he slid down the cabinet on to the floor, his eyes starting with horror. Dr Jarvis bound behind the counter to shield Faith. The robber with the revolver aimed it at him.

'Get back here and down on the floor. Both of you. Put your hands behind your heads.'

'Don't shoot,' Gerald Hornsey pleaded, as he and his brother edged round the counter away from the third robber who was emptying the contents of the till into a large bag.

'You two stay where you are.' The one with the revolver pointed it at Cyril Hornsey, at the same time throwing another bag at him. 'Open the safe and fill that up and no one will get hurt.'

Faith recognised the voice as that of Hugh Kavanagh. She was still shielded by Dr Jarvis who had pulled her behind him as they moved around the counter to sit on the floor. There was a smashing of glass as the robber with the shotgun hit the silver cabinet with its butt. He scooped the silver into his bag. When the customer on the floor didn't get out of his way fast enough he slammed the gun's butt at his head. The man keeled over, blood pumping from a cut on his temple.

'Stop that! There's no need for violence,' Faith remonstrated. Her anger at the unnecessary brutality overrode her fear. The man with the shotgun wheeled round, his dark eyes blazing with hatred. Her own eyes narrowed as she held the venomous stare of Ernie Durham. She didn't flinch and was unable to contain her loathing.

She felt Dr Jarvis tense. Afraid he might do something to endanger himself, she grabbed his arm and whispered, 'Don't, it's too risky.'

'None of you move. Or the woman here gets it.' Ernie Durham aimed the shotgun at Faith's head. She had suspected that he was a villain, but she had not realised how ruthless he could be. How had Ruby stuck with him so long? She was under no illusions that Ernie would use the gun. Her body was bathed in a freezing sweat. All she could think of was Nathaniel. If anything happened to her, what would happen to her baby?

The till empty, the third robber dragged some rope from his pocket. With the shotgun remaining on her, Faith could feel Ernie's evil grin. He was just waiting to get even with her for taking Ruby into her house. She struggled to hide her fear. Durham would feed on it.

The third robber advanced towards Dr Jarvis. With the gun on Faith he submitted to having his hands and feet tied. It wasn't a meek submission. A muscle pumped in his neck and his eyes were sparking with fury. It was the threat to her which stopped him acting. What could he do against two armed men? He was being wise, not weak. Her admiration for the doctor intensified. She felt safer for having him next to her, but they were both powerless to do anything.

After the doctor was tied, it was Faith's turn. Then Gerald Hornsey, who was clutching at his heart, his lips turning blue.

'Let me tend that man,' Dr Jarvis rapped out. 'He's having a heart attack. He could die.'

His plea was ignored. The two women huddled together were also bound. Both were sobbing. The man with the cut head was bound.

'You won't get away with this,' the doctor ground out.

'You better pray that we do!' Ernie barked. His stare razored into Faith. The warning was unmistakable. 'Unless you're ready to meet your maker.'

Hugh Kavanagh pushed Cyril Hornsey to the back of the shop where the safe was kept. 'Be quick, old man.' His command was impatient. 'We ain't got all day.'

Seconds later there was the report of a gunshot. 'Stupid fool!' Kavanagh raged. 'No more tricks. Empty it.'

The two women customers began to whimper; Ernie swiped them both across the face to shut them up. Kavanagh sprinted out of the back of the shop clutching his bulging bag.

Dr Jarvis shouted, 'For the love of God untie me so I can tend the wounded. Robbery is one thing. Do you want to be hounded for murder? Because if either of the Hornsey brothers dies that's what it will be.'

'The one out back ain't badly hurt,' Kavanagh snarled. 'Tried to press the alarm bell, stupid fool. He's got a bullet in his shoulder.'

Dr Jarvis began to rise. 'But that man is having a heart attack. I must tend him.'

Ernie was already at the shop door; Big Hugh hesitated. 'I want your word that you don't call the police or free the others until we've been gone ten minutes.'

'I agree.'

Ernie tossed his shotgun to Kavanagh then rounded on Faith. 'Make sure he sticks to his word. I think you know the consequences.'

Ernie brought out his knife, pressing it against Dr Jarvis's throat. 'You mind what you say to the police. Anyone grasses on us and I've got friends who will make sure you don't live long enough to gloat about it.'

The knife slashed viciously, slicing the flesh around the doctor's wrists before the rope fell away.

'That applies to anyone who blabs to the law,' Ernie barked out before leaving the shop with the others.

'Thieving scum,' the doctor grunted as he freed his wrists and slid across to Gerald Hornsey. He loosened the jeweller's tie.

'Take it easy, Mr Hornsey. The heart spasm has passed. I don't think it was serious. I'll phone for an ambulance to take you to the hospital.'

Faith looked at the clock. She felt so helpless trussed like a Christmas goose. It was twenty-five minutes past one. The robbery had taken no longer than seven minutes. It had felt like hours.

Cyril Hornsey staggered into the shop, a bloodied hand clenched against his shoulder. His face was grey. Dr Jarvis went to him. 'Looks like the bullet passed clean through. Best sit down and I'll see to the wound in a moment. Is the phone in the office at the back?'

'They cut the wire. The sweet shop on the corner has a phone.' Cyril sank weakly down on a stool behind the counter. He was pale and trembling. 'Robbed. Everything of value. All our takings. Fifty years ago our father opened this shop. We've never been robbed before.'

Faith struggled helplessly to release her bound wrists. 'Dr Jarvis, release my hands. I'll go and phone the police and an ambulance.'

'It's not ten minutes yet,' one of the women screamed. 'They'll come back and kill us.'

'I'll take my chance on that,' Faith said once her wrists and feet were free.

Dr Jarvis touched her arm. 'Be careful that they're not outside.'

'They'll be long gone.' She ran out of the jeweller's to the sweet shop. On her return people were crowding outside the jeweller's but none had ventured inside.

'The ambulance and police are on their way,' she announced.

Dr Jarvis was still tending to Gerald so Faith untied the customers, helping them to their feet and consoling them. The elderly man with the wound to his head reeled to the door.

'Sir, you have to wait to speak to the police.'

The man's eyes rolled in terror. 'I didn't see nothing. You heard that villain. I didn't see nothing.' He stumbled out mumbling incoherently.

344

Faith calmed the two women. 'I'll make a cup of tea. I'm sorry but you should stay and talk to the police. They will need some kind of statement.' They nodded dumbly, too shaken to move. She went over to Dr Jarvis who had helped Cyril Hornsey into the back room, removed his jacket and shirt and had ripped up a clean tea towel to staunch the blood from his shoulder wound.

'How is he?' Faith asked.

'It missed his lung and doesn't appear to have broken the bone. It will be painful but there is no danger to his life.'

'Thank God for that.' Faith closed her eyes and pressed a shaking hand to her brow. The sight of Ernie's eyes glittering with hatred was etched in her mind. She had been appalled at the merciless violence Ernie used. It had been so unnecessary. How could she allow a man like that to remain free? But how could she inform on him? His threat was no idle one. It had been levelled directly at her, but reached out to Ruby and Nathaniel.

Chapter Twenty-Six

The police arrived at the same time as the ambulance. Gerald Hornsey was too shaken to give the police much of a statement and Cyril was in too much pain to relate more than the briefest details.

Inspector Wharton was middle-aged with a fat paunch and aggressive manner. When he harangued Cyril Hornsey who was in acute pain, Faith took a dislike to him. She hated bullies in any form.

'Just give me the facts, Mr Hornsey,' Inspector Wharton snapped. 'I want those men in the nick before teatime.'

'Ease off, Inspector,' Dr Jarvis intervened before Faith could. 'Mr Hornsey is in pain and his brother needs rest or he could risk a serious heart attack.'

'I've got all night to talk to you, Doctor.' The inspector stared coldly at him. 'Christmas Eve or not.'

One of the women, an obvious gossip, was falling over herself to give him information. She was rattling on, giving an exaggerated account of the robbery and adding details which had not occurred. 'And it appeared to me that the young lady who was serving knew one of the men.' Her voice carried shrilly.

'Is that so, Mrs Tempest?' Inspector Wharton rounded on her, his expression sharpening to one of accusation.

It dawned on Faith that they might believe that she was an accomplice if she knew one of the robbers. Her honesty would not allow her to protect Ernie, but Wharton's attitude made her loath to speak out. Ruby had spoken of Ernie boasting of the policemen on his payroll. Wouldn't they have chosen a district where an inspector had been paid not to be too strident in his investigations? She hated bent coppers more than she hated villains. They abused the trust of the public.

'I think the customer has been over-enthusiastic in her observations,' she evaded. 'The lady had her hands over her eyes and was sobbing throughout the robbery.'

'You calling me a liar?' the woman shouted. 'I know what I saw.'

Faith raised an eyebrow at the inspector. From his belligerent stance he was prepared to believe the customer and not herself. 'One of the robbers directed his threats at me,' she hedged. 'But I was so frightened . . . and it all happened so quickly. They were wearing kerchiefs across their faces, so I couldn't see them properly. A voice sounded vaguely familiar but I can't place it. I've been trying to rack my brains.'

'They seemed to know what to take and where the safe was. An inside informant could have helped them,' the inspector accused.

Cyril protested, 'Mrs Tempest is most trustworthy.' He swayed on his feet as the ambulancemen helped him outside to where his brother was already in the ambulance.

'It's been an ordeal, Inspector,' Dr Jarvis interceded. 'The gunman picked on Mrs Tempest because she was the shop assistant and she had already spoken up against them using violence. That took courage. I feel I should have done more, but with a gun held on Mrs Tempest . . .' He broke off, his voice angry. 'They were ruthless men. The way Mr Hornsey was shot proved that.'

'This is the second jeweller's which has been robbed in half an hour. The other was only a short distance away,' the inspector said tautly. 'We think it could be the same gang.'

The inspector studied Faith for several moments in silence. Could he tell that she was lying? If Ernie was arrested and put behind bars, Ruby would be safe from him. But men like Ernie had men on the outside. Men who could do his dirty work for him.

What if they came for Ruby or Nathaniel?

Even as this fear and argument formed, Faith knew that she would be shielding herself from danger at the expense of other lives. Ernie and Kavanagh had shown that they had no respect for humanity. If they weren't put behind bars the deaths from their villainy would rise. She couldn't live with that on her conscience.

Yet still she hesitated to speak. Her dislike of the inspector made her cautious. She put a shaking hand to her head and deliberately played on her weakness as a woman. She burst into tears. 'I've tried so hard to think. All I can see is that horrid gun pointed at my head.'

Dr Jarvis put his arm around her. 'It's been a frightening experience for us all. Do you need to persist in this questioning, Inspector? Wouldn't it be more important to question the people hanging round outside the shop? One of them may have seen the getaway car.'

'You telling me how to do my job?'

'I'm giving you my professional advice as a doctor. Mrs Tempest is in no state to be questioned. She placed her life in danger to curb the robbers' violence. I'll give you what details I can.'

'So you didn't recognise any of the robbers, Mrs Tempest?' Inspector Wharton barked at her.

'The robber's accent was cockney.'

'That's not much help.' Inspector Wharton continued to stare at her. She forced herself to hold his assessing glare. Her feelings of distrust intensified. She was right not to talk to him. Finally he added, 'For now my officer here will take written statements from all of you. If you later remember anything about the robbers inform Walthamstow or Chingford police station. That's where the other robbery was committed this morning.'

When the police left, Dr Jarvis commended the two women customers on their bravery. Faith collected a broom and swept up the glass from the shattered silver cabinet.

'You shouldn't be doing that,' Dr Jarvis declared. 'Go home.'

'I can't leave Gerald and Cyril to come back to this mess.

Gerald was devastated. He had such pride in this shop. At least they didn't take the paintings. Some of them were worth far more than the silver they stole.'

'They wanted what can be melted down or disposed of easily. Now I must insist that I take you home.'

She nodded gratefully. She was feeling sick and shaky inside and still had the Christmas goose and tree to purchase. Fortunately she had bought all her presents and decorations for the tree and Ruby was getting the rest of the shopping. This was Nathaniel's first Christmas. He was only a baby but she wanted it to be special.

She was about to lock the shop when she paused and looked up at Dr Jarvis. 'Your sisters' presents. We forgot them. The robbers didn't touch that tray of brooches.'

He stared at her in amazement. 'Do you never stop thinking of others?'

The brooches chosen, Faith locked the money in the safe and secured the shop. As they drove down Wanstead High Street, Faith said, 'Would I be imposing on you terribly if we picked up the tree and goose? I don't feel up to struggling home with them on my own.'

'Certainly,' he smiled. 'A few days' rest over Christmas is just what you need. But are you sure the work will not be too much for you?'

Faith laughed. 'I'm not made of porcelain. But I could murder a gin and tonic.'

'You are a remarkable woman, Mrs Tempest.'

'No, I'm not. I was terrified during the robbery. All I could think of was my son and what would happen to him if I was shot.'

Her fears and doubts crowded back and she closed her eyes to conquer them. They would destroy her resolve to put Ernie and Kavanagh behind bars if she gave in to them. She had to be strong. She had to keep herself occupied then the fears could be kept at bay.

A half-hour later the tree was installed in the front room and the goose lay trussed and sacrificial in its roasting tin. Ruby was not in the house. Madge had knocked to tell her that Ruby had taken Nathaniel shopping and would be back shortly. Faith had desperately needed to hold her son in her arms after her ordeal. She felt her panic rising that Ruby and Nathaniel might be in danger from Ernie.

'Is anything wrong, Mrs Tempest?' Dr Jarvis was looking at her with concern.

She was tempted to tell him of her fears, but he had already done so much for her in recent days, she did not want to impose on him further.

'I think I'll have that gin. Do you want a whisky?'

He shook his head. 'I've my surgery in an hour. I hope it will be a quiet one. I was called out to a heart attack and a birth last Christmas Eve.'

Again his steady look held hers and his expression softened. 'I could call back later. You look as if you've a heavy burden on your shoulders. It's not just reaction from the robbery, is it?'

She shook her head. 'I need time to think and be alone.'

'I'd be happy to share those burdens, Mrs Tempest. I have come to admire you greatly. I'd like to see more of you in the New Year.'

Faith stared at him. She didn't fool herself that he was in love with her, but if they saw more of each other he might fall in love with her. That would be unfair. He had been a comfort to her since Ruby's accident and now during the robbery. She admired him and liked him a great deal. She didn't want to hurt him.

'I have much to be grateful to you for, Dr Jarvis. I have come to think of you as a friend. A special friend.'

He saw her discomfort and smiled. 'I understand, Mrs Tempest. You are still in love with Nathaniel's father.'

'I will always love Nathaniel's father.'

She held out her hand and he took it in a firm grasp. 'Then I hope you find the happiness you deserve.'

Ruby returned to the house bubbling with excitement. That morning she'd posted a letter to Ernie telling him she wanted a separation. He'd get it by the afternoon post. Nathaniel's pram was piled high with presents and two bottles of gin. 'That was just the tonic I needed to forget my no-good husband. I never had a family Christmas. You're my family, Faith. We're gonna have a Christmas to remember. And look at these.' She held up a box of tiny electric lights. 'I couldn't resist these for the tree. I splashed out and got two boxes down the market. Since Dan forked out to have electricity laid on we might as well make the most of it. The stallholder even put a plug on them for me and knocked a bob off the price as I gave him a kiss under the mistletoe.'

Faith summoned a smile. 'They're lovely.'

It wasn't until Nathaniel had been bathed and put to bed that Faith told Ruby of the robbery.

'The bastard! God, I knew Ernie weren't no saint when I married him! But shooting old Hornsey who was such a sweet old man . . .' She sank her head into her hands then scraped her fingers through her blonde hair. 'I never knew he was so evil. I swear. It ain't just robberies. It's gambling, vice . . . any racket you can name. Including drugs. And no doubt murder. Kavanagh has a reputation for putting his enemies six foot under.'

Ruby lifted her head to regard Faith. 'What about us? Do you think Ernie means trouble?'

'If he's any sense, he'll be lying low until the heat dies off the robberies.'

'Ernie's got more muscle than sense,' Ruby groaned. 'That's the problem. You did right not to talk to Wharton but I think Armitage should be told. If Ernie knows you recognised him, he's gonna make sure you ain't gonna spill the beans. I'm certain I was followed when I took Nathaniel shopping. Ernie don't give up. We'll get Madge or Dave to phone Armitage and tell him I'm here. Also that you were a witness to the robbery and we both have information he's interested in. They must stress how important it is.'

Faith protested, 'It's not fair to involve them. What if Ernie's spy is watching?'

'I don't see we have much choice. It's Christmas Eve. The police will be dealing with drunks and stretched to the limits. At least we've still got our copper outside. Ernie always strikes when he thinks it's least expected. This time we're one step ahead of him. Dave can also phone Mike. Thank God there's a telephone in the hallway leading to his flat. I won't feel safe without a man in the house tonight.'

Faith nodded. She went into the front room and put on the light. 'If there's anyone spying on us, we'll show ourselves putting up the decorations and doing the tree. I'll ask Dave to come in and check the tree lights. That will sound innocent enough. We can tell him our plan then.'

Dave arrived and looking at the lights scratched his head. 'Don't know nothing about these. Bit grand for us. We ain't got the electric like you.'

'Actually the lights are fine, but we're not sure if Ernie has someone watching us. I need you to do me a favour. I'll tell you while we fix the lights to the tree. That way it all looks innocent.'

Faith hastily told him about the robbery and their need for him to phone the inspector. He agreed. When Faith showed him out, he called back. 'Want anything picked up down the pub? I'm off down there for a pint.'

'I could do with a bottle of port.'

'I'll bring it in to you in about an hour. Madge wants me to help her with the decorations.'

Faith shut the door and let out a long breath. It all seemed like some melodrama from a second-rate B movie. The conversation had been agreed as a ruse to stop any spy of Ernie's getting suspicious when Dave came back to report on the telephone calls.

It was over an hour before Dave returned and by then Faith's nerves were jagged.

'I didn't have much luck. Armitage was out on duty. I left a message with his wife telling her it was vital the inspector contacted you tonight. Also Mike Rivers was out. There was a party going on in one of the other flats and the owner was a bit the worse for drink, but he said he'd put a note under Rivers's door.'

'Ain't that just our luck,' Ruby groaned and poured herself a large gin.

'I had a word with the copper outside,' Dave said. 'I mentioned you were worried that as it was Christmas Eve Durham might turn up if he's had a few. Do you want me to kip on the sofa?'

Faith shook her head. 'No, Dave. It's kind of you to offer. I'm sure we're just overreacting.'

'Ay, but one scream or sudden noise from in here, and I'll have me head out the bedroom window yelling blue murder. That will scare Durham off and keep the police on their toes.'

'Thanks, Dave,' Faith said as she escorted him out.

Ruby was pacing the floor when she came back in. She took a couple of drags from her cigarette then said heavily, 'Perhaps we should get out of here. Book into a hotel for the night.'

'I'm not being chased from my own house or have my first Christmas with Nathaniel ruined, because of Ernie Durham. He's probably celebrating his victory over the police. He won't worry about us tonight.'

'Even so, I'm keeping this close to my side just in case.' Ruby patted the gun in her handbag.

Ernie had a bad feeling in his gut. The third robbery had caused problems. The only customer in the shop was an off-duty policeman buying his wife's Christmas present. He'd gone for Ernie and tried to grab the shotgun. It had gone off in his face, killing him. They hadn't waited round to clear out the safe, just grabbed what jewels were easily to hand and emptied the till. With the copper's blood over his suit, Ernie needed to change. He'd stopped off at his house before going on to Big Hugh's where the two cabinet minister's daughters would provide their alibi.

There was a letter on the mat in Ruby's flamboyant handwriting. He scanned it and scowled. So she wanted a separation did she? That's what she thought . . . 'Stupid tart. Do you think having a statement with a solicitor will stop me getting back at you?'

He knew that with a copper dead he had to get out of the country. Kavanagh had a private plane for just such an emergency. They'd use that. But first he needed to change then meet with Kavanagh.

He crumpled Ruby's letter in his hand. 'And before I go, sweetheart, I'll have your blood.'

Ernie did a lightning change and threw his bloodied shirt and suit into the coal boiler which heated the water. He paused to watch it start to smoulder, but his fear of being caught by the police made him eager to get away. He grabbed a bag of clothes and all the cash hidden in the wall safe, stashing them in a canvas bag. He checked outside before leaving the house.

He decided against using the car. It was too well known to the law. Instead he wheeled out of the garage his old motorbike. No one would look twice at him on that. The leather helmet and goggles were a good disguise.

It was a fifteen-minute drive to Kavanagh's house. Throughout it Ernie was on edge. He kept looking over his shoulder, his back and palms slick with perspiration. He was a fool to have been so trigger happy. Even the bent cops would be after him now that he had killed a policeman.

He slowed down as he approached Kavanagh's house which was set back in a long drive. A black Daimler sped out of the gates at top speed. It wasn't Hugh's car. There were four men inside. It wasn't Hugh and his brothers and it wasn't the police. Ernie's unease increased. He turned into the drive. The front door of the house was ajar. Hugh was never that careless.

Pulling the revolver from his shoulder holster he cut the motorbike engine and went inside. There was an unnatural stillness to the house. Pete was lying face down in the hall with the back of his head blown away and Reg was lying in a pool of blood just inside the sitting room. There was no sign of Hugh or the loot. He was torn between the need to run and the necessity to find out if Hugh was there.

He ran up the stairs. Three naked bodies were splattered with bullets from a machine gun: Hugh and the two women.

Ernie wheeled away fighting down nausea. He ran down the stairs. It must have been the Greeks. They must've learned of the robberies and decided to take all Kavanagh had stolen and pay him back for fire-bombing the River Boat which was under their protection. They would have seen that act as a declaration of open war against them. Ernie had never let on to Hugh that he was involved. Hugh would have killed him for starting a gang war over a private matter. Ironically, Hugh was dead and he was still alive. But for how long?

Now he had the police and the Greeks after him and no plane to escape in. There was a moan from the back of the house. Ernie saw Squinty Watkins try to pull himself up and then flop back down on to the carpet. He didn't bother to stop and help him. If Watkins wasn't dead yet he soon would be.

Ernie knew his days were numbered. It was all Ruby's fault. If she hadn't made him so damned angry he'd never have fire-bombed the River Boat. And with him banged up by the police or mown down by the Greeks she'd be sitting pretty. As his widow she'd claim all the money in his bank account which now ran to several thousand. And she'd probably marry Mike. That grated the most. Ernie didn't believe in happy endings. Especially for someone who had been instrumental in the mess he now found himself in.

At eight o'clock there was a strident knock on the door. Ruby and Faith looked at each other, fear stark on their faces.

Ruby recovered her wits first. 'It ain't gonna be Ernie at the front door, is it? Perhaps it's Armitage or Mike.'

Faith nodded. 'I hope so.'

It was Inspector Armitage. He looked grave as he followed Ruby into the front room.

'I received your message,' he said curtly.

'It's about Ernie Durham,' Ruby plunged straight in. 'My husband. He did a jeweller's over Walthamstow at lunchtime. This is my friend Faith Tempest. She worked at the shop and recognised Ernie. She didn't tell the inspector who was investigating as she wasn't sure if she could trust him. I'd told her how Ernie bragged about having coppers on his payroll. I was the woman who tipped you off about the Gilded Lily the other week. And about there being three jobs on for today. I couldn't find out where.'

356

He looked at both women sternly. 'Withholding information is a serious offence.'

'I'm sorry, Inspector,' Faith said. 'I was frightened. Ernie threatened to kill me and my son if I spoke out. But I knew I couldn't let him go loose after the violence of the robbery. Mr Hornsey was shot.'

'I know the details,' Inspector Armitage rapped out. 'And I have to inform you, Mrs Durham, that during a robbery on another jeweller's this afternoon a policeman was killed. It's believed it was the Kavanagh gang. Acting on the information you supplied they were our first suspects. We went to Kavanagh's house. We found three members of the gang dead, also two women. Another gang member was seriously wounded. He's in hospital, but I doubt he'll pull through. There was a suit of Durham's covered in blood and partially burned in the boiler at your house. It incriminates him as the murderer of the policeman.'

'Was Ernie one of those killed at Kavanagh's?' Ruby demanded.

'No.'

'Did he kill them?' Ruby was deathly pale and began to shake.

'It looked more like a gang killing. Watkins was the one who was injured, the three Kavanagh brothers were murdered.'

'So Ernie is still out there.' Ruby put her hand to her head and slumped into a chair.

Throughout the interchange Faith had stood rigid with shock.

Inspector Armitage continued to address Ruby in a clipped voice. 'You were injured in the fire at the River Boat. Were the Greeks behind that? Mike Rivers is Ernie's brother.'

'Mike has nothing to do with Ernie or Kavanagh. He knew nothing of the rackets they were into.'

'And you do?'

Ruby nodded. 'Some of them. But not Mike. I swear not Mike. Mike was paying protection money to some Greeks. He hated that, but said he had no choice. That it was common practice. Don't that prove he had nothing to do with Kavanagh and Ernie?'

The inspector did not answer. He turned to Faith. 'Has Durham contacted you since the robbery?'

'No. Do you think he will?' Fear for Nathaniel chiselled through her.

'I'll put another man out the front. We want to question Durham. But since this is an obvious place to look for him I doubt he'll show up. There were signs that Durham had been at Kavanagh's house after the massacre. I should think he'd be in hiding. He's got the Greeks after him as well now.'

'So he's still out there loose,' Ruby said shakily.

'Every policeman in London has his description and is looking for him, Mrs Durham,' Inspector Armitage said before leaving. 'We shall need statements from you both later. But it's Christmas Eve. We've more than enough on Durham to charge him. Come down to Bow Street police station the day after Boxing Day and we'll take your statements then.'

'Looks like that's the last I'll see of my husband,' Ruby said with false bravado. 'And good riddance. Could be this is the best Christmas present I've ever had.'

Faith wasn't taken in by Ruby's manner. She knew that her friend was as frightened as she was. But at least the police were outside and now knew the whole story. Ernie would be a fool to risk coming here. But she wouldn't relax until she learned that he had been captured by the police.

For the rest of the evening Faith and Ruby tried to act normally as they finished putting up the paper decorations and sprigs of holly and mistletoe. Throughout they boosted their courage by sipping gin. When Faith swayed and nearly lost her balance on the step ladder, she decided she'd better lay off the booze. If Ernie did turn up and they were drunk they would be sitting targets for whatever evil he planned.

The last of the presents were wrapped and placed around the Christmas tree. It was one thirty.

'I suppose we'd better turn in,' Ruby slurred. 'It don't look like Mike's coming. I'm gonna take those two coppers a snort of brandy each. It must be freezing out there. Not that I think Ernie will dare show his face round here. He'll be hiding in some bolt hole.'

Faith turned off the tree lights and climbed the stairs for bed. She stared into the darkness, longing to be with Dan. Outside the street was quiet as befitted a respectable residential area. It was Christmas Day. The most special day of the year and she would spend it without Dan. Was every Christmas going to feel incomplete like this?

'Be safe, Dan,' she whispered into the darkness. 'And be happy.'

She yawned and emotionally and physically drained fell asleep as soon as she got into bed.

A silent form climbed over garden walls. Not even a sleeping dog stirred to bark a warning as he dropped down on to the lawn at the end of the terrace. He still wore the leather helmet and goggles. At seeing the two policemen in the street he'd been forced to sneak round the back and wait. For over an hour he'd been crouching in the shadow of a shed until the lights went out in Faith's house. As an extra precaution he waited another half-hour to ensure the two women were asleep. He was now cold which added to his murderous mood.

It was years since, as a child, he had robbed houses by entering through the kitchens at night. The good life might have made him less agile but he hadn't lost his stealth. No police sentinel out the front was going to stop him from exacting his revenge on his treacherous wife.

Ruby had drunk so much gin she thought she would fall asleep as soon as her head hit the pillow. Instead her mind was fizzing with chaotic thoughts. She had been looking forward to spending the night with Mike and was disappointed he'd been out. Belatedly, she remembered that he had arranged several bookings for the River Boat musicians in various venues until his new club opened. Tonight he was playing at the Ringside Hotel near Richmond. She resented being unable to sing with him. It would have given Ernie power over her again because of her wretched contract.

'Biggest mistake of my life was getting involved with Ernie

Durham,' she groaned. 'He promised me the earth and what did I get . . . sweet nothing.'

All his promises to make her a star were just hot air. The tour he had arranged was second-rate, like her marriage. She had made her own publicity during her disappearance. She had wanted fame more than the fortune. Being raised in an orphanage she never wanted to feel unloved and deserted again. When she was singing men adored her. She was someone special.

Yet that achievement was nothing. It didn't lay the ghost which had haunted her all her life. Only by becoming famous could she prove to herself that she had succeeded – that she was important. The foundling no one had loved, and who had been abandoned in a threadbare blanket on the orphanage steps, would no longer be a nobody. To have her name remembered and upon everyone's lips was an obsession.

Throughout the years only Faith had been true to her. Faith had never let her down. That friendship was more precious than gold. It meant everything to her. She would do anything for Faith.

Once Ernie was behind bars, her future with Mike would be very different. Mike loved her as she had craved to be loved all her life. Mike would make her famous. She could dance now as well as sing. She would marry him and star in a West End musical. At last the producer was setting up auditions for the New Year. Her name would be headlined in every newspaper in the land. Now that was fame.

Ruby was jolted back to the present by the sound of the parlour clock chiming two in the morning. She was still wide awake. The bright moonlight penetrating the brocade curtains illuminated the room, making sleep difficult.

Nathaniel began to cry. Faith would be exhausted after the traumas she had experienced today. Ruby slipped out of bed to warm Nathaniel a bottle of milk so he would not disturb his mother. She had never expected to feel maternal about any child, but being Nathaniel's godmother had made her fiercely protective of the baby. When she held him and he snuggled his head against her neck, it roused a longing to possess a child of her own. That wasn't in her plans at all. A child would ruin her figure and the schemes for her career. Yet if the kid was like Nathaniel ... and was Mike's child ... ?

She grinned to herself. She was getting soft in her old age. Motherhood was not for her. She always made certain of that. The thought halted her descent of the stairs abruptly, and she was suddenly aware of the passage of time without her monthly visitor. A befuddled count on her fingers told her she was two weeks late. It could be the shock of the fire-bomb. Somehow she knew it wasn't. Fate was paying her back for giving Squinty that dose of senna pods. She'd been so desperate for Mike to make love to her that day at the club neither of them had remembered to take precautions. Her first slip up and she'd been caught out. It wasn't bloody fair.

Plenty of gin in the morning and a steaming hot bath might yet get rid of it. Yet as soon as the thought formed, she shuddered. Was that how her mother had felt when she knew she'd conceived? Had she tried everything to get rid of her and when all else failed abandoned her? Protectively her hand covered her stomach. A baby! Mike's baby was growing inside her. Her baby! Someone she could love and who would love her entirely for herself.

She felt her eyes sting with tears. How could she think of destroying her child, or of not wanting it as her mother had not wanted her?

Ruby leaned against the wall both shattered and elated by this turnaround in her reasoning. This really was a Christmas of surprises.

She hummed softly as she wrapped her dressing-gown round her waist and glided into the kitchen feeling as though she was floating on a euphoric cloud. Just wait until Mike heard the news! He'd be delighted.

The hand in a leather glove which suddenly clamped over her mouth caught her completely unawares. Her scream was cut off before it reached her throat. Terror speared her. The smell of cologne was chillingly familiar. Ernie had broken into the house.

And her gun was still upstairs in her bag. After carrying it around for weeks, she had left it behind at the very time she needed it!

Seized by panic she started to struggle. She kicked out at Ernie and sent a kitchen chair clattering across the linoleum. Then she was pushed back over the kitchen table, Ernie's body between her sprawled legs.

'You ain't getting away from me this time,' Ernie rasped. The moonlight revealed the sadistic light in his dark eyes. She saw her death written there but it would not be before he had made her suffer.

His hand was like an iron talon over her mouth, preventing her from screaming.

'Thought a letter with a solicitor would stop me getting even with you, did you?' Ernie jeered. 'Kavanagh and his brothers are dead. Mown down by the Greeks. All because of you. They're after me. So are the law. A copper got shot in the last robbery. I'm going down but you ain't gonna be around to see it. You were the woman who phoned Armitage when the club was raided.'

Even if she had been able to speak Ruby knew it was pointless protesting her innocence. Ernie intended to kill her. Her struggles became frantic. It wasn't just her life, it was her baby's she had to fight for. Determination to survive pumped strength into her muscles.

'No, Ernie. No!' The words were distorted against the leather-clad palm.

'You made a fool of me!' His voice was without mercy. 'You and me brother. You thought you were clever shopping me to Armitage. The last laugh's on me.'

Her strength was no match for his. He used his weight to crush her on the table, both his hands warding off her attack.

She gagged on rising vomit as she felt him fumbling with his trousers. Did he intend to rape her as well? The jutting pressure of a shaft against her bare skin was cold, not warm. It was the blade of a knife he had drawn from his waistband.

A guttural scream ripped from her throat, her hand closing over his wrist to deflect the lethal blade.

'First you, then I'll get that interfering bitch upstairs,' Ernie snarled. 'She thought she was so clever helping you get away from me. No one gets one over on me.'

Oh God, not Faith as well! Ruby increased her struggles, knowing it was useless. Ernie had overpowered her so many times in the past. Even as she fought him, her mind reeled in torment. She might have brought all this upon herself by marrying Ernie, but Faith didn't deserve his wrath. Faith mustn't die because of her sins. The dagger scraped her breast as the last of her strength deflected it. Ernie wrenched back his arm for the death blow . . .

'Die, bitch!'

There was a flash of orange light and a loud crack. Ernie jerked, his eyes behind the goggles widened by surprise. Then he fell away from her.

The flash of gunpowder followed by the kick of the pistol made Faith stagger. She'd meant to fire the gun as a warning but her hand was shaking so violently the bullet must have struck the man. His body toppled sideways, enabling Ruby to slither away from him. It slumped over the side of the table, dripping blood on to the floor.

Faith stared at the horrific tableau in front of her. Ruby was safe but the man looked dead. She was a murderess. She would be hanged. What would happen to Nathaniel?

The revolver fell from her lifeless fingers, her eyes staring as Ruby flung her arms around her. 'You saved my life! He had a knife. He was going to kill us both!'

'I saw it. Oh my God, I killed him!'

'He was going to kill me.' Ruby saw all the implications of Faith's brave act. Imprisonment. Scandal. The ordeals of a trial. Her name reviled. The hangman's rope. Nathan motherless. Headlines in every national newspaper.

Ruby's eyes were wild. Her mind tried to focus. Someone was banging on the front door. A policeman's whistle was being blown furiously.

Dave shouted, 'You two all right in there? Faith! Ruby! Open up!'

Faith crumpled on to the floor shaking uncontrollably, and murmuring, 'Oh Nathan, my baby. My poor baby.'

Ruby knew then what had to be done.

When the policeman on duty in the street smashed a glass pane in the front door he heard two more shots. Undoing the latch he drew his truncheon and advanced cautiously inside.

'Whoever is in there is armed, cornered and dangerous,' he warned Dave Taylor who was white-faced beside him. 'Stay back.'

Dave ignored him and when the two men entered the kitchen they found Faith huddled on the floor and Ruby standing with a smoking gun barrel inches from a man's shattered head. Then Ruby began to scream hysterically.

Chapter Twenty-Seven

Dan arrived in England on New Year's Eve, docking at Southampton. To pay off Imelda had taken all the money from the Los Angeles exhibition. Fortunately Dan had the native American Indian paintings to sell and his agent in America had raved over them.

'Hollywood will love these with Westerns being so popular,' his agent promised.

Dan insisted that only half of them were sold in America. He wanted the rest for the European market.

His jubilation on his return faded when he arrived at the station to catch the London train and caught sight of the newspaper headlines on a newsstand. TWO WOMEN ARRESTED FOR THE MURDER OF EARNEST ERNIE DURHAM — GANGSTER. Next to it was a second placard announcing: GREEKS TO FACE TRIAL FOR THE KAVANAGH GANG MASSACRE.

He bought a copy of the paper. The women's names were not mentioned. Kavanagh and Durham were named as partners. The two incidents had to be connected. He had a gut-wrenching feeling that one of the women involved in Durham's murder was Ruby. Who was the other? It couldn't possibly be Faith – or could it? Had Ruby involved her again? Had Durham threatened them?

His questions and fears were endless. Just as he thought the future was rosy for him, it looked bleaker than ever.

Collecting his car from the studio garage he went straight to Wanstead and tried to convince himself that Faith was not involved. She couldn't be. She could never kill anyone. But what if her child's life or her friend's had been threatened? Even the most gentle creature can become a raging tigress when someone they love is in danger.

To his relief the lights were on in Faith's house. Madge opened the door. 'Thank God it's you, Mr Brogan. You're just who that poor woman needs. I was worried it was another reporter. We've had so many sniffing round since the murder. Now Faith has been released they all want her story. The police got rid of them. Faith's been sedated but wouldn't have anyone but me with her.'

Dan walked into the front room and saw Faith huddled on the sofa staring wide-eyed into the flames of the fire. Every few moments a tremor shook her body.

'My love,' he said softly.

Faith turned to them. Her eyes revealed a mind locked in some cavern in Purgatory.

'Dan. Is it really you?' A sob broke from her.

Madge briefly touched Dan's arm, 'Nathaniel's next door with me husband. I've the kids' tea to cook. I'll leave you two together. If you need me to come back, don't hesitate to fetch me. She's had a rough time. Poor luv.'

Dan took Faith into his arms. She clung to him and burst into tears.

It took an hour to get the story from her. Cradled against his chest, he soothed and coerced her to speak of her ordeal. Tears streamed down her cheeks. The traumatic shudders continued to vibrate through her. When she finally found her voice, her sentences were disjointed. Gradually he pieced together the events of Christmas Eve.

'They let me go free after two days of questioning,' she said, becoming calmer as he continued to murmur reassurances to soothe her. 'Madge looked after Nathaniel. I couldn't bear the thought of him being taken into a home. The police said Ruby confessed to everything. She said it was her shots which killed Ernie, that I had only wounded him. She said he was going to attack her again. Ruby said I'd saved her life. And that Ernie was going to kill me to stop me giving evidence about the robbery.'

'You did save Ruby's life. If Durham came here to kill Ruby he couldn't let you live to give evidence,' Dan placated. He was appalled at how she had suffered. He should have been here for her. 'You were brave and courageous. I'll never forgive myself that I left you to face so much danger alone. You should have written telling me that Ernie had threatened you because you helped Ruby.'

'What could you have done? You had enough problems with Imelda. We'd agreed that for Nathaniel's sake we'd live apart.'

He tensed and his voice was hoarse, 'I should have been here for you.'

'That wasn't possible, we both know that.'

Her defence of his actions had brought a change in her. The trembling had stopped and she lifted a hand to his cheek. 'You're here now. That's what's important. I've missed you so much. Whatever happens to me, Nathaniel will have a father.'

'Nothing will happen to you,' Dan reassured, although he was tortured with the thought that he could still lose her. The police might have released her but had they dropped the charges? There was still a murder to be accounted for. No matter that Durham had it coming to him. Someone would have to pay the price for his death.

Faith looked at him steadily. 'I can't let Ruby take all the blame. It's my fault Ernie wasn't arrested earlier. If I'd told Inspector Wharton at the time of the robbery that I recognised Ernie and Kavanagh, this would not have happened.'

'Armitage was here. You told him. He even put an extra policeman outside. You did everything that you could. You don't know if you killed Durham, or not. You said you wanted to warn him off. I can't see Ruby confessing to a murder she didn't commit.'

A shudder rippled through her body. 'After I fired the gun the events became confused. Ernie looked dead. All I could think of was that I had killed him.'

Faith sighed; the sedative was adding to her inability to think straight. She kept going over that night in her mind, trying to

367

make sense of it. 'By the time the police arrived I couldn't stop crying. I'd been so frightened during the robbery and all evening we were worried that Ernie would come. Dr Jarvis was called to attend me. He said I was in shock and in no state to be questioned.'

'And you shouldn't be talking now,' Dan counselled. 'You should be resting.'

'How can I rest with Ruby in prison and Ernie dead . . .' She shook her head in bewilderment. 'I really thought that I'd killed Ernie.'

'Stop thinking that way.' Dan held her tight. 'Your evidence will save Ruby. She shot Ernie in self-defence.'

'That's what she was screaming when the police broke in. Ruby and I were arrested and put in separate cells. I don't remember much of that. Except that the cell smelt of vomit and urine. And a drunk kept shouting abuse.'

She put a hand to her head. 'There were questions. So many questions. I tried to answer them honestly, but they kept making me repeat things over and over. They kept shouting at me, why hadn't I told Inspector Wharton about Ernie. They seemed to think I was an accomplice to the robbery. They wouldn't tell me how Ruby was. I heard her shouting once.'

Dan shuddered as he listened to her. The thought of Faith in a cell harrowed him. She was such a sensitive woman yet that part of it she had taken in her stride. 'My darling, how could you have borne it?'

'They didn't arrest me until two days ago. Twice they'd taken me in for questioning and this time they were going to charge me. They must have thought I did it. Then they let me go saying Ruby had confessed to everything. On her evidence they hauled in the Greek gang for questioning and they were facing several charges including murder.'

Dan's voice was rough. 'Then stop blaming yourself. You wounded Durham, that was all.'

Faith pulled back from him, her expression stricken with anguish. 'But what about Ruby? Her life with Ernie must have been hell.'

Dan could no longer control his anger. 'And she dragged you into it. That's typical of her.'

'No, it isn't,' Faith declared. 'Why does everyone think the worst of Ruby? It's all an act she puts on. For years Ruby protected me at the orphanage from the bigger bullies. She had her arm broken by one for sticking by me. I'll never forget that.'

Dan kissed her hair and held her tight. 'You saved Ruby's life.'

'But she'll be hanged if they find her guilty. What if it is me who is the guilty one, and not her?'

There was no reasoning with Faith. She'd make herself ill if she kept blaming herself. Dan gripped her shoulders and shook her. His voice was gruff as he insisted, 'You were in shock, which is hardly surprising after all that happened that day. Ruby looks after number one. She wouldn't be owning up to a murder she hadn't committed.'

Faith drew back from Dan and sank her head into her hands. 'You only ever saw the wildness in Ruby. Our friendship is stronger than any family ties.'

There was a loud rap at the door. Dan cursed the intrusion and answered it.

A man of about sixty in a trilby and overcoat stood on the doorstep. He looked Dan up and down assessingly, before announcing, 'I'm Detective Inspector Armitage. I'd like a few words with Miss Tempest. Who are you?'

'A friend.'

Inspector Armitage's eyes narrowed. 'You're Brogan, aren't you? Recognise you from a photograph and article about your paintings in the newspaper.'

'Come inside, Inspector. Faith is upset and has been sedated by the doctor. I'm not sure she's fit to answer questions.'

The inspector entered the front room and stood at its centre looking down at Faith. She rose unsteadily to her feet.

'How can I help you, Inspector Armitage?'

'Mrs Durham has been extremely helpful in our enquiries concerning the Kavanagh gang. Watkins is out of intensive care. He's answered all our questions. He told us about several run-ins

369

between the Greeks and the Kavanagh brothers. Every member of the Greek gang has been arrested and we've enough evidence to keep them all inside for life. Watkins also gave the names of the police on the payroll. Wharton was one of them. You were right to be suspicious of him. I understand Durham came here and threatened you once before.'

'Yes.'

'Durham was behind the fire-bombing of the River Boat. He intended to kill his wife and brother that night, according to Watkins.'

'No!' Faith swayed, a hand flying to her mouth in horror. Dan put his arm around her.

The inspector went on, 'Mike Rivers has also given us information about his brother's involvement with Kavanagh. It was the cause of several arguments between them and why he ended his partnership in the Gilded Lily. In Kavanagh's safe was evidence that they'd been blackmailing eminent politicians, judges and doctors.'

'And Ruby?'

'She will be charged with manslaughter, in self-defence. The number of bullets will go against her, but she was hysterical at the time and unsure of her aim. One bullet grazed Durham's temple and could have stunned him. One was in his back and another shattered his skull. Mrs Durham swears that your bullet was the one which stunned him. She saw her husband begin to rise from the floor and knew that he intended to kill you both.'

'Will she be hanged?'

The inspector shook his head. 'No. In view of Durham's reputation and the evidence we've got to hand to put so many vicious criminals away, it's likely she could get off with a suspended sentence. Even if she doesn't, she won't serve more than a couple of years at most with time off for good behaviour.'

Faith breathed more easily, but she was still worried at the charges Ruby must face. 'Will she be given bail?'

The inspector fixed Faith with a hard stare. 'She's best kept in custody for her own protection for the time being.'

'And after the trial? Will she still be in danger if she goes free? I imagine the Greeks will go for his contacts outside prison.'

'Mrs Durham will not be called as a witness. Some of the Greek gang confessed to crimes and implicated the others. Watkins will give evidence against Durham, in the hope of getting his own sentence lessened.'

'Ruby finally has the blaze of publicity she always wanted,' Faith said. 'She'll be famous for all the wrong reasons.'

Dan was more cynical. 'For the rest of her life she'll be famous as the woman who killed her gangster husband. People will flock to see her sing.'

The visit to Ruby in prison was heart-rending for Faith. Her friend was taking it stoically in her stride. She might be without make-up and the prison clothing was far from flattering but Ruby entered the visiting room like a duchess receiving guests at a ball. She also looked surprisingly well. Faith had expected her to be thinner and gaunt.

'It ain't so bad, if you keep on the right side of the screws,' Ruby assured her. 'Being the wife of a gangster gives you some status here. But I keep meself to meself as much as possible.'

'You look so well, unlike I expected,' Faith commented.

'Ah, that's me little blessing. I'm pregnant. It's Mike's of course, but if the jury think it's Ernie's and he was trying to kill me and the kid, it will go in my favour. Mike's employed the best defence lawyer in London. He reckons I'll get off and be given a suspended sentence.'

'I pray so, Ruby.' Faith's voice was still troubled.

Ruby shrugged. 'I've finally learned that fame ain't all it's cracked up to be. Becoming Mrs Rivers sounds a good compromise. And I'll be singing at the River Boat, so it's not as though I'll lose all the limelight. I'll settle for that.'

There was a twinkle in her eyes as she added, 'Some bloke has contacted Mike. He wants to write my biography. How's that for fame? A whole book about me life, not just a few headlines!'

Faith hung her head. 'I still can't believe that I didn't kill Ernie that night. He looked dead to me.'

'Shush. Forget about it,' Ruby said with impatience. 'It was a nightmare. Ernie's dead. I ain't mourning him. I dragged you into something I had no right to. Your loyalty and friendship could have lost you everything. Nathaniel. Dan. You didn't deserve that. This is the best way.'

For a long moment Faith held Ruby's glittering stare and her voice dropped to a whisper. 'I have to know. Did I kill Ernie?'

Ruby's eyes did not flicker. '*I* had the satisfaction of doing that. Now get back to that man of yours. Just you see, I'll be out of here after the trial in time for your wedding to Dan. Everything will work out fine.'

Faith felt the burden lift from her shoulders. 'You're a good friend, Ruby. The best.'

Ruby stood up as the warder touched her arm, warning her that the visit was over. She paused by the door to watch Faith from the far side of the room. Faith was a survivor but she had never shaken off her middle-class upbringing. Prison would have destroyed her. She would have been humiliated by the publicity which would have surrounded her release. Ruby was looking forward to it. What were a few months to her in another kind of institution? It was like water off a duck's back to Ruby. And when she got out, she'd have the fame she'd always wanted.

Thank God, Faith had believed her.

The Foundling

Philip Boast

To burglar Jack Riddles five-year-old Joy Briggs is a valuable commodity he can sell in the child-brothels of Victorian London. But in the hue and cry following her kidnap from her parents' opulent home, Riddles abandons Joy – deaf and so deemed stupid – in a canal tunnel. To his distress, for the child's silent knowingness has touched him, she is gone on his return. Drowned, he thinks, or, as the Scotland Yard men called in by her outraged parents believe, lost to the city's vice-infested underworld.

They are wrong. For Joy is found by a family of canal folk who bring her up as their own, giving her the kind of open-hearted love she has never received at home. But as Joy reaches womanhood it becomes clear that her past cannot let her live in peace and that events she witnessed as a child on that terrifying night mean there are those who want her dead . . .

0 7472 4882 6

HEADLINE

The Millionaire's Woman

Tessa Barclay

Condemned by her grandparents for being illegitimate, Ruth Barnett brings more shame on herself for being 'different'. Unfulfilled by what a sheltered rural village has to offer, Ruth has a thirst for adventure. So when she is offered a job in London by famous motor-racing driver, Ethan Coverton, she knows she'll be leaving Freshton for good.

At first London isn't quite the hub of excitement she'd expected. Not least because it's weeks before she sees Ethan, who's also the company managing director. But when Ruth is sent to cover for his secretary things begin to change. Attracted by her fresh looks, youthful vigour and passion for the racing circuit that is his life, Ethan begins to fall in love against all the odds.

Despite the fact that he is already trapped in a loveless marriage, and that she is half his age, Ethan and Ruth fight against the moral and social expectations of the 1920s and maintain an intimate happiness that seems invincible. Until, that is, a motor-racing accident leaves Ethan weak and vulnerable. And it's then that his embittered wife and ambitious son make their move to destroy all that Ruth holds dear . . .

0 7472 5006 5

HEADLINE

A selection of bestsellers from Headline